SIERRA SIX

TITLES BY MARK GREANEY

THE GRAY MAN

ON TARGET

BALLISTIC

DEAD EYE

BACK BLAST

GUNMETAL GRAY

AGENT IN PLACE

MISSION CRITICAL

ONE MINUTE OUT

RELENTLESS

SIERRA SIX

RED METAL

(with Lt. Col. H. Ripley Rawlings IV, USMC)

SIERRA SIX

MARK GREANEY

BERKLEY
NEW YORK

BERKLEY
An imprint of Penguin Random House LLC
penguinrandomhouse.com

Copyright © 2022 by MarkGreaneyBooks LLC
Penguin Random House supports copyright. Copyright fuels creativity, encourages diverse
voices, promotes free speech, and creates a vibrant culture. Thank you for buying an authorized
edition of this book and for complying with copyright laws by not reproducing, scanning, or
distributing any part of it in any form without permission. You are supporting writers and
allowing Penguin Random House to continue to publish books for every reader.

BERKLEY and the BERKLEY & B colophon are registered trademarks of
Penguin Random House LLC.

Library of Congress Cataloging-in-Publication Data

Names: Greaney, Mark, author.
Title: Sierra six / Mark Greaney.
Description: First edition. | New York : Berkley, 2022. | Series: The gray man ; 11
Identifiers: LCCN 2021040891 (print) | LCCN 2021040892 (ebook) |
ISBN 9780593098998 (hardcover) | ISBN 9780593099001 (ebook)
Subjects: LCGFT: Novels.
Classification: LCC PS3607.R4285 S54 2022 (print) |
LCC PS3607.R4285 (ebook) | DDC 813/.6—dc23
LC record available at https://lccn.loc.gov/2021040891
LC ebook record available at https://lccn.loc.gov/2021040892

First Edition: February 2022

Printed in the United States of America
1st Printing

Interior art: Black-and-white Paris map © Nicola Renna / Shutterstock.com
Book design by Kelly Lipovich

For Ava Carrington Wilson,
Sophia Kemmons Wilson, and
Charles Kemmons Wilson IV.
Your stepdad loves you!

Death is not the greatest loss in life. The greatest loss is what dies inside us while we live.

NORMAN COUSINS

Pain is the best instructor, but no one wants to go to his class.

CHOI HONG HI

CHARACTERS

COURTLAND "COURT" GENTRY: aka Golf Sierra Six, aka Violator, aka the Gray Man; former CIA Special Activities Division (Ground Branch) paramilitary operations officer; freelance intelligence operative

ZACK HIGHTOWER: aka Golf Sierra One; CIA Special Activities Division (Ground Branch) paramilitary operations officer

KENDRICK LENNOX: aka Golf Sierra Two; CIA Special Activities Division (Ground Branch) paramilitary operations officer

KEITH MORGAN: aka Golf Sierra Three; CIA Special Activities Division (Ground Branch) paramilitary operations officer

JIM PACE: aka Golf Sierra Four; CIA Special Activities Division (Ground Branch) paramilitary operations officer

BERNADINO (DINO) REDUS: aka Golf Sierra Five; CIA Special Activities Division (Ground Branch) paramilitary operations officer

MURAD KHAN: Operations officer, Foreign Coordination Unit, Inter-Services Intelligence agency (Pakistan)

OMAR MUFTI: Major, Pakistan Army Aviation Corps

TERRY VANCE: Director of analysis, CIA Special Activities Division (Ground Branch), Task Force Golf Sierra

JULIE MARQUEZ: Junior tactical analyst, CIA Special Activities Division

PRIYANKA BANDARI: Freelance intelligence, surveillance, and reconnaissance specialist

ARJUN BANDARI: Freelance intelligence broker

TED APPLETON: Former CIA operations officer, former CIA chief of station, Islamabad, Pakistan

MATTHEW HANLEY: CIA chief of station, Port Moresby, Papua New Guinea; former deputy director for operations, CIA; former group chief, Special Activities Division (Ground Branch), Task Force Golf Sierra

SUZANNE BREWER: Assistant deputy director for operations, CIA

AIMAL VIZIRI: Code name Leopard; Inter-Services Intelligence agency (Pakistan) operative, Foreign Coordination Unit

NASSIR RASOOL: Pakistani counterintelligence technical specialist

SIERRA SIX

ONE

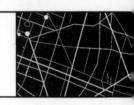

TWELVE YEARS AGO

Zack Hightower and the five other men of Golf Sierra watched the scene before them as if they were merely spectators, when in fact they were the stars of the show, waiting in the wings for the play to begin.

Fifty yards away from them, the ramp lowered slowly on the Lockheed C-130 Hercules. A scarlet glow shot like a soft ray from inside the cabin, illuminating the tarmac, and the plane's four massive turboprops spun at idle, growling in the cool night.

Ground crew worked feverishly around the aircraft, moving this way and that as they readied it for its upcoming flight.

The light from the cabin did not quite reach Hightower and his men on the tarmac; they remained in the dark, gazing on, interested but unconcerned.

The six men were armed and armored, festooned with heavy equipment and bulky parachutes, but they endured patiently, embracing the suck of the weight on their bodies. The sixty pounds of gear strapped to each man made unnecessary movement ill-advised, so all of them knew better than to waste energy now, before their arduous evening had even begun in earnest.

The ground crew in front of them did not engage with or even look at the operators in the dark. That was considered bad form, so the six men were left alone with their thoughts, gazing at the glowing rear of the hulking aircraft in front of them and waiting for their cue.

All six operators wore quad-tube night vision goggles stowed in the up position on their helmets. They were also equipped with rifles, pistols, and extra ammunition, as well as fragmentation, flash bang, and thermite grenades.

They'd be dealing with extreme cold soon enough, so they wore efficient merino-wool base layers under nondescript black Gore-Tex flight suits, which were themselves under plated ceramic body armor that was housed inside load-bearing vests.

Additionally, each man wore two parachutes: a main chute on his back and a reserve in front, low, cinched around his midsection. Oxygen masks were snapped tight to their faces, with two small tanks strapped just as tightly to their bodies.

The men were already consuming bottled O_2 even though they were still on the ground. Tonight's mission would begin with a HAAM, a high-altitude airdrop mission—a leap from the Hercules at twenty-eight thousand feet—and breathing from the tanks now would eliminate the risk of nitrogen buildup from the rapid change in air pressure as the men descended.

These six were ordinarily a talkative bunch, but as team leader of the tiny unit, Zack demanded a strict decorum before an operation. All extraneous conversation had ceased as soon as they'd arrived on the tarmac; no one shouted through their rubber mask about what was to come.

They all just waited, heavily laden statues in the night.

Eventually the aircraft's loadmaster came down the ramp and then made his way over to the group. He looked around for a moment, obviously for some indication of who was in charge.

Zack Hightower, virtually identical in dress and load-out to the others, took a single step forward.

The loadmaster shouted, "Sir, you can board whenever you're ready."

Zack answered back through his mask in an easygoing tone. "I'm not 'sir,' chief. Just call me Bob."

The loadmaster was in his forties, thick and brawny. He nodded; he understood what was going on. "Thought you fellas were Special Forces."

It wasn't really a question, and he received no response. "Sweet. To be honest, we don't get a lot of ops like this. Doubt anyone in the Air Guard does." He shrugged. "I mean, this is just a milk run. For *us*, I mean. Can't imagine what *you guys* have planned."

Zack stared back at the loadmaster, his eyes slightly narrowed.

"Right. No worries. We'll take care of you and your boys, Bob. The pilots are ready to get this bus a-rollin' as soon as you men board and strap in."

"We're following you, chief."

The operator who called himself Bob turned back to the other five now. All but shouting through his mask, Zack said, "U.S. taxpayers bought us half a plane ride, gents. Let's go."

The team of six lumbered towards the waiting aircraft, following behind the wide-eyed chief master sergeant, who couldn't wait to tell his friends back in Nebraska that he'd flown a mission with the CIA.

The dark gray Lockheed had taken off from Camp Chapman not forty-five minutes earlier, but already its engines sucked the night sky high over the mountains, just inside Afghanistan's border with Pakistan.

The four-engine propeller-driven aircraft could accommodate sixty-four paratroopers, but inside the red-glowing cabin, the six men from the Central Intelligence Agency were the only passengers. They sat on the webbed benches in the rear, near the closed ramp.

The loadmaster stood up by the bulkhead, and after conferring over the radio, he raised his fist in the air and extended two fingers, garnering the attention of the team leader in the rear of the cabin. The TL stood, adjusting the Heckler & Koch rifle hanging from a sling over his body armor as he did so.

Hightower then used one gloved hand to grab onto a bulkhead railing, knowing from experience that the air here above the Spin Ghar mountain range could be rough. He raised his other hand high and, just like the loadmaster at the far end of the cabin, he held up a pair of fingers.

The five men seated around him hadn't noticed the loadmaster. They *did* notice Hightower, however, and they understood.

The men shouted in unison. "Two minutes!"

The five climbed to their feet, made adjustments to weapons and gear and dump pouches and parachute harnesses. Now all six operators of CIA Special Activities Division Ground Branch Task Force Golf Sierra checked and double-checked buckles and reserves and O_2 hoses and pouches and Velcro closures one last time. It was second nature to do so; nothing was left to chance.

Most of this team had been together for a year now, combating the global war on terror by performing high-threat incursions all over the world. They'd rotary-winged in, fixed-winged in, HALO-jumped in, armored-personnel-carriered in, Zodiac-boated in, even inserted through national immigration under false passports. And then, no matter how they'd gotten there, they'd executed their mission, then exfiltrated whatever denied territory they'd found themselves in.

Most of this team.

Hightower turned to look at the closest man on his right, who now adjusted the webbing affixing a combat tourniquet to the shoulder strap of his body armor. Hightower was Golf Sierra One and the operator adjusting the tourniquet was Golf Sierra Six, the newest member of the tiny but formidable group.

Sierra Six had only been part of the element for the last two months; he'd made a pair of helo incursions into Pakistan in that time, and both had turned out to be dry holes, devoid of enemy contact. He'd also assisted with one relatively easy rendition of a high-value terror threat off the street in Ankara.

As the junior man, Sierra Six got the shit work, that was just part of the deal, but to his credit, the new guy did his job without protest. Hightower was satisfied with Six's effort, he had high hopes for the younger man, but Six was still the FNG—the Fucking New Guy.

Zack turned away from Six and lowered the visor on his black helmet, and all five of the other men of CIA Task Force Golf Sierra around him followed suit.

The loadmaster motioned again, and Zack turned and shouted over the wail of the four Pratt & Whitney engines.

"Ramp!"

The five other men repeated the word in a shout, ensuring that the message got through to them all. They then each immediately detached the hose from the tank they'd been breathing from and reattached it to a fresh tank lashed under their left arms. They opened the valve on the new tank, then unhooked the depleted stainless steel tube from their gear and stowed it in webbing behind their seats. As one they all sucked in the fresh bottled air.

Just then, the massive ramp lowered at the rear of the aircraft. The night sky screamed back at them, louder than the engines but just, and the men walked in the direction of the wail, lumbering towards the ramp.

Twenty-eight thousand feet below and some twenty-nine miles from where this C-130 flew in far eastern Afghanistan, the men had an objective waypoint the size of a basketball court, and every fiber of their being was focused on hitting it.

This was a HAHO jump, high-altitude, high-opening, meaning they would pull their rip cords not long after exiting the plane and then use their winglike canopies to fly over the border into Pakistan, towards a precise geographical waypoint.

A CIA UAV was on station above the target location now. It reported a few security milling about, but command in Virginia had talked to the task force's intelligence shop at the CIA base in Afghanistan and green-lit Zack's hit. So the six Americans stood near the ramp, the loadmaster of the aircraft now strapped to the wall next to them, and they all waited for a cue from the cockpit.

One last look around from Hightower to make sure the men were arrayed correctly in the cabin, and then he focused on the loadmaster. The chief master sergeant conferred on his radio, then gave Zack a thumbs-up, and Sierra One walked down the ramp and stepped off into the dark night without breaking stride.

The others followed right behind him, like men striding off a bus on their way in to the office.

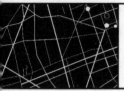

TWO

Thirty-three minutes later, the six members of the task force all hung under canopy, each roughly twenty-five meters apart from the next man, arrayed in a descending line through the moonless night. Their O_2 masks were off and stowed now; the men wore their night vision goggles over their eyes as well as radio headsets with earpieces that suppressed loud noises and enhanced soft noises, so they were able to stay in comms with one another without uttering more than a whisper.

Golf Sierra One was in the lead; he was the lowest to the ground and would be the first to land. He scanned his landing zone; the rooftop of the three-story structure they called the command building was now in sight, just a few hundred feet below and a few hundred yards away.

Triggering his mic, he said, "Phase-line Delta. Omega is clear. Lights are off in the command building. If they pop on, Bravo will take down the generator."

Behind him, Sierra Two said, "Sector east is clear to the wall. Beyond that is a technical, looks like a patrol. Negative contact in front of it."

To this, Hightower replied, "No factor."

Three clicked his own mic. "Sector south, three pax in the airfield control tower with the Dishka. No signs they're alert. We're good."

"No factor," Golf Sierra One repeated.

Four now. "West sector. One pax in the guard tower at the front gate. He's got an AK. Dude looks asleep."

"Roger. Focus on your landing."

"Check."

Five said, "North to the structures on the hillside outside the wall; no movement, no lights. The glow from Pesh is whitening out everything on the top of the hill and beyond."

"Understood."

Sierra Six was highest still and in the rear of the stick; he wasn't given a sector to scan, but he'd have plenty to do soon enough.

Zack Hightower clicked the transmit button on his chest again. "One copies all. Hit the Omega or pull hard left, turn around and land to the west. Take your chances with the dude with the AK. Pull right and you're gonna get smoked by that Dishka in the tower."

And then he looked to the north, thinking about what Five had just said. There was a cluster of little homes just beyond the wall of the compound. The dwellings looked dark and quiet, but beyond them, the team did not have a good view because of the hazy distant light affecting their NODs. If danger came in numbers, then danger would come from Peshawar, a city of two million that was less than thirty minutes to the north. This disused military base was located a couple of klicks south of the village of Kalaya, and it was surrounded on all sides by low dusty hills, and then just beyond, wheat and sugar beet fields that ran to higher hills that hid the location from Peshawar proper.

If the shooting started, the Pakistani military would be here by land in twenty minutes or by air in one third that time.

This operation wasn't one where Golf Sierra would lollygag around after the fact for a sensitive sight exploitation. No, Zack and his men were here to find a high-value target, roll him up, and get him back over the border. Failing that, they were here to find the HVT, and to kill him.

And failing *that*, they were here to find somebody, *anybody*, who might have intel regarding the HVT.

Their extraction helo was already en route, flying nap of the earth through the rugged Spin Ghar mountains to the southwest. Golf Sierra wouldn't have a single moment to wait here at the target once their work was done.

The HVT was supposedly billeted somewhere in the command building, protected by a small security force, and Zack had given the team four minutes to search the structure, a difficult task for a group of six, and this meant they would split up once they went internal. It wasn't ideal, but the intel was hot, JSOC forces back over the border weren't available, and the other CIA Ground Branch team positioned at Camp Chapman had been running a hit against an AQ base up north in Damadola and hadn't made it back in time to be integrated into Zack's raid tonight.

So, six men against an unknown number of enemy, but the intel folks were saying no fewer than six and no more than ten.

And included among them, so they'd been told, was tonight's jackpot.

All the men on the Ground Branch unit carried a picture of the man. The HVT was a helicopter pilot and officer in the Pakistani army named Omar Mufti, now supposedly second-in-command of a newly formed terrorist organization called the Kashmiri Resistance Front. Virtually nothing was known about the leader of the organization, a man who carried the war name of Pasha the Kashmiri. His chief lieutenant, Mufti, however, *was* now known to coalition forces. And he was, if the intel out of CIA Station Islamabad was correct, right here, right now.

Nabbing Pasha's top deputy, it was thought, would provide the intel to take Pasha down.

The KRF's well-equipped and well-motivated fighters had conducted raids against coalition targets over the border in Afghanistan, and that was more than enough to earn Pasha a capture/kill order from the CIA, along with Major Omar Mufti, and to hell with what the Pakistanis had to say about it.

Hightower's boots touched the concrete rooftop of the command building at a run, and he pivoted on them and dropped to a knee pad. He popped the left riser strap of his chute so that a stray evening gust didn't drag him over the side of the building, then collapsed his canopy quickly, unfastened the chest and leg straps that harnessed both the main chute and the reserve chute to his body, and began quickly balling the canopy and lines up tightly and cramming them into a massive empty dump pouch staged on his belt for just this purpose.

He disconnected the pouch from his waist and let it drop to the dusty roof, then reached back for his rifle slung over his shoulder.

The intel officer monitoring the Reaper feed thirty-three thousand feet overhead chirped into Zack's ear that there remained no hint the team had been detected, and Zack could hear his other men landing behind him on the rooftop, their boots running and then abruptly stopping.

Zack brought his weapon's optic up to his night vision goggles and began heading towards the stairwell door, not even looking back at his men as he advanced.

He had done this so many times, first in the Navy and then in the CIA, that the moves were not only automatic but virtually silent.

Softly, he said into his mic, "One is on the ground. Sound off."

"Two is with you," came a voice, partially through his headset and partially over his right shoulder. A big and broad African American with a short but bushy beard appeared on Hightower's right, his own weapon high and sweeping.

"Three is on the ground." Sierra Three had already moved to the side of the rooftop, and here he lay on his chest, extended the bipod on the front rail of his suppressed rifle, and took aim at the guard tower.

"Four is with One."

"Five coming to One."

There was a delay, just long enough for Zack to arrive at the side of the closed stairwell door and look back into the dark in time to see Sierra Six balling up his canopy, then triggering his mic.

"Six is on the ground and moving to One."

Sierra Six made it to the door, the four men stacked up behind him, with Zack Hightower now the third in line.

They all knew what was behind the door, at least in theory. This base was originally constructed by America to house UAVs in the early days of the war on terror. The Americans left before ever occupying the facility, and then the Pakistani army moved in for a while to billet troops in the command building and to use the small runway and hangars for their helicopters here in the badlands of Pakistan, known as the Federally Administered Tribal Area. But the Pak army had moved out two years earlier; the place had been abandoned since then, until the intel came in that the KRF was using the command building inside the walls as a forward staging area for attacks into Afghanistan.

A blueprint of the structure had been made available to the CIA by the Air Force. Zack and the team had studied it, and the Golf Sierra intelligence cell's structure and geospatial intelligence officer had assured them of the blueprint's accuracy.

Into his mic, Zack said, "Three?"

Three lay on the roof, peering through his optic towards the guard tower. "I've got visual on all targets in the tower, boss."

"You need Five over there to support you?"

"Negative. Easy pickin's here. You hit the stairwell and I'll link up and provide rear security before you make it down a flight."

Zack nodded. "On your signal, Three." He flipped a switch to transmit to the tactical operations center back at Camp Chapman. Softly he said, "Sierra One for Homeplate. Phase-line Echo."

The reply was brief. "Homeplate. Sierra One, copy, Echo."

Golf Sierra Three was Keith Morgan, the best sniper on a team full of excellent snipers. His carbine rifle with its eight-power scope was more than adequate for the two-hundred-meter distance to his target, and all three sentries there were standing or seated within a couple meters of one another.

Taking a life, taking three lives, was not necessarily a difficult thing for a person who had the right training.

Morgan thumbed the safety off his weapon, having already decided the order in which he'd engage the men. He steadied his breathing, taking no more than a couple of seconds to do so, and then he put his gloved finger on the trigger of his rifle.

"Engaging."

With a slow exhalation, Sierra Three opened fire.

Even with the long silencer on the end of the rifle, the 5.56-millimeter rounds pounded the night. Someone in the building below could easily have slept through it, but if they were awake, they would recognize shooting, although they likely would perceive the gunfire as coming from somewhere off in the hills and not a floor or two above them.

At the snap of the first gunshot, Zack reached forward and squeezed Golf Sierra Four's shoulder, and he, in turn, squeezed the shoulder of Golf Sierra Six.

The sniper on the roof fired a pair into all three targets around the only heavy weapon in the compound so rapidly that the third sentry only had time to look around at the noise and see the other men falling before he himself tumbled off the side of the tower and down to the hard earth.

Two hundred ten yards away from the carnage, and thirty feet from the American sniper who'd created it, the youngest man on the team tried the latch on the door and found it to be unlocked.

As the four men in the tactical train entered the stairwell, Zack whispered into his mic. "Second deck. Keep it tight, Six."

With night vision goggles projecting a hazy green view for all the men, Golf Sierra Six shouldered up to the stairwell wall and began descending, his suppressed 416 with its laser sweeping the stairs beyond the landing below.

In his headset he heard the call from the tactical operations center. "Sierra One, Homeplate. All targets at the Dishka are down. We see no reaction from other visible opposition. We record main Golf Sierra element proceeding internal at this time. Time oh three, oh one, fourteen seconds."

Through his NODs, Golf Sierra Six saw the lasers of the other men sweeping all the angles as well.

Zack was behind Four as they cleared the corners at the bottom of the stairs, his eyes, his ears, even his nose strained for any sensory input that might alert him to the presence of danger.

He heard Sierra Three catch up and fall in at the back of the stack.

They arrived on the second floor; the stairwell was in the center of the building, and a hallway led off to both the left and the right. Alpha squad—One, Three, and Five—broke to the right without a word, while Bravo—consisting of Two, Four, and Six—went left. The men did not rush; there was no sense in running to one's death, after all. Instead they were meticulous and efficient with their progress.

In the hallway on the left, Sierra Six was the lead man in his three-person train. He kept both eyes open, soaking in all the information he could from the soft green image in front of him. His right eye also peered through an EOTech holographic weapon sight mounted on his rifle, a red circle around a tiny red dot hovering in the center of the glass, showing him approximately where his bullets would strike if he fired, depending on the distance to his target.

The hallway was narrow and dark; he knew there should be two doors on his right and three on his left, and he also knew he'd be the first man through all five of them.

It sucked to be the Six, but that was the job.

Six, Two, and Four stopped at the first door. While Six waited, the other men took positions on either side of the doorway, and once Four squeezed him on the shoulder, Six tested the latch, opened the door silently, and moved quickly into the room, heading for the wall on the left.

At virtually the same moment, Two pushed in behind him from the left side of the doorway, focusing right, and just after this, Four went center.

The men did not actuate their weapon lights; they could see all they needed to see through their NODs, and they took in a dormitory-style room with eight sets of bunk beds.

The beds were empty.

Quickly looking around, Six found no obvious false doors, and the window seemed to be locked, so he passed the other men; they stacked up just inside the doorway, then returned carefully to the hallway.

This they did again at the next door, and here they found a small kitchen. There was no food, and there were no personnel.

Golf Sierra One reported over the radio that his squad wasn't turning up anything on the west side, either, and the UAV had seen no fresh activity outside beyond that which had already been reported.

This was starting to feel like another dry hole to Six.

. . .

The three-man Bravo squad checked all the rooms on their side of the second floor save for the last door on the left. They stacked up outside it, and to their right was a window on the wall at the end of the hall. Sierra Two glanced out it quickly, looking down one floor to the concrete courtyard. There, just as he'd learned from the intelligence briefings on the facility, was a large generator, a meter or so away from the building.

His orders were to leave the generator alone unless an alarm was raised and the lights came on, in which case he was to destroy it, plunge the command building back into darkness, and continue on with his mission. All was quiet for now, so he decided to concentrate on this door and then proceed downstairs.

They entered the room; again they found nothing.

The two teams of three formed back up in the stairwell to head down to the lower deck.

Two minutes later Golf Sierra Two and the two men with him approached the end of the ground floor east hallway. There was just one more door to clear on their left, and right in front of them, a chained exit door that led straight outside to the courtyard where the generator sat just feet away.

The last door on the left, they knew from their briefing, led to a small storage area, only three meters by three meters, but the men stacked up just the same, even though the seven rooms they'd cleared both here and above had all been empty.

Six put his hand on the latch, found it, like all the others, to be unlocked, and Four again squeezed his shoulder.

Just as he began opening the door, the rumble of the generator outside the chained door on their right reverberated through the men's boots, all the lights in the hallway flashed on, and the storeroom door flew open, knocking Sierra Six backwards into the other two men. The American operators lifted up their night observation devices; the tubes had flared out, leaving them blind, and as soon as they had done this and gotten their guns back up to scan for targets in the now brightly lit hallway, they saw a lone man running away, down the hall, towards the small central lobby of the building. There was a main exit there to the left, and to the right was the stairwell the Golf Sierra men had just exited.

The running man seemed to have no weapon on him, but still Sierra Six raised his weapon in his direction.

Golf Sierra Two said, "Hold fire!" He looked to Four. "Is that our guy?"

"Don't know! My NODs bled out."

"Same." Two flashed his weapon light quickly into the storage room; unlike the brightly lit hallway, the generator wasn't powering any light source in there. He saw shelves and boxes but no other movement, so he flipped his light back off and spoke quickly now to Sierra Six. "Clear this last space, then cut through this chain and blow the genny outside. Four and I will grab the squirter."

Sierra Six had already turned on his own weapon light and focused his attention on the storeroom. "Clearing here, then redirecting to disable the genny."

Two and Four took off up the hall at a sprint, with Two radioing Hightower what was going on. Zack and his men would be in the hall on the other side of the lobby, and they needed to know about a squirter in case he ran straight on past the front door and the stairs and found himself on top of Sierra One.

Sierra Six knew he had to get that generator off, and fast. The Americans had a great advantage with their night vision equipment, an advantage that was rendered moot with the electronic lighting. But he also knew he had to first sweep the dark little storeroom.

There was a single two-meter-high shelf on the far side of the space, filled with what looked to be truck or car parts. It was pushed slightly away from the wall, and Six assumed the unarmed man had been hiding behind it before racing off.

He doubted there was space back there to hide anyone else, but he took no chances. He stepped forward, his HK aimed at chest level, his bright, white light still cutting the dark, and he spun around the shelf, scanning for a target.

A metal hatch in the floor stood wide open, right at his feet. Six was surprised by this, as the blueprints given to the team by the Ground Branch intelligence unit had made clear there was no subterranean level at the location.

He lowered his weapon slightly; the light made its way down a narrow stairwell in advance of the point of aim of his gun, and then his eyes took in the gravity of his situation.

He saw movement. One, two, four . . . at least a half-dozen men, all wielding Kalashnikov rifles, and they were rushing up in his direction.

Six fired first, dropping the first man in the stairwell, and he began to retreat back around the shelf and out into the hallway, but before his boot landed a single step, five AKs opened fire. He felt the impacts on his body armor, a heavy round sliced into his shoulder, then another in his thigh, and he fell backwards against the wall as he desperately returned fire.

THREE

Two and Four were on the heels of the unarmed man as he stumbled out the front door. It was essentially a foot race, although the Ground Branch operators had to go slower than they would have liked so as not to run straight into any as-yet-unnoticed armed opposition. There was a sentry on a tower by the gate, but a wall running off the command building hid the Americans from the man's sight line.

Gunfire suddenly erupted behind the two, stopping them in their tracks. Without saying a word, they called off their pursuit, turned, and began running back to support their colleague.

It was the right thing to do, but they already knew their help would come too late. The unmistakable sound of AK-47s rocking in full auto had drowned out the short crack of the suppressed HK416 almost immediately, and the sheer number of guns rattling now told them their lone teammate didn't stand a chance.

As Two ran along with Four, he transmitted through his radio. "One! Six is in contact! The squirter is out front, heading towards the gate. Returning to support Six."

Zack Hightower's voice responded quickly. "Negative! Get that squirter! Alpha is moving to Six."

Two and Four stopped their run, spun around, and raced again back towards the fleeing man, who was halfway across the courtyard now, running in the direction of a massive tin-roofed warehouse the size of an air-craft hangar that the imagery analysts had determined to be empty of personnel. But both Americans knew they had to stop him before he got into the warehouse and found a place to hide.

Sierra Two slowed, stopped, aimed his weapon carefully, then fired a single round, striking the running man in the right calf and sending him tumbling to the ground, just feet away from the warehouse. With cacophonous gunfire continuing in the building behind him, he shouted to Four. "Go around the east side of the building and blow the genny. I got this asshole."

Four ran off, and Two closed on the wounded man lying on the concrete.

Zack Hightower, along with Golf Sierras Three and Five, fired their weapons up the brightly lit hallway at a group of men desperately trying to find cover from the onslaught. During the exchange, Zack heard through his earpiece from the TOC back in Khost.

"Sierra One, Homeplate. Be advised: the technical is approaching the front gate at this time, ETA your poz, one mike. The sentry at the front gate is holding his position but alert."

Zack had been hoping to avoid calling in a Hellfire from the Reaper on this mission; it always made things a lot messier for the CIA when they used anything larger than a hand grenade while inside Pakistan. But his little force was dealing with too much right now to handle three more enemy approaching from another vector. Without hesitation he said, "Homeplate, take out the technical for us when it reaches the gate. Smoke 'em all."

Hightower had execute authority for the UAV's two Hellfire missiles on its wings, and the TOC understood this. "Launching Hellfire." A moment later: "Missile off the rail. Impact in six seconds."

Zack ducked in the stairwell and changed his magazine, then leaned back into the lobby and fired up the hallway to the east.

Outside, the boom of the Hellfire's eight-kilogram warhead slamming into a pickup truck, just 150 meters from the building he stood in, told

Zack that one of his many problems had been solved. The disembodied voice in his earpiece confirmed this an instant later, adding that the sentry at the gate was down from the blast, as well, so Zack returned to his main focus: recovering his missing man.

With gunfire raging in the building behind him, Sierra Two held his pistol to the head of the runner he'd shot in the leg. With his knee in the man's back and the man's face pressed into the cool concrete of the courtyard, Two produced zip ties and bound his prisoner efficiently. He then reached into a pocket on his right biceps and pulled a laminated three-by-five card from it. On it was the grainy photo of a man in a military uniform.

Two flipped up his NODs, slid forward the button on his helmet-mounted flashlight, and glanced quickly at the card. He'd studied it briefly already, but tonight's hit had come up too fast for him to spend much time memorizing every aspect of the HVT's visage. Once he had a fresh look, he rolled the zip-tied man onto his back and turned his head till the six-hundred-lumen spotlight attached to the left side of his helmet blasted the bearded man in the face.

It took Two only an instant to make his determination.

"Shit," he muttered, and then he put the photo back in his arm pocket and leaned down close to the man's ear.

In Pashto, Sierra Two said, "Cherta Omar Mufti?" *Where is Omar Mufti?*

He received no response from the man lying on the concrete, so he then said, "Taaso noom sa dey?" *What is your name?*

The man did not answer.

"Taaso Pakto weyley shee?" *Do you speak Pashto?* Nothing still. He switched languages. "Al Arrabiyatu?" *Arabic?*

Still nothing.

"English?" he tried, but he didn't expect a response.

To this, the man looked up at him and answered in a British-laced Pakistani accent that was also twinged with the pain of his leg wound. "I speak . . . fuck you, America."

Sierra Two nodded. This man was a terrorist; he wouldn't break instantly. No, he'd have to be softened up over time. The big African American stood, then reached down for the man's shoulders. "Let's see how that attitude works out for you where you're headin', my man." He yanked the terrorist up to his feet, ignoring his bleeding leg.

Two pressed his transmitter now. "Two to One. I have one enemy zipped. Negative jackpot. He's not our boy."

Hightower answered back quickly. "Roger that. Get him to the roof. The lobby is clear, we're advancing on eastern hallway. Helos are inbound, extraction in five mikes."

"Roger that."

Zack Hightower had killed three men in the hallway near the side door and the storage room. Keith Morgan, Sierra Three, had killed two more, and Bernadino Redus, Sierra Five, had stitched rounds up the pelvis and chest of the last man they'd encountered, leaving him mortally wounded and gasping for air on his back in the doorway to the storeroom.

Sierra Four was Jim Pace, and he came over the radio now, announced he was cutting power to the generator, and when the lights went out, Zack and his men again pulled their NODs over their eyes and moved warily up the hall, searching for Sierra Six.

Hightower kicked the AK away from the wounded Pakistani, looked him over through his image intensifier tubes, and determined he was not the man they were hunting. He could also tell that the man was too badly wounded to capture for intelligence value. He raised his rifle a few inches and shot the fallen man in the forehead, blasting bone and brain and blood six feet from where he lay, then raised his weapon and swung into the storeroom.

As he had feared, Sierra Six was crumpled in the corner on his right, his weapon by his side. Another man lay facedown at the lifeless American's feet, a Kalashnikov jutting out from under his body. Hightower kicked him and found him to be dead, but knelt and pulled the weapon away nonetheless, sliding it back into the hall.

He ignored Sierra Six for now, kept his eyes in the optic of his rifle as he stepped around the shelf, and then, when he saw the open hatch that led below, he knelt down and covered the space.

"Five, check him out!" he shouted. Redus entered the cramped room and knelt over Six while Zack examined the stairs.

Hightower saw two bodies at the bottom of the narrow shaft down to the underground level, but he detected no movement below. He shot both of the motionless figures with his suppressed carbine while inwardly fuming that the intelligence he'd received had maintained there *was* no underground level to the compound. He stood and began descending the stairs, and he spoke softly while he did so. "Three, stack up on me."

Three tried to get in front of his boss; Sierra One wasn't supposed to be the first man to or through *anything* during close-quarters battle, but Zack elbowed him back. He had payback on his mind as he descended into the darkness, protocol be damned, and he wasn't going to give Three the first shot at anyone down here.

But there were no targets to be found. At the bottom of the stairs, Zack turned on his weapon light because his NODs were no good to him without ambient light for the tubes to work with.

He saw in front of him a low and narrow tunnel that led off beyond where his light could reach. It headed north, towards the little homes outside the compound, and if Omar Mufti had, in fact, been here, he was probably long gone by now.

Golf Sierra didn't have the number of men required to raid a tiny hamlet house-to-house style, nor did he have the time. He heard the thumping of the extraction Blackhawk growing above the building, and he backed up the stairway, his weapon trained on the distant darkness and pure, unadulterated anger seething inside him.

The five operators, the prisoner, and a single body bag rode in the rear of the specially designed Blackhawk helicopter as it raced west in utter darkness through the Spin Ghar mountains on the Pakistan-Afghanistan border.

Hightower's back was against the front bulkhead; he looked down at where Sierra Six lay, encased now in plastic. He turned and spit tobacco juice out the open hatch, then fumbled with the commo gear on his chest a moment, turned the dial till his satellite phone was connected to transmit through his headset. He pushed a button on the phone, secured tightly to his body armor with nylon straps and plastic quick-release buckles.

Then he leaned his head back against the bulkhead.

The prisoner was next to him, zip-tied and head-bagged. Kendrick Lennox, Sierra Two, had expertly bandaged the man's leg wound while secretly wishing he'd hit the man a few inches higher, through the back of the knee, where the pain would have been exponentially worse.

Zack didn't expect he was bringing back a lot of intelligence value in the wounded man; he just looked like some young Jihadi shithead. But in an operation where one of his men had been killed, he was glad he was returning to Khost with *something*.

Just then, the satellite connection crackled to life.

Zack spoke first. "Sierra One to Rooster. Sierra One to Rooster, how copy?"

"Rooster for Sierra One. Read you five-five." The tone of the other man's voice told Zack he knew tonight's mission had gone to hell.

"You saw that shit from the UAV?"

"I didn't see the internal, obviously. Saw the body bag on the roof. Who was it?"

Zack Hightower was team leader of Golf Sierra, but the group chief who ran both this Ground Branch task force and another based at Forward Operating Base Chapman, as well as the intelligence and logistics for the entire operation, was named Matthew Hanley, call sign Rooster.

Hightower said, "Matt Kiefer is KIA. How copy?"

"Jesus Christ," Hanley growled. "Sierra Six. We've lost two Sixes in, what, five months?"

"Little over four. And Pete got wounded in the Philippines six weeks before that."

Hanley sighed audibly. "What happened tonight?"

Hightower looked out the open hatch; the sound was so loud that normal conversation would have been impossible, but his noise-canceling headset and unidirectional mic made it easy to communicate over the sat link. "I'll tell you what happened. There was a *goddamned motherfucking* tunnel. Intel said, without a doubt, 'No subterranean to worry about.' Six was clearing a ground-floor storeroom, shooters poured out of a hole and overran his ass. We finally smoked them, and the Reap took out the technical with two enemy along with one sentry. We count fifteen EKIA in all. *Fifteen!*"

"Anybody else hurt?"

"Not yet. But soon. The intel puke who gave us the blueprint to the facility and assured us no construction had taken place since, that motherfucker's as good as dead when I get back to Khost."

Hanley replied with a softness in his voice. "I'll have him on the next flight back to the States. He's done, Zack. Forget about him."

"I can't forget about—"

"Zack!" Hanley was more forceful now. He'd been an officer in U.S. Army Special Forces; he knew how to speak with authority. "You don't touch him, you don't confront him. You let me replace him. We understand each other?"

Hightower didn't like it, but he rumbled out a "Yes, sir."

It was silent over the connection a moment. The Blackhawk banked hard to the left; Zack felt the weird gravitational pull on his body, but he didn't even look around. It seemed to him like he'd spent years of his life in the back of helos whipping around mountain passes under cover of darkness. These night flights didn't raise his blood pressure in the slightest anymore.

Hanley said, "All right, One. We'll talk when you get back to Chapman. They tell me you're a half hour out." He added, "Matt Kiefer was a fine man. I'm sorry."

"Gil Nunez was, too, boss. Ditto Pete Vassar." Hightower sighed. "I guess I need you to find me a *new* fine man. Let's see how it shakes out for the next poor son of a bitch."

"Yeah. We're returning stateside tomorrow. I'll get you somebody good."

Hightower looked down at the body bag just beyond his boots. He said, "Kiefer was good, but nobody's good enough to go one-v-ten in a fucking *closet*."

"I know," Hanley said. "See you when you get here."

"Roger that, Rooster. Sierra One is out."

The helo passed between two snowy mountain peaks and into Afghanistan, carrying death in its belly and leaving death in its wake.

FOUR

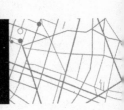

PRESENT DAY

The young brunette sat in the lotus position on the floor of her suite at El Djazair, one of Algiers's most luxurious hotels, her eyes closed, her hands on her knees, palms facing up. She breathed in slowly through her nose and then out through her mouth, even more slowly.

The doors to the balcony were on her right, and they were open; a warm evening breeze blew in along with the distant sounds of traffic, neither of which wrestled her away from her deep state of mindfulness.

Soft flute music played on the suite's stereo, with the sound of gently falling water behind it, adding peace to her yoga practice, but when the Apple Watch on her wrist beeped one time, she slowly opened her eyes.

She took in the room around her: the desk near the balcony, the suitcases, along with the mess of room service trays, empty Coke cans, and candy wrappers. She rose to her feet adroitly, walked across the untidy but ornate space, and sat down at the desk in front of an IBM ThinkPad. Also on the desk was a small but high-end VHF radio, a joystick, and a wireless headset hanging off the side of the laptop's screen.

Before touching any of the technology, the woman conducted one more slow breathing exercise. Yoga had always calmed the woman, helped her make her way confidently through stressful situations, and right now she required the utmost calm.

But the yoga wasn't working as she'd hoped.

The woman wore off-white denim pants, a thin black merino sweater, and a smartwatch that tracked her steps. She had a dark complexion, almond eyes, full lips. Her hair was past her shoulders but held back in a ponytail, and a cup of tea remained hot in a thermos next to the computer.

She looked at the image on the monitor for several seconds, enhanced it with movements and clicks from the mouse, then put her headset over her ears, adjusting the microphone over her lips. Taking a moment more to compose herself, the woman closed her dark eyes, took one last long, slow breath, and then opened them while tapping the transmit key on the VHF system.

"Radio check. Radio check. Copper is on the net. How do you read, Cobalt?" She spoke English, but she was Indian, her voice a soft and beautiful lilt. She sounded relaxed enough, because that was the mood she was trying to convey, though in truth, despite the calming effects of yoga, her stomach churned and her blood pressure was up.

Her heart pounded in excitement when a response came through her earphones, loud and clear. A composed American male voice she'd never heard before answered with, "Cobalt receives, Lima Charlie. How me, over?"

She nodded, happy the connection had been made. "And I receive you loud and clear, Cobalt. How are you, sir?"

There was a brief pause. Then the reply, "I'm just dandy, unless you tell me otherwise."

"I have eyes above the target location now, sir. Everything looks fine. Normal patterns of activity."

"How do *I* look?"

Copper furrowed her eyebrows. "I do not know. You have not activated your tracker, so I do not have a fix on your location, sir."

"Yeah . . . about that. I flushed it down the crapper yesterday."

The woman in the hotel suite cocked her head. "You . . . *what*?"

"I don't *do* tracking devices. Sorry."

"But . . . your instructions were to wear the—"

"I'm right here at the target periphery, south side. If you have eyes on, then you should be able to find me."

She didn't see anyone at first, so she leaned closer to the computer screen.

The image on the fifteen-inch laptop monitor showed a straight-down view of a darkened and winding street that ran alongside a narrow row of trees and bushes, which itself ran alongside a chain-link fence. On the inside of the fence were more trees and lush gardens, all the way to a cluster of buildings.

This was the Turkish embassy of Algeria, here in a leafy neighborhood of the capital city, on a hill and within a mile of Algiers Bay.

Scanning left and right, she saw absolutely no one through the low-light camera but a small group of men at a guard shack at the front of the driveway, so she switched the feed to infrared.

Instantly the image before her changed, and she detected something new. A form the size of a human body in the bushes near the street. She zoomed in on it. The body was lying flat, unmoving.

With worry in her voice she said, "Are you lying down?"

"Yes."

"Are you injured, sir?"

"Nope, just chillin'." He added, "I *really* hope you have IR or thermal and can't just see me on your regular camera."

"I am using infrared, yes. You are well hidden, sir."

"I'm Cobalt, Copper. Not 'sir.'"

"Oh . . . yes. Sorry."

These two had never spoken, and Copper could tell Cobalt was much more used to this kind of thing than she. Copper also could sense that he had already detected her relative inexperience, and this was a problem, because the man in charge of both of them had told her to hide the fact that she wasn't exactly seasoned at this sort of fieldwork.

The American asked, "What's the disposition of security?"

She took her time before answering. She was analytical by nature, and that made her good at this. Staying with infrared, she looked over the entire compound off the left shoulder of Cobalt. When she saw nothing that looked in any way out of the ordinary, she said, "No movement at the rear garden or gate, no movement in the south garden near you. I see one team of two patrolling on the north side now; they will be back around to your position in a moment, then they will pass. Their normal pattern of activity suggests an average of eleven minutes for a complete circuit of the grounds. Eleven minutes and nine seconds is the recorded median patrol route." She was pleased with herself for bringing this level of detail to the tactical intelligence picture.

The American did not compliment her, though. Instead he asked, "How long have you been watching the target?"

"This is my third night."

"No hint they've spotted your UAV?"

"Oh, no, sir." She caught herself. "I mean, Cobalt. Impossible. The vehicle is only forty centimeters square, and it's loitering at two hundred meters in the darkness. Impossible to see or hear."

There was a pause. "Well, if you've gotten away with it for two nights, I guess we're okay. Just don't do anything different with your patrol above. UAV pilots think their little gizmos are invisible. I've seen enough of them buzzing over my head to know that they're not."

"Of course." With a little defensiveness, she said, "This is not my first time doing this."

She was telling the truth. This was her *second* time doing this.

Copper sat silently and watched the feed from the drone for two more minutes before saying, "The roving sentries are passing you on the other side of the fence now."

There was no reply.

"Cobalt? Copper for Cobalt?"

Still no reply, but when she next said that the sentries had passed around the corner, he spoke up again. "This isn't my first time, either, Copper. If I don't respond to you, I have a reason. Don't stress. Just keep reporting."

Chastised, she said, "I'm sorry."

"No worries. Relax, miss, you're doin' great."

She had expected a voice with a harder edge, more tension, more menace. But this man, while obviously careful and competent, seemed rather tranquil considering the situation.

And now it was time for her to go over that situation with him. "It is my understanding that you will move to the fence, cut a hole, then pass through the southern garden to the eastern garden. There you will place the device in a hidden location in the trees within ten meters of the center of the three freestanding bungalows there."

Cobalt replied, "That's the plan. But if it looks a little different on the feed than what you are expecting to see, don't worry too much, okay?"

"Sorry, what does that mean?"

"It means, shit happens."

"What does *that* mean?"

"Don't worry. We'll get it done, Copper, but we're doing it my way."

Copper let it go. This operator seemed almost flippant in his duties, but she had been assured that he was more than proficient.

The young Indian woman sat in her hotel suite, sipped her tea with a hand that wasn't quite trembling, and moved the joystick on the drone she piloted over the Turkish embassy in Algeria. She saw a pair of guards milling at the front gate, the two on patrol, and a lone man walking in the grass next to a covered passageway that led from the embassy towards one of three bungalows in the rear garden behind the embassy proper. This man tossed a cigarette on the ground, entered the first of the bungalows, and shut the door behind him.

Only when she was certain he was inside did she say, "Cobalt, your area is clear. You are authorized to execute at the southern fence."

"Roger," came the reply. "Keep me updated on any movements."

The young woman watched intently as the infrared image of the man lying down outside the fence began to move.

Courtland Gentry climbed up to his knees, hefted a black backpack loaded with twenty pounds of equipment, and pulled a pair of nine-inch wire cutters from under his jacket. After checking back over his shoulder to make certain there were no pedestrians on the road who might notice movement, he began low-crawling towards the wire fence.

He wasn't dressed in military gear or even in all black. Instead he wore blue jeans, a charcoal hoodie zipped up over a burgundy T-shirt, and brown hiking boots. His dark hair and short beard helped keep his face concealed in the darkness.

He had a pistol, a suppressed Glock 19 in an open-framed holster, although his job tonight called for no gunplay.

When he had scrambled all the way to the fence, he placed the wire cutter's hardened-steel jaw around the lowest of the chain links. With a strong squeeze the edges bit in, slicing the metal link with a soft snap. He then moved the jaws up to the next link and repeated the process, opening a vertical line in the fence. This was slow work, especially if he wanted to keep the noise level down, which he most definitely did.

His own research of the property had ruled out any audio surveillance measures he needed to worry about. Of course there would be security cameras around the buildings themselves, and these would likely be equipped with capabilities to pick up audio, but he'd seen no microphones, cabling, or electrical outlets just inside the fence line that would suggest the presence of DAS—distributed acoustic sensors.

The woman on the other end of his encrypted communications had confirmed the same thing in a text the day before, but he didn't know her, and he barely knew anything about the man who had contracted him for this job, so he'd decided to do his own recon of the property by arriving in Algiers three days earlier and taking several walks in the neighborhood, eyeing the embassy and the adjoining grounds through the fence as he did so.

This work was freelance for Court; he'd taken the contract through a broker he'd connected with on the dark web. But Court had been doing this sort of thing for so long he had a good idea from the mission itself of who was employing his services tonight. It was the Indian government—or, more specifically, the Research and Analysis Wing, Indian foreign intelligence.

Court figured R&AW needed some work done, and they couldn't get themselves compromised to any of the other parties involved, so they farmed out this job to the broker, who in turn contracted Court.

The equipment he'd been given to do the job was first-rate, and he assumed it came from R&AW. Among the items he'd picked up in a locker in a bus station the day before was one of the smallest stick-on GPS tracking devices he'd ever seen, the size of a nickel and just as slim, and he'd been ordered by his broker to affix it to his body so that his technical specialist would know his whereabouts during the op to help route him away from danger.

Court had marveled at the impressive piece of tech, then tossed the cool little device in the toilet. He wasn't the type to broadcast his movements, but it provided him even more evidence that he was, by proxy anyway, working for an upper-tier intel organization and not just some shadowy jackass on the dark web.

His job tonight was to get into the trees inside the fence line, skulk his way to the right, back towards the rear garden, and then find a place to secret a device that, right now, was folded up in his backpack. It was an IMSI-catcher, a shoebox-sized machine with a telescoping antenna that could dupe a nearby mobile phone into thinking it was the closest cellular tower attached to the provider's network. Through this means, known as a man-in-the-middle attack, the Indian government could eavesdrop on any calls made from any mobile phone used in or around the rear bungalows of the property.

It had been very important to Court's broker that he put the device in place this particular night, because the people conducting the eavesdropping needed to pick up cell phone traffic from a man who was thought to be a guest in one of the bungalows here at the compound for this evening only.

It was an easy mission, as far as Court's freelance contract work went. Not much of a challenge to him at all.

So it was too bad, he thought as he snipped the next wire up in the chain-link fence, that the mission he'd been contracted to undertake was not, in fact, the mission he was planning on carrying out tonight.

Yes, he would plant the equipment for India's Research and Analysis Wing. But once that was done, he'd get down to his true objective here at the Turkish embassy.

He felt bad for the woman behind the disembodied voice in his headset whom he'd been talking to. She seemed like a nice enough person. But he wasn't here simply to do the job she thought he was here to do. Instead, Court had only taken this assignment when the broker informed him that the target they were trying to obtain intel on was not just a member of Pakistan's Inter-Services Intelligence agency but was, in fact, a member of a secretive branch within the agency called the Foreign Coordination Unit. FCU were bad dudes, in Court's estimation, and he held them personally responsible for an incident that had happened nearly a dozen years earlier.

America had let ISI off the hook for an event that took place long ago, but Court Gentry most definitely had not. In all the years since, he'd never knowingly come face-to-face with someone from FCU.

But tonight, he hoped, he'd finally get his chance.

As soon as he was finished placing the equipment in the garden, he'd go inside one of the bungalows out back and he'd look for the Pakistani national. He didn't know the identity of the man; the intel hadn't provided that, only his affiliation with this small branch of the Pakistani intelligence services.

And that was good enough for Court.

Court wasn't here to kill; he was here for information about the events of a dozen years ago, and if this man *was* senior FCU, then either he would have been around himself back then, or he'd at the very least be aware of the operation.

Court wanted to know names of those involved in the incident, and although the mastermind had been killed, his underlings were probably now running the show at FCU, and Court wanted a word with them.

He wasn't going to tell Copper about any of this for two reasons: one, if she didn't know, then she wouldn't be implicated in whatever kidnapping or shit-kicking he was about to perpetrate. And two, if she didn't know, then she wouldn't be able to tell their mutual broker after the fact. She would wonder why he went through a window or a door—that certainly wasn't part of the plan tonight—but he'd come up with some sort of excuse to appease her.

He snipped another wire and decided the vertical row of cuts was now large enough to pry open and shimmy through. Just as he started to open it up, however, Copper's tense but somehow comforting voice filled his head.

"Copper for Cobalt. Patrol just switched out with another two-man unit. The original pair has gone inside the embassy, and the new pair are in the rear garden. They are crossing through the walkway connecting the buildings and not following the fence line. They will be on the south side at your position in sixty seconds."

Court could have made it to a hiding place inside the grounds in the next sixty seconds. If he had more experience working with the woman running his tactical overwatch he might have pushed forward, but something held him back. Copper seemed too raw and unsure, though she was definitely doing her best to hide her inexperience. She said the Turkish guards would be on him in a minute, but what if she was off by fifteen seconds? It wasn't worth chancing it.

He checked the fence to make certain it wouldn't appear to be cut without someone shining a light on it and inspecting it carefully, then grabbed his pack and rolled into the deeper bushes alongside the road, back where he'd been lying since nightfall.

Once he arrived there, Copper came back over his comms.

"I have you on infrared, Cobalt. The patrol is thirty seconds away."

He was pleased that it seemed as if she had estimated the time correctly, and his confidence in her grew a little.

He lay there, unmoving, staring up at the sky, wondering where the little UAV was and wondering if the woman watching him through it was going to get really pissed off at him when he went off mission.

Yeah, she'll be livid, he told himself, but if that was what it took for him to get his hands on the neck of some piece of shit from Pakistan's FCU, then so be it.

He spoke softly, quickly, before the sentries arrived. "I'll execute as soon as you tell me they are out of view."

"Roger, Cobalt. Await my notification."

She was good, he told himself. New at this, apparently, but precise. There was careful calculation in her words and, Court recognized, there was already a unique professional chemistry between the two of them, despite her relative inexperience. He liked this woman. Quickly he reminded himself that she, on the other hand, would begin to loathe him in just a matter of moments.

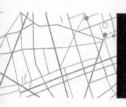

FIVE

The Turkish embassy in Algiers on Chemin des Aqueducs was rarely any sort of a hive of activity, but this evening there were more people on the property than normal. This fact, along with the identity of the new arrivals, had caused significant stress to the property's security office.

Earlier in the day, a guest had arrived from Switzerland, put his luggage in his room, then gone out alone to meet with others in the city in advance of a meeting he had scheduled here in the embassy tonight.

Just after eight p.m. he returned, fed from a dinner of lamb and tired from travel, and went back to his quarters, bungalow one in the rear garden. Here the man planned on taking a long hot shower to freshen up for his meeting at eleven p.m.

Shortly after the return of the Swiss businessman, a two-car entourage pulled through the verdant compound's front gates and drove through the trees up to the main entrance, and eight men climbed out. They were Pakistani, and they were on the approved visitors list.

The Pakistanis unloaded cases and cases from the trunks of the cars, and then they headed up the steps while the Turks looked on.

Their attendance at the property tonight had been sanctioned by Turkish intelligence, but that didn't mean Turkish diplomatic security here at the embassy had to like it.

The men from Pakistan were led by the security men from Turkey into the embassy's security office, where a dozen monitors hung from a wall in front of a desk where two suited men worked day and night. A small table had been set up in a corner, and here the leader of the Pakistanis set up his own monitoring station, solely for this evening.

The Turks thought the Pakistanis were foolish and paranoid, but they stayed out of their way.

It was a weird arrangement; no Turk on the property had any idea what this was all about, and if the Pakistani security guys knew, then they weren't talking.

More visitors went to the roof, and here they placed directional microphones, high-tech cameras, and other equipment.

The rest of the eight-man detail headed out the back door, under an open walkway through the garden, and into bungalow two, checking it out in advance of the arrival of their VIP later in the evening.

In the office, the surveillance tech sat at the table, and after getting a message from his team on the roof, he clicked buttons on a laptop attached to three monitors. He radioed back that all equipment was working nominally, and then when the site survey team pronounced the bungalow free of listening devices or other threats to their principal, the Pakistani man in the corner of the small security office dialed a number on his phone.

It was answered on the first ring, and the Pakistani man in the embassy security office said, "This is Rasool at Observation One. We're set. Bring him in."

Court Gentry had no idea there was any extra coverage on the property tonight. He'd been told the Pakistani from the Foreign Coordination Unit would arrive shortly before his eleven p.m. meeting and then spend the night, and Court figured the man would have a bodyguard or two with him, but he had no clue there would be an advance party sent in hours earlier.

Copper, for her part, was not to blame. Her own operational security protocols meant she had not begun operating the UAV until it was fully dark outside, shortly before nine p.m., to erase any chance that the Turks could see the tiny craft. By then the Pakistanis had arrived, their vehicles were parked in the underground garage, the equipment on the roof had been set, and the new security detail had taken up duties inside the main embassy building.

Twenty-four-hour surveillance on the embassy would have necessitated a much larger operation than Court and his recon specialist.

Even the site survey of the bungalow by the Pakistanis had been missed because Copper's UAV happened to be patrolling directly over the roof of the walkway at the time, so she couldn't see the men approach the small two-story building.

Without any of this crucial intelligence in hand, Court began moving slowly and carefully through the woods around the property's edge, heading directly to the wall of the main embassy building. He expected he'd hear from Copper about this soon, and he was not wrong.

"Copper to Cobalt. As I said before, you can avoid the main building by remaining along the fence line as you travel to the east garden area. Then you can turn north to arrive at the bungalows from the rear."

"I'm heading that way now," he said, and he was; he just wanted to look in any windows in the embassy he could see inside, in case there was activity there related to his search.

Copper's voice came through his earpiece a moment later. "Cobalt, be advised, a vehicle has entered the grounds, proceeding up the driveway to the main entrance."

"Make and model?"

"Appears to be a Mercedes. Four-door. Black. Possibly E-Class."

"Have you seen it before?"

"Negative."

He whispered back, "Roger, let me know what it does."

Court ducked under a pair of darkened windows, then poked his head up again in the lower left corner of the second lit window.

The room was empty.

Copper spoke again. "Four men exited the Mercedes. They are moving towards the front door of the embassy."

"Can you get a look at their faces?"

The delay was short. "Negative. They were under the front door awning too quickly. I just had their backs in my lens."

"Understood. What's the disposition of personnel around me?"

"You are clear to proceed to the rear garden." There was unmistakable confusion, and no small amount of frustration, in the young woman's voice. "Again, I recommend you get back in the foliage on the southern side and—"

"My way, Copper. Remember?"

She did not respond. She was already pissed, Court realized, and she hadn't seen *anything* yet.

Pakistani national Nassir Rasool sat at the temporary monitoring table in the security office, where he kept a relaxed eye over his equipment; he wasn't expecting trouble tonight, but his job was to stay vigilant, to be ready for it if it came.

And then, just as he rubbed fatigue from his eyes, it came.

A red square began blinking on and off on his monitor on the right, the image coming from a camera on the roof and pointed at the night sky above. The square indicated a small speck high above, and it moved slowly across the screen.

Nassir Rasool sat up and leaned closer. Soon several lines of data appeared next to the blinking square. The security officer triggered his microphone and spoke in Urdu to all the Pakistani security men inside the walls of the property.

"Rasool to all staff. I have a UAV overflight . . . actually . . . it appears to be loitering above the location at this time. Altitude one hundred ninety-nine meters and steady, size of aircraft approximately forty centimeters. It's a quadcopter. It will have a camera only. Too small to carry a warhead."

Behind the man at the table, the three Turkish security men obviously did not speak Urdu, because they continued to monitor their screens and chat among themselves.

Rasool heard a response from one of the detail. "You want me to go to the roof?"

"Affirmative. Power the counter drone and standby. I'll watch this a moment. Send two teams out onto the property, eyes open for anything out of the ordinary."

A new voice asked a question. "How do we know what's ordinary? We just got here."

Rasool snapped into his radio, "A raid by Algerian special forces would be out of the ordinary, wouldn't it?"

Chastened, the officer on the radio replied, "Yes, of course. We'll check out the grounds right away."

A UAV hovering over the Turkish embassy did not necessarily mean anything ominous for the Pakistanis on the property. Any kid with a little money could fly a drone around, and though Turkey and Algeria had a good relationship, there were, no doubt, others locally with an interest in what Turkey was doing. There was no chatter anywhere that anyone had word about tonight's meeting between nationals of two other countries, so the man monitoring the UAV above told himself he'd get his counter drone ready, but otherwise he'd just continue to look for signs of danger.

After a full minute of peering in windows of the embassy, Court Gentry continued on towards the back garden of the property.

His eye in the sky noted this and replied with relief. "I see your movement east, Cobalt. Once more, you are advised to return to the trees along the fence. It is safer to—"

She stopped speaking suddenly, and Court immediately dropped low in the dark, behind some landscaping that ran along the wall of the main embassy building. "Copper? What's wrong?"

"I . . . I see men leaving the side doors on both the north and south sides of the main building."

"How many men?"

"Three on the north, two on the south." Court was on the southern side; the doors would be off to his left but out of his view around the uneven wall of the embassy. He was about to ask how the men appeared to Copper—were they just ambling along, or did they look like they had some sort of objective in mind? But she gave Court what he needed unbidden.

"I think they are searching the grounds. Not just patrolling. Flashlights are on, they are heading towards the perimeter, scanning back and forth."

Shit. This was just what Court did *not* want to hear. He'd been detected somehow.

"No chance your drone was spotted?" he asked.

"No chance. You would need very specialized equipment to identify a UAV of this size at this altitude in the dark, and there is no evidence the Turks have this equipment."

Then maybe it was Court himself who'd slipped up. It didn't matter, though; he was *not* leaving. Not when he was so close to getting some alone time with a senior man from Pakistan's Foreign Coordination Unit.

He said, "Keep me updated. Operation continues."

"Yes, sir."

She was back to "sir" again. She was nervous, and he didn't need his overwatch nervous, but he *did* need her full attention and focus, so he let it go. He headed on to the bungalows, just another twenty yards on through the dark and then across a small garden. He'd position himself with a view of the covered path that bisected the garden and connected the three small buildings to the main embassy. This way he could see anyone coming or going back to the residences. Copper would go apoplectic when Court squatted down in a hide to lie in wait, and he didn't want to listen to that, but he couldn't turn his radio off because she was the one who could keep him apprised of the movements of the search parties.

The Pakistani VIP had been shuffled into the embassy with no fanfare, his three body men alongside him. As soon as he arrived he was told the man he was here to meet was staying in bungalow one, and he would be in bungalow two. The Pakistani VIP informed those around him that he would go straight to his quarters to change from his day of travel, and then he would head back to his meeting.

As he approached the rear of the building, heading for the covered walkway to the back garden, one of his security men stepped up to him and told him a small UAV had been spotted overhead. From the size of the device, they were certain it would have nothing more than a camera on board, so the VIP was surrounded by four officers, and together they all walked out back under the cover of the roof over the walkway.

The VIP wasn't concerned. He was assured by his men that he could stay out of the line of sight of the device above. Plus, if he cut and ran every time there was a drone somewhere nearby, he'd never get anything done, and he had a hell of a lot to do.

Court moved around the back of the bungalows, then around the side of number three. There was thick, lush Mediterranean landscaping here, and he was able to position himself on the northwest corner of the building, kneeling down between thick bushes and the wall. From here he could get eyes on anyone who came out of the embassy or any of the three bungalows. He knew that the men searching the grounds now might force him to vacate this hide and go defensive, slipping the search parties as he moved around the property, but he had Copper to help him avoid the guards.

Copper broadcast into his ear, but it wasn't fresh information about the men checking the grounds. It was, in fact, exactly what Court expected to hear. "Sir? Why are you just sitting there? This is *not* your mission. You can place the IMSI-catcher and turn it on, and then you can evacuate via the northern fence. There is no one there now, they are all moving around the front of the property at this time. We can finish this operation safely, but only if you—"

Court spoke calmly but firmly. "I need you to stay off the net unless you see personnel approaching my position. Understood?"

"But I don't know what you are—"

"Understood?"

There was a pause, and then, "Yes, sir."

"Good. I'm going silent for a minute. Just watch my back and report."

Copper did not reply. *Yep,* Court thought, *here begins the adversarial relationship between me and my support.* It was inevitable, he'd known from the start, but he hadn't expected to actually *need* her help during this phase of his op.

Across the garden, the back door to the embassy building opened, and five men in dark suits stepped out. They walked along the covered path in Court's general direction, though he was hidden off to their left between the corner of bungalow three and a bushy eucalyptus plant.

The five men carried themselves differently than the others he'd seen milling around the embassy during his three days of recon.

This group was visiting; he was certain they were from the vehicle Copper had alerted him to at the front of the property.

Copper came over his headset once again. He assumed she wouldn't be able to see these men since they were under cover, so he expected she'd have other news for him.

"There is a man on the roof now. I don't know what he's doing, he's just opening a black container. Can't see what's inside it. I will notify you if he comes to the edge of the building where he can see the garden and—"

Court interrupted her in a whisper. It was perfectly quiet out here save for the footsteps of the approaching men. "Copper, give me a second. Do not transmit."

"But—"

"Copper."

"Yes, sir. I will wait to hear from you, but again, you are not following the—"

"Copper." He snapped her call sign in an angry whisper, and she went quiet.

There was pathway lighting, but it didn't reach the approaching men's faces, only illuminated them from the waist down. They neared the American's position, and once they arrived at the entrance to bungalow two, Court was no more than fifty feet away. He was hidden, perfectly still, even holding his breath now, but more than anything, he was peering into the night, desperate to ascertain if one of these men might be the unknown FCU officer he'd come to find.

The man in the middle, obviously, was the most likely to be a VIP, so Court strained for a look at his face.

And then, at the entrance to bungalow number two, the man in the middle stepped under a gas lamp at the door, turned, and spoke to those who had been shielding him.

Reflecting back later, Court was amazed that he had recognized the face so quickly. It was as if the past twelve years of his life had never even happened.

He knew this man. This wasn't some FCU operative who might or might not be able to tell him details of the events that he'd spent over a decade hoping to someday understand and exact retribution for.

No, this was the man responsible for it all, the mastermind, here in the flesh. And this, to Court, was strange on very many levels, not the least of which being that the mastermind was dead.

This can't be, Court thought.

He recovered quickly. Instinctively, impulsively, he reached to his hip and drew his suppressed Glock 19, popping it out of the molded holster and lifting it up slowly.

But before he raised the weapon to eye level, the man disappeared out of view and into his bungalow. Only one of his bodyguards followed him in; the rest fanned out around the garden. Flashlights flipped on; they didn't seem agitated or certain there was an infiltrator in their midst, but they were clearly intent on securing this location.

Court backed up around the edge of the third bungalow and leaned his back against the wall. His heart pounding, he reholstered his weapon with a jittering hand, then rose and began running.

He found himself on the east side of bungalow three, pushing his way into thick vegetation and away from any electric lighting. He backed up to a tree near the chain-link fence at the edge of the property here, then slid down the trunk, ending up in a squat in the dark.

And then, he just sat there, a thousand-yard stare on his face, his mouth slightly agape, his skin ice cold.

He said a word softly, the sound lost in the rustle of the fir and the cypress around him. Then he said it again. Louder this time. "Khan."

His hands began to shake. "Murad Khan. What the fuck?"

SIX

After allowing himself a few seconds to recover, Court removed his pack from his back and pushed it into the nearby eucalyptus, the IMSI-catcher inside and forgotten. He pulled his Glock 19 pistol from the holster on his belt again and held it with one hand between his knees. After taking just a moment to decide on his course of action, he tapped his transmitter. Forcing calm into his voice, he said, "Copper, you reading me still?"

The young woman sounded like she was on the verge of panic. "What the hell are you doing? Why were you running? There are lights on in the middle bungalow. Men looking over the rear courtyard with flashlights. Sir, there are ten men outside the embassy now, and they are all searching for someone."

Court did not respond to any of this. His heart was racing as he tapped the transmit key again. "Copper, listen carefully. Spin the ball."

There was a short delay. "Spin the . . . spin the *what*?"

"I need you to spin the ball."

"I . . . I don't know what that means, sir. That is code? Sir, I don't understand anything about what is happening right now."

Court sighed. He forgave her. He was using American military slang, but even though her English was flawless, she was obviously from India. Of course she'd have no clue what he was asking of her. His mind was racing right now, he wasn't thinking straight, and he needed to get his shit under control. He explained himself, speaking softly and quickly. "When a military unit wants the UAV overhead to stop monitoring their actions, they tell them to 'spin the ball.' On the American Predator and Reaper drones, there is a ball in the nose cone that houses all the cameras. 'Spin the ball' means 'turn the cameras away.'"

He clarified for simplicity. "It means 'stop watching what I'm doing.'"

"Why would a military unit not want what they were doing recorded or watched?"

This, in Court's estimation, was a dumb question, but he didn't say this. Instead he cut to the chase. "There's a man here on the embassy grounds. A man I recognize. I had no idea I was going to see him tonight, but I did, and there is only one thing I can do about it."

"What?"

Court did not hesitate. "I have to kill him. Trust me, this dude has it coming."

The pause on the other side came just as he expected it to. When she spoke, her voice was weak, hoarse. "No, no, sir. *No*, sir, you *can't*."

"Spin the ball, Copper, *now*. In fact, break off all surveillance of this location, recall the drone to your position, pack up and get out of the country as soon as you can. Ending transmission. Good luck."

He reached for the radio on his belt to turn it off, but the woman said, "Wait! Wait. I have to report this to Arjun."

Arjun was Court's broker, the man who hired him for the mission.

"Of course you do. You're fine, you had nothing to do with this. This is me." Court looked around in the dark a moment, his pistol at the low ready. Softly, almost to himself but still transmitting, he said, "It's always me."

"But—"

Court turned off his radio, stood, turned, and began moving back towards the rear of bungalow two.

The guards patrolling the embassy grounds found the breach in the fence on the southern side of the property, and they radioed this news back to Nassir Rasool in the security office. The Pakistani had been speaking softly over the net about the drone and his additional search of the property, but now that he knew without a doubt that some sort of intrusion had taken place, he turned his head and shouted to the bored Turkish security men sitting at the monitors of the fixed cameras here at the embassy. In English he said, "You have an incursion! South-side fence has been cut. Get all the lights on and everyone searching!"

The Pakistani had no authority to give orders here, but his news was more than adequate to get the men on their radios, barking instructions to the Turkish security staff all over the property. While they did this, the Pakistani at the table reached to his own radio.

"Roof! Release the counter drone!"

It took just seconds for the response. "This is the roof. Counter drone is in the air."

Rasool opened a control panel on one of his screens and reached for his joystick. After a moment to make certain everything was working nominally, he said, "Observation One confirms good control of the vehicle." He manipulated his mouse and tapped a few keys. "Vehicle lock on enemy aircraft initiated." And then, "Lock on, acquired."

Almost instantly, the speed and trajectory of the tiny UAV he was tracking changed. Into the radio he said, "I think it's leaving the scene. They must have detected the security sweep. Enemy aircraft is heading east-southeast, speed increasing. We are going after that drone; its range isn't far, and that means whoever has been watching us is nearby. Roll a car of men and I'll vector them as able."

The man at the desk knew UAVs; he had personally acquired this state-of-the-art countersurveillance equipment from China, technology that could protect any location from the spying eyes of a drone. And he knew that a UAV the size of the one he was tracking could probably last about seventy-five minutes tops before it needed to have its battery changed or recharged. A small battery meant a limited range, and whoever was operating this device would probably be somewhere within five or ten minutes' flying time of the Turkish embassy.

"I'll send the Indian along with four men," the Pakistani security director said through the radio. "We will stay to help the Turks find out whoever is on the grounds."

A minute later the black Mercedes screeched out of the underground garage and began racing towards the front gate and the street.

Copper initiated the recall of her UAV, then began pacing around in circles in her suite with a phone to her ear. Her call was answered on the third ring by Arjun, and both the man on the other line and the woman in the hotel suite spoke Hindi to one another.

"Is it done?" the man asked.

"It's *not* done! It is *shit*! Absolute *shit*! What have you got me involved with?"

"Calm down! What are you talking about?"

"The asset just informed me he is going to kill a man on the premises."

Arjun was clearly gobsmacked. "*Kill a man?* Why?"

"I don't know."

"I did not hire him to kill anybody. He was only supposed to plant the equipment."

"I told him this! Then he told me to bring the UAV back to my location and to leave the country. I am doing that now. I don't want to be a part of an assassination!"

There was a slight pause, and then the man said, "I want you out of there."

"Believe me. I am leaving!"

"Get to the airport. I'll put you on the first flight to anywhere."

"Okay." After a pause she said, "What is happening?"

"I . . . I don't know. It's the fucking American. He is ruining everything."

She ended the call, then ran into her bedroom to begin packing.

Court couldn't believe his luck. He found an unlocked ground-floor window on the north side of bungalow two. There were blinds on the window, so he couldn't see into the room, but he was, at least, able to tell that the lights were off in this part of the building.

A search of the inside of the window satisfied him that it was not wired with a security alarm. Court figured the Turks assumed that their cameras, guns, gates, and staff protecting the property itself provided enough protection, and the internal structures didn't need to be overly secure.

This bungalow was large enough for Court to consider entering here, somehow disabling the one security man he'd seen enter with his target, and then killing his target. It would have to be as quick and as quiet as possible, considering the fact that the two-acre property was literally crawling with opposition. So while he would have loved nothing more than for Khan to suffer a demise as slow and excruciating as it was overdue, he'd have to slit the man's throat or, if unavoidable, just shoot him in the face with his suppressed Glock.

He decided to go ahead with this plan, so anxious he was to kill this man, though he was seasoned enough to know his plan was riddled with holes. Copper was gone, and that meant his overhead recon on the disposition of security forces was gone, too. Goons could start raining down on him from all angles at any second, and he'd have no escape.

But it didn't matter. The events of twelve years ago were as fresh in his mind as if they had happened just yesterday, and he was certain Murad Khan needed to be held accountable for his actions.

Court knew he might well die tonight in the process of assassinating Khan, but as far as he was concerned, paying that price would be a bargain.

Court rose at the window and began slowly pushing the wood-framed glass up, remaining perfectly silent as he did so. The lights were still off on the other side of the blinds; it was quiet around this part of the property, though he heard yelling and shouting off in the distance.

Soon he had the window open high enough to climb through; he'd heard nothing to alert him to any danger, so he started to push the wooden blinds apart for a peek at the room he'd be entering. He reached for them, all his senses on fire now, and he almost had a hand on the blinds.

Then the slats snapped open.

He pulled his hand away, but he did not run.

There, just three feet from his face and staring right back at him through the open blinds, was Murad Khan, former officer in the Foreign Coordination Unit of the Inter-Services Intelligence agency of Pakistan.

Khan was clearly as alarmed to see Court as Court was to see Khan.

Court knew his own face telegraphed that he recognized the man in front of him, and he regretted this, but he cut himself some slack.

Khan's face had been a part of his nightmares for a dozen years now.

He realized the man was standing alone in a dark little bathroom. He'd stepped up to piss in the toilet when he'd obviously heard the window a foot away from him slide open. The two men's eyes stayed locked on each other for a second more, but then Court's right hand shot down and grabbed his Glock. His plan was to jam the end of the silencer in the man's chest and shoot him through the heart at contact distance.

And then Court would run for his life.

The pistol was rising up for the impossible-to-miss kill shot, but then a firearm cracked close off to Court's right, and he felt a round streak right in front of his nose, impacting in the trees off to his left somewhere. Another shot sent Court spinning in the direction of the gunfire, and aiming at the shooter now, he squeezed off two quick rounds.

A man at the northeast corner of bungalow two dropped his pistol and grabbed at his thigh before falling back behind the wall and out of Court's view.

The American now swung his weapon back to the open window inches from his face.

Khan was gone, clear of Court's field of fire.

Another gunshot boomed off to his right, this one hitting the wall near the window and peppering Court's face with brick and plaster.

The American turned and ran into the trees on the east, racing towards the perimeter fence in the darkness, cussing aloud at the situation he'd put himself in, and at the fact that he'd achieved nothing at all tonight other than learning one thing—not only had he failed tonight; he'd failed long ago, as well.

Copper grabbed all the clothing strewn around her bedroom and threw it into a rolling suitcase. After zipping it shut and leaving it on the bed, she tossed the toiletries arrayed around her messy bathroom into her shoulder bag, and this, too, she threw on the bed.

She rushed back to her computers to check the status of the UAV and saw that it was just coming to a hover above her hotel. As she watched the onboard camera on her monitor, the aircraft began lowering from two hundred meters down to her balcony.

She couldn't power off her equipment until she recovered it, so she ran back to the bedroom, grabbed her suitcase and her handbag, and brought them back out, placing them at the front door.

Just as she headed again back to the computers, her wireless headset came alive in her ear. She had forgotten she was still wearing it.

"Cobalt for Copper. Are you still up on this net?" It was the American asset. The man who went off mission and destroyed this entire operation.

She snapped at him. "I am shutting down and leaving. Why are you even contacting me?"

"Just checking in. Are you okay?"

"I will be better when I stop talking to you! Are you still in the compound?"

"No. I'm clear. Back out on the street a couple blocks away." After a pause he said, "Listen . . . that thing I said I was going to do? It didn't happen, so you can relax about that. Still, you need to get out of wherever you are, there's some dangerous people involved in all this."

"*Really?* Well, I think I am talking to one of them right now, aren't I?"

"Fair point. What about the UAV?"

"It is descending above my location now, I was just about to land it and pack it up." Her eyes looked up to the monitor to check the camera feed, and she saw that it was down to forty meters and descending on course.

The American said, "Something tipped off security to some trouble. I don't know what it was."

"Well, don't blame me. Maybe if you had stayed on mission, this wouldn't have happened. As I said, it would be impossible to track my UAV without—"

She stopped talking when she saw something on the camera feed that confused her. Quickly she tapped a button that stopped the drone's descent—just thirty-five meters now from landing.

The man on the other end of the connection noted her sudden silence.

"Copper? You there? Something wrong?"

Softly, almost in a whisper, she said, "The black Mercedes. From the embassy."

"What about it?"

"It is . . . I don't understand this."

"Talk to me, Copper."

"It's parked outside my suite, just below the balcony."

"Shit," the man said. *"Shit!"*

"I don't understand . . . How could they know where I am?"

"Where *are* you?"

She hesitated; Cobalt was not supposed to know her location, but the terror of realizing she'd been identified and fixed by the enemy overpowered her desire to remain beholden to her orders or her operational security. "I am at the Hotel el Djazair. It's only five minutes from the embassy."

"They tracked your drone somehow." And then, for a third time, the man shouted, "Shit!"

"How could they possibly—"

"It doesn't matter. They are there, and you are going to have to deal with it. Listen very carefully to me. You won't be able to get away. They *will* take you."

"What? No. Take me where?"

"They will want to know who you are, what you know. That means they won't kill you. I need you to do something for me."

"What?"

"Do you have another little stick-on GPS tracker like the one I was given?"

Copper turned and looked at one of her backpacks. "Yes."

"What's the battery life?"

"Thirty hours. Why?"

"Hide it on your body. *Now.* I will track you wherever they take you, and I will get you back. You're going to have to hurry."

Her mind raced; she felt light-headed, nauseous. "You . . . you need my phone to see the tracking information."

"Damn. They won't leave your phone behind."

She looked down to her wrist. "My smartwatch. You can read the tracker location from the smartwatch."

"That's it, then. Hide it in the bathroom, under the vanity, around the plumbing. I'll find it. What room?"

"Suite 211."

"I'm on the way, but I won't get to you as fast as they will."

Copper heard rushed footsteps in the hallway just outside her room. Men running.

"They are here! I can jump from the balcony and—"

"They are too smart for that. They will have a man in that car, and he will get you. Do what I said to do, and I *will* get you back." There was a quick pause. Then, "I promise."

She yanked off her headset, grabbed a tracker from the backpack, and ran into the bathroom. She took off the cover over the adhesive and placed the small, flat cylindrical device high on the back of her neck, then took out her ponytail so it was hidden by her dark hair, and she pulled off her watch. Outside in the suite she heard a violent bang against the door. They weren't knocking on it; they were breaking it down.

Looking around, panic welling inside her, she opened up the cabinet below the vanity, then placed the smartwatch in the joint in the plumbing, making it impossible to see unless someone got down on the floor and looked up for it. She hoped the American was smart enough to find it, because she only had time to step back into the living room of the suite before the door to the hallway crashed open.

She stood there next to all her surveillance equipment. Her UAV had landed on the balcony, and the backup drone rested on the charging station next to it.

She had been caught as red-handed as one could be.

She expected the men who filed into the room to be Pakistani or Turkish, perhaps even Algerians who worked at the embassy, so she was surprised and confused when the first man approached her and spoke.

"Tum kaun ho?" *Who are you?* It was Hindi, the woman's native language.

She stammered but did not answer.

The man said, "Tum kiske liye kaam kar rahi ho?" *Who are you working for?*

An Indian? Here? Working for the Pakistanis? She tried to figure it out, but not for long, because another man stepped up without speaking and swept a powerful backhand across her face. She fell to the ground, clutched at her battered jaw, and fought back tears of both pain and terror. The man who struck her turned to the others in the room and spoke in Urdu. Copper knew a little of the language—she'd studied it at university—but she didn't understand what the man said.

Two men reached down and grabbed her, yanked her to her feet, while others rushed towards the desk full of computers and began grabbing equipment.

SEVEN

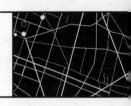

TWELVE YEARS AGO

The long rectangular table at the center of the well-lit space was surrounded by men and women who turned Matthew Hanley's way when he entered the sterile conference room, and this made him uncomfortable. The seventh floor of the CIA's McLean, Virginia, headquarters held that kind of vibe for a man who, just three days prior, had been running lethal operations from an Agency outpost in eastern Afghanistan. He didn't have friends here at HQ, though he saw faces he recognized. He nodded at no one in particular, then found an open chair halfway down the table on the right.

Once seated, he felt enveloped by the strange quiet, and he looked around more carefully. There were eleven at the table plus himself, and all were silent, even though the meeting had not yet begun.

Fun crowd, Hanley thought.

Hanley had done stints working at headquarters, but not many, and not in a long time. He was a field man; he'd been with the Directorate of Operations and the National Clandestine Service since leaving the military nearly fifteen years prior. He was in his midforties now and had served as a case officer in four countries before being moved over into the Special Activities Division, where he now worked as a group chief leading a combined Ground Branch and Intelligence task force composed of two teams: Golf Sierra and Lima Foxtrot. Lima Foxtrot was still over in Afghanistan, along with the SAD intelligence cell under Hanley's command, but he'd brought Golf Sierra back to the States with him so the five surviving men could bury their fallen teammate and get to work finding and training up a replacement for him.

To this end, Matt had some ideas, and he planned on discussing them just as soon as this meeting was called to order.

He scanned the table around him. It was, at first glance, nothing but mid- and high-level executives from different departments, and he felt like the only outlier in the bunch. Men and women from the Special Activities Division, from Legal, from Personnel, and from the D/O, which ran both SAD and other all-operations divisions.

Max Ohlhauser from Legal, along with a deputy, a kid who didn't look twenty-five and dressed like he'd been on his way to a *GQ* photo shoot when yanked into the meeting, sat across from him.

Gray-haired Jordan Mayes, the assistant deputy director of SAD, sat next to the empty chair at the head of the table on Hanley's left.

Looking down the table, however, Hanley saw one man he did not recognize. He sat at the far end, across and down from Hanley, and he looked as out of place as Hanley felt. The man wore his rumpled gray suit like it both pained and angered him to do so; his thinning curly hair was only perfunctorily combed, as if it had been done in a cab on the way here. He was past sixty, and rough-looking, and he doodled on a pad of paper in front of him while eyeing all the others in the room, Matt Hanley included.

Matt Hanley *especially*, in fact.

Hanley had been at this long enough to know that this guy was Operations, and old school, *very* old school. There was no way he was any kind of an exec; he looked and acted foreign here at HQ, even more so than Hanley himself, and he was way too battle-hardened and weatherworn to be in Analysis or Science and Technology.

He was a grizzled old spook; normally a man like that at that age would have been put out to pasture, so Hanley wondered if he was part of the training cadre at the Farm or one of the other CIA facilities. If so, he couldn't imagine what the hell the man was doing here for this meeting about a dead Ground Branch operator in Pakistan.

Maurice Cahill wondered what the hell he was doing here for this meeting about a dead Ground Branch operator in Pakistan. He wasn't Ground Branch, he hadn't trained the man, and he didn't know anything about what had happened to him because he wasn't read in on the op, other than the fact that the man died and a Hellfire was launched in Pakistan.

It sounded like a shit show, but it wasn't Maurice's shit show, so he couldn't imagine what any of this could possibly have to do with him. Nevertheless he'd received the order the afternoon before to put on a monkey suit, come to HQ, and plop his ass in this conference room at this time, so here he was. As he looked around the room, he saw Mayes, Ohlhauser, and Ohlhauser's pretty-boy number two, whatever the fuck his name was. Athena Barnett from Personnel was here; DeFalco, deputy director for operations, sat morosely, probably because SAD was the redheaded stepchild of D/O, and another dead operator, along with a hasty drone strike, meant headaches for the DDO.

Yes, just as Maurice had expected, the table was filled with the usual suspects for a dry and inconsequential meeting on the seventh floor.

These weren't the men and women who actually did the work at the Agency. These were the men and women who *talked* about those who did the work at the Agency.

But then Maurice saw Matt Hanley.

Maurice knew Hanley, though only by reputation. An ex–Green Beret, then a move to the Agency, a meteoric rise as a case officer, working rough stations, then a sideways shuffle into the Special Activities Division at the vanguard of the global war on terror.

Maurice had heard that Hanley was a royal prick but also damn good at his job. Not a man you'd want watching your back when it came to office politics, but exactly the man you'd want watching your back out in the field.

The Agency needed men like Hanley, Maurice told himself.

He just didn't want to know him.

Well, Maurice thought, *at least Hanley's a doer and not a talker, like the rest of this pretentious bunch.*

The older man doodled on his pad, wishing this meeting would hurry up and get going already, because he wanted to get out of HQ before he started to smell like the rest of the starched shirts around him.

Mercifully, the door beyond the far end of the table opened, and a man in his fifties entered. Denny Carmichael was the head of the SAD, himself former military, having reached the rank of lieutenant colonel in the Marine Corps. Carmichael didn't smile, didn't acknowledge anyone at the table; he just sat down, took some papers from Mayes on his left, and then looked up at the room. His eyes almost immediately locked on Hanley's, and Maurice knew this was about to get ugly.

Hanley saw his boss glare across the table at him, and he knew this was about to get ugly.

Carmichael said, "Matt. We meet again under the same circumstances as four months ago. Another fatality on your task force."

"Yes, sir."

"And this time, to top it off, we shoved a Hellfire missile up the ass of a pickup truck with two nobodies inside. That, as you know, makes deniability of our operation a hard sell to the Pakistanis. State and the White House are running Greg DeFalco and me through the fucking coals." He motioned to DeFalco, who didn't even look up from his briefing papers.

Hanley took a slow breath. "My men were attempting to recover their teammate, and the decision was made to engage the technical and guard tower with a Hellfire in order to—"

Carmichael waved a hand in the air and interrupted. "How'd you lose *another* man, Matt? What's the story this time?"

"I—"

Carmichael didn't wait for the response. "I read the after-action report. Six men dropped into a heavily defended compound. I guess we should count ourselves lucky your entire team wasn't wiped out."

Matt Hanley cleared his throat, glanced down at the opposite end of the table from Carmichael, and saw the old Operations man he couldn't identify looking at him with a stare that went right through him. He shook away the unease this caused and said, "Sir, our intel shop had been right on everything they had given us since we got to Forward Operating Base Chapman last month. We had solid information on the target location. All the overflights we needed were approved and carried out. We saw six guards on site, widely dispersed, plus the arrival of the man we thought to be an HVT with two security. We expected no more than nine enemy in total."

"But?"

"But a tunnel had been constructed that led out of the compound. Somehow infiltrators came into the location while we were conducting our search for the HVT. We presume the HVT used that same tunnel to escape."

"So somebody knew you were coming. A leak in your operation, perhaps?"

"I don't see how. We certainly didn't inform Pakistani authorities we were conducting a raid near Peshawar. This was Ground Branch, sir. Done in the black. If there was a compromise, it happened *during* the mission. A sentry the UAV didn't spot, something like that."

Carmichael nodded, looked down at his papers. "The team. Golf Sierra. They've been all the fuck over in the past year."

"That's correct, sir. They have conducted more high-threat ops and taken more hits than any other team in Ground Branch, bar none."

"You suffered two deaths along with a career-ending injury on the team, all in the last six months. You are certain your problem isn't with your Number One?" Carmichael glanced at his notes again. "Hightower?"

Hanley shook his head adamantly. "Absolutely positive about that, sir. Zack Hightower is former Naval Special Warfare. A DEVGRU operator. Decades of experience. He's a hard charger, no question, but that's exactly what we need. He's intelligent and careful without being carefree."

Carmichael looked around the room. "Other thoughts?"

The young man with slicked-back dark hair sat directly across from Hanley. Hanley didn't recognize him, but he was seated next to Ohlhauser, the top lawyer for Operations at CIA, so Hanley took the man to be part of the legal team. He said, "Why not stand down Golf Sierra for a few months? Do a safety review. Ascertain if there are gaps we need to fill in the—"

Carmichael shook his head. "We need them in the field and producing. Especially now." He turned back to Hanley. "The target of the mission was a deputy for the terrorist known as Pasha the Kashmiri. Did you recover *anything* of value about this Pasha guy or his organization?"

Hanley cleared his throat uncomfortably. "Golf Sierra captured a subject at the base. He claims he was security, brought in for Major Omar Mufti's arrival that day. This man wasn't armed when we encountered him; we're guessing he tossed his weapon to make a run for it. He doesn't know much, but he admits to being a member of the Kashmiri Resistance Front. He did confirm other intel that we've picked up on the KRF in the past few months. He says the KRF is planning . . . how did he phrase it?" Hanley looked to his own notes now. "Something the West has never had to deal with before."

Carmichael said, "Threats don't impress me." Then he sighed. "What about our working theory that Pasha was military as well, just like his number two?"

"The prisoner claims to not know of anyone higher in the hierarchy than Major Mufti. The complexity of their raids, however, definitely lead us to believe the fighters are organized and well trained, and that leads us to the conclusion that they are run by someone with military experience. Maybe that's just Mufti exerting his influence as second-in-command, maybe that's Pasha himself."

Carmichael shook his head. "Mufti was a damn helo pilot. He's not organizing land raids and rocket attacks against American outposts."

Hanley acquiesced with a shrug.

Carmichael added, "I think Pasha is former military as well, a colonel, perhaps. If true, then he might well have dangerous contacts, and he might very well know a lot more about Agency activities in Pakistan and Afghanistan than we want any terrorist knowing." He thought a moment, and then with a nod he said, "Golf Sierra will stay on this. As soon as you replace the fallen paramilitary operations officer, I want you, and them, back over there. Let Lima Foxtrot fill the gap in the meantime." Carmichael barked now, "And fix your damn intelligence section, Matt! You and I both have worked operations where we were sent into unknowns after the analysts claimed to know it all. I didn't like it when it was me, and I don't like it for Hightower and his men."

"Yes, sir. I'm looking at replacing the analyst who failed." He drummed his fingers on his notepad. "About replacing the paramilitary, though, I want to pick from Ground Branch's best. I've brought a few names along who I think would be suitable for the—"

Carmichael shook his head. "Disallowed. I have another idea. I've looked at your missions over the last year, and I'm looking at what's ahead for you and your boys, going after Pasha in Pakistan. This is a marathon, not a sprint. I might need your team to infiltrate deeper into denied territory. Much deeper."

Warily, Hanley said, "Okay."

"I have decided, then, that you need a different kind of operator on your team."

Hanley was instantly on guard now. *What do any of these suits know about what the hell Hightower needs out there in the mud and sand?* He controlled himself and asked, "What do you mean by that, sir?"

"Not just another shooter. You need someone with the ability to work on a team for kinetic actions, but also someone able to infiltrate a target."

Matt Hanley sniffed. "My boys did a HAHO drop at twenty-eight thousand feet, Denny, landing on a rooftop thirty miles away. Golf Sierra infiltrates targets just fine."

Carmichael shook his head. "I'm not talking about that type of infiltration. You need a man with real tradecraft. I want your new Six to be a spook. A spook who can shoot."

"My Ground Branch men aren't just trigger pullers. They have all the tradecraft skills they need to—"

"Your men are former DEVGRU or Delta or HRT guys who operate in teams. They have more tradecraft than military special operations forces, no argument there, but I'm talking about something else. Not a jack of both trades, but an ace of *both* trades. Both soldier and spy. *That's* what you need."

Hanley said, "In my experience here in Operations, that man does not exist."

Suddenly Hanley heard movement across the table. He turned to see the old man he didn't recognize sitting up straighter suddenly, putting his pen down, and then crossing his arms. Clearly he understood something about what Carmichael was saying, and clearly he didn't like it.

Hanley, however, remained very much in the dark.

"Sir," Hanley said to Carmichael. "Do you have someone in mind?"

"I do. But first, I asked some people to come to this meeting who might have ideas of their own. I suspect their thoughts will coincide with mine." He scanned the table. "The rest of you know details about code word ops using Agency field assets. I want a name. A name of a man who might fit in on a rendition team, but a man who also excels at thinking outside the box. I need a man who can help Golf Sierra conduct unconventional operations in and around Pakistan."

It was silent for a moment. Hanley looked around, unsure who would reply.

To Hanley's surprise, the young man from Legal was the first to speak. He said, "Sir?"

Carmichael turned to him. "Lloyd?"

"You're talking about Violator."

Carmichael nodded. "I am, indeed."

Hanley looked to the young man now. "What's Violator?"

Lloyd said, "Not what. *Who*. He did that thing in Murmansk, a year or so ago."

There were twelve at the table in total. Hanley noticed that only a few nodded in understanding.

"I agree," DeFalco from Operations said. "That took incredible tradecraft, staying in deep cover like that for so long, and it obviously also took a lot of martial ability. There was a significant body count at the end of it, if you remember."

Hanley couldn't believe what he was hearing. He knew some details of the operation in the port city of Murmansk in northwestern Russia, but it was code-worded, and not an SAD initiative, so he didn't know much. "The Murmansk operation. Are you suggesting that was accomplished by only *one* asset?"

Carmichael nodded at this. "Affirmative." It was clear to Hanley that this was the exact same asset Carmichael himself had been thinking about.

Hanley then asked, "And he's ours?"

"He's in the D/O, yes," DeFalco confirmed.

"Okay," Hanley said, sitting back in his chair now. "You have my attention."

Carmichael turned to look down the table now. Hanley followed his eyes, didn't know which of the two men and one woman sitting there was going to speak. When no one did, he looked back to Carmichael.

Hanley took the floor again. "Sir, Golf Sierra is getting more hits, more high-threat, high-impact raids, than anyone else in Ground Branch. I'd put their activity level up against anyone at JSOC, and I can guarantee the complexity of their work is more than anything the Army or Navy is doing. Whoever this asset is . . . I need to, at *least*, take a look at him for myself. To put him with Hightower and the rest of the team, and see if we can work him in."

Carmichael kept his eyes on the far end of the table while he addressed Hanley. Now it was clear that the head of the Special Activities Division was staring at the older man in the rumpled gray suit. Carmichael said, "The asset who conducted the Murmansk operation . . . *alone* . . . is code named Violator. Maurice Cahill built him, quite literally, from the ground up."

Matt Hanley spun his head to the right, stared at the older man. *So this is the infamous Maurice.* He didn't know Cahill personally, but he knew the man's reputation.

Holy shit, Hanley thought. *This old bastard is a living legend.*

Cahill hadn't said a word during the meeting, but now he spoke up.

His voice was raspy, like these were the first words he'd uttered today. This week, even. "Violator is not a good fit for a rendition team, Denny."

"But—"

"He's in cover right now, on a national security directive, and he is in a role he knows. We should leave him right there."

Hanley spoke up now. Intrigued. "Can he shoot? Is he a paramilitary?"

Maurice brought his shoulders back a little. "He has overlapping skill sets with the type of work Ground Branch does, I won't deny that, but that's not the point. The point is, he's needed exactly where he is to—"

Carmichael interrupted. "*I'll* determine where he's needed, Maurice. You trained him. You know him. Do you think he could integrate with the rendition task force if called upon to do so?"

Maurice shrugged. "He's done every last thing we've ever asked of him, I don't see why he couldn't run and gun with some team of Ground Branch door kickers, but that's not where his true abilities lie. He's a force multi-plier, not a point man on a kill squad. He needs to be—"

Carmichael turned to Hanley, ignoring Maurice. "You want him?"

Hanley said, "I want to see his file, at least."

To this, Carmichael answered flatly. "Denied. He was hired into the Agency in a sub rosa program that is not in your purview. Not in the pur-view of anyone in this room except for Mayes, Max Ohlhauser, Greg De-Falco, and myself."

Jordan Mayes took the opportunity to say, "I think, sir, considering what Matt and Golf Sierra have been doing in the past year, and consider-ing what we'll likely need from them in the near term on the hunt for Pa-sha the Kashmiri, Violator would be a perfect fit."

Maurice spoke up again. Imploringly this time. "Look, Denny. Not this one. Not this asset. Please, find somebody else."

Carmichael stared him down. "You sound like an overprotective parent."

"I'm the one man in the room who knows the man's competencies. He's been run ragged. Let's save him for when we *really* need him."

"Mr. Cahill." Hanley spoke up now. "If he did Murmansk, alone, then *I* know his competencies, too. A little bit about them, anyway. That was an incredible display of just exactly the skills my team needs. I want him. Even if I can't read his file."

Carmichael whispered to Mayes for several seconds; the rest of the room remained quiet. Finally he looked again down the table at Maurice. "Violator will be reassigned to Ground Branch. He'll be the new Six on Golf Sierra." He turned to the woman from personnel. "You can make it happen, Athena?"

The head of Personnel said, "If someone brings him in from the cold, I can paper him into Ground Branch, a regular SAD paramilitary opera-tions officer." She shrugged. "No big deal."

The head of SAD looked to Maurice now. Maurice's face showed dis-pleasure as much as Hanley had ever seen anyone show their displeasure in a seventh-floor meeting with a senior exec, but the old man at least held his tongue.

"Where is he?" Carmichael asked.

Maurice answered, "I don't know."

Jordan Mayes said, "I checked this morning. He is in Belarus currently. Temporarily on stand down. He checks in from time to time; we don't have a direct line to him."

This sounded weird to Hanley, but Hanley didn't know anything about this sub rosa program, so he didn't question it.

Carmichael did not hesitate. "Maurice, I want you to go personally to pull him out and bring him back here. Explain to him why this is in his best interest."

"First, Denny, you'd better explain to *me* why it's in his best interest."

"He will have my everlasting appreciation."

"And if he refuses?"

"Get him here. Tell him he can always return to his former tasks if he can't hack it in Ground Branch." Carmichael's craggy, thin, and stern face formed a sinister smile. "I know men like him. He'll see that as a personal challenge."

Maurice did not respond to this, nor did he hide his displeasure. He stood, though the meeting had not been adjourned. When everyone turned his way at what they all took to be a show of disrespect, Maurice just addressed Carmichael. "I assume, Denny, that neither you nor Mr. Hanley here want me to delay a moment when I could be back in my office booking a flight to Minsk."

Carmichael smiled the smile of a weary parent to his recalcitrant child. "Go, Maurice."

The older man headed for the door, and Hanley realized he was going to get a new Six for Hightower, and he wouldn't be able to tell Hightower a thing about the man before they met.

Zack would not be pleased.

Denny Carmichael walked alone along the seventh-floor hallway back to his office. He'd just arrived in his outer lobby when he saw Maurice sitting there waiting for him. A glance at his executive assistant and a shake of her head confirmed to him that she'd not given the older man any assurances he was going to get an audience.

There was a protocol to arranging a meeting with a seventh-floor exec, but this was Maurice, and he'd been flouting the rules at CIA for as long as Denny Carmichael could remember.

He didn't break stride when he saw the older man sitting there; he kept heading for the door to his office, but he said, "Had a feeling you weren't rushing out to book a flight."

Maurice stood. "I need to talk to you about this. One on one."

Carmichael waved him in behind him, then looked to his EA. "Rachel. I need five minutes. No more."

"Yes, sir."

Carmichael closed the door behind Maurice, went to his desk, and put his folio down.

"You can make your case. It won't change a thing, but I don't want you saying I wouldn't even listen to you bitch."

"Denny, you, more than anyone else, know what the men in the Autonomous Asset Program have accomplished in the last few years. And Violator is the best of the bunch."

Denny sat down behind his desk. Maurice sat in front of him, though he'd not been invited to do so.

Denny said, "This HVT. Pasha. He's intertwined somehow with the political and intelligence fabric of Pakistan. He's not some Muj in a cave wearing man jammies. What it's going to take to bring him down . . . we aren't talking about smash-and-grab stuff anymore. This is real espionage, but espionage that will end with bullets cracking foreheads. Violator is *exactly* what a small Ground Branch cell tasked with infiltrating Pakistan to terminate a protected HVT needs."

"Violator doesn't know Pakistan, he doesn't—"

"The program he's in, the program we built, was designed to create assets who could go anywhere, melt into the landscape, and get jobs done. Right now, I don't need that in Russia one *tenth* as much as I need it in Pakistan."

"Then why not send him in as part of an Autonomous initiative? Why does he have to be folded into a Ground Branch operation?"

"*Hanley's* in command of the hunt for Pasha. Not Islamabad station. Ted Appleton's doing a damn good job running the station in Pakistan; he gets incredible intelligence product from his sources, but he's not a killer. He's always looking for a political solution with the Paks, and there *is* no political solution that can eradicate a terror organization the size and scope of the Resistance Front, especially if they've infiltrated the military. This is a job for SAD, and front and center in that fight will be Hanley and his gunmen. We need hard men who can suppress and then exploit targets in a denied area, and for that I need Ground Branch. I also need more surveillance skills, B&E skills, black bag skills, social engineering skills, all the shit you taught Violator. Golf Sierra will be a formidable unit if you can get your boy to comply."

Denny continued. "Shit, Maurice, I've read every word of his file. He's a ghost, he can shoot, he can fly aircraft, he can pilot boats, he speaks three languages, he can work deep cover, he can—"

"I know what he can do, Denny. I just don't see him doing it with five other guys. They'll only slow him down."

Carmichael laughed angrily. "Golf Sierra is more tip-of-the-spear than that oddball of yours hiding out in Belarus, I can assure you of that."

Before Maurice could reply, Denny said, "Get out of my office. Go get Violator, bring him in from the cold."

Maurice stood, but Denny added, "But first, old man, take a good look around at the seventh floor, because this is the last time you'll ever be anywhere near it."

Maurice Cahill nodded wearily. "Suits me just fine. You used to be a field man, Denny, but I have to say, I can hardly recognize you here, in your three-grand suit and your master plan to move pieces on a chessboard you don't even understand."

Carmichael picked up some papers on his desk and made a show of reading them. After just a few seconds he looked up. "You and I are both military men, Maurice. Different generations . . . but whatever. I am your superior officer. Right now, your job is to 'roger up,' turn around, walk out that door, and execute your orders. Have you forgotten how all that works?" Denny looked down at the papers again.

Maurice stood there, unmoving.

Carmichael looked back up at him slowly. "Are you still here?"

This time Maurice turned and left without another word.

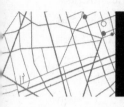

EIGHT

PRESENT DAY

Court's rented Honda Fit subcompact raced the winding and hilly streets of Algiers, arriving at the Hotel el Djazair less than ten minutes after his reconnaissance technician, the woman he only knew as Copper, last spoke to him from there. He expected her, and her captors, to be long gone by now, but he took no chances. He accessed the suite from the balcony, climbing a drainpipe and then kicking his leg over the waist-high wrought iron rail. Two tiny UAV chargers sat on the balcony, but the drones they charged were missing. He saw that the sliding door to the suite was ajar, so he entered the living room and cleared the space with his pistol quickly, though he was pretty sure he knew what he'd find.

This was not the first time in his career he'd shown up too late, and it was always like this. A broken chair, a ransacked room, equipment and luggage strewn in all directions. Cords sticking out of walls but no longer attached to the laptops or other electronics they had once powered.

He bypassed all the mess for now, swept the bedroom and the bathroom and the closets with his weapon to make sure no one had been left behind. Only when he was done with this did he return to the bathroom and kneel down below the vanity. He fished around for a moment, then found the watch Copper had hidden by setting it on the S-turn on the drain pipe. Looking it over, he saw that the woman had activated the tracker app, and he could easily make out her position as a blinking green dot that moved along a tiny display.

He didn't take time to see where she was going; he'd do that later. Instead he ran to the balcony, looked over the side to make sure no one was down there in a little alleyway that ran between two sections of the hotel, then climbed off it, dropping down the last few feet.

Five minutes later he was back in his white Honda, driving through the nighttime streets of Algiers, desperately trying to identify where the little blip on the watch was heading.

He could tell it was moving east, and this was bad news. The airport was east; he was at least twenty minutes behind them and not making up any ground, since at this time of night he knew better than to flout the city's traffic laws.

He was still carrying a pistol, after all.

He told himself to ignore the watch for the next few minutes, to concentrate on driving towards the airport, and to make a call.

The man Court knew as Arjun answered quickly. In his earlier conversations over the phone with his new broker, Court picked up on the fact that the man was clearly Indian, and he spoke English in a somewhat aristocratic British way that Court suspected might have been a put-on.

"Yes?" Arjun was breathless when he answered. Nervous and not even trying to hide it.

Court, in contrast, spoke calmly and methodically. "The operation failed. The technical asset has been kidnapped by the opposition. I have a low-profile tracker on her, and I am in pursuit, but I think they are heading to the airport. I might not be able to retrieve her before they fly her out of the country."

Admittedly, it was a lot of information to take in, and a full serving of bad news, but when the man did not reply after several seconds, Court's frustration grew.

"Are you there? Did you hear me?"

"She's been . . . kidnapped?"

"The Pakistanis must have traced her UAV's origin. They sent men."

Now the man shouted. "Of course they did. They sent men because you decided to assassinate someone!"

"That's not why they came for her. I didn't kill anyone. They were on the way to pick her up before I'd even been identified on the property."

"Where are they taking her?"

"I don't know. That little GPS tracker won't work on an aircraft, but assuming they fly her somewhere, and assuming they don't find the tracker en route, I should be able to see her on the app wherever she lands."

"These men, what will they do to her?" There was pain in his voice. He seemed, to Court, to be uniquely concerned about his employee.

"They will keep her alive. For now. But these are bad people."

"The ISI? Yes, they are bad people, but this isn't that type of a mission. You are the only one with murder on his mind!"

Court gripped the steering wheel and thought about what to say next.

He made the decision to level with his broker. "I don't know who you are, but I can guess. You are obviously Indian. I don't think you are with their intelligence services presently, but my guess is the Research and Analysis Wing is using you for this op to keep their hands clean with Turkey. How am I doing so far?"

"None of that matters. Copper is our priority now."

"It *does* matter," Court countered. "Because whoever you are, I'm going to assume you have some knowledge of intelligence matters yourself. Specifically, knowledge of Pakistani intelligence. *More* specifically, about events in the past."

Arjun hesitated; he was obviously confused by what his American asset was trying to tell him. But then he said, "Go on."

"Tonight I saw someone at the Turkish embassy, and if you know anything about the past, you will know why I tried to kill him, right then and there."

Arjun said nothing, and Court continued. "The man who arrived for the meeting tonight was Murad Khan. Don't even pretend not to know who—"

"That's bloody impossible! You've made a mistake. There is no way you could have—"

"Trust me, Arjun. I'd know that face anywhere. I was one meter from the tip of his nose, and it was him."

"But it can't be. He died . . . ten years ago."

"Almost twelve," Court corrected, and then he amended himself. "Except he didn't really seem all that dead when I bumped into him a few minutes ago."

Arjun wasn't having it. "The Americans killed him. Everyone knows what happened."

"I don't know what to tell you, chief. He's alive, and his people have Copper. I'll help you get her back, but if I'm going to do that, I'm going to need a lot out of you."

Court drove along in silence while his broker thought it over.

Finally Arjun said, "If it *was* Khan, if it really was him, then I need to notify authorities in New Delhi."

"Not till we know where the woman is. He saw me. He doesn't know me, but he had to have seen that I recognized him. That will buy her some time; they will need to try to find out who I am, who I'm working for, who I might tell. Their unknowns in this are our leverage. But if it gets out wide that he's been seen alive, we won't have that leverage anymore, and then they'll kill her."

The man from India spoke in a soft lament. "This was supposed to be easy. No great danger. Just a simple mission."

"Believe me, I hear that shit all the time."

"A mission to intercept counterfeiting ink coming in from Switzerland. That's all. The Pakistanis were in Algeria working on an operation to produce counterfeit rupees to insert them into India and affect the economy. It was a malicious operation, of course. But . . . but it is *not* . . . it's *not* murder."

Court hadn't known why he was sent to plant the IMSI-catcher at the Turkish embassy for the meeting between the Pakistani and the Swiss national, but he was surprised to learn it had to do with counterfeiting rupees. That seemed too small for Murad Khan. If history was to be any guide, Khan was up to another play.

Court put that thought out of his mind. "Can we work together on this? We get the woman back, then you can go to the Indian government about Khan."

"Why won't you go to the American government?"

"Because I'm not with the American government."

"I'm not with the Indian—"

"Trust me," Court interrupted. "Whatever your relationship with *your* people is, it's better than my relationship with *my* people."

"Very well. If you are right, if this is Khan, then we must hurry. You *must* find Copper. There is nothing this man would not do to protect his identity now, after what he did twelve years ago."

"Yeah," Court muttered. "Tell me about it."

The American held the Apple Watch up to his face as he drove and saw that the blip representing Copper was now stationary. As he feared, the men had taken her to the airport. They were far from the terminal, so he assumed there would be a private plane there on the tarmac. He was twenty minutes behind still, and he saw no chance whatsoever that he could get there, get onto airport grounds, locate Copper, and then get her away from a group of men before they managed to take off.

Shit, he said to himself. He'd have to find a flight himself, but he did not know where to go. If the men who held Copper took her to Pakistan, as he feared, he'd have to find a way in, but he wasn't about to just climb aboard a domestic flight to Karachi right now. No, he'd go somewhere in that direction and prepare the next phase of this mission, which had already crept far out of control.

Court hung up the phone and continued on through the night towards another airport, towards another journey, towards another foreign country and another kidnap victim and another group of assholes who so richly deserved to die.

This was his life, but he wasn't thinking about any of this now. He was thinking about the past.

It occurred to him that he had never stopped thinking about the past.

NINE

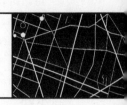

TWELVE YEARS AGO

Slonim, Belarus, was a quiet city with a population just under fifty thousand, roughly an hour's drive east of the Polish border. It was off the tourist beat, even by the minimal standards of Belarus: a mill, factory, and timber town surrounded by fields and forests, intersected by rivers and highways.

The Shchara River runs north to south through the center of town, and just on the western bank, a barren construction site stood far enough away from the lights of the rows of apartment buildings nearby to be pitch-black in the night.

Prirechnaya Road passed along the western side of the property; a chain-link fence separated it from the building site. The road was empty of vehicular traffic at this time of the evening, and only a single pedestrian walked through the dark, his silhouette disrupted by his hooded jacket and his backpack. With his hands in his pockets, he looked—if there had been anyone around to see him at all—as if he were heading north towards a quiet neighborhood of small apartment buildings just a few hundred meters away.

But as he reached the edge of the property, he abruptly turned right, leapt up on the chain-link fence, and climbed it deftly and without any obvious concern that someone might be watching. He moved like he belonged, like he did this every damn night and it was no big deal.

He dropped down on the other side onto a pile of earth, then made his way to asphalt that had been recently poured and leveled for a parking lot. Here, he pulled off his backpack and dropped it on the ground, then took off his coat and dropped it, as well. Under it he wore a dark green fleece jacket with a hood, blue jeans, and black running shoes. He stopped, listened, and waited for a full minute in the black.

Courtland Gentry was twenty-five years old and an employee of the Central Intelligence Agency, operating under the code name Violator. He was a non-official cover officer, meaning if he was captured here, or anywhere for that matter, he could be subjected to a long imprisonment, or worse.

Much worse.

His personal security was important to him, so he stood here in the dark, ears tuned to any hint he'd been discovered.

Finally he convinced himself he'd not been detected, so he unzipped his backpack and pushed his hand down into it, rummaging past a collection of small empty tin cans, reaching around a medical kit and a plastic bag and a bottle of water, before finally retrieving the largest item in the pack. He stood back up with a set of night vision goggles attached to tactical headgear, slipped the device over his head, adjusted the chin strap tightly, and then lowered the two image intensifier tubes down in front of his eyes.

He turned on the device, and the near pitch-black darkness shifted into a hazy green as the tubes took in the tiny bit of ambient light from stars above the cloud cover. In front of him on the construction site, he saw what he knew he would see, what he'd seen most every night for the past week. A three-story skeletonized building. The exterior walls were open to the elements, but the floors, stairwells, and inner weight-bearing beams were in place, as was some of the interior wallboard, the plumbing, and the electrical wiring.

Court figured this would be a big, ugly office building someday soon.

Leaving his coat on the asphalt but picking up his pack, he zipped it shut and put it back on his back, then took off through the construction site at a jog, heading for the building.

An hour later Court Gentry sat on the rooftop of the construction site, looking down at the black river through his NODs and eating from a bag of granola with dried cherries he'd bought at the produce market that afternoon. His heart was still beating hard, his muscles sore.

He'd been training in parkour, and he'd jumped, vaulted, dropped, run, and rolled all over this building. He had a high-quality pellet gun on his hip, right in front of his real firearm, and he'd used the pellet gun to shoot targets while on the move, adding difficulty to the already complex art of free running.

At one point he'd failed to get one of his legs up high enough during a monkey vault over an iron waterpipe, and this had sent him tumbling awkwardly onto his right arm.

He rubbed his elbow, thinking of his mistake. It would be fine in a day or two, he knew, and it took his focus off last night's shoulder injury.

Overall, however, he felt better tonight about his performance than he had on the other evenings he'd come here to train.

Training was tough work, but this type of disciplined practice was so ingrained in the young man that it was an integral part of his life. The man who'd taught him everything about spycraft a few years earlier had a saying that played in Court's mind every day.

Stay ready so you don't have to get ready.

Court Gentry did everything he could to stay ready, because his country needed him.

The American had been living here in sleepy Slonim for the past month, lying low after doing a job down south in Kharkiv, Ukraine, near the Russian border. The mission had been the political assassination of a separatist hit man who'd killed a high-level Ukrainian diplomat, a politician the United States had put a lot of hope and resources into.

Court had pulled it off; he'd quickly and cleanly killed the killer, and then he'd come here to hide out before returning to his home base in Moscow.

Gentry worked for the Central Intelligence Agency, but there existed not a single document proving that in his possession. He was a singleton, a lone operator, employed in a sub rosa outfit known only to a few at Langley as the Autonomous Asset Program.

Court had been at this for nearly four years now, and he'd conducted dozens of operations in the field.

Court was *always* in the field.

And now, years after he'd been recruited, he found himself alone in a foreign land, waiting for his next operation, waiting for someone else to kill.

He climbed to his feet, just on the edge of the roof of the construction site, wiped the granola off his hands, and rubbed his sore elbow as he headed back for the stairs, ready to begin the drive home to his apartment.

TEN

PRESENT DAY

Priyanka Bandari didn't know where she was, exactly, but she had a feeling she knew where she was going. If she wasn't heading to some dungeon in Islamabad or Quetta or Karachi, then she couldn't imagine where else they could possibly be taking her.

When they kidnapped her from her hotel suite, headphones were immediately placed over her ears. Music blared at a volume that made it impossible to hear anything going on around her, and a pillowcase from her bed was pulled over her head. She was led to a waiting car, and though she hadn't been bound in any way, she could feel men seated on either side of her, pressing up against her, and this, along with the sensory deprivation of the hood and the music, was more than enough incentive for her to behave herself on the drive through Algiers.

Priyanka wasn't a fighter; she wasn't a spy or an agent or a soldier or anything of the like.

In fact, up until four months earlier, she'd been, primarily, a college student. This was the first real full-time job she'd ever had in her life, only her second time out in the field, and it had somehow led to all this.

After a half hour's drive, she'd been led out of the car, and through the music she felt the vibration of jet engines on her right; then she'd been escorted roughly up jet stairs, and panic welled within her as a hand was placed on the back of her head so that she didn't bump it entering the cabin of what seemed to be an executive jet. She'd placed the tracker high on the back of her neck behind her flowing hair, and the hand that guided her briefly touched it, but apparently both the pillowcase and her thick hair were enough buffer that he didn't recognize the outline of the little metal disk under his fingertips.

She was pushed down roughly in the aircraft, and she felt it take off minutes later.

Once the plane leveled, the headphones and pillowcase were removed, but all the cabin lights had been turned off, including the emergency lights, so she could see nothing around her.

Four men spoke from different directions in the darkness. In Hindi, but with accents, they asked her name, over and over, and she refused to answer, as if she did not understand. They asked her who she was working for and she refused to answer; they asked her what she knew, and she refused to answer this, either.

They tried speaking to her in English, but she did not respond. Most educated Indians of her age would likely know at least some English, but she played dumb, desperate to think of some strategy to extricate herself from this situation.

She was so new to this world—she didn't even know she was *in* this world until things had gone so terribly wrong tonight. She thought she was just a technician working semi-remotely to assist an operation that was for the benefit of her nation.

When the men in the cabin made no headway with her after five minutes, one of them moved closer, wrapped his fingers around her throat, and squeezed firmly. Priya brought her hands up to his, tried to pull them away, but the man was just too strong.

This man spoke to her in Hindi, but he sounded Indian, not Pakistani like the others. She realized it was the same man who'd addressed her in the suite back in Algiers.

"The person who entered the embassy tonight. He is all we care about. Unless you care about him more than your own life, you will tell us who he was."

She wasn't trained for this shit, and she knew in her heart that the minute they started playing hardball with her, she would crack.

But the man close to her face did not play hardball. Not yet. When she did not reply to him, he slowly released his grip. He leaned closer to her; he was almost visible in the darkness, but not quite.

"We've been told to take you someplace where we will have the time and the tools to extract whatever we want from you. You will regret not having a pleasant conversation with me now, I can promise you that."

The woman said nothing, though her stomach roiled with panic. She believed every word the man said, but she knew she had to fight the urge to simply blurt out everything she knew.

"Very well, young lady. Relax, for now. Enjoy the flight. The true unpleasantness will begin when we land."

The headphones were snapped back on her ears, and the hood was returned to her head.

ELEVEN

TWELVE YEARS AGO

Court Gentry returned to his apartment building from his late-night training shortly before two a.m. He kept his thoughts on his personal security, making certain he'd not been followed, keeping an eye out for anyone who didn't fit or for any other discernible changes around his flat that would serve as an indicator of danger.

He saw nothing amiss, took the stairs to his floor, and unlocked and opened his door slowly. He slid his fingers around the door frame until he put his hand on a piece of thread he'd taped loosely to both the inside door frame and the top of the door itself. It was still affixed, so he pushed the door open and stepped inside.

Walking through his living room in the dim, he made certain the same single light was on as when he left, and he looked for footprints on a small shag carpet in the entryway. Satisfied his place was undisturbed, he went to his kitchen, just off the living room. Here he put down his keys; took off his backpack, his ball cap, and his jacket; and opened the refrigerator.

He reached into one of the cases of beer and retrieved a cold bottle, then popped the top with a handheld opener. He closed the fridge and casually faced his apartment. He drank a long, loud swig of beer and took in his surroundings with a bored sigh, then began heading towards the bedroom, drawing his pellet gun from his holster as he did so.

This he placed on a table next to his TV, putting it down with the thud of a polymer-and-steel weapon being laid to rest.

Then he carefully placed the beer down on the same table on a paperback so that it, in contrast to the gun, made no sound.

He burped as he ambled lazily towards the bedroom, but when he stepped inside the darkened room, he went from moving with nonchalance to moving with astonishing speed and purpose. He spun around on his right foot as he reached under his shirt to his hip, dropped to a combat crouch, and aimed his nine-millimeter handgun at the chair in the corner.

A man sat there in the dark.

It was quiet in the room save for the sound of a streetcar outside. The man in the chair did not move a muscle; he faced the gun pointed at him, but he did not reel back in terror.

Court spoke to the silhouette in Russian. "Kto tey?" *Who are you?* His finger rested lightly on the trigger of his Walther PPQ.

The seated man slowly raised his hands in surrender, then reached even more slowly to the table next to him and pulled the cord on a small lamp there, bringing the corner into view with a click. A nearly empty bottle of beer sat on the table under the light.

The man spoke English. "The thread on the door, the shag carpet. Did I miss a third telltale, or was it the damn beer I snuck?"

Court lowered his weapon. "The third telltale *was* the beer you snuck. Should have been seven left in that case. I put my hand in and found two rows of three."

"I'll be damned," the man said, and then he smiled. "I taught you well, didn't I?"

"I knew how to count to seven before I met you, Maurice."

Court rose to his feet, slipped the Walther back into the waistband holster at his four-o'clock position, went to retrieve his beer just inside the living room, and sat down on the bed.

Maurice turned the light back off and remained seated there in the dark. He said, "It's been a while, kid. How you doing?"

"Fine."

Maurice looked around. "Nice place. Very nice. You aren't going soft, are you?"

The younger man just stared back at him.

"Where were you tonight?"

"Am I out past curfew?"

"Cute. You aren't running around with any women, are you?"

Court looked at himself in the wall mirror next to where Maurice sat. His jeans and fleece were coated in the dust and lime of a construction site, his hands were scratched, and his beard still had bits of wallboard in it.

"Not that kind of running around."

"Training, then?"

"What did you always say? 'Never stop sharpening the blade.'"

Maurice nodded at this as he looked around at the apartment. "This place . . . too clean, too neat. Too nice. Books on the shelves and paintings on the walls and a kick-ass stereo." He motioned to the bed Court sat on. "Even a big fluffy bed. Slept in, left unmade. I turned you into a hard man, son. That's an important asset in this business. One you can't afford to lose."

"You think I'm the interior decorator here? I rented this place furnished. The books on the coffee table are mine, but the rest was here when I got here."

"You could have rented a barn."

"Why would I rent a—"

"You should sleep in a fuckin' barn, kid, it would do you good."

"You first."

The older man rolled his eyes. "Yeah, it *was* me first. I once went three days alone with a broken kneecap, without water, sleeping in the jungle and staying alive drinking rainwater off of palm fronds while dodging Charlie."

Court turned his head and looked out the window at the cool night. "I sure have missed all your 'There I was, in the shit' stories about Vietnam."

"Really?"

"Nope." Court sipped his beer.

Maurice chuckled a little. "That was in Laos, anyway."

"Right."

The older man reached into his jacket; Court's hand moved to the gun on his hip. He had it out in the blink of an eye.

Maurice stopped. "Settle down, Roy Rogers. Just grabbing my Marlboros."

"No smoking," Court said.

"You'd shoot me if I lit up?"

Court holstered the weapon but kept his hand on the grip. "Not to kill."

Maurice laughed a raspy laugh now, put his hands back in his lap. "Well, that's one way to quit, I guess."

Court put his own hands on his knees, but he said nothing. He was stiff, utterly on guard for whatever Maurice was here to tell him.

The older man sensed the unease. "Listen. The two years we spent together, way back when. Everything that happened . . . as tough as it was for you . . . it all needed to happen, every last bit of it, in order to make you into the asset you are today."

"Don't patronize me. I know all that."

Maurice smiled. "*Patronize?* A ten-dollar word. Those books in the front room aren't just to backstop your legend as a student, then."

"I read a lot in my downtime. I've been reading for the past four years."

"And studying Russian, as well?"

Court shrugged. "Other languages, too. When I'm not working."

"I've heard a little about your work. Murmansk, specifically. You did that colonel? I'm not read in on it, but I picked up some scuttlebutt. Sounded like some crazy shit went down."

Court shrugged at this. "It didn't go down, it went sideways." He added, "But the mission objectives were achieved."

Maurice nodded. "They usually are with you, I hear. And the reason you've been so successful is due to what I put you through in training."

Flatly, Court said, "You almost killed me. Multiple times."

"Exactly. And that made you hard to kill." Maurice added, "All that was out of love, not out of hate, although I know how building somebody up can seem a lot like tearing somebody down when you are the one on the receiving end."

"What are you trying to do, Maurice?"

"What do you mean?"

"I mean, now. What are you doing? You came here to tell me I'm awesome and you're the one who made me that way? Look, I've already got a dad, and he's an even bigger asshole than you, so if you're trying to be some kind of a father figure, you're wasting your time."

The older American regarded the man seated on the bed for a long time. "What's wrong, son? I didn't expect a hug and a sloppy kiss, but you seem . . . unhappy."

Court shook his head. "No."

"Angry, then?"

"No."

The older man looked hard into the younger man's eyes. Finally he said, "Different, anyway."

Now Court answered him. "The job . . . I thought *it* was going to be . . . different."

"Different, how? More fun?"

"Less lonely."

Maurice regarded the comment for a moment, weighing his options for a response. "When we found you, you were in prison in Florida. I bet you weren't lonely there."

Court glared at him, then turned his gaze out the window once again. It was silent for nearly a minute. Court remembered that Maurice had no problem weathering pregnant pauses.

Eventually, however, Maurice polished off his beer and held the empty bottle up in the dark. "Another round, barkeep?"

A minute later the two men sat on bar stools at the kitchen counter, each with a second bottle of Stavka in his hand.

Court said, "You've never dropped in on me in the field, Maurice. And you sure as hell have never kissed my ass. What's this about?"

To this, the older man sighed with a smile. "So much for small talk. Okay, kid. Down to it. You are being recalled. Immediately."

Court put his beer down on the counter with a loud *thunk*. "What did I do?"

"You did every last thing that's ever been asked of you, just as I knew you would. Now, the powers that be are asking something else of you."

"Where am I going?"

Maurice grimaced a little, giving Court the impression that he wouldn't like what he was about to hear. "There's an SAD task force that suffered a casualty the other night. Your name was fielded as a replacement. You'd be a paramilitary operations officer in Ground Branch."

"Ground Branch?" Court was genuinely surprised. "But . . . I'm a singleton. I haven't worked with anybody in . . . well . . . I've *never* worked with anybody."

"Yeah, this will take some getting used to. The rest of the team are all SEAL Team Six or Delta, I'd imagine. You'll have to show them that you do know how to run and gun with the squad. You have the background for it, you just might be a little rusty. They'll fix you up."

"When you say they had 'a casualty,' I'm gonna guess the officer is KIA."

"That's correct."

Court was unfazed by this news. "Why do they want me?"

"They are getting some tough hits, dynamic work, not just kicking doors. They need an operator with your diverse skill set."

"Sandbox shit?" Court was asking if the team's work was in the Middle East.

"Primarily. Some sub-Saharan Africa. I believe they were the task force that got involved in that shit in Indonesia last year. They want to train with you stateside for as short a period as they can and then get back to Afghanistan. They've been inserting into Waziristan, Khyber, Kurram. All the tourist hot spots. I imagine you can expect more of that."

"I don't speak Pashto. Or Arabic."

Maurice said, "Most Pakistanis speak Urdu."

Court shook his head in bewilderment. "I didn't even know that. I'm *not* the right guy for this, Maurice." His eyes narrowed, looking into his mentor's. "And you *know* I'm not. You've been sent here to pull me out and talk me into it, but you know it's bullshit, just the same as me."

"I taught you how to read people. I didn't expect you'd be reading me." Maurice smiled for an instant at this, then turned serious again. "The group chief running Golf Sierra, that's the task force you've been assigned to, said his team would benefit from having a shooter who also had some first-rate tradecraft. I guess they want to use you as advance force operations, scouting out hits before the rest of the team shows, that kind of stuff."

"Right. But . . . again, you think this is a bad idea."

"It's a job. Jobs come with bosses, and bosses come with orders, and orders come with . . ."

"Bullshit?"

"Bullshit. Yes, indeed."

Maurice was almost finished with his second beer. He said, "Hanley, he's the suit running the team, and Carmichael, he's—"

"I know who Carmichael is."

"Right . . . Anyway, don't trust either of them."

"Why do you say that?"

"Because *I* don't trust them. Good enough?"

Court started to ask for more clarification. Instead he just shrugged. "Good enough."

"And don't trust the ISI."

Now the twenty-five-year-old cocked his head. "Trust Pakistani intelligence? I'm not an idiot."

"No, you're not, but our agencies do 'work together' from time to time." The older man made air quotes with his fingers as he said this.

"Got it."

"Watch your back, son. As a singleton, you only had yourself to rely on, but that was all you needed. Now . . . you'll be a cog in a bigger machine. You're the best, I don't doubt that for one second. But I've lived long enough to see the best get killed, time and time again. You've grown on me over the years. I'd like to see you live to be thirty."

Court stood and threw the two empty bottles in the trash. "Thirty? A little optimistic, aren't you?"

"A man can dream." Maurice stood. "Start packing, I'm gonna go outside and have a smoke. We're wheels up in two hours."

TWELVE

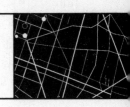

Matthew Hanley's stateside office was far away from CIA HQ, down in Virginia Beach, in a converted office complex that was guarded and gated, equipped with cameras and other security measures. His two Ground Branch teams each had a floor of their own, sublevel one and sublevel two, but Matt's office was aboveground, on the second story, along with the intelligence and logistics teams.

Promptly at nine a.m. on the fourth day after Hanley returned to the United States, his executive assistant told him someone was waiting outside to see him. He looked at his watch, appreciated the punctuality of his visitor, and stood up from his desk. "Send her in, Leah."

A young woman entered Hanley's office wearing black slacks and a gray sweater, her dark hair back in a ponytail and simple glasses covering large brown eyes. She had dark Hispanic features and a lean frame of about five-four. Hanley found her attractive but dressed down and understated, and this he appreciated.

He stepped around his desk; he hadn't bothered to put on his suit coat, and he hiked his pants up a little before he came over and shook the woman's outstretched hand. "Matt Hanley."

"Marquez, sir." Her voice was low, serious, and professional. She looked him directly in the eyes, and this he also appreciated.

"Been reading all about you, young lady. Julia Marquez, from El Paso, Texas."

"I go by Julie, sir. And I was born in Las Cruces, New Mexico. Moved to El Paso with my family when I was ten."

"Details," Hanley said with a tired smile. "I appreciate details."

Hanley offered her a chair in front of his desk, and she sat stiffly. He returned to his own chair and plopped down. "Former Army specialist. Thirty-Five Foxtrot. Intelligence analyst."

"Correct."

"I was Army myself. Fifth Special Forces."

Julie Marquez said nothing.

Hanley gave her a moment, then continued. "You did two years with Third ID. Just two years. Then you were moved into JSOC. Tactical intelligence. That's a hell of an accomplishment. Tactical intel for special operations command at, what, twenty-one years old?"

"Correct, sir."

"Damn impressive."

Again, she just looked back at him. He waited a moment for an acknowledgment of his compliment, and then, when it did not come, he said, "Glowing reports and accolades in your four years there at JSOC. And then you left the Army and worked at DIA for the past two years."

"Nineteen months," she corrected.

Hanley chuckled a little. Analysts could be annoyingly precise, but this one seemed downright pedantic. "Okay. Nineteen months. And then you left there to come work at the Agency. That's a lot of moving around for a woman as young as you. How old are you again?"

"My DOB isn't in that file in your hand?"

Hanley now wondered if this woman was being insubordinate, she was so matter-of-fact about all this. If so, it was one hell of a weird tactic for a job interview.

He allowed a little of his frustration to show. "It *is*, Marquez, but I don't want to look down at it. I want you to tell me."

"I turned twenty-seven last Tuesday."

"Well, then. Happy belated." He wasn't smiling, and neither was she. "You've worked tactical, you've worked strategic, you come highly recommended. You might be a suitable fit for the position I am hiring for. What have you been told about the job?"

Without hesitating she said, "I was told SAD had an opening. My current job here at the Agency is below my capabilities. A misuse of my skills. I hope this one is better."

Hanley was good at reading people; it came from his career as a spy. Marquez gave nothing away with her face. She was attentive but unemotional.

He said, "I run a task force composed of a pair of asset teams, along with their field support staff. Are you familiar with Ground Branch?"

She nodded. "The paramilitary unit. Basically doing what SEAL Team Six does. What Delta does."

Hanley shrugged. "The military mission is a little different than ours, but some of the basic skill sets are the same. Anyway, we're looking for a new junior tactical field analyst in our intel shop."

"Okay," she said. Hanley couldn't tell if she wanted the job or not.

He said, "I'm going to be honest with you. The position you would be filling . . . the last person who held it made a critical error. An error that led to the death of one of my officers."

Marquez asked, "What was the error?"

"He provided schematics of a facility we raided. There was a tunnel. A tunnel we knew nothing about. He'd had days to assess the location, a location that the U.S. military built. There was a lot of data about the site, and he assured us the blueprint he gave us was correct." Hanley added, "No tunnel on the blueprint."

Marquez said, "The site was altered. The tunnel was added after the blueprints were generated."

"Obviously. But it was his job to ascertain that information, or to say it was an unknown. He did neither. He signed off on the schematics, and that got a good man killed."

Julie Marquez did not reply.

"Do you disagree?"

"I neither agree nor disagree. I could only determine if an error was made by looking at all the raw data."

Hanley leaned back in his chair now. "Would that interest you?"

For the first time, Hanley saw emotion on the pretty young woman's face. He even heard a slight excitement in her voice. "I would like to examine the data and see if I would have come to a different conclusion than the previous analyst."

"Good. I have a conference room with a laptop set up and all the paperwork in a file. Just down the hall, second door on the right. You have two hours to find out if the last guy fucked up or not."

Julie Marquez blinked now. "You fired him without knowing for sure if he made a mistake?"

"A man died. The analyst lost the confidence of those who have to go outside the wire. The analyst had to be removed, regardless of whether he made any error at all." Hanley sighed. "It's a tough gig, absolutely unforgiving. You need to be aware of that if you want to join us."

She responded in her flat tone. "Second door on the right, you said?"

Hanley nodded, looked at his watch. "Two hours, and the clock is now ticking."

In the end Marquez didn't need two hours. She needed forty-eight minutes. She stepped into Hanley's office, unannounced, the laptop in her hands. When Hanley looked up at her, she declared dryly, "You were correct to remove the analyst. He *did* make an error."

Hanley glanced down at his Tag Heuer watch.

"You figured that out in forty-five minutes?"

"I would correct you and tell you it was actually forty-eight minutes, but I understand some people get annoyed when I am overly specific, so that might be the wrong thing to say."

Hanley waved her comment away. "Sit down. Tell me how you could have avoided this."

Marquez sat, placing the laptop on his desk. "The schematics are of the entire compound, and the previous analyst was correct to use them, correct to cross-reference reports of U.S. personnel as well as allied personnel to verify details. But other than running a request through NGA for any intelligence on the cluster of freestanding homes just here on the hillside to the north, and looking at the raw data of some ISR flyovers, your analyst did no more research on anything outside the compound's walls." She looked up at him. "I would have made that a priority."

"Why?"

"Because intel on the compound was solid and easy to obtain. Intel on the village was not. I wouldn't have gone after what was easy. I would have gone after what was difficult, because that would be the most likely threat vector to the Ground Branch team once they hit the location." When Hanley did not speak, she said, "ISI would be aware that we had data on the compound. We're talking about Pakistan. The ISI is riddled with compromises. Whoever we were after at the compound could have been aware we knew our way around inside."

Hanley looked back down at the aerial photograph on the laptop. "Continue."

She said, "So, I pulled up every single overflight of the area for the past five months, overlaid them on the computer, and created a sort of motion picture of the progress, focusing on the movements in the village. Look at this." She touched a pen on the monitor, indicating a concrete-block house twenty-five meters up the hill from the north wall of the compound. "Three months ago, construction began on this structure." She pulled up other images on different days around that time.

Hanley said, "Trucks coming. Trucks going. So?"

"On seven different images, over a two-month period, we see trucks coming up the one road out of the village or parked at the house. On five different overflights we caught trucks leaving."

"Two months to build this little house? That seems excessive."

"Not to build it, sir. The structure was already there. No, the two months were spent renovating something inside the existing building."

"What were the trucks bringing in?"

"From my calculations looking at the imagery of the approaching vehicles, I'd say they were carrying nothing of any great weight. They were partially loaded with something, but I won't speculate. And when the trucks left, they were heavily loaded."

"With . . ." Hanley got it now. "With dirt."

"Correct. The Pakistanis were building a tunnel into and out of the compound. I saw there was a question as to why a heavy machine gun and guards had been posted at an empty facility. Perhaps it was to keep people away while the location was being altered."

"And the previous analyst should have noticed this construction in the town?"

"I guess I am not saying what he should have done, Mr. Hanley. I am saying what I *would* have done. It's my job to separate signal from noise, sir. That's what I do. The trucks represented an important signal as to what was going on."

Hanley nodded, impressed. "If you take this job, you'll be sent all over the world. You have a husband, a family? A boyfriend who means something to you?"

She answered without hesitation. "No," she said, then pointed to the data on the laptop. "This. *This* means something to me. This means *everything.*"

Hanley smiled. "You're an odd duck, you know that, Marquez?"

Without showing any signs of being offended, she just shrugged and said, "I'm sure all that's in my file, too."

"It is. Is that going to be a problem for me if I hire you?"

"That's up to you. Some people find me strange. But I'm just me, and I don't see me as strange in the least."

Now the big man nodded, appreciative of the way she took his jab and turned it into *his* hang-up, not hers. He stood, extended a hand. "The job is yours if you want it, and I sure as hell hope you want it."

Marquez herself stood now. She shook his hand. "I'll take it."

THIRTEEN

PRESENT DAY

Priyanka Bandari had no idea how long she'd been sleeping, but a vigorous shake to her shoulder brought her to. She was helped to her feet and pushed forward, and only then did she remember that she was on an aircraft.

She realized now that the plane she'd been flying on had landed, and when she was escorted down the jet stairs and pushed into a waiting car, she felt incredible heat and humidity. She'd never been to Pakistan, which was where she assumed she was now, but the hot air sure felt a lot like home.

She was driven for an hour, and still the music blared in her ears, until finally the car came to a stop and she was led out into what felt and smelled like some sort of a service elevator. When it reached its destination—she had no idea how many floors she'd ascended, but she'd definitely ascended—she was led across a room, or down a hallway, and then she was pushed through a door. Here the pillowcase was removed, her headphones were yanked off, and she was shoved forward while she blinked against the sudden exposure to light.

A door slammed behind her, and she found herself in a small and dingy storage space that had been set up like a cell. A cot in a corner, a bucket across from it. There was no plumbing; she assumed the bucket would be for her waste, but she didn't want to think about having to use it.

She was hungry, thirsty, exhausted, and scared. But at the forefront of her mind was the worry that she would, through her actions in the next few minutes or few hours, blurt out a name that might put someone very close to her in danger.

Priyanka Bandari didn't know the identity of the man who had breached the fence of the embassy in Algiers under the watchful eye of her drone—she only knew his code name—but she *did* know the identity of the man who had brokered this entire operation.

And this knowledge in her brain terrified her now.

Sometime later the door to her cell was opened, and a man wearing a mask entered, carrying a bottle of water, a paper plate of naan bread, and a plastic bowl of lentil soup. The bread was stale and the soup was luke-warm, but she ate ravenously between gulps of water, consuming a fourth of her meal before the man left and locked the door behind him.

She didn't know if lentil soup was popular fare in Pakistan, but it was in her own country of India, and she appreciated this taste of home, such as it was.

When the masked man returned, he threw her a blue jumpsuit and told her to dress in it, now, while he watched. He spoke to her in Hindi, with an Indian accent, but he was not the Indian man she'd spoken to on the aircraft.

Why are these Indians working for Pakistan? she wondered.

She refused at first, but he calmly explained that his orders were to check her body and her clothing for any hidden items that weren't found when she was originally taken. She remembered the GPS tracker, still affixed to the back of her neck, and she realized her best option to keep the device on her body and undetected was to comply with the man, despite the fact that this would be brutally humiliating. Still, she realized that if he could put his hands through her clothing and see her naked body from across the little cell, there was hope he wouldn't begin touching her, then feeling around in her hair, where he would certainly uncover the tracker hidden there.

As she took off her clothes, she felt sickened to stand nude in front of this stranger, but also hopeful that by subjecting herself to this insult now, she would improve her chances for rescue.

Once the man checked through all her clothing, he tossed it onto the floor outside the cell, again instructed her to dress in the jumpsuit, then picked up the empty plate and bowl and left without another word.

Priya did as asked, then sat down in her jumpsuit on the edge of her tiny cot and tried to regain her composure. As she thought about everything she'd been through since Algiers, it slowly dawned on her that things could have easily been so much worse. She hadn't been incessantly badgered for information, she wasn't hit or manhandled past a threatening but ultimately painless hold on her throat. Other than the humiliation she'd just endured and the promise of bad things to come, she felt she had gotten off relatively easy.

So far.

An hour later she was certain her luck was about to come to an end. She was again given the headphones and hooded before being walked out of the cell and down a corridor. She was pushed down, not roughly but firmly, into a metal chair. She was bound by a metal chain so thin it would slice into her skin if she tried to move, and it had been wrapped around her wrists and forearms a dozen times or more before she'd heard the click of a small padlock, so she didn't even bother to test its strength.

Her terror regarding the entire situation had her imagining men standing right in front of her with knives, ready to plunge them into her body.

It was the unknown that scared her, and deprived of most of her senses, virtually *everything* was an unknown right now.

Finally, hands took the hood off her head and the music out of her ears. She kept her eyes closed for a moment, until she heard a soft voice right in front of her.

He spoke Hindi, and it sounded like the Indian from the hotel in Algiers and the same voice as the man on the plane. "It's okay, dear. You may look at me."

She blinked her eyes open; tears of terror had formed on her long lashes, and they dripped onto her cheeks. It took a moment, but soon she focused on the man sitting before her. It was, in fact, the man from Algeria. He wore comfortable and casual clothing, his brown silk shirt open halfway down his hairy chest. He was heavy but well kempt, as if he'd just bathed and changed for his talk with this prisoner.

He looked to Priya as if he were someone's kind and doting father.

Behind him, however, were three younger men, and they looked to Priya to be men of the street. Gangsters. Thugs. She saw the grips of handguns sticking out of belts, cold dark eyes, and the cruel sneers of those who looked at her as if she were prey.

She had been expecting a Pakistani military prison, but what she saw instead looked like members of some sort of criminal element from her home country.

This made no sense.

The older man smiled at her, his bushy mustache rising above white teeth. "Young lady, you may call me Jai."

She did not respond to this.

"And what shall I call you? Your phone is locked, so we must admit we know very little about you."

Finally, she spoke her first words. "Where . . . where is this place?"

"In the spirit of openness and truthfulness, I will tell you. We are in the heart of Mumbai. I would say you are home, but I do not know where you live. From your dialect I detect you are from somewhere else . . . Goa, perhaps?"

Priyanka had gone to university in Mumbai, and she lived here now, but she was, in fact, from Goa. She did not reveal this through words, though she wondered if she'd telegraphed it with her surprised expression.

The man called Jai said, "But . . . wherever it is you hail from, my guess is you work in New Delhi now."

"Why New Delhi?"

"Because that is where the R&AW is headquartered. You are a field agent, I understand, but surely you see New Delhi as your home base, yes?"

R&AW was Indian intelligence, this Priya knew, though she had no relationship with Indian intelligence whatsoever. "I don't work for R&AW."

The man smiled. "That sounds just a bit like something someone who works for R&AW would say, doesn't it?"

"I . . . I *don't*."

"Then, pretty one, who *do* you work for?"

She surprised herself by replying with a question of her own. "Who do *you* work for?"

He smiled, and spoke with pride. "Bari."

Priya recoiled. "Palak Bari? You are . . . B-Company?" B-Company was the most powerful mafia group in India; they had a controlling hold of vast swaths of the underworld.

"You've heard of us. Good. This might make tonight go a little quicker."

"Everyone has heard of B-Company."

The man smiled. Prideful still. "That is to my advantage right now, that you know something about us. Let me tell you, young sister, that we wish you no harm at all. We only hope to learn from you about the incident last night. But before we begin with that unpleasantness, tell me about yourself."

She wanted to give this man something, but to keep it vague. "I am no one. I just graduated from university in May."

"Congratulations," he said without smiling.

"Dhanyavaad," *Thank you,* she said. "Computer studies. I was hired by a man, I don't know who, to do a job in Algeria. It had nothing to do with India at all."

In fact, she was sure the original job had everything to do with helping India and hurting Pakistan. The fact that Indian mobsters had kidnapped her for it still had Priya perplexed.

Jai nodded thoughtfully, made a show with his hands as he called for chai to be brought for both of them. She drank the hot liquid greedily, and he smiled while he sipped.

Finally, as if he were in no hurry, he said, "I need the name of the man who hired you. Perhaps you are who you say you are. Perhaps you are not a spy." He winked. "But I think you are a spy."

"I am not a spy. My employer is not a spy. We only take technical jobs."

"On behalf of India's intelligence service?"

"No."

The man looked at her a long time, then said, "Do you know why you have been so well treated over the past day?" When she didn't answer, he said, "You must be wondering this."

"I . . . I don't know."

"Because we think you are R&AW. We . . . I am speaking of myself and the others here, and of my entire organization . . . we do not have any problems hurting people when we have no choice but to hurt people. But we do our best not to bring the Indian federal government down upon us if we can avoid it. We are not your enemy, young lady, unless you make that inevitable."

Priya said nothing.

"You were caught supporting a foreign intelligence operation that would have benefited India. That sounds like the Research and Analysis Wing to me. In fact, that's the *only* thing it sounds like."

She shrugged. "I was not told who we were targeting other than the Turkish embassy in Algiers. My job was to watch over things."

"So that an infiltrator could break in."

"I . . . I didn't know about any infiltrator. I flew the drone."

He shook his head. For the first time, he showed that he was annoyed with her, and that uneased her some, almost as if she were disappointing a relative and not pissing off a gangster.

Jai said, "The communications gear in your hotel room. You were in contact with someone on the ground."

"I . . ."

"And your drones had thermal imaging. There was a man on the property. You saw him. You talked to him. Denying it will only anger us." He smiled a little. "Listen. We are all just doing a job. I do not hate you for doing yours, and I hope you do not hate me for doing mine."

"No, sir. I don't hate anyone."

"We are both Indian. I have every intention of being nice to you. You tell me what you know and this is all over for you. You will be treated well and released unharmed." He leaned closer. "I do not wish to threaten you with my actions."

Priya was anticipating a "but."

"*But*," the man said, "just like you work for someone, I work for someone." Gravely, he said, "Someone in Pakistan." He let the comment hang in the air.

"The Pakistani is on his way here now, only a few hours from arrival.

We both know that if he has to come here with his people to get information from you, he will not hesitate to use any tool he has at his disposal."

"But . . . I don't know anything."

Jai's face darkened for a second time, and Priya began to wonder if the entire friendly disposition was merely some sort of an interrogation technique, a facade that would soon disappear. In a voice lower and more serious than before, he said, "You know how to get into your phone, now don't you?"

Priya looked at the floor in front of her a moment. What could she possibly say? Finally, she looked up. "I can't tell you."

Jai nodded, sadness on his face. "Our agreement with our business partners in Pakistan is that we ourselves will do nothing against our own nation that will bring the weight of the government down upon our enterprise." He shrugged. "If you are, in fact, Indian intelligence, then torturing you for the information we seek would be very much against our own nation." He sat back in his chair. "But . . . if you are, as you say, just a recent university graduate who happened to be caught working in Algeria, then we could do with you whatever we wanted. The government won't care if you simply disappear."

She trembled but remained silent.

He leaned forward. "Now . . . very carefully answer this one question. Do you, or do you not, work for the Research and Analysis Wing?"

He was imploring her to confirm that she worked for R&AW, whether it was true or not, because he did not want to torture her himself. Tears filled Priyanka's eyes. She did not know what to say. Finally, with a little nod, she lied. "I do."

Jai put his hands on his knees and then stood. "You have bought yourself a little time, young lady, but you have also brought yourself immeasurable pain for not giving us the information we seek. The Pakistani will come here, he will get what he wants from you, and I am terribly concerned that he will not allow you to leave with your life. My organization will have nothing to do with this, we aren't killing R&AW officers, but it won't matter to you, because you will be just as dead when this is all over."

Priya Bandari began sobbing uncontrollably as the big man left the room.

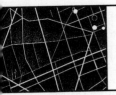

FOURTEEN

TWELVE YEARS AGO

The handoff of the new Ground Branch asset happened in a parking lot at Dulles International Airport surrounded by tourists and business travelers. Maurice Cahill led Court Gentry out of the terminal, both men carrying duffel bags, towards a broadly built and middle-aged man in a gray suit standing next to a black Yukon XL. A younger man was behind the wheel of the vehicle, and a third man in a suit stood near the big man. Court took the middle-aged guy to be an Agency exec and the other two to be bodyguards, but he had no idea why an SAD executive would need security while stateside.

That said, he'd heard that the Ground Branch guys could be wired a little tight. Unable to leave the enemy theater behind, even when they left the enemy theater behind.

As the two men just off the plane walked towards the Yukon, Court spoke softly to Maurice. "I guess this is goodbye. Any last words of wisdom for me?"

"Same as ever, kid. Don't get got."

Court smiled a little. "Same as ever."

At the Yukon, Maurice said, "Court Gentry, this is Matthew Hanley. Matt has made quite a name for himself since moving to the Agency from the Army. Currently he's group chief of an SAD task force, and he'll be your new boss."

Court and Matt shook hands, though Hanley looked at Court with no small amount of skepticism. He even flashed his eyes towards Maurice, an obvious show of confusion.

Court Gentry did not look like a Ground Branch asset, and he knew it. He'd shaved his face clean, though his hair was a little long, and for today's meeting he wore a tie and a blazer. Court understood he was here to join a team of paramilitary operations officers, but he imagined he wouldn't be climbing off the flight from Minsk and heading directly to some rifle range to shoot machine guns. This was the CIA. He figured there would be meetings, paperwork, bullshit.

And he was dressed like the suits he imagined he'd encounter today. His entire modus operandi was built on fitting in, not standing out. Being invisible, living gray.

Matt Hanley thanked Maurice perfunctorily, Court said his goodbyes to his mentor with a quick handshake and brief eye contact that to both men reflected back to the two years they'd spent together, and then the big SAD executive led Court to the backseat of the Yukon, putting Court's lone piece of luggage, a tan duffel bag, into the SUV himself.

Hanley sat next to Court and spoke to him as the vehicle began rolling. "Murmansk. That was some wild shit. I'd love to hear the real story."

"Me, too," Court replied dryly. Hanley wasn't code-worded into that op, so, new boss or not, Court wasn't talking.

Hanley chuckled, and he didn't press. He said, "I don't know if you had some fantasy that you'd be heading in to HQ. By the way you're dressed, I'm assuming that to be the case. We aren't going to Langley. We're heading to a facility we have down in Virginia Beach. You'll meet other members of the task force there and . . ." Hanley looked Court up and down. "We'll see what we're going to do with you."

Court nodded and just looked out the window. He'd not been back to the United States in over a year, and then it was just for some specialized classes at CIA's training center in Harvey Point. The last time he'd spent any meaningful time in the United States, he was preparing to go into the field as a singleton operative in the Autonomous Asset Program, to be cut free of the tether of the Agency and communicate with HQ only sporadically to get intelligence or mission directives.

He'd gone native to some degree in the past four years, Court decided while looking at the Virginia countryside around him. It didn't feel like home; it didn't look like home. It occurred to him that he probably shouldn't get too used to it even now, since Ground Branch was always jetting around the world running various ops. Virginia Beach was just a stop along the way to some armpit of the earth where he and a group of hard dudes would go and kill people.

He put all the unknowns out of his mind. As soon as Hanley began sending texts on his phone, ignoring his new asset, Court put his head against the window of the Yukon and fell asleep.

They passed through the high, barbed-wire-rimmed gate of a well-protected office building just before lunchtime and parked in front of the main entrance. Hanley handed Court his duffel and led him inside, perfunctorily flashing his credentials to multiple layers of security. They entered an elevator and the task force leader pressed the button that read U2, which told Court his new workplace would be two stories below ground. As the elevator began descending, Hanley turned to the younger man.

"Here's what you need to know before we go in. The TL of Golf Sierra is Hightower. He's as good as they come. We got him a few years ago from SEAL Team Six, and he was pretty much a legend there."

Court said nothing, although the phrase "whoop-de-doo" was going through his head.

"But Zack can be . . . he can be . . . resistant to authority. I don't mean he won't execute any mission he's given. Just that he can show a certain . . . obstinance about things. A disagreeableness. He'll come along, if managed correctly, but it takes work to deal with Zack Hightower."

My new team leader is a whiny asshole. Great, Court thought. But he just said, "Why are you telling me this, sir?"

"Because you need to be ready if he doesn't greet you with a hug and flowers. He knows nothing about you, at all, just knows you've been assigned to his outfit. He doesn't get a say in the matter. You can quit if you can't hack it, but he can't fire you without going through me and Carmichael first. You can imagine what that might be like for an alpha male who is responsible for executing difficult missions while keeping the men under him alive."

And with that, the elevator lurched to a stop, and the doors opened.

A tall man with short blond hair and a bushy beard stood feet in front of them in a small and otherwise empty entry hallway. His body was squared off to the elevator, and his hands were on his hips. It was an aggressive posture. While Gentry wore a blue blazer, a burgundy tie, khakis, and dress shoes, the man before him was dressed in a flannel shirt, jeans, and dirty roper boots. He was nearly four inches taller than Court, probably fifteen years older, with shoulders several inches broader. He didn't seem to wear an ounce more fat on his frame than was necessary to keep him functional, and his steely gray eyes bored into Court, then into Hanley, and finally back into Court.

The two men stepped off the elevator and Hanley said, "Zack. Meet your new Six. This is Gentry." Looking to Court, he said, "This is Hightower. Sierra One."

Court extended a hand, but Hightower did not. He just glanced Hanley's way with an angry look on his face. "Is this a joke?"

Court lowered his hand.

Hanley did not answer, so Hightower added, "Is it 'bring your kid to work day,' Matt? Is that it?" He turned back to Court. "What are you, seventeen?"

Court's jaw muscles flexed, and he barked out a reply. "Nailed it. How old are you? Fifty?"

Court didn't think Zack looked fifty, but he didn't think he looked seventeen, either.

"Prior service?" Hightower asked Court.

"I've been in Operations for almost six years. Two in training, four in the field."

"I'm asking about your military service history."

"No."

"No, *what*?"

"No, I'm not former military."

Sierra One cocked his head and looked at Court with bewilderment. After a time he turned to Hanley. "Matt, can I talk to you in private?"

Hanley sighed, but Court got the distinct impression the task force leader was not in the least bit surprised about his team leader's reaction. The two men stepped through a door after Hanley asked Court to wait in the hallway. He found a bench and sat down, and he caught himself wishing he were back in Slonim, or Saint Petersburg, or Moscow, or Budapest, or *anywhere* else, preparing for his next job.

Alone.

Hanley shut the door to the floor's small break room and stepped in a few feet deeper towards a row of tables so Gentry couldn't hear what he expected to be a heated discussion.

And Hightower didn't let him down. "Seriously, Matt. You send me some assclown from D/O who never served in the military, who looks like he should be taking my niece to prom, and I'm supposed to turn him into a tier-one operator?"

"Nobody's asking you to train him. He already *is* a tier-one operator."

"How the fuck so, boss? He plays Xbox in between his dead drops? That make him an operator? Or is he running around the woods with the airsoft kids when he's not chatting up the Chinese attaché at a cocktail party?"

"He's not that kind of an Operations guy. That's all I know." Before Hightower could speak, Matt added, "Denny Carmichael vouched for this man. I know you don't exactly walk the halls of the seventh floor, Zack, so I'll remind you Denny is the director of the Special Activities Division. I work for him, you work for me, and now, because Denny and I have spoken, Violator works for you."

"*Violator?*"

"Sorry, that was his code name in D/O."

Hightower just shook his head at the insanity of this. "What kind of a stupid-ass code name is—"

"Look, he's your new Six. You don't have to like it, you don't have to understand it, but that's the way it is. You can't say no, but if he quits, that's on him. If he quits, we'll go looking for someone else."

Hanley could see the sudden spark in Hightower's eyes, and he knew instantly that Gentry had a very difficult day in store, because Hightower would try his best to force the young man to quit.

But Zack wasn't finished with his arguing. "Have you ever heard of anyone joining Ground Branch as an operator without serving in the military?"

Hanley thought a minute, then nodded. "Jeff Russell, used to be on X-Ray Charlie. No former military service."

Hightower waved a dismissive hand. "Russell was a cop in Oakland, then he made federal SWAT, then FBI HRT, then CIA in the D/O." He motioned in the direction of the younger man sitting on the bench outside the room. "You gonna tell me your wonder boy was on the FBI's Hostage Rescue Team before turning into some secret squirrel for the Agency?"

"No, I'm not saying that. I don't know what he was doing before he joined D/O."

Hightower shouted now. "He was a fuckin' middle schooler before he joined D/O!"

Hanley ignored the outburst. "And I don't know what he was while he was in the D/O. I just know Carmichael wants you to integrate him." Hanley thought a moment before saying, "I am aware of an operation last year in Russia, and I've been told this asset carried out that operation alone. If that is true, then he's all the Six you need, Zack."

"Being a little vague, aren't you, boss?"

"It was a code word op, but I picked up some of the deets from open source after the fact. Denny says Violator pulled it off single-handedly." Quickly, he added, "But that's between you and me, that's not for dissemination to the boys."

Hightower clearly knew when he was beat. This wasn't Hanley's doing, so Hanley wouldn't be able to undo it. "What do I do with him?"

Hanley said, "Take him down to U3. Gear him up with sims. See how he works with the team. If he can't stack up and run clean with you guys, keep at it. If he throws in the towel, then call me, and we'll talk. Come on, Zack, you've dealt with new blood before."

Hightower's eyes grew distant, and his face turned to steel. "Yes, sir. I have. In fact, this is my third time in five months. I've been covered in new blood recently." He was clearly furious, but Hanley had been a military officer, then a CIA officer. He had given the order that was given to him, and he didn't give a shit if his man liked the order or not. He turned back to the door, opened it, and beckoned the younger man in.

As Gentry entered, he spoke matter-of-factly. "You guys might wanna work on soundproofing these walls just a tad."

Hanley didn't acknowledge this. He said, "Okay, I know how this is gonna go. You two have to do a little butt-sniffing to see who the pack leader is here. Well, Gentry, the answer is this. It's Hightower. I don't know or care what you did before today. You are a soldier in his unit. What he says goes. Full stop. You got that?"

Court spoke softly. "Got it, sir."

Hanley turned to Hightower. "Now, bring your men in."

Hightower went to a door on the opposite wall and opened it. "On me, guys."

Court watched as four men entered. They were older than Court, bigger, more muscular, and all dressed in casual attire. Three were wearing ball caps. Two wore flip-flops. An African American had a freshly clean-shaven face, but the other three wore beards and mustaches.

They looked at Court, then at their TL. None of them seemed to get that Court was now part of their unit.

Hightower motioned to the African American. "Gentry, this is Lennox, Golf Sierra Two. Morgan is Three, Pace here is Four, and Redus, Five. Gents, this here's the fuckin' new guy. Our overlords, in their infinite wisdom, have determined that young Mr. Gentry will be our new Sierra Six. We're going to run him and see what he's made of."

"Da fuq?" muttered Redus, a tall, dark-complected thirty-eight-year-old wearing a Sammy Hagar T-shirt and flip-flops.

Hanley, apparently, was done with all this. "I've got to haul ass up to Langley for a meeting at three." He turned to Hightower. "Figure this out, Zack. Call me later."

"Right, boss."

When Hanley was back in the elevator, Hightower looked Court over, then at the duffel on his shoulder. "That all your shit?"

"Yeah."

"Take it down the hall, second room on the right. That's your temporary hooch. Don't unpack, you won't be staying, but do change out of that monkey suit. Don't know what you've been told about Ground Branch, but we don't lunch at Capital Grille. We're going downstairs."

"What's downstairs?"

"Our armory and shoot house."

"Cool."

"Hanley says if I can get you to quit, then I don't have to keep you."

"I won't quit."

Hightower eyed the younger man when he said this. "Why do you want to be on this team so bad?"

Court held the bigger man's eye contact. "I don't. I *don't* want to be on your team. I've been here five minutes and can tell you guys are a bunch of arrogant dickheads. I just . . . don't . . . quit."

Morgan sniffed out a laugh. "I've heard that shit before."

"That you're arrogant dickheads?" Court deadpanned.

Morgan smiled. "All the time, slick."

Hightower started moving for the stairs. "Let's go shoot some people."

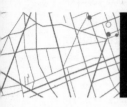

FIFTEEN

PRESENT DAY

Court Gentry had flown from Algiers to Istanbul, mainly because that was the first international flight of the day. Upon landing in Turkey, he took out Copper's watch and pulled up the GPS tracking app. Her tracker wasn't broadcasting, which meant either she was in the air, or else the device had been found on her body and destroyed, in which case the young Indian woman would more than likely be found floating in a river in Pakistan.

He shook off this thought, told himself he just had to wait a few hours, so he found a quiet corner in the airport, settled in with some food and coffee, and focused on recharging the woman's watch and his phone.

An hour later he walked the shops in the airport; bought new clothes, toiletries, and tech gear; and cleaned himself and shaved in a bathroom. He exited looking like a new man.

Minutes later he felt a vibration in his breast pocket. It was Copper's watch, and it was notifying him that the tracker was transmitting again.

He yanked it from his pocket and zoomed in carefully on the location. He blinked a few times to make sure he wasn't seeing things, and then he all but lunged for his cell phone.

A minute later Arjun answered.

"Cobalt? Is that you? Have you found her?"

"Yeah. She's in Mumbai."

"Mumbai?" The man sounded genuinely astonished. "*I'm* in Mumbai. What's she doing in—"

Court interrupted Arjun with the same question. "Why would Pakistanis take her to India, Arjun?"

"I don't know. I certainly didn't kidnap my employee to bring her home." He thought a moment. "Maybe you were wrong. Maybe it wasn't Pakistani intelligence."

Court ignored the man and said, "She's at the airport. Looks like she came in on a private charter flight."

"I have friends at the fixed operating bases there. I'll reach out to them."

Court was certain Arjun was a former intelligence man himself, so he suspected he had contacts all over, though he doubted they would be friends. He also suspected he wouldn't learn much at the fixed operating base. If the ISI was operating in India, they sure as hell would have a plan to cover themselves.

Arjun said, "You must come to Mumbai immediately. You must help me get her back."

Court just said, "I didn't think I understood what the hell was going on before, but if she's with Murad Khan, in Mumbai, then I am *really* confused."

"I know people all over the city. If they take her somewhere, and if you see that on the tracking monitor, just tell me, and I will find out what I can."

"Don't expect to hear from me till I arrive. I don't want you trying anything without me. If someone goes in to get her, it's going to be me."

"I agree. But . . . but I can arrange men. To help."

"I'll let you know," Court said, and he hung up.

He checked the closest departures board, scanning it as quickly as he could, hoping like hell there was a direct flight to Mumbai and that he hadn't missed it. To his relief, he saw a Turkish Airlines direct flight that was leaving in just a few hours.

He'd need a visa to get into India, so he cleared Turkish customs and immigration with his forged credentials and jumped into a cab to head to the Indian embassy here in Istanbul. There he talked his way into a tourist visa for same-day travel with no issues, and he booked his flight online while riding in another cab that raced through the city's crazy afternoon traffic. A one-way trip for a tourist would have raised eyebrows at immigration in India, so he paid for a round trip, returning to Istanbul in six days.

He had no intentions of being on that return flight. He hoped he'd be able to free Copper from her captors, then either find Khan himself or at least find out where he'd gone.

Court fully expected to end up in Pakistan, hunting Murad Khan, before this was all over.

Again.

Khan was behind Copper's kidnapping, but he couldn't imagine that Khan was actually with Copper in India right now. It made no sense for a senior ISI officer who had been declared dead by both his own agency and the CIA to be walking around in a country that was, for all intents and purposes, enemy territory. The conflict between Pakistan and India was at one of its lowest points these days, even considering the three wars that had been fought between the two nations since the 1940s.

No, Copper's arrival in India made no sense to him, but he kept monitoring the tracker, and by the time he'd checked in for his flight to India, he saw that the GPS was indicating it had been stationary for several hours at a location in the Andheri East neighborhood of Mumbai.

Court didn't know Arjun well enough to trust him with this information. While he'd love to have help surveilling the location for hours in advance of his arrival, Court decided he'd keep this intel to himself and only reveal it to Arjun when he had established himself in Mumbai.

He boarded a Boeing 777 and took his seat in coach, tucking himself in with reading material he'd downloaded on his phone about Pakistan and the ISI. Maps and history and flow charts of government organizations. A long time ago this had been very much on his radar, but in the past decade he'd not kept up with what was happening in Pakistan, though what *had* happened in Pakistan never seemed to leave his thoughts for long.

The aircraft took off and banked to the south over the Sea of Marmara, banked again to the southeast, and Court kept reading, telling himself he needed to be ready for whatever he encountered at his destination, because right now, everything that had happened in the past day seemed like such a confounding and impenetrable riddle.

SIXTEEN

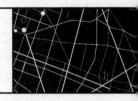

A half hour after Court Gentry was told he'd get a trial run in the Ground Branch shoot house in the basement of the Virginia Beach compound, he was decked out in body armor, a helmet, and an Avon C50 gas mask. Just like the other men, he carried a rifle and a pistol loaded with Simunitions, actual bullets filled with a dusty paint in a plastic capsule that, when fired from these specially modified weapons, struck their targets at seven hundred feet a second and were known to cause cuts and heavy bruises along with the telltale splatter of a paint round. Court had been shot thousands of times with sims while working at his father's law enforcement training facility, and he knew that getting hit in the chest, face, or head where he was most protected by armor, a rubber mask, or a helmet was far superior to taking a hit to the legs or arms. He also knew that knowledgeable shooters using sims liked to aim for their opponent's crotch; the sting of a plastic projectile to the balls could bring a man to his knees and keep him there, so Court pulled a folded hand towel from a shelf of gun-cleaning products in the armory, then slipped it down his pants, with half its length going down one leg and the remainder going down the other. This would blunt impacts to his privates or inner thighs, should he catch a round there.

Even at his relatively young age, Court Gentry had more close-quarters battle training than most anyone else on Earth, but one thing he did not have a lot of experience with was working in a stack, being one man in a group taking down targets. Sure, as a trainer in his father's firearms school, he had taught the techniques from time to time, but that had been seven years ago, and even then he was much more comfortable playing the lone-wolf opposition force member than he was telling FBI Hostage Rescue men with decades of SWAT experience how to flood a room together and take down a target.

Court figured these Ground Branch guys, while all clearly douchebags, at least would be damn good at functioning as a cohesive unit, and Court didn't have as much confidence in his own abilities to integrate.

Despite Court's bluster about never quitting, Hightower might have been right. There might be no need for him to unpack his gear in his room, because this could turn into a short stay if he couldn't prove himself as adequate.

The six men left the armory and walked down a hall to a door with a sign that read:

SHOOT HOUSE. LIVE FIRE. EAR AND EYE PROTECTION MANDATORY.

**ANYONE ENTERING THE DOOR WILL FOLLOW THE
INSTRUCTIONS OF THE RANGE SAFETY OFFICER.**

The team encountered the safety officer waiting for them in the front lobby of the shoot house, a barrel-chested man of about sixty who appeared to be a grizzled former Marine gunnery officer right out of central casting. He checked each man's weapons, then frisked them from top to bottom to ensure that only Simunition rounds were being used during the upcoming evolutions.

A metal staircase led to a catwalk above the shoot house proper, and from here the safety officer could watch the action in each room and hallway, because while there were walls and floors in the various spaces, there were no ceilings to block the view from the catwalk.

Five other men were also in the lobby out front waiting, sitting around on a bench and geared up for a fight. Hightower explained to Court they were all ex–Ground Branch operators who now worked in the training cadre, and they would serve as the OPFOR, the opposition force.

The five older but obviously strong and capable former operators had already been frisked and armed with submachine guns, and soon they walked through the main shoot house door, disappearing into the warren of rooms and hallways that made up the facility.

Zack looked at Court now. "Tell me you have operated in a stack before."

"I have," Court said. "But . . . it's been a minute."

Zack shrugged. "All right, then, Rambo. Stack up."

Court started to put himself in the middle of the row of men standing by the entrance to the shoot house, but the African American introduced as Lennox pushed him towards the front of the pack. "Fresh meat goes to the front." With a shrug he said, "Sucks to be the Six."

Court pushed ahead and found his place, with all five men behind him. A few seconds later he felt a squeeze on his shoulder telling him to breach, and he tried the latch on the door. Finding it unlocked, he entered the lighted space, a small entry hall. He could feel the others tight behind him as he looked through the EOTech optic on his weapon, and he cleared the space before him.

This done, he started to move to a door on the left, but a hand grabbed the drag handle on his body armor and yanked him roughly back to the right, towards another door.

The team wasn't using radios; there were hand movements and other signals for small teams in close-quarters battle, and Hightower wanted to be sure Gentry knew, at least, this much.

Court moved into the first room and cut hard to the left, his weapon lights strobing through the darkness as he dug his hard corner. Finding it clear, he turned to the center of the room, the blaze of white revealing a man who was well covered behind a plywood bar area. He fired a burst, striking the wall just above the man's head. *Shit.* He went to follow up, sensing the rest of the team flowing into the room around him, but before he had a chance, rough hands shoved him out of the way.

"Stay in your fucking lane."

Others in the stack engaged the man, so Court shifted aim towards a dark open room on his left.

He flashed his light again and saw nothing in this space, but he knew he had to clear it quickly, because a hallway fed into the barroom he now stood in from a far corner, and if the opposition put a man in both the hall and the dark room to the left, they could pin the Golf Sierra unit tightly together by the bar and pick them off one by one.

Court broke left, rushing towards the dark room with his weapon sweeping in front of him.

He didn't know it, but no one followed.

Court blasted his light on the dead space to his left as he entered, and first detected the telltale outline of a man's elbow. From the position of the extremity, the man connected to it was tight against a wall and holding something in his arm. Court launched through the air to his right, fired his HK while doing so, and when he landed on the floor, he rolled onto his shoulder, ending up in a crouch with his rifle still aimed in and firing at the enemy. The opposition player crouched in the corner took one to the arm and then two to the mask, and he dropped his rifle to his chest and held up his hands, a look of astonishment on his face that he had somehow missed a target he'd had the drop on.

"Hit!" the man announced.

Just then, gunfire erupted back in the room where Court had left the rest of the team. As he rushed in that direction to support them, he saw Redus already down on the ground in the middle of the space. Morgan crawled forward on his knee pads and grabbed Redus's drag handle on the upper back of his body armor, but Morgan took a string of hits in the leg and right side. He went down as well, falling next to Redus and raising a hand, shouting "Hit!" in the process.

Hightower was behind the bar with Pace, and the origin of fire was the open corner-feeding hallway on Court's left. Court sprayed the remainder of his mag up the hall as he ran out of the dark room and back into the bar area, then he executed another roll and came up behind Hightower behind the bar.

"Reloading!"

Hightower rose high on his knees to shoot over the bar, and as soon as he did so, he caught a round in the top of his mask, right on his forehead. He fell back onto his butt and sat there, out of the fight.

He yelled loud enough to be heard by the man who'd tagged him, "I'm hit!"

Court stopped working the reload on his rifle, let it hang on his chest, and drew his Glock pistol. Dropping down onto his left shoulder, he had a low angle on the hallway and only his head and gun arm exposed. An OPFOR player showed just a few inches of his knee as he hugged the wall at the corner, and Court shot him in the center of it. The pain of the paint round caused the man to lose his balance and expose more of his body as he fell, but Court did not fire on him. He waited for another opposition player to come retrieve his fallen man. When an ambulatory OPFOR exposed his arm to grab the drag handle on the back of his fallen partner's body armor, Court tagged him in the forearm.

Court then redirected his aim to the man lying on his back, shooting him twice in the face mask now.

"Hit!" the man called.

The twenty-five-year-old CIA operations officer rolled out into the middle of the barroom for an angle on the man who'd been shot in the arm. Court placed two perfect rounds in the center of the man's chest while fully prone. The opposition player fell to the ground and announced he was hit, and then Jim Pace, the only other member of Golf Sierra still operational, leapt over the bar and moved to the edge of the hallway in search of the last enemy.

Court holstered his pistol, reloaded his rifle, then moved to assist his surviving teammate, but Pace didn't wait for him. He instead dropped to a knee, leaned into the hallway, and began spraying automatic weapon fire.

Within seconds Court heard a man shout from far up the dark hallway. "Hit!"

The safety officer above on the catwalk spoke into a wireless mic on his vest tied into the facility's PA system.

"Cease fire! Cease fire!"

"Goddammit!" Morgan shouted from the floor when it was all over.

Pace was no more pleased than Morgan. "Four men down in the first fuckin' room! This is some amateur-hour bullshit!"

Court safed his weapon, took off his mask, and wiped sweat from his forehead. He had a strong suspicion he was about to get blamed for this mess.

He was not wrong.

Hightower climbed back to his feet from behind the bar and stuck a finger in Court's face. "*Never* go into a room alone! That fuckup is on you! You don't leave the stack without being ordered to leave the stack. *Ever.*"

"I saw the room on the left and—"

The safety officer had watched the entire evolution from the catwalk. He shouted into his mic now, his gravelly Marine Corps voice booming against the walls. "And you cover it, but you don't enter it till the stack is with you. You left your team, Redus realized your mistake, and he broke off to try to support you, but he had to enter the line of fire from the far hallway. He caught a round from one of the shooters there. Morgan went to drag him back to the bar, and then he got popped because he was exposed. Zack and Pace made it to the bar, but by the time you got back to them, you had three operators pinned in an eight-foot space with no egress, and then Hightower took a round trying to cover your mag change."

Zack Hightower said, "You break from the stack, and the stack breaks down. You got that, Gentry?"

"Got it," the younger man replied, chastened.

Pace stepped up to Court now. He was covered in perspiration due to the exertion, all the gear, and the gas mask he'd just removed. "Are we gonna run this again, asshole, or are you going to admit this shit isn't for you?"

Court looked him in the eye. "We're going to run it again."

Hightower said, "You're wasting our time, kid."

Court turned to him, moved close. "Then why am I the only one who doesn't look like an Andy Warhol painting? Bet against me. That'll be fun."

Hightower looked at the younger man with derision, but nevertheless he glanced up to the safety officer and nodded.

The safety officer took the TL's cue. "Reload, rehydrate, and get set for another run!"

The second run wasn't much better than the first. Court's inability to see the men behind him caused him to misjudge the speed at which they moved, and twice he was grabbed and yanked back, "encouraged" to slow down by Redus, Sierra Five. The third time the man in the train behind him let him go, Court got too far ahead and turned a corner into a hail of gunfire.

He'd expected his team to be on his heels, but he was wrong.

He shot two of the oppo, but a third took Court out with a round to the neck that hit right below his full face mask and hurt like hell.

Hightower called a cease-fire, and then the men again took off their masks and stood in the middle of the hall under the catwalk *and* under the disapproving eyes of the safety officer.

Court rubbed his neck and coughed.

Hightower said, "Okay, we tried. We're done. This isn't for you, Gentry. Time for you to ring the bell."

"Ring the bell" was Navy SEAL speak; it meant it was time for him to give up.

Court's head hung low. He couldn't argue that he'd been at the center of the failures of both evolutions. Part of him wanted to throw in the towel, but he was telling the truth when he said he didn't quit. He had to convince Sierra One to grant him one more try.

The men around him began removing their gear. Court ignored the pain in his neck, looked to Hightower, and said, "I have an idea. Don't integrate me with you. Stand down the oppo and let me take their place."

Hightower said, "The *oppo*? *You* want to be part of the oppo?"

"No. I want to be the *entirety* of the oppo."

"You want us to come at you? *All* of us?"

"Yes."

"At the same time?"

Court nodded. The rest of the team laughed, save for Redus, who just spit on the sawdust-covered concrete floor and began reloading his rifle. "The new kid wants to play OPFOR. Five on one."

Hightower addressed Court. "What will that prove?"

"That he's a cocky prick," Pace blurted. "But let's do it anyway. I'm gonna shoot this dude in the nuts for ruining what was supposed to be a perfectly lazy afternoon."

Court implored Hightower now. "What do you have to lose? You guys are so obviously hot shit, this should be easy, right?" Court took his rifle off its sling and handed it over to Lennox. "I'll run with a pistol only."

Lennox looked up to the safety officer. "This motherfucker's insane."

The older safety officer just said, "If you boys haven't been keeping score, the new kid has zipped five out of ten of the oppo on the two runs. He's sloppy as shit with his team movement, but he's stacking bodies, and if you can't see that, you're blind." He added, "He's not going to make it onto Golf Sierra, I'll go on record with that right now, but he's a hell of a lot of fun to watch." He nodded to Zack. "Let's see him work on his own, just for fun."

Hightower reluctantly agreed. "Fine." To Court he said, "We'll run the exercise against you, just so you can't go back to Hanley whining that we didn't give you every chance. But you can have a carbine, an SMG, whatever you want. We will be fully kitted up. You do *not* want to face us with a pistol."

"All I want is a handgun. You guys have a Walther PPQ in the armory?" Court asked.

Hightower replied. "You have a Glock on your hip."

"I prefer the—"

"I don't give a shit what you prefer," Hightower said. "We all use the G19. *You* will use the G19, and you will like it."

"Fair enough," Court said. He'd always preferred Walthers and HK pistols to Glocks, but he wasn't going to fight this battle right now. He said, "Give me a couple of minutes, and then raid the shoot house. Let's see what you guys can do."

Pace stepped up to him. "You're dead, fuckface. You realize that, right?"

Court put his mask back on. "When I'm looking down at you on the floor in five minutes, that's me awaiting your apology."

Pace moved closer, aggressively, but Hightower just barked his name. "Jim."

Sierra Four stopped, eyed Court a moment more, then turned away and began moving back to the front of the shoot house lobby with the other men, while the safety officer on the catwalk looked to Gentry.

"Three minutes and I'm sending them in." He turned away, then began walking back towards the beginning of the warren of rooms. As he did so, he muttered one word that Court could hear down below. "Dumbass."

SEVENTEEN

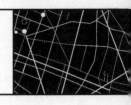

Hightower and his men stood outside a different entrance to the shoot house now, readying themselves for the evolution to come. The team leader spoke softly. "Morgan, you take point. Listen up, don't get cocky. Hanley said this dude had some skills, and the safety officer's right, he can shoot. We haven't seen anything all that special yet, but don't make yourself be the one that proves he's the real deal. I do *not* need the aggravation of running drills with this kid all day. I've got shit to do."

Morgan said, "Fuck this guy. Let's hit this door, find that squirrelly little bastard and smoke him, and then go get some lunch."

Hightower said, "Nice and slow. Keith, hit it."

Morgan reached for the door latch.

The Ground Branch team breached the side door of the shoot house, then cleared the first three rooms without incident. At a T intersection at the end of a hall, Hightower signaled for Golf Sierra Four to follow him to the right while Two, Three, and Five went to the left. This was a departure in tactics from their earlier evolutions, but that was also the point. Zack didn't want Gentry to know what to expect, so he made the call to split the force.

Jim Pace came to the first open doorway and spun in expertly, and then he kept moving, making way for Hightower to follow him in. They split at the entrance, Pace went left, and Hightower shifted right.

They found the small room clear.

Just as they began to restack to move back into the hallway, the sound of Simunitions fire came from the direction the other team had split off to.

Pace knelt down low, then took a quick peek around the corner of the door that led into the hall. After looking down to the far end, he yanked his head back to safety and then used hand motions to convey what he saw to his Sierra One.

Lennox, Redus, and Morgan were all down in the hallway in front of an open doorway some thirty yards away.

Hightower had been crouching, but he stood up slowly. Dumbfounded. He headed towards the hall, then peeked out for himself. His three men sat with their rifles in their laps, their backs to the wall of the hallway and facing the last doorway on the left. They'd all been "killed" either in the doorway itself or outside in the hall, and Hightower couldn't envision one man accomplishing that.

The safety officer was on the catwalk right over the fallen men, looking down at them.

Hightower turned to Pace, said nothing, just indicated with his hands that they would proceed down the hall, and then he would make a left at the T and approach the room Gentry had been shooting from via another route, while Pace himself would continue down the hall, past his fallen teammates, and hit the room simultaneous with Hightower's arrival.

One minute later Pace stepped over the "bodies" of his three teammates, keeping his weapon high, only lowering it to shield it from anyone in the room on the left. He put his shoulder on the wall near the doorway, then spun into the room, raising the gun to bring the holographic weapon sight to his eye.

At first, he saw nothing, but then Gentry appeared, upside down, a few feet above and in front of him.

Before Pace could shift fire to the figure above him, Court shot him twice in the chest, knocking him back out into the hallway.

"Hit!" Pace shouted as he fell onto his back, right on top of his three teammates.

Court's legs were hooked around a steel beam that ran along the bottom of the catwalk over the room. He continued aiming his pistol at the doorway while still hanging upside down by his legs, but only for an instant, because he heard a noise on his right. He'd seen the closed door there when he entered, but he hadn't had time to check where it led before the first three men closed on his position.

The door opened; Court shifted his pistol to the movement and fired but missed. Zack Hightower lay on the floor, rolling into the doorway on his left shoulder and firing a spray of fully automatic fire, tagging Court multiple times and causing him to fall from the beam down to the concrete.

Court stood up and holstered; his left side was riddled with fresh welts and racked with pain. He ignored Zack now, stepped out into the hall, looked down at Pace, and smiled.

He didn't expect an apology from the man and wasn't particularly disappointed when no apology was forthcoming.

Instead the man on the floor said, "That's some fuckin' epic beginner's luck. Won't happen again."

Zack walked up to Court now, while the other men climbed back to their own feet.

Court had not taken down the entire Ground Branch unit by himself, but he *had* eliminated four out of five.

The men were quieter than before, their bemused faces now masks of anger and frustration.

Zack ordered everyone to reset, and he handed a pair of Glock magazines to Gentry. "We'll go again," Hightower said, determination in his voice and on his face.

"Thought we might," Court quipped.

Pace moved up into his face now and repeated himself. "It won't happen again."

But it did, in fact, happen again. On the second run-through, Court took out three of the five before Lennox shot him, and on the third evolution, he again eliminated three Ground Branch officers before Morgan and

Pace both caught Court during a mag change and stitched him across the crotch with red paint cartridges.

Two more runs each saw Golf Sierra losing men against a single opposition, something that rarely happened during training when facing an entire team.

After ninety minutes in the shoot house, Hightower finally announced the end of the session. "Everybody take your weapons and gear back to the armory; meet me in the break room in thirty." He nodded up to the safety officer, who had not left the catwalk for the duration of the drills.

The safety officer just looked at Hightower, slowly shaking his head in disbelief. Clearly he'd never seen anything like what he'd just witnessed, either.

Most of the men headed for the armory, but Court caught up to Zack. "How about one more time, me running in the stack with you guys again? I'll get it tight."

Zack just shook his head. "We're done for today."

Court just looked at him. "So . . . you're the one ringing the bell, then?"

Hightower didn't like this one bit. He raised a finger into the smaller man's face. Court did not back away from it, but neither did he adopt an aggressive posture himself.

Zack said, "Listen to me, Gentry. You have made your point that you are one hell of a CQB shooter. I haven't seen anybody do the shit you just did. Not in the teams, not on DEVGRU, not here, and not in any of the opposition I've faced.

"What we need, however, is not some loose gun running around our target area, we need a sixth man in our cohesive team."

Court knew Zack was right. He'd not proven himself as anything more than a singleton, and Golf Sierra wasn't the place for singletons. He said, "I'll get there. I just need some practice. I've been doing some . . . some different things the past few years. I'm rusty on my team tactics." He added, "But I won't be for long."

"This isn't the place to learn, kid. Trust me, you've never seen anything like the hits we get sent on."

"You don't know what I've seen."

"I know you didn't see your pubes until about five years ago."

Court rolled his eyes. "I'm almost twenty-six, for God's sake. What is the deal with my age? Do you fuckers need a sixth man to help you hit targets out there, or do you need a sixth man for bingo night at the retirement home?"

Zack cracked a little smile at this, but he hid it quickly. "Drop your gear in the armory and go back to your hooch. I'm going to talk to the guys, then I'll send for you."

Court stood. "Fine. I'll be unpacking."

Zack said nothing as the new guy left the room.

Two hours after the men first kitted up in the shoot house, the five veterans of Golf Sierra sat in the break room on sublevel two.

Morgan said, "Boss, I gotta say it. That dude can move."

Pace said, "He's fifteen, of course he can jump around. And he can put rounds on target. But can he work with a team?"

Hightower took a swig from a bottle of water. "We need two weeks. Long days, long nights. But we can get him where we need him before we redeploy to the sandbox."

It was Redus who spoke up now. "Doesn't it bother you that we aren't allowed to know shit about who this guy is? Where he came from? How he learned to do what he did down in the shoot house? It creeps me the fuck out that this unknown shows up and schools us like that, and we're supposed to just take him in and not ask questions."

Hightower thought this over a moment. "I hear you. But the raw materials are there, no matter how the hell he came upon them. And there's something more important than his CQB abilities."

"What's that, boss?" Pace asked.

"I don't know if you guys were paying attention, but I was. Forget about all the shucking and jiving he did. Did you look into that kid's eyes?"

No one answered.

"Well, *I* did. There's an almost feral look in there. He's a killer." Zack spit dip into a cup, then said, "A stone-cold fucking killer."

Lennox had been quiet. He nodded now. "Saw it, too, boss."

"We're all killers," Morgan countered.

"We aren't like him," Hightower said flatly. "They won't tell us what he did in Operations because he was an assassin."

Morgan sniffed. "The Agency doesn't employ assassins."

Hightower said, "Sub rosa shit. I guarantee that kid has been sent out on kill missions. Alone. It's in his eyes."

Redus said, "All the more reason I don't want him shouldering up behind me in the train. He's the breach bitch, or I'm not going out with him."

"Fair enough. He's on point. I'll use him solo when I can, God knows we sometimes need an extra pair of eyes and a gun."

The team left save for Hightower, and Redus leaned into Court's hooch and told him the TL wanted to talk with him in the break room.

Court arrived at the table a minute later. He was icing an elbow he'd smacked when falling off the catwalk beam.

Hightower said, "You pick up a boo-boo?"

"It's nothing."

Hightower nodded, then looked into the younger man's eyes. "How do you do it?"

"Do what?"

"Do *what*?" Zack mocked. "All that. I saw you firing on targets you didn't even have an angle on. I saw you reloading faster than anyone I've ever seen reload in my life. I watched you engage three oppo on three compass points, taking down two of them. Twice."

Court put his elbows on the table, ignoring the injury to one of them. "What you saw? That's all I did between about the age of eight to eighteen. My dad ran a shooting school in Florida. I worked there. Pretty much seven days a week. Pretty much eight hours a day. Sometimes more. Sometimes a *lot* more."

Zack's eyebrows furrowed. "I was playing baseball at that age."

Court shrugged. "I couldn't hit a baseball if my life depended on it. It was guns. It was CQB. It was moving and shooting. That's all it ever was for me, until I got into the CIA."

"And then?"

Court wasn't going to talk about his work at the Agency. Instead he said, "Do you know what tachypsychia is?"

Zack shook his head.

"It's a neurological condition that alters the perception of time."

"So?"

"For me, time seems to slow down when my adrenaline is up. I'm calmer under stress, I react more efficiently than most people. That, and the training I've been given, have turned me into what I am." He shrugged. "Whatever that is."

"Some CIA shrink told you all this?"

"Pretty much, yeah. But there's more to it. I can see shadows within shadows, recognize shapes and movement quickly. I don't know why. Back in the shoot house—those guys you said I engaged without being able to see them? I knew they were there. I cut the pie moving into the rooms, caught just a sliver of an elbow of a man holding a gun, or a kneecap, saw the oppo before he saw me, and then moved my weapon to engage before putting myself in the line of fire. Doesn't always work . . . hell, I got smoked a half-dozen times today. But I'm fucking good at this."

The older man looked him over for a long time, then spit into his cup. "You went into some code word program that I don't get to know about. Hell, even Hanley doesn't get to know about. And now they think you're a good fit for our team."

For the first time, perhaps, Court and Zack were in agreement.

"Yeah," Court said. "It's bullshit, right?"

"But you won't quit."

Court said, "I *don't* quit."

"You are hardheaded and cocky. I respect your talent, but I'll tell you this. If you join Golf Sierra, I'm in charge, you are the low man on the totem pole, and your arrogance will only fuck you up."

"I'll be honest with you," Court said. "I don't have people skills. They weren't assigned to me. I don't work well with others, and I see this position as a major demotion from what I was doing before. As to me being cocky . . . Guilty as charged. I'm pretty certain I'm one of the best in the world at this shit."

Hightower cocked his head. "Do you have a point?"

"The point is, you're gonna have to deal with a little self-assuredness out of me. Comes with the package. But I bow to no man when it comes to commitment to the mission. And I know that you are the head honcho here." Court shrugged. "Doesn't mean you're always right."

"But it does mean you do what I say."

"I understand that."

Zack didn't look happy, but he said, "Okay, kiddo, you're my new Six. We'll spend the next couple of weeks working to get you tighter with the guys. Lots of low-light drills, we'll do a couple days in West VA working on mountain ops." Zack asked, "Are you jump qualified?"

"*Qualified*, yes."

Zack made a face. He realized Court was saying his parachuting skills were nothing to write home about.

"How's your driving?"

Court winced a little now. "Not good."

Zack laughed. "See, we're making progress already. You aren't cocky about everything."

Court laughed, the first time today. "I had a little training on driving at Harvey Point, but where I've been living the last few years, I didn't even have a car. Putting me behind the wheel for anything more technical than a Sunday drive would be a mistake on your part."

Zack said, "Noted. You are our point man, that's your specialty. We'll get you squared away on the rest of it."

Court nodded, then motioned with his head down the hall, in the direction of the hooches. "They don't like me."

"I don't like you, either." Zack put his hand on Court's back. "But they'll respect you if you give them a reason to. That's about all you can ask for around here."

Court didn't love being touched. He stood up, breaking the contact. "Fair enough, One."

Zack shook his hand now. "Welcome aboard, Sierra Six. You might live to regret this, but . . . let's be honest. You probably won't."

EIGHTEEN

PRESENT DAY

Gentry landed in Mumbai, India, with the September evening's temperatures hovering around ninety. While the aircraft was still taxiing, he pulled Copper's Apple Watch out of his pocket and looked at the GPS app. On it he could see she was still in the city, stationary by the looks of it. Zooming in on the tiny map, he saw she remained in the Andheri East district, in the center of the sprawling coastal metropolis.

He breezed through immigration with his forged documents and his visa, then made his way to a cabstand with a suitcase he'd purchased at the airport in Istanbul, loaded with clothing and the computer he'd bought there, as well.

He took a cab to the Oberoi Mumbai on Nariman Point and used his forged credentials to rent a room. His plan was to keep moving, no more than one night at a location, although he would reserve rooms for three, four, or five nights each time, just so that if facial recognition picked him up and he was flagged by one of the many organizations around the world pursuing him, they would think they had more time to prepare for a raid.

Once in his room, he sat down in a chair at a desk and pulled out his phone, turning it on for the first time since arriving in country. He used his encrypted Signal app to dial his broker, Arjun, and while he did this, he looked at Copper's watch, ensuring that the blip he hoped still represented her location had not moved since he'd landed.

Arjun answered on the first ring. "Cobalt?"

"It's me, I'm here."

"Can you see Copper on the GPS?"

"I see the tracker. We don't know if it's still attached to the woman, but the fact that it's broadcasting is a good sign. Usually when someone finds one, the first thing they do is disable it."

"Yes, that is good. Where is she?"

"She's in Andheri East."

"That is a big place. Millions of people. *Where* in Andheri East?"

"Arjun, we're doing this my way. First thing I need from you is some weapons and other gear. You can provide that?"

"Absolutely. I know people in the underworld. It should be no problem to acquire what you need."

"I will text you a list. Get as much as you can now. Tomorrow morning, first thing, text me where I can pick it all up. Have it left in a storage locker, a rental unit, something like that."

"I can bring it to you personally."

"No, you can do exactly what I just asked you to do. You and I won't be meeting face-to-face."

"But . . . how do I know you will not take the equipment and leave Copper to her fate?"

"You think I just raced halfway around the world to steal some shitty guns from the Mumbai mob?"

Arjun reflected on this. "No . . . of course not. I will try to get you everything you ask for. What will you do in the meantime?"

"Reconnaissance of the location where they are holding her."

"A white man, doing that alone? In Andheri East?"

"Just get my stuff. Let me know when you have it." Court hung up the phone and began texting his list of items.

It was after eleven when a lone American climbed out of a rickshaw on Makwana Road, surrounded by locals on foot, in cars and taxicabs, on scooters and bikes. Even this late in the evening, horns honked all around; vendors shouted, peddling their wares. Police whistles blew in intersections; a pack of dogs ambled by like they had someplace else to be.

The city of Mumbai pulsed like a living, breathing entity.

He made his way onto the side street where Copper's beacon had indicated, although in the past hour it had stopped updating. He took this to mean the batteries had worn down, but he also knew either she or one of her captors could have destroyed it.

He located the building where the last GPS signal had been broadcast from, but he continued on past it, noting that it was seven stories high, not particularly wide or deep, and built in early gothic style. Two balconies on every side of every floor indicated it might be a lower-end apartment complex, with eight units per floor.

There were signs outside at ground level; some were in English, and they represented a wide array of industries. Apartments for rent, office supplies, warehousing, computer hardware sales and repair. But these places of business all seemed to be on the first couple of floors, leading him to believe the six higher floors were, indeed, living spaces. Laundry hanging from some of the balconies all but confirmed this.

Court saw no sign indicating the floor and suite number of a Pakistani intelligence holding facility here on the premises, and that was disappointing, if unsurprising.

He then began walking the nearby blocks, drifting down alleyways, moving through buildings with unlocked doors: restaurants still open, twenty-four-hour dingy family-run manufacturing operations. Virtually no one noticed him as he slipped past their lives like a black alley cat in the night.

He made his way around to the eastern side of his target building and immediately saw something promising. The next building over was identical in shape and size, a twin of his target, but it was darkened and appeared empty. There were no windows, and the entire structure was enveloped by an intricate network of bamboo scaffolding. The building didn't look new at all, so it was obviously undergoing some renovation or repairs.

He looked back and forth between his target building and the building with the scaffolding, separated by no more than thirty feet, with a quiet one-lane street running between them.

And he had an idea. He walked over to the bamboo on the dark building and ran his hands over the joints within his reach, getting a feel for how they were lashed together with cordage. He took a few steps back and looked at the lengths of the vertical stabilizing pieces, saw a single tied-off joint indicating where one pole stopped and another started on its way up the side of the building, and this told him the vertical poles were some fifteen meters in length.

Court looked back over his shoulder a moment.

Shit, he said to himself, and not because he didn't have a plan. He said *shit* because he *did* have a plan, and he wasn't exactly in love with it.

He thought he had a way to enter the target building from above, as opposed to going through one of the ground-floor doors. Top-down structure raids were usually preferable to bottom-up raids, as almost always a structure's defenses were designed to protect from attackers entering from the ground floor.

Court decided that once he had some weapons and some more intelligence on the location, he would raid the place and be inside their defenses before they knew he was there.

He didn't really have a solid plan for getting the woman out of the building once he got in, but, he told himself, he was used to making up shit on the fly.

He did some late-night shopping in the neighborhood, clothes and food primarily, and by the time he was ready to leave the Andheri East neighborhood, he felt he had a good mental blueprint of the area and an idea about what it would be like during the day. He didn't want to wait twenty-four hours to attempt to rescue Copper, so that meant he'd go as soon as he had his equipment.

A daytime raid, despite the dangers, might be her only hope, because the enemy would be trying to extract intelligence from her. Once they had it, they would no longer need her.

He took one more pass by the target building just before midnight, then climbed into the back of a taxi and asked the driver to take him to a location a few blocks from the Oberoi. He'd conduct a surveillance detection route before returning to his suite to catch a few hours' sleep, and then, in the morning, he'd get his guns and go to work.

Six floors above where Court Gentry had been skulking around the parking lots and alleyways of Andheri East, twenty-four-year-old Priyanka Bandari sat chained to a chair in the middle of the same nondescript room she'd sat in for the interrogation hours earlier. She'd spent the time since in her tiny cell, mostly practicing yoga to the best of her ability, and she'd been fed and was relatively well looked after, other than the fact that she'd been robbed of her liberty.

But now the Indian men in the room with her seemed more grave, more serious, almost nervous as they waited around.

Waiting for what, she did not know for sure, but she had a guess.

The Pakistani that the Indian gangster named Jai had mentioned that afternoon. His arrival was imminent; she could see it on the strained faces of the men.

A couple hours earlier she'd removed the tracker from the back of her neck—she assumed its batteries were depleted and doubted it was still signaling—and then she had rolled the adhesive-backed disc into a tiny little ball. She needed a place to hide it in the room, and finally decided on her waste bucket. She dropped it in and felt reasonably certain no one was going to go looking for it there.

The waiting in the interrogation room was endless, and it was stressful, but the stress did not dissipate when the door finally opened in front of her and she saw Jai. Big, almost flamboyantly dressed, a thick mustache. His eyes were all but blank and unreadable, and this sent a cold chill throughout her body.

When he stepped into the room, he moved to the side, allowing another man to enter. This individual was smaller, fitter, and easily a decade older than Jai. He was clean-shaven, his dark hair flecked with silver and his almond eyes peering at her. He was dressed in white cotton slacks and a long white linen shirt known as a kurta that hung to his midthigh. His hands were empty and his gaze impassive, even when he fixed it on Priya, obviously the woman he had come to question.

She just looked back and forth between the new man and Jai, waiting for someone to speak.

Others entered the room now, and this seemed to cause the Indian gangsters to push off the walls, to step away a little, to give more space to the new arrivals.

The new men were casually dressed, but their bearing was very different from that of the Indians. They were more professional, more organized; even her untrained eye could detect this easily.

Soon there were at least a dozen men in the room with her; she couldn't see behind her to get a clear count, but she was terrified of what was in store.

Finally the new man in the kurta pulled a stool over in front of Priya and sat down. Nonchalantly he waved his hand around the room.

He said, "My friends who have been watching over you, your fellow countrymen, have been exceedingly kind to you so far. These men, do you know who they are?"

Priya nodded her head. "B-Company."

The Pakistani said, "So, why are the gangsters of Mumbai treating you so well, you might ask. The answer is simple. Your countrymen here are afraid to touch you. They think you are Indian intelligence, and they are . . . fearful about hurting someone from the Research and Analysis Wing. They dread that the wrath of New Delhi will fall down upon their operation here. Frankly, it annoys me that they are afraid. They work for me, and I want information from you, and they should have been able to acquire it without my personal intervention."

Priya said nothing.

"So, yes, I am angry that they are afraid of what is to come." He pointed a finger in her face but his voice was chillingly calm. "But you. You on the other hand, I *want* you to be afraid. The more certain you are that I will do something terrible to you now, the quicker you will give up the ruse that you can hold out, that you can keep that information in that pretty little head of yours." He put his finger on her forehead, pressed hard. She pulled away and looked at him with revulsion.

"A defiant spirit. Admirable. Did they teach you that at R&AW?"

"I am not R&AW."

The man looked around, found Jai smoking near the window, and said, "She's not R&AW."

Jai shrugged. "She told me she was."

The man in the kurta nodded slowly. "Very well. Do you have the items I requested?"

Jai kept his eyes averted from Priya. He ordered a couple of his men about, and they left the room. While they were gone, the man with the Pakistani accent said, "What I urgently need to know from you is this: the identity of the man who breached the embassy in Algiers, and the identity and affiliation of the people you work for. Two simple things. Notice I haven't asked about you. You are too young and junior for me to worry about. You are the little girl with the brain for computers who flew the drone and helped others violate my privacy and my safety, but I am not interested in hurting you. I am interested in knowledge. Only knowledge."

Just then the door opened back up, and the two men reentered. One carried a car battery and jumper cables in his arms, and the other carried several liters of ice water sloshing around in a large plastic jug.

The Pakistani looked at them, then back to the woman. "I will amend what I just said. I am not interested in hurting you, as long as you answer my questions truthfully."

The two men placed the battery and other items on the floor between the bound Priyanka and the Pakistani, and he scooted his seat closer and went to work attaching the cables to the battery.

As he did this, a man walked past Priya from behind, headed for the door without acknowledging anyone else in the room. He was one of the new arrivals; she took him to be Pakistani.

The man in the kurta kept working on the jumper cables, but he spoke in Urdu to the man. "Too much for you, Nassir?"

Priya understood, and she understood the man's response. "I hate this part."

The man left and the door shut, and Priya's body began to shake uncontrollably as her eyes misted over. "I don't know anything," was all she could say, her voice so meek and wavering it sickened her to hear herself.

The Pakistani looked away from his work, seemingly fascinated by her terror, and then he said, "Let's get started, then." Turning to the men against the wall, he said, "Put her on her back. We will begin with the electricity. I will apply the charge to her feet. I find that is the most intolerable." He added, "And put something in her mouth so she doesn't bite her tongue off." He made a face as he looked back into her eyes. "I've seen it happen."

They started to lay her chair back onto the cold concrete floor, but she screamed, stopping them.

"I do not know the identity of the asset. You have to believe me!"

The Pakistani motioned for the men to wait. To Priya he said, "Why? Why do I have to—"

"Because if you *are* Pakistani intelligence, then you know the technician isn't told the asset's identity."

"So, you are now admitting you *are* Indian intelligence."

"I'm *not*. I worked for a man, a man in the private sector. He was hired for the job, and he found me and the asset. That is truly all that I know."

"Then let's see if I can spark your memory a little." He tapped the positive and negative clamps together, and a shower of sparks cracked just a foot from her face. The two men standing next to her chair laid her on her back, her bare feet up in the air. One man took off his belt and knelt to shove it in her mouth.

"No!" she screamed.

The Pakistani stood over her now, looking down, the clamps of the jumper cables in his hands. "I don't have to do this. You merely must be smart enough to know this is a battle you cannot win."

She stared up at him through puddles of tears in her eyes and said nothing.

He tapped the clamps together again, for a longer time. Sparks showered, fell over her body, and she screamed. The Pakistani said, "We have plenty of batteries, my dear. And more importantly, we have all night."

She began to hyperventilate; she was near shock, and the Pakistani saw this and understood what was happening. He tossed the cables behind him by the battery and then grabbed the large jug of ice water.

He poured half of the jug's contents onto the bound woman's face and upper torso. She screamed some more, and when he placed the jug to the side, he straddled her body. Looking down, he said, "You will not go into shock. I will not allow it. You see, I know what I am doing. You do not. You have no idea what you are about to endure."

Her eyes were bloodshot; water matted her long black hair across her face. She nodded distantly. "Please . . . please don't hurt me. I will talk."

He raised a skeptical eyebrow.

"I will tell you everything I know."

The man stood and smiled. "Pull her chair back up."

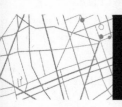

NINETEEN

After taking a moment to compose himself, the Pakistani said, "Very well. Let us try to have a conversation. You will see I am a man of my word. What is your name?"

Her voice cracked as she spoke. Her eyes downcast. He had broken her spirit completely, and he knew it. She said, "Priyanka Bandari."

"Priyanka. Now, tell me about the asset."

Still softly, she said, "He . . . he was American."

The Pakistani nodded. "American. Very good. His name?"

"I was told to call him Cobalt. He called me Copper."

"Code names. Very smart. You were speaking with Cobalt while he was in the Turkish embassy compound in Algiers. What did he tell you about what he saw?"

"He only told me that he saw someone he recognized." She paused.

The Pakistani leaned forward. "Continue."

"He . . . he said he had to kill this man." Priya flashed a glance up towards the Pakistani. "Cobalt said the man deserved to die."

"What else?"

"Nothing else. He told me to leave the country. I recalled the UAV and began breaking down my surveillance station. Then he radioed me back a few minutes later and said he didn't do it after all. I don't know why he wanted to do it, and I also don't know why he didn't do it." She sniffed congestion along with water that had made its way up her nose when she was doused on the floor.

The Pakistani said, "You are doing an excellent job so far. Now, let us discuss the man you both were working for."

Priya looked down and to the left. "I . . . I don't know who he is."

"Yes, you do. You can tell me now, or you can tell me after you suffer indescribable pain. The choice remains yours."

Priyanka said nothing, and the man turned to reach for the cables attached to the battery. Just as he turned back for her, she spoke through sobs.

"Arjun."

The Pakistani cocked his head. "Arjun? Arjun who?"

She did not answer.

But from behind her, a man answered the question for her. It sounded like Jai's voice, but she could not see him. He said, "She might be talking about Arjun Bandari. Former R&AW. He works private intelligence now."

"Arjun . . . *Bandari*?" the Pakistani said. "Is this the man you work for?"

She nodded her head, her face registering utter shame.

"Two Bandaris on the same mission. He is your . . . father?"

Priya bit her lip. "He is my uncle."

"Your uncle. Very nice."

Jai stepped around to the side, into Priya's peripheral vision. Looking at the Pakistani man in the kurta, he said, "We've employed him in the past, but only on little matters. Foreign business in Bangladesh and Dubai mainly. He is not a big player for us, he mostly works with the government. But he goes where the money is. He's been helpful."

Priyanka knew nothing about her uncle working for the mafia goons of B-Company; she wanted to believe that the man was lying, but she honestly had no idea.

The Pakistani smiled at her. "Priyanka, where might we find your dear, dear uncle Arjun?"

"I do not know."

He looked at her dubiously. "You don't know where your uncle lives?"

"I do, but he won't be there waiting for you. He is too smart for that."

"But . . . you have his phone number. What niece does not have her uncle's phone number, especially a niece who travels the world conducting exciting missions with him? Let us give him a call."

Priyanka looked at the battery, the cables, the water. She closed her eyes, forcing more tears down her wet face, and then she nodded.

"Excellent." The Pakistani looked to the Indians in the room. "Get her phone." Also to the Indians, he said, "And while you are doing that, tell me everything you know about Uncle Arjun."

Arjun Bandari sat at his desk in his fortress of a home on Malabar Hill, in the far south of the city, just off the water, some fifteen miles from where Priya was being held, and he told himself that he needed to get some sleep. He'd had just a couple of hours' sleep since his niece was kidnapped thirty hours earlier, and he felt his body shutting down.

He knew he should have left his home the moment he found out Priya had been compromised, but he had remained right here, with his computers, with his phone, with his safe that contained everything he might need to win his niece back from the Pakistanis, and he was unwilling to leave any of his resources behind just to protect himself.

No, he got Priyanka into this, and if he didn't get her out of this, then he had no will to live anyway.

Arjun had never married, never had children; he'd only had Priya, his sister's daughter and the focus of every ounce of affection Arjun had to give to this world.

He decided to put his head down on his desk, but just as he did so, his mobile phone dinged. He had private detectives combing the city searching for Priya, but the American asset, he knew from the small amount he'd gleaned about the man, was her best bet, so he hoped like hell it was Cobalt on the line now.

He lunged at the phone, yanked it up, then saw that the call was coming from Priya herself, or at least her phone.

He answered with a wary but hopeful tone.

"Is it . . . is it you?"

But it was a man's voice that replied. In Hindi, but with a definite accent. "Arjun Bandari. I have learned a lot about you in a short time. In fact, five minutes was more than long enough for me to be filled in on your modest career."

Arjun's heart pounded. The man's accent was Pakistani. "Who is this?"

"It's up to you who I am. I can be the man who keeps her safe and returns her to you unharmed, or I can be the man who will make it so that you will never see her again."

"Please, sir . . . please. How . . . how do I know she is alive?"

Arjun heard a shuffling, movement of the phone, and then his heart sank to the floor.

"I am so sorry, Uncle. Please forgive me."

He faked optimism. "I am so happy to hear your voice. It is all fine, Chiki, I promise you we will—"

But the Pakistani was back on the other end now. "We don't care about her. We don't care about you. We only want to know who hired you, what the mission was at the Turkish embassy in Algiers. That, plus the identity of the American asset, will save you both from death and further distress."

Arjun said, "I give you this information and . . . and Priya will be released unharmed?"

"You would be a fool to trust my word, but *you* have put us all where we sit right now, Bandari, not me. And unfortunately, Arjun, my word is all I have to offer you. So, don't trust, but do hold out hope, because that is the only hope your darling niece has. Talk, talk truthfully, now, or she dies."

There was a long pause. And then, "What do you want to know?"

"Tell me about your contract."

"I was contracted to—"

"Contracted by who?"

He paused. "I . . . I don't know for certain, I was hired through a cutout. But I assumed my actual client was the Research and Analysis Wing in New Delhi."

There was a chuckle on the other end of the line. "Look at that, my friend. You and I have something in common. I am assuming the same as you. Continue. You were contracted to do what?"

"To hire and support a small team, two persons only, to place an IMSI-catcher on the grounds of the Turkish embassy of Algeria."

"Why?"

"I was told a Swiss counterfeiter had been wiretapped, by who I don't know. Someone picked up that he was going to have a meeting with a Pakistani member of the ISI at the Turkish embassy in Algiers on that evening. The ISI operative was interested in producing counterfeit rupees in Algeria that could then be infiltrated into India. My contractee assumed it was to disrupt the Indian economy."

The Pakistani paused for a long time after receiving this information. When he spoke, he seemed utterly confused. "Where did they get this intelligence?"

"Sir, I promise you, that is not how this works. I am never told where the intelligence comes from that sends me out on my operations. I am merely sent out on my operations with mission directives I must accomplish."

After another long pause, the man seemed to get past his confusion. "So . . . you brought in your niece and showed her how to operate the drones and the communications gear and the IMSI-catcher?"

"It . . . it seemed like a simple operation. I thought it would be fine. We would listen to a few phone conversations and then shut down. She is not a trained technician. Just an IT expert, but I didn't think the job would be too—"

The Pakistani interrupted. "And the man you hired to install the device. The American. Who is he?"

"I do not know."

"That answer might go a long way towards saving the American, but it won't get you anywhere with saving your niece."

"It is the truth, sir! I swear it. I have a site on the Darknet. I had been given his contact information, just a string of numbers, and was told he would be suitable. I reached out to him, and he accepted the job."

"You never met him?"

"No. And neither has my niece. We don't even know what he looks like. We called him Cobalt."

The Pakistani seemed to think a moment before moving on. "After the operation, after your niece was captured by my associates, did you hear from the American again?"

Arjun thought carefully about what he should say. Finally, he nodded at the phone and uttered a single word. "Haan." *Yes.*

"Tell me about this conversation."

Arjun hesitated again. Every word he said from now on had to be perfectly calculated. He would give up the American for Priya, but if the man who had her knew the American had given Khan's identity to Arjun, then there was no way either he or his niece would survive this. "He told me he failed to install the IMSI-catcher. He told me he was getting out of the country."

"That's all?"

"In that conversation, yes. But then, a short time later, he called me from the airport. He said he saw Priyanka. She was put on an aircraft. He told me that he would help me recover the woman." This was a lie, but it was a lie designed by Arjun to protect his niece.

"How did he happen to come upon them at the airport?"

"He . . ." Arjun thought quickly now. "He didn't just come upon them. He followed a car, he said. I don't know whose car."

Arjun was freestyling. Lying through his teeth.

There was a long pause now; Arjun almost spoke again when the voice said, "And what did he tell you about me?"

For the first time, Arjun Bandari realized, without question, that he was speaking with Murad Khan, formerly an operative with the Foreign Coordination Unit of the Inter-Services Intelligence agency of Pakistan.

His mouth went dry.

Khan shouted now, "What did he tell you?"

"About *you*?" After a pause, Arjun Bandari did his best to sell a new lie. "Nothing. Nothing at all. I don't know who you are. He was just an asset I found on the Darknet; I am sure he did not know who you were, either."

Khan took this in for a moment. Then he said, "Priyanka has told me he conveyed to her that he needed to kill me. He did not tell you this?"

Dammit. Arjun closed his eyes and held the phone against his forehead, desperately trying to think of something to say.

When he didn't answer for several seconds, Khan said, "I am beginning to doubt your commitment to your lovely niece, dear uncle."

"He told me there was someone there who he intended to kill. He did not say why, he did not say who. A Turk, I only assumed."

"And what did he tell you he was prepared to do to get the girl back?"

"He called me this evening. He is in Mumbai as we speak, sir." Arjun sighed. "I will lead you to him if you release Priyanka."

"How did he know to come here?"

"The flight. The flight from Algiers. He was able to track it somehow. He didn't tell me."

Arjun had lied to the Pakistani about how the asset knew to come to Mumbai. His niece had been wearing a geolocator, and it obviously had not been found, because if it had, the Pakistani would not have asked the question. He didn't lie to help the American asset. He lied to protect Priya from men who would be beyond furious with her if they knew what she'd done.

At the B-Company hideout, the Pakistani in the kurta glared across the room at Jai, the head of this cell of Indian gangsters. He said nothing, but his look conveyed his disgust with him.

Priya saw this, and she had the impression that it was the B-Company man's responsibility to ensure that she was brought to Mumbai without being picked up by surveillance.

She doubted the American had somehow tracked the aircraft as her uncle had said. She suspected Arjun was lying to protect her from being punished for having the tracker. It made her sick to her stomach. He was trying to save her life, and she had so willingly given up his name to protect herself.

In front of her, the Pakistani muted the phone. He snapped his fingers and shouted in Hindi.

"Search the woman, from top to bottom. Search her cell, as well."

"For what?" Jai asked.

"A tracking device."

"A tracking device? But Bandari just said they followed the aircraft to—"

"People lie. If we find a GPS locator on her, then that means the opposition is aware of where we are right now." When Jai didn't immediately order his men into action, the Pakistani said, "You proved yourself to be inept in Algeria, allowing the American to follow you back to Mumbai. I want to make sure you aren't equally incompetent on your own turf."

He returned to Priya's phone while the men began pawing over the young woman's hair, looking down her throat, touching her with rough, angry hands. Other men rushed towards the hallway to the closet where she'd been kept to check it from top to bottom.

The Pakistani returned his attention to the man on the phone, releasing the mute to speak to him. "Does the American know where the woman is now? Think carefully before you answer."

"No, sir. But I amassed some gear for him, by his request. I will put it in a locker at a railway station for him to pick up tomorrow morning. If you send people there, you will certainly find him." The man added, "I will help you."

The two men continued speaking for a few minutes more, working out details of Priya's eventual handoff to her uncle after the American was in Khan's custody. But Priya wasn't listening to this conversation at all. She realized that by her weakness, she had condemned the American to certain death and her uncle to the very strong possibility of death. The American was risking his life to help her, and she'd betrayed him. And her uncle was her uncle; he would die for her, this she had always known. And now . . . he would more than likely do just that.

Her own predicament, while it had been the driving force minutes ago when she'd sold her uncle out, now meant nothing at all to her.

She was dead inside.

Her mind drifted, but it came back to the here and now when the man hung up the phone and tossed it to one of the Indian gangsters.

Men came back from the closet where they had been searching. They reported to their leader, Jai, and not to Khan. "Nothing in there, boss. Nothing at all."

A man standing by Priya confirmed, "Nothing on her body, either."

The Pakistani stood and pointed into Jai's face. "Double your guard force."

"We have a dozen guys here and downstairs who can take care of—"

"Then make it two dozen!" the Pakistani shouted. "He is in the city because of your poor security measures. You need to pray that your poor security measures don't reveal this building, as well.

"And send another dozen men to the station to watch for him tomorrow. I can't send my men, we are Pakistani, they don't know the city like your people do. I want him captured alive and cut apart, piece by piece, till I know everything there is to know about him."

Still, Jai pushed back. "Two dozen men? We're talking about one target!"

Khan shoved the larger Jai up against the wall. The other Indians of B-Company in the room looked on with concern, but the Pakistani force that had arrived with the man in the kurta kept them in place with their own withering looks.

Khan said, "He knows me! I saw it in his face! He knew *exactly* who I was, and he could not believe his eyes." He motioned to Priya now. "She said as soon as he recognized me, he said he had to kill me."

Softer, anxiously, Jai said, "It's one man."

"It's *not* one man. It's the CIA. It's the U.S. military, it's whoever the hell the American was working for when he last saw my face." The Pakistani released his grip on the bigger man's collar and took a half step back, smoothing the man's rumpled shirt as he did so. "I am not afraid of one man. I am afraid of everyone he talks to about what he saw in Algeria. We need him captured and brought to me. Send your best people to the railway station tomorrow. Remain covert, but get the job done, Jai, do you understand me?"

The Indian just nodded.

The Pakistani patted him on the chest now. "Good. I'd hate to have to go back to your boss and tell him I was having trouble with you down here."

Softly, Jai said, "There is no trouble."

"Good. Four more days, Jai, and then I leave. Give me what I want for four days."

The heavyset Indian nodded.

The Pakistani started to walk out the door. His two underlings moved quickly to catch up with him. When he was almost in the hall, Jai called out to him.

"The girl? What about the girl?"

The man said, "Keep her alive, until we have the American. Then . . . make her disappear. We will eliminate the uncle, as well." He looked at the young woman lashed to the chair. "My dear, it's a pity. You know so precious little, but with everything on the line, it turns out you know way too much."

He turned back to Jai, who nodded compliantly, all but a bow to the man who was clearly calling the shots, and then he left, the rest of the Pakistanis following him.

TWENTY

After two weeks of daily training evolutions to get his new Sierra Six up to speed, each day a little better, a little smoother, a little more solid than the last, Zack Hightower and his team boarded a Boeing 737 converted for cargo use that was owned by the CIA and bound for Frankfurt, Germany. From there they would continue east, landing in Khost, Afghanistan, some twenty-one hours after taking off from Virginia.

Court hadn't connected with any of the other men on his team, and other than his team, the range safety officer, and a few equipment handlers, armory personnel, and parachute riggers around the Ground Branch compound, he hadn't spoken to another soul in two weeks. He kept to himself, spent his downtime in his room reading, or, while the other team members worked out in the gym, ran a makeshift parkour route he'd both discovered and created around the complex.

He lived not as part of a unit but as if he were still out in the cold, in some sort of deep cover, worried at any moment that he might be exposed.

It didn't make sense; everyone around knew he was CIA, but he'd been trained for one thing above all else, and that was moving low-profile through the ether of life.

He watched people, he learned from them. He didn't interact with them.

The rest of the team, with the possible exception of Hightower, thought Court was a young, cocky prick. Court had no interest in bonding with any of them, and during the drills he still had a tendency to call audibles. Hightower secretly marveled at the young man's abilities, though he took him to the woodshed every single day for some sort of flamboyant maneuver the younger man conducted that Hightower felt could lead to the team being decimated in action.

Court listened, nodded, and did one percent better on the next evolution of the drill.

Zack realized the kid still thought he knew everything better than the Ground Branch team around him that had been together for over a year.

Now the team was on its way back to Afghanistan to continue the hunt for Pasha the Kashmiri and the rest of the Kashmiri Resistance Front, and all the men, save for Court, had reservations about this. They knew what they were in for and felt like they were operating at five sixths capacity, with a renegade operator tagging along who would do God knows what when the shit hit the fan.

Court Gentry sat alone on the flight to Afghanistan, leaning back into a webbed bench, a book in his lap and his Salomon boots up on his large desert-sand-colored duffel bag on the deck. He wore jeans, a flannel shirt with the sleeves rolled up, and a black Carhartt baseball cap that shielded his eyes from those around him.

He'd taken to dressing like the other men around him; it was simply part of his nature.

He was deeply engrossed in his book about the Russian mafia—he had a more than passing professional interest in the subject, after all—when he suddenly sensed a presence above him.

Court looked up to find a young woman standing there. She wore a red Under Armour hoodie, jeans, and combat boots. Her jet-black hair was tied back in a ponytail, and her black-rimmed eyeglasses were just thick enough to slightly obscure her brown eyes.

He'd noticed her briefly at the airport before the flight, carrying a heavy webbed black duffel and rolling a massive black Pelican case behind her. She was obviously logistics or something with the task force, but he hadn't seen her around the Virginia Beach compound, and he hadn't even noticed that she was on the flight until now.

She appeared Hispanic, in her twenties, and as Court just stared up at her now, he found her close presence and her bold eyes mildly discomforting. By her look, he had the impression he'd done something to annoy her. They were over three hours into this flight, however, so he couldn't imagine she was coming to tell him he'd taken her seat.

She said nothing. He took off his ball cap, running his fingers through his messy hair.

"Help you?"

"Thinking about a career change?"

"Huh?"

"The book."

It was a joke he was slow to get. He looked down at the cover, then forced a little smile. "You never know."

"The Russian mob probably pays better," the woman said, continuing the joke, though she remained as deadpan as she could be.

Court motioned around at the spartan cabin of the ugly CIA aircraft. "But we get so many cool amenities."

"Yeah," she said. "With them, you probably just get all the vodka you can drink and a free bullet in your head."

Court nodded, waiting for the woman to end the joke and tell him what she wanted with him.

"I'm Julie Marquez," she said. "You're the new Six on Golf Sierra."

"Gentry." Even after two weeks on the team, telling someone his real name still felt unbelievably weird to him.

She sat down, causing him to kick his boots off his ruck and sit up with his back against the fuselage. He stiffened a little more and brought his shoulders back, still ready to hear what he'd done wrong, because that was basically all he'd heard from anybody around here for two weeks.

But instead she just said, "I'm new here, too."

"Oh. Okay." He looked her over discreetly, trying to figure out what she did for the Special Activities Division. She was dressed like a college kid, but Court himself was dressed like some sort of a farmhand, so that didn't mean anything. She was about his age, attractive, but her eyes all but bored through him, so he kept his averted from hers.

Finally, he said, "Logistics?"

"Intel."

Court nodded. "Right. A targeting officer?"

She said, "Me? No. Just level two tactical analysis."

"Okay." He nodded, then said, "What's that?"

She seemed surprised by his reaction. "You don't know what tactical analysis is?"

"Remember? I'm the new guy."

He felt those eyes digging into his face; he gazed at a point on the opposite end of the fuselage, right past her ear. Finally she said, "I do mostly structural and geospatial stuff. Building blueprints, patterns of life, that sort of thing. I've got a strong background in BDA, as well."

Court nodded blankly. He had no idea what she was talking about.

Marquez slowly took in that he was clueless. "BDA is bomb damage assessment. Structural and geospatial means, in my case, that I don't find the bad guy, but if someone else finds him, I tell you what his house looks like on the inside, how thick the walls are, how far away the police are, what their response time is. Does he have dogs? Security? If I can, I put together a complete 3D blueprint of the location, as well, so when you gunfighter types hit it, you'll know whether to turn left or right at the top of the stairs to find the bedroom."

Court nodded now, glanced back at her eyes, but only for an instant. Marquez would be pretty low on the intelligence totem pole, but if he was making his way through a dark structure full of assholes, the information she was tasked with providing might just be the most important intel he could possibly ask for.

"Thanks for what you do, then," he said.

She shrugged. "Well, I haven't actually done it yet. Like you, I guess. When we get to Camp Chapman, we'll see what it's really like on the ground."

Court said, "Right."

It was quiet for a moment, and then she said, "I was Army intel. Enlisted. Some people thought I should become an officer, but I don't really like managing people."

Court said, "Me, either. I mean, I don't think I would. I've never tried."

"You are way too young to be ex-Delta. You were a SEAL? A Ranger?"

Court sighed inwardly. The fact that he hadn't served in the military had never shown up as a blemish on his career in the CIA, primarily because he had been operating deep in the shadows, so there was no knowledge of his career in the CIA by that many people. But now, with Ground Branch, it felt very much like an old boys' network that he'd crashed. He said, "I don't have any prior military service. I was hired out of the Directorate of Operations into Ground Branch."

"What were you doing before?"

Court's eyes narrowed. This wasn't a question he was going to answer.

He thought she'd get the hint, but when he said nothing, she leaned a little closer and spoke louder, as if he hadn't heard. "What were you doing be—"

Court put his book down on top of his duffel bag. "Nice talking to you, Miss Marquez. I'm going to rack out for a while till we get to Frankfurt."

She looked at him with confusion, and then she understood. "You can't talk about what you were doing before." She said it as a statement, not a question.

"Right."

"That's fine. You could have just said that."

Court eyed her curiously, and not because she was only the second or third person to introduce themselves since he'd joined Ground Branch. She was acting a little strangely, her heavy gaze and her questions, but she didn't seem threatening. Just odd. Finally he just said, "Yeah, sorry."

"I understand now. Sometimes I don't pick up on subtlety. Thanks for explaining it to me." Apropos of nothing, she added, "I miss the Army. It's more . . . clear-cut, I guess. Regimented. I find I need that." She looked down at her clothes now. "Traded in my uniform for this. Can't say I miss BDUs, but I liked not having to think about how to dress all the time."

Court was starting to become uneasy with the seemingly pointless banter. He just waited for her to leave.

Marquez said, "How is your team?"

But she wasn't leaving.

"The guys know their shit," he replied. "I'm the weak link, or so they keep telling me."

"Haven't made any friends yet?"

He did not answer, but she took his silence for a response.

"Me, either."

To this, Court quipped, "Why not? You sure are chatty."

"Because I am too direct for most people. I came in a couple weeks ago, on my first day, and told everybody that the guy I was replacing made a mistake that got a man killed." She shrugged. "They liked my predecessor, so they don't like me, even though I told the truth."

"The guy who got killed. Was that—"

"Sierra Six. *Your* predecessor did *not* make a mistake, and he died anyway, and you are replacing him. That's probably why your team doesn't want to be friends with you. They figure you will just die."

Court blew out a sigh. "You *are* very direct, aren't you?"

"And you are very guarded. Which is worse?"

"I'm sorry, Marquez. I don't really understand the point of this conversation."

"You are guarded because you are trained to be, because you work in Operations. I am direct, as you say, because I am on the spectrum."

"The *what*?"

She shrugged. "My parents had me tested when I was a kid. Found out I was high-functioning spectrum. Did your parents ever have you tested? You don't seem exactly neurotypical yourself, although I'm not really one to say."

Court shook his head. "I don't think we had anything like the spectrum where I grew up."

She smiled now, the first time he'd seen her do so. "You did, you just didn't know about it." She thought a second. "It might be good to not know about it." With another shrug she added, "But it's fine. I don't mind it. Sometimes other people do."

"Marquez, I'll be honest. I'm not following a word you're saying."

"Oh." She thought a moment. "Do you watch *The Big Bang Theory*? Sheldon?"

"The . . . the big . . . *what*?"

"It's a TV show."

"No," he said, still looking at her blankly.

"Who hasn't seen *The Big Bang Theory*?" She seemed a little crestfallen. "That's usually the best way to explain it. Better than saying it's Asperger's."

Court knew what Asperger's was, more or less. The young woman had just met him, and she was telling him she was autistic. He didn't know what to say. Most interactions with people were uncomfortable for the twenty-five-year-old. But now this was off-the-charts stressful for him.

Marquez said, "There are good aspects about it, too. Nobody talks about that. Intellectual interest. Increased attention to detail. Persistence. Even high integrity."

Court was still uncomfortable, but he said, "All things that probably make you a kick-ass analyst." After a pause, though, he asked, "Why are you telling me all this?"

"You looked lonely."

"I'm reading a book."

"Exactly."

"Do you read in groups?"

She shook her head. "At the airport, too. You are in your own world. I know what it's like to be an outsider. It's not bad, but sometimes it's okay to have a friend. Mind if I come and talk to you at Camp Chapman sometime?" She added, "I mean, when you aren't running around doing something crazy."

Awkwardly, Court replied, "Yeah, sure. I'll be around."

She nodded, almost to herself, like she'd checked off a box on her to-do list. Then she stood and headed back down the cargo cabin without another word, disappearing between high pallets of gear boxes.

After she was out of view, Court grabbed his book off the top of his duffel, but he didn't open it. Instead he just looked off in Marquez's direction for a moment. If this was what it took to make friends . . . then he wasn't sure he was up to it.

Finally he laid his book down on his chest, closed his eyes, and tried to sleep.

TWENTY-ONE

PRESENT DAY

The Sandhurst Road Railway Station teemed with life at eight a.m. Commuters on the Central and Harbor lines entered and exited the doors to the passenger station, cooking stalls and kiosks lined the road in front of the entrance, and long lines formed at the ticket booths and counters just inside the door, visible from the sidewalk outside.

Court Gentry walked among the crowd carrying a small gray backpack that he had stuffed with another shirt and a heavy serrated knife—essentially a small saw with a pointed tip—that he'd purchased, along with the backpack, at a street stall in Andheri East.

Court wore a black polo shirt over faded jeans he'd also picked up the evening before. He had dark hair and something of a tan, and with his beard and mustache covering the majority of his face, he thought he could fit in as a local if he didn't get too much additional scrutiny.

Avoiding additional scrutiny had basically been his job for the past twenty years, so he felt comfortable enough as he approached the location where Arjun had told him to pick up the equipment he asked for.

The text had come on his Signal app at seven a.m., giving the locker number and location of the station, along with a request that he contact

Arjun just as soon as he picked up the equipment to tell him what the next step was.

By now Court had accepted it as fact that Copper meant something to Arjun. She was his girlfriend or wife or kid or sister, or maybe just a close friend. Court had dealt with brokers, handlers, and technical support personnel in the private sector for many years, and Arjun's passion about the well-being of Copper was utterly unique. This meant trouble, as far as Court was concerned, because he knew Arjun would feel pressure to do something himself to find the girl, and this might well put her in more danger.

Court had no idea if she was even still alive. Two days was a lot of time for the enemy to extract what they needed from her and then dump her body. He kept telling himself they would keep her alive until they had him, or Arjun, in pocket, because she was obviously a small cog in whatever machine was involved in the operation that compromised Khan.

He didn't know that she was alive, but all his actions were based on the assumption that she was. As far as he knew, she was still in the building in Andheri East, but he'd have no way of verifying that until he went there for himself, so that was the plan.

And this morning's equipment pickup would allow him to do that.

The station itself was full of people, many wearing bright colors. Large fans spun lazily from the high ceiling, stirring the warm air. Signage all around in Hindi, Arabic, and English gave instructions and directions for commuters. Colorful advertisements hung on walls and poles.

Court entered, passed the ticketing area in the main concourse, and then headed down the hallway that led to the tracks. As he neared the area where metal lockers lined the wall of a small alcove, the crowd thinned, and he was able to look at individual faces as he passed the alcove by on his first security sweep of the area. This, he knew, was a potential failure point in his entire operation. If Arjun wasn't playing straight with him, and Arjun knew he would come here to this station to pick up items, then Court would be in serious danger.

So he decided to recon the area first.

He had no reason not to trust Arjun other than the fact that he didn't trust *anyone* these days. Arjun, Court had told himself, was just like everyone on Earth—a duplicitous, backstabbing asshole—unless and until proven otherwise.

Court walked past the locker area, past the cloakroom, then up a flight of stairs to one of the platforms. Here he stood for a moment, looking back down onto the main floor of the station, then scanning the area close around him.

His brain began running calculations at phenomenal speed. Threat assessments of everyone around him. He looked at each person's age and gender, their dress and mannerisms, where they were directing their attention and how they positioned themselves. There were myriad ways to detect someone in the process of conducting surveillance, and Court did his best in the fast-moving crowd to focus on as many people as possible.

During one of his scans he saw a man on the stairs; commuters hustled around him while the man stood still, a phone to his ear, and Court centered his attention on him more closely.

He appeared to be Indian, he was in his twenties, and he had neatly parted hair and a mustache. He was dressed for an office job, like many of the others around, but his focus was clearly back down on the floor of the station, near the locker alcove next to the cloakroom, same as Court's.

What Court noticed most was that the man seemed to be in a perfect static position to surveil the area.

Armed with the knowledge that there was at least one person here who was acting suspiciously, Court went back down the stairs on the opposite side of the man, positioning himself right in the middle of a group of commuters descending. The locals didn't seem to notice Court in their midst; he was just another traveler who walked along in the same direction, but this afforded him the freedom to survey the area more carefully.

He was past the locker alcove and almost out into the main station concourse when he saw the second man. This person was older, thicker, more haggard-looking than the first, and he squatted down against the wall with a newspaper in his hand, a paper cup of chai next to him. Other than the fact that he was static, there was nothing special that drew Court's attention to him at first, but as he focused on the person's face, Court realized that his eyes were not sweeping the newspaper but rather scanning over the top of the page, pointed in the direction of the wall of lockers.

Court didn't see an earpiece or a radio or anything overtly identifying the man as surveillance, but his actions telegraphed his role.

Court passed him by and then continued on towards the main concourse.

The American was now nearly certain that the location he'd been sent to by Arjun was being watched. He didn't know if that meant that Arjun was simply protecting the locker full of equipment and weapons until his asset retrieved the gear, or if Arjun was looking out for Court, giving him some unwanted backup. But if it was neither of these two things, Court knew there was only one more option—Arjun had dimed him out to the enemy.

No matter the reason for the men watching the locker, Court knew there was no way in hell he was going to approach it now.

His first impulse was to leave the station, to contact Arjun and tell him his team had been made, but then he decided he should just retreat back to a safe position and try to draw out any more watchers.

He pulled out his phone, opened Signal, and typed out a message to his broker.

Approaching locker now. I'll have package in five minutes.

He sent the message, then stepped up to the back of the longest ticket line within view of the hallway where the locker alcove was located. He knew that even most trained surveillance professionals look right past a line of people, because the line was always there—it was part of the landscape.

All but the very best countersurveillance experts only look for what's different, not what's expected.

And then, as the line slowly shuffled forward, he turned to face the concourse and asked the woman behind him if she knew what line he needed to take to get to the Taj Mahal Palace hotel. As he then asked about the fare, he used the opportunity to look behind the woman. Dozens and dozens of people passed or milled around, so it took a while to pick out anything anomalous, but eventually he locked on to a pair of men standing close together, simultaneously looking down at their phones in their hands as if they'd both received a message. They had no luggage, no shoulder bags. Examining more carefully as the men came into and out of view through the passersby, he registered the pair's hard faces. Their cold, calculating eyes. He saw the printing of a knife's hilt jutting under one man's shirt, and though he couldn't identify a weapon on the other man, he suspected these were both career criminals, and they were here on the job.

He had a couple more questions for the lady; her English was excellent, and he asked her about tourist hot spots in the city, knowing that anyone who noticed him would absolutely discount him as a potential target because the man they were expecting would be here alone, and he would likely *not* be buying a ticket before picking up his gear.

He thanked the lady, then glanced up once more at the two men before turning back around.

He was sure now. These weren't watchers. They were in the busy main concourse, and they had no view to the hallway where the lockers were located. No, this was either the roll-up team, men here to kidnap him, or the wet team, men here to kill him.

He suspected they were the former; Khan needed to know who he was, who he was affiliated with. The same unknown keeping Copper alive would also keep Court alive, at least in the short term. That was the good news. The bad news, for both Copper and Court, was that this unknown meant Khan would be desperate for information. He'd probably already beaten everything out of Copper, and now he had men here ready to do the same to Court.

He stayed in the ticket line for the next five minutes and bought a one-way to Nashik, a town to the northeast of Mumbai. But he didn't head up to the platforms; instead, he went outside the main entrance and began looking around there.

If the two men he'd seen in the main concourse were here to kidnap him, which he strongly suspected, they would have some means of getting him out of the area after sticking a gun or knife in his ribs in a crowded station. That meant a car, probably with a driver, waiting close to the nearest exit.

He would have found the roll-up team's getaway vehicle faster if it hadn't been a taxi, as taxis lined both sides of the street. But finally he noted a single cab backed into an alleyway across the busy road from the entrance to Sandhurst Road station, and not in the queue to pick up fares.

This wasn't altogether uncommon—Court knew cabdrivers took breaks like everyone else—but he decided to investigate it anyway.

As soon as he walked by the cab, he knew he had the right vehicle. The driver was looking down at his phone, completely unaware of Court's passing, and this afforded Court a chance to look the man over closely. The imprint of a shoulder holster showed from under the man's light linen jacket. Further, in the backseat of the cab, a green duffel bag sat unattended. This taxi wasn't in service, it was being driven by an armed man, and there was a bag in the back.

Court passed two more times to get a better look at things to prepare his plan, and then he stepped around a corner, out of view of the taxi but within view of the front of the station, and he took out his phone.

Quickly he typed out a message to Arjun.

Aborting.

Almost immediately, he received a reply.

What is the problem?

Court typed out, **Police in area. Had to get on a train. I'll come back tonight.**

Arjun pressed him twice in subsequent texts to go to the locker, but after the second time, Court stopped responding.

Instead he just pocketed his phone, did a few neck rolls to ready himself for what was to come, and watched the exit.

The two hard men from the concourse exited a few minutes later and headed towards the taxi in the alleyway. They would need to pass within ten feet of Court to get there, and the men weren't looking around at their surroundings, obviously taking on faith the intel they'd received that their target had left the area.

Neither of the men was particularly tall, but the younger of the two was slimmer, with a short beard, and he was the one carrying the covert blade. The other man was a few years older than Court, perhaps forty, with a bushy mustache and a thick midsection. Both men, to Court's practiced eye, looked comfortable in their element, as if they'd waited around to snatch people at knifepoint many times before.

Court took the opportunity to check them over more carefully as they neared, and now he made out the outline of a handgun with a short, squat suppressor attached to it, jammed in the waistband of the belly of the older of the two thugs.

Court now had a plan to find both the weapon and the vital intelligence he would need to execute the next phase of his operation in Mumbai.

As the men passed him by at the corner on their way to the taxi with the armed driver, Court slipped his serrated knife out of its cheap canvas sheath, then palmed the weapon, hilt down at his fingertips, with the blade running up the inside of his forearm.

The two men from the kidnap crew went to opposite sides of the taxi while their driver fired up the vehicle. They simultaneously opened the back doors, and just as the heavyset man leaned down to enter the cab, Court stepped up behind him, adjusted the knife in his hand, and pressed the tip against the man's left kidney. The man froze in place, and Court reached around the front of him and yanked the pistol free from his waistband. Without looking at it, Court could tell he was holding a Makarov, a Russian pistol he knew well. He thumbed off the safety and racked the slide on his belt with one hand, ensuring that the weapon was ready to fire. Before the man could even stand back up, Court kicked him in the ass, knocking him into the backseat, and then he opened the front passenger door and climbed in.

"Shut the doors!" he commanded the two men in back, and then he jabbed the tip of the suppressor against the driver's temple. The man started to make a fast move for his pistol in his shoulder holster, but Court pulled back the hammer on the little Russian weapon, and the man froze.

The passenger behind the driver was the one Court had seen with a knife, so as soon as he retrieved the little .25 caliber pistol from the driver's shoulder holster, he thumbed the safety off this weapon and racked the slide, this time on the steering wheel of the taxi. He pointed the weapon at the man with the knife. "Take out the blade with your fingertips. Carefully."

The man did as he was told.

"Roll down your window and drop it." The man did this quickly, and Court said, "Now, all of you. Your phones. Drop them in the alley."

When this was done as well, Court smacked the man behind the wheel in the head with the Makarov. "Drive, asshole."

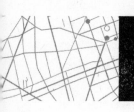

TWENTY-TWO

The taxi rolled out of the neighborhood, heading north. Court both felt and saw the pure malevolence of the other three, men who had come here to kidnap him and then probably to kill him. Their morning wasn't turning out as they'd planned, but things were moving right along for the American with the pistol in each hand as he continued to cover the three men.

He couldn't take them to his hotel, and he didn't have another location in the city. But he had spent a half hour on Google Maps earlier in the morning and then another half hour in a taxi, and he had an idea of where to take these three men so he could have a chat someplace quiet.

They got on the Western Express Highway, the main north–south artery through the city, and after less than five minutes, Court had them take a service road to the east. They drove past a Buddhist temple, then a slum, and soon they pulled up the drive of a large ruined factory complex, destroyed by time, neglect, and vagrancy. The locked gate at the entrance had been broken open, and Court ordered the driver to push through slowly with the grille of his taxi.

There didn't seem to be anyone around at present, so Court had him drive around to the back of the dilapidated building, then pull to a stop.

Just as the driver put his cab in park and pulled the parking brake, his left hand reached into the pocket of his door.

Court saw the movement, and when the man's hand came out quickly, he registered something sweeping in the tight space towards him. Court leaned back and reactively fired once with the suppressed Makarov into the man's face.

Blood sprayed out of the driver's mouth and nose, and his head snapped to the side, and his left hand dropped. A switchblade fell into his lap, into the blood draining there, and then it tumbled down to the floorboard between the dead man's feet.

Court kept the .25 on the men in back through it all, and they did not move despite the orgy of blood and violence in front of them.

After banging the Makarov against the driver's head to make certain he was dead, Court looked into the eyes of both men in the backseat.

Though his ears were ringing from the loud crack in the small vehicle, he said, "Anybody else feel as lucky as this guy did ten seconds ago?"

The men just stared back at him.

He ushered the roll-up crew out of the taxi and frisked them quickly for the first time. He found a couple more magazines for the Makarov on the thicker man, along with wallets on both of them, all of which he crammed into the pockets of his jeans. Then he led the men into the ruined dirt-floor factory.

Inside they entered a room that looked like it had been used for storage but now served as a refuge for the homeless in the nighttime hours. There were trashed sleeping mats and refuse all over the floors, graffiti on the walls, and a smell of urine throughout the small space.

Sufficient light from a row of broken windows shone in, and Court led the men into the room, then ordered them to drop to their knees.

Reluctantly, the men complied.

Court moved around the front of them, chanced a quick look out the windows to the taxi outside, and saw that the area remained clear.

"What was your plan at the train station?"

Neither man spoke.

Court gave them a hard look. "Do you know why I grabbed three of you?" Both men shook their heads. "So I can kill one of you in front of the others. That way, the remaining two pieces of shit would know just how goddamned serious I am right now."

Neither man responded.

"I didn't know your driver was going to make a play, so now when I kill another one of you assholes, the last guy left will be doubly sure that I'm not fucking around."

The men's eyes were downcast now, and they still did not reply, but it was clear they understood their predicament. Court knew men like this. They'd spent their lives preying on others. Beating, robbing, killing. They had no idea how to deal with someone threatening them, and their brains were essentially unable to process the situation they now found themselves in.

Court tried again. "What was the plan at the train station?"

The heavy man sighed after a moment. "We were to take you somewhere and find out who you worked for. What you were doing in Algeria."

"And then?"

The man shrugged now. "Let you go."

"Bullshit."

The other man said, "We do what we're told. Just like you."

"I *used* to do what I was told. Now I do what I want."

"We don't know anything," the heavy man interjected.

Court knelt in front of them. "I don't have much time, so I'm going to just pick one of you." He grabbed the heavier of the two by the throat, pulled his face up. "You lose." Court drew his heavy serrated knife. The man struggled against the choke hold as the American held the blade up in front of his eyes.

The other said, "We will talk. We will both talk if you show us mercy."

Court lowered the blade and looked to the other man. "Where's the girl who was kidnapped in Algiers?"

The heavy man spoke through Court's grip on his throat. "She's . . . in . . . Pakistan."

Court shook his head. "Wrong. I know she landed here yesterday. You are already lying to me, and I don't have time for that shit." He put the tip of the knife between two of the man's ribs, then looked at the man's partner. "I want you to watch this. It's gonna be brutal, even nastier than whatever you guys had in store for me. But pay attention, and realize that you can be fifteen seconds behind him on your way to hell, or you can avoid this."

The heavy man with the knife in his ribs said, "No. I will tell you what you want. Just promise me mercy."

"If you *earn* mercy, then you *get* mercy. Talk."

The younger man said, "I'll talk, too. I'll talk, too!" They were sufficiently scared, Court determined, and now he might finally get somewhere with them. He lowered the heavy man back down and put the knife away, but the suppressed Makarov remained trained on the pair. He asked, "Who do you work for?"

The thick man said, "B-Company."

Court had heard of the Indian criminal organization, but he knew next to nothing about them.

"What is your relationship with Murad Khan?"

The men looked at each other, seemingly confused. "Who?" the thinner man said.

Court's jaw flexed. "The Pakistani."

He saw it in both men's eyes. They knew exactly who he was talking about now.

The younger man looked down at the floor. "The Kashmiri, they call him. Our boss does jobs for him."

"Okay. The girl. Where is she?"

The men were defeated. Their answers rang truthful. "She's here in Mumbai."

"*Where* in Mumbai?"

"Andheri East. I can show you on a map."

Court nodded. They were confirming what he already knew. "I know the building. What floor? What room? How many guards?"

"I don't know. The Kashmiri ordered the guards doubled last night. Maybe a dozen now."

"He called the location?"

The man looked up at Court for a quick moment, then glanced to his partner. "Yes. He called us."

Court could tell this was a lie. "Like hell he called. He's here. He's here in Mumbai. He was there, last night. Is he still there?"

Both men shook their heads now.

"What does he want?"

"He wants to know how you know who he is. Who you work for."

"Why is he in India?"

The older man shrugged, and Court pressed the pistol into the forehead of the younger man. Immediately he said, "We don't know. Jai . . . our boss . . . he does things for the Kashmiri."

"Why?"

The other man said, "Because he's ordered to."

"Ordered by who?"

"Bari."

Palak Bari was the head of B-Company. Court only knew the man's name.

"What have *you* done for the Kashmiri?"

The thinner man said, "We pick up people. Bring them to wherever. Do whatever we're told with them. It's just a job, bro."

These were assassins for the Indian mafia, that much was clear, and there would be a lot of blood on these men's hands.

The two spent the next five minutes giving him a decent picture of the layout of the apartment being used as a holding facility in Andheri East and the disposition of the guards around the building.

Finally Court asked, "What happens when you don't check in?"

One shrugged, but the other said, "We should be back there now. They would have called our phones. They already know we're missing."

"How did you know I'd be at the train station?"

The younger man said, "Arjun Bandari."

"Who is he to B-Company?"

After a shrug, he said, "He has worked with us. He's nobody, but we know who he is."

Arjun was not Indian intelligence, that much was clear. But what was he? Court had dealt for years with Darknet brokers in the trade he plied, and he knew they were never saints; they almost always worked with the underworld.

Court hadn't been identified by the ISI. No, he'd been set up.

By his own broker.

Son of a bitch, he thought, But he didn't fixate on it for long. It was one hundred percent clear that Arjun had a personal reason for recovering Priyanka alive. Arjun, at the beginning, anyway, felt Court was the man who could save her. But something had changed along the way, that much was obvious. And now Court's usefulness to Arjun was purely as a bargaining chip.

The Indian broker had gone to the people holding Priya, or they had come to him. Either way, Arjun had sold Court down the river.

"What will happen to the girl?"

The younger man shrugged. "When they didn't get in touch with us, they probably killed her."

Court didn't believe this. She, like Court, remained a bargaining chip. But they would definitely move her from the Andheri East safe house, and he would lose his one chance to save her.

He believed these two would have killed her themselves if they'd been instructed to do so.

He knelt down slowly, directly in front of them. He was angry at them not just for their plans for him today, the danger they posed to Copper, and the fact that they were hit men for the Indian mob. He was also *especially* angry at them for serving Khan. He said, "Murad Khan . . . the man you are working for. Do you two have *any* idea what he is capable of? Any understanding of what he's done?"

The heavier man looked at Court with eyes teeming with hatred. "I don't know what he's done. I don't know what he's doing now. But I do know how dangerous he is. And if you do, too, you will realize that if you do anything to us now, then he will come for you."

Court just laughed in the man's face. "I should be so lucky. You are just two of his nameless servants. He won't give a rat's ass if something happens to you; at this point he only cares about who knows he's still alive. For the time being, that's just me. I also know what he did twelve years ago, so I know I have to stop him."

The younger man cocked his head. "What did he do twelve years ago?"

Court looked at the man but did not reply.

After a long moment of stillness, the heavier of the two men said, "Remember, sir. You promised mercy."

Court rose slowly. Then he nodded. "I *did* promise mercy, and I keep my promises."

Both men breathed audible sighs of relief.

Court Gentry raised the Russian pistol and fired twice in impossibly quick succession, shooting both gangsters through the crowns of their heads. Their bodies tumbled against each other and landed on the dirty floor, coming to rest above a singular pool of expanding blood.

Standing over their still forms, then stepping back away from an approaching rivulet of crimson, Court said, "A quick death is as much mercy as I can spare right now, gents."

Court Gentry turned and walked out of the factory, made his way to a busy street, then flagged down a passing taxi. Giving the address to the B-Company location in Andheri East, he ordered the driver to hurry, because he knew if Copper was still alive, they'd be rushing to get her out of there now.

TWENTY-THREE

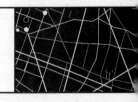

TWELVE YEARS AGO

Court Gentry had never set foot on a foreign U.S. military or intelligence base of any sort, so when his aircraft landed in Afghanistan and he climbed down the jet stairs with the rest of his team, he was struck by the size, the scope, the overwhelming blandness of the scene in front of him.

In front of a beautiful backdrop of rugged snow-peaked mountains to the east, he saw low white and brown buildings, dozens of them. There was a lot of activity about; a pair of Osprey tilt-rotor aircraft landed like helicopters on the other side of the runway, a C-130 cargo aircraft bearing the insignia of the United States Air Force taxied for takeoff, and men and women, many in uniform but just as many in civilian dress, hustled about in the near distance.

Court watched a pair of big red and white dual-rotor helicopters flying slowly through the hot air at no more than one hundred feet in altitude before passing over the scene and landing a football field's distance away.

Court slung his duffel up over his shoulder and followed the other Golf Sierra men from his flight towards a waiting bus. He found a seat halfway back and looked up to see Julie Marquez coming his way.

Before she made it to him, however, Zack Hightower dropped his heavy bag onto a luggage rack and plopped down next to him.

Julie took the first available seat after exchanging a brief glance with Court.

Hightower said, "Kid, welcome to FOB Chapman, or what everybody here likes to call it, Rocket City."

"Do I want to know why they call it that?"

"You do *not*, but I'll tell you anyway. This place gets hit by the Taliban with some regularity."

"Some regularity?"

"Every day, pretty much. We're seven miles from the Pakistan border," Zack said as he pointed towards the jagged mountain range to the east. "Infiltrators slip over, fire rockets, mostly, but occasionally mortars, too. Hell, sometimes assholes drive up to the front gates and blow themselves home to Allah, but the Agency security folks guarding this shit hole are pretty good about keeping the hajis back."

Court had never experienced a barrage of rockets or mortars, or an IED for that matter, and he felt helpless about the prospect of incoming fire from an unseen enemy.

His Ground Branch team had their own building on the complex, one of a multitude of low-roofed metal prefab structures surrounded by sandbags to catch shrapnel from incoming munitions. When the bus stopped in front of their facility, he and the rest climbed out with their bags, then headed for the entrance. Julie got out, as well, but she headed off in another direction with her big pack and Pelican case.

He stepped out of the sun and into the relative cool of a dark and cavernous space. Inside, large wire-cage structures—eight feet high with locking doors and a table, bins, and hooks on the wire inside—lined the right side of the room. Individual cots with small desks and shelving units lined the left side, and in the center of the room was a large empty table. A coffee machine, a refrigerator, a microwave, and some particleboard cabinets ran the length of the back wall.

Hightower slapped Court on the back in the doorway as everyone else filed in past them. "We call this the pit. This is your new home. We anticipate a good five days to acclimate and to do some training inside the wire before Langley sends us out, so settle in." Hightower turned to Lennox, who was just now entering with his own pack. "Two, keep an eye on him."

The tall and powerfully built African American spoke to Gentry now as he placed his duffel on the desk next to the second cot. "Since you've never served in an SMU, I'll tell you how this works."

"First," Court said, "tell me what an SMU is."

Pace muttered, "Jesus fucking Christ," as he sat down on a bunk and began unlacing his boots.

Lennox sniffed out a little laugh before answering Court's question. "Special mission unit."

Court realized he'd heard the acronym back in his time training military and intel types at his dad's school in Florida, but not since.

Lennox added, "Anyway, you get your own bunk and desk, there's a locker here on the left, and then, over there"—he pointed to the far side of the room—"you have your own personal cage for all your weps and gear. You'll be issued said weps and gear immediately, and it's up to you to keep your shit in optimal working condition."

Court nodded.

But Lennox kept looking at him.

"What?"

"No military background at all? Really?"

"My dad was in Nam."

"Not what I'm asking."

"Then . . . no."

Lennox heaved his powerful shoulders. "Lots of acronyms and other names you're gonna have to learn. Radio protocol, all that shit. Everybody else in Ground Branch comes into the team with all that easy stuff locked down tight, but you are gonna be a handful, brother."

Redus stood at the table in the middle of the room. After he put a wad of dip under his lip, he said, "I ain't gonna be his tutor."

Hightower was unpacking on his bunk, and he heard this. "Yes, you are. We all are. Get the kid up to speed on how shit runs around here."

He looked to Court now. "There's already body armor in your cage. Put it on. We wear plates and helmets any time we walk out that door. The other Ground Branch unit, Lima Foxtrot, has a pit in the next building over, then logistics is in the building past that. Then intel, then the TOC." Hightower himself sighed a little before saying, "That's the tactical operations center."

"I know," Court said, but he did not know.

Lennox smiled now and looked at Court. "You wanna take a stab at what number cage is yours?"

Court didn't answer; he threw his bag down on the sixth bunk, then walked over to the cage with a handwritten "6" on a board zip-tied to the wire. He unlocked the door and pulled the key out of the lock, pocketing it.

Inside he put on a desert-camouflaged load-bearing vest with ceramic protective plates inside it, and he lifted a helmet off a rack and found it to be a decent fit. He'd been jocked up like this for most of the past two weeks while training in Virginia Beach, so he was comfortable with the equipment.

Keith Morgan said, "Don't know about y'all, but I'm ready to go. Let's find this Pasha dude and smoke him. We need to get this shit squared away so we can get back to Vah Beach."

Court stood in his empty cage. Distractedly he said, "What's Vah Beach?"

Redus said, "Virginia Beach. Where you live, dummy."

Court didn't respond. He wasn't going to start shit every time somebody criticized him; he didn't have that kind of energy.

TWENTY-FOUR

For the next few hours Court and the rest of Golf Sierra moved around Camp Chapman together. They signed out for weapons and gear, night vision equipment, medical, communications equipment, and ammo. They went to a large gun range and zeroed their weapons, then broke for dinner in the dining facility.

As he left dinner and headed back towards the pit, he caught a glimpse of Julie Marquez, still wearing her red hoodie but now also donning black body armor and a black helmet. A walkie-talkie swayed on her hip. She moved along at a brisk pace towards the tactical operations center, like she was on her way to a meeting, and in her hand she held a massive iced coffee. Despite her rush, she looked calm and confident, and to Court, she appeared to be a hell of a lot more comfortable here in her new job than he was in his.

He'd not called out to her, he didn't know what to say, and she didn't notice him though he was just steps behind her.

Soon she entered the TOC, and Court continued to his building.

Back in the pit, Court found the men working through their gear, with Hightower on his radio in the corner, conferring with someone. And before Court could make it to his bunk, Sierra One put the radio down and called out to the five other men.

"Don't get too comfortable. Just got off the horn with Hanley. He's on his way over. Sounds like he's spinning us up tonight."

"*Tonight?*" Redus said. "No, man. Six is *not* ready to go outside the wire."

Court knew Redus was right, but he wasn't going to let the man challenge his abilities without arguing back.

He said, "I haven't seen you dudes do anything I can't do."

Pace got into his face aggressively, and he spoke up to Hightower behind him. "*I'm* not ready to operate in two-way live fire with Gentry. We haven't had time to fully check him out yet, boss. Comms, night ops, you name it. We haven't even tested this little fucker in hand-to-hand combat." He stepped even closer into Court's personal space, their chests all but touching now. "How are your ground fighting skills?"

Court didn't blink. "Fuck around and find out."

Pace chuckled, but his eyes didn't mirror the sound. Court recognized the man was gearing up to throw a punch.

Court said, "I'll drop your ass on the floor before that right uppercut you're loading up gets anywhere near my chin."

Pace's eyes widened a little at this. Clearly that had been his plan.

Lennox intervened after picking up on a glare from Hightower. "Both of you, stand down."

Pace didn't move. "We're all good here, Two. I was just about to teach Six a lesson."

Court said, "And I was just about to put Pace on a medevac home to Vah Beach."

Lennox repeated himself in a booming voice. "Stand the fuck down!"

Hightower said, "Pace, Gentry is a young and cocky know-it-all. You, on the other hand, are a fucking grown-up. Anything starts up between you two, and it's your ass."

Pace sniffed hard in Court's face, like he was trying to smell fear, and then he smiled.

"Roger that, One."

Just as the pair separated and the tension in the room lowered, Matt Hanley entered. Gone was his suit and tie; now he wore 5.11 tactical pants and some sort of lightweight adventure-wear shirt that strained against his big back and belly. He nodded to Hightower, who then ordered the rest of his team to form around the particleboard table in the center of the pit.

Hanley sported a five-o'clock shadow, just like Court. They'd flown all day yesterday and through the night, and then they had spent most of this day hard at work, and there'd been no time for a shower for any of the men, their group chief included.

Hanley put his hands on the table and leaned forward. "Gentlemen, I thought you'd have a couple of days before getting caught up in the OP-TEMPO, but Langley is sending you out. I've already talked to the intel shop here, and they're in the process of working up a tactical profile of the target location."

"Boss," Hightower said, "we'd planned on some more time with Six before heading into the field. You sure you don't want Lima Foxtrot to run this one?"

"Negative. They've got a raid up near J-Bad tonight. Meat-and-potatoes stuff, we expect. I need you guys to go a little deeper into Indian country."

"Where are we headed?" Hightower asked.

"Lahore."

There was a map of Afghanistan and Pakistan on the table, and some of the guys looked at it. Court didn't know where Lahore was, either, but he was too proud to be caught stealing a glance at the map.

Redus said, "Shit. That's the other side of the country, almost all the way to the Indian border."

"Yeah, I know where it is, Dino," Hanley said. "We'll slip you into the country with covert covered docs; your legend will be that you're diplomatic security agents. We're still putting that together with Islamabad station. From there, non-official cover assets already in country will get you to a safe house southwest of the city and hook you up with pistols, vics, everything you need. You leave in the morning."

Hanley knew what the men would say next, so he headed them off. "Pistols only," Hanley stressed. "You are relocating State agents, you aren't a team of pipe hitters on this op."

None of the other men on Court's team loved this, but all of them had done this sort of thing before.

Apart from Court, of course.

"What's the mission?" Lennox asked.

"We've picked up chatter that the Kashmiri Resistance Front is going to perform reconnaissance at a factory complex outside Lahore sometime in the next seventy-two hours."

"What kind of factory?" Lennox asked.

Hanley answered matter-of-factly. "Explosives."

"Explosives. Awesome," Morgan muttered sarcastically.

"Why the recon?" Lennox asked.

"It's thought the KRF is planning to steal some material."

Now Hightower said, "Where does this intel come from?"

"Islamabad station. Beyond that, we don't get to know," Hanley replied. "But I can give you my best guess. It's coming from within the ISI. We have a mole in their operation, I suspect, so we're getting these nuggets. Whether it's a gold nugget or fool's gold, like the hit near Peshawar where Matt Kiefer bought it, well . . . I guess we'll find out."

Court had been warned by Maurice not to trust Pakistani intelligence. He wondered if that included not trusting CIA informants within Pakistani intelligence.

"Intel briefing is at ten p.m.," Hanley said as he looked at his watch. "Three hours from now. Tomorrow a.m. you'll be flown from Kabul to Dubai, where you will receive credentials to get you into Pakistan. In the meantime, take it easy."

Court was about to infiltrate into Pakistan; he realized he wouldn't be taking it easy for a while.

The intel briefing took place in the intelligence building, next door to the tactical operations center and three doors down from the Golf Sierra pit. Hightower and his men wore casual civilian clothing under their armor, and they sat in plastic chairs in front of a large computer monitor. Analysts were all around the room at workstations.

The director of analysis for the task force was Terry Vance, an African American in his fifties with a noticeable southern accent. He would be Julie's boss, Court realized, and everything about him, from his serious eyeglasses to his razor-cut silver hair, exuded an air of experience, intellect, and gravity. He was ex-military, there was no doubt about it, and in determining this, Court realized even most of the desk jockeys on this task force had served.

There were easily twenty-five analysts and technicians from the intel side of the task force present for the meeting, including Julie Marquez, who appeared to Court to be the youngest of her team. She sat at a computer terminal in the back of the room, and her attention seemed to be divided evenly between the proceedings and something on her monitor.

Terry Vance explained to the men of Golf Sierra that a CIA phone intercept picked up a call between someone who worked at the factory and a man with ties to Omar Mufti, second-in-command of the KRF. The conversation was cryptic, but, essentially, the man who worked at the factory notified the KRF man that the industrial chemical factory would be easy to surveil for the next three days only because soldiers at a nearby military garrison would be away conducting exercises. The factory itself wasn't a military installation, and only locally hired guards would be present.

There was no talk reported by Langley that the KRF was planning anything more than running a surveillance operation at the location, but the implication was clear: the KRF had designs on the factory and, more importantly, what was being manufactured and stored there.

Lennox asked, "Why don't we just tell the Pakistanis, assuming they don't know? They can recall the troops. Set up countersurveillance. Find out who is watching the factory and why."

Vance had a ready answer. "Because we want and need to get Pasha in pocket more than we need to break up the theft of a few crates, or even a few tractor-trailers, of industrial chemicals. Conventional munitions are everywhere in that country. We don't see this as a grave threat, and if ISI gets involved, they might be able to round up the perpetrators of the reconnaissance, but they won't break up the organization, and they won't play fair with us in sharing the intelligence product they get out of the op."

Court wondered why, if conventional munitions were everywhere, a U.S.-designated high-value-terrorist target would need to steal industrial chemicals.

He didn't mention this, but behind Vance, Julie Marquez looked up from her computer. "Sir, that factory produces primarily AN. Ammonium nitrate. Mixed with diesel fuel, it makes ANFO—ammonium nitrate/fuel oil. Do we have a theory as to why Pasha would be after ANFO? I mean . . . we know from past KRF hostile acts that they have access to machine guns, mortars, rockets. Why do they need powder or pellets to build their own weapons?"

Court saw one of the other analysts sitting near Julie look to a colleague and roll his eyes.

Vance looked back over his shoulder to his junior analyst. "That's strategic, Julie, not tac, so it's not in our purview, but it's a good question. My guess is they figure he wants to build some IEDs for his forces. Yeah, he could do that with military munitions, but on a large scale, he might need something he could get in greater quantities. He grabs a few tons of AN, mixes it with diesel fuel, puts it all in cans or drums, and that will build him a couple hundred IEDs."

Julie said nothing else, but Court appreciated the fact that she'd given voice to his concerns.

"What is our mission, specifically?" Hightower asked next.

"Observe and report. We need photographs of KRF operatives, preferably top lieutenants of Pasha the Kashmiri. Omar Mufti wasn't seen in Peshawar where Islamabad station's source intel put him, but maybe he'll be here. If not him, we can get more faces, and a better picture on the organization's leadership."

Hightower said, "Why don't we just kill any KRF forces we encounter?"

To Court's surprise, none of the men or women from the intelligence shop reacted to this at all. It was clear to him that around here, these analysts were all assassins, just like him. America had been fragging targets in this endeavor for a decade or so; it was no big deal to discuss killing a target, even by the eggheads who worked at computer terminals.

Matt Hanley answered Hightower's question. "It's a political decision. Lahore is in the interior of Pakistan. We send a wet team in that deep and there will be serious repercussions. The chief of station in Islamabad is risk-averse, more in line with the ambassador and less in line with those of us trying to fight the terrorists, but that's just my opinion.

"If we get photos and other nuggets of intel in Lahore, then we can build a comprehensive intelligence package on Pasha and his deputies. We'll be better prepared to deal with them when they show up again to run strikes over the border in Afghanistan."

"How do we know the KRF will be back in the FATA?" Morgan asked, speaking of the Federally Administered Tribal Area of Pakistan, which ran along the border.

"Eleven raids into Afghanistan from FATA in four months. Bagram once, Jalalabad four times. Kabul two times. The rest were against small U.S. FOBs and even a civil-affairs installation right at the border. They haven't conducted an attack here at FOB Chapman." Hanley shrugged. "They're leaving us for the Taliban, apparently, but Pasha is obviously gunning for the coalition in Afghanistan.

"The good news about that is we don't imagine he'll be expecting for us to be watching his activities in Lahore."

Hightower asked, "Any idea of the force that is going to be running the recon of the factory?"

"No idea at all," Vance replied. "As you saw at the base on the border, however, Pasha is able to command a significant number of men to do his bidding. You have to be ready for anything."

A targeting officer spoke next, and then there was a discussion of how the team would be infiltrating Pakistan under official cover. After this, Julie Marquez opened a PowerPoint she had built in the previous few hours showing the terrain around the factory.

As she advanced photos of the site on the large wall monitor, she said, "The town is densely populated, but there are woods and farms all around, and the factory is on the southern edge of the urban area, so a layup position to the south in the trees might be your best bet.

"Again, this is an industrial chemical facility, not a military installation. The AN fabricated here is used in civil engineering and mining, mostly. But make no mistake; this is high-explosive." She flashed a look in the direction of the Golf Sierra men in the center of the room. "I'm not an expert on AN, so I can't tell you if firearms can set it off or if you need a different means of detonation."

Hightower said, "Well I *am* an expert in weapons, so I can tell you that, depending on the state of the chemical, firearms and grenades most definitely can and will cause an ammonium nitrate explosion."

Hanley chimed in instantly. "So it's a good thing that you and your guys won't be doing any shooting. Right, Zack?"

Hightower shrugged a little, but he said, "Shooting? Wouldn't dream of it." It was a joke, and people laughed, but Hightower himself did not.

When the meeting broke up, Court filed out of the room and headed towards the dining facility to grab something to drink to take back with him to the pit. He was halfway there when Julie caught up from behind.

"So much for settling in to your new job."

"Right." Court kept walking; she walked with him.

"Are you nervous?"

"Not as nervous as the rest of my team is because I'm coming along with them."

She thought about this a moment. "They have a point. This is a deep infiltration. You're new. I'm actually surprised we are being this aggressive with Golf Sierra, considering what happened the last time you guys went outside the wire."

Court just said, "We'll get it done."

"I'm sure you will. There is a field to the south and then some trees, and if you guys—"

She stopped talking suddenly, stopped walking, too.

Court stopped as well, and looked at her quizzically.

"What's wro—"

Julie shouted, "Incoming!"

She tackled him to the ground; he was a man trained to be ready for everything, but he sure as hell wasn't ready for this. A second later, when the scream of rockets filled the air, he understood what was going on.

Muffled explosions, sounding as if they had detonated some distance away, rolled over them. Julie lay on top of Court, who lay on his back in a pile of gravel in front of a row of portable toilets, their faces inches apart in the dark. A second barrage was closer than the first, hitting no more than two hundred yards off to their left. They could hear shrapnel and debris raining down on metal roofing around them, and sirens began to wail.

A thin but noticeable cloud of dust blew slowly over their position seconds later, but the attack seemed to be over.

"Holy shit," Court said. "Every day? Really?"

"I was here in Khost three years ago. Not here at Chapman, but up at Salerno, a Special Forces base only five klicks northwest. It was worse back then. You just experienced eight, maybe ten rockets. We had days when we counted sixty. They aren't accurate, it's just luck as to whether or not they hit you."

They were still prone, still close, still more or less embracing. They both became aware of this at the same time, and Julie sat up from him. "That wasn't so bad."

Court climbed to his feet as well, ignoring the dust all over him. "Well, I'm lucky you were here. Thanks."

Julie shook her head. "You'd have been fine."

"I appreciate it anyway." He listened to the sirens. "Hell, I can't wait to get to Lahore."

She stared at him a long moment. "That was sarcasm?"

"It was."

She nodded. "Please be careful over there."

Court had been sent into harm's way dozens of times in his life, and no one had ever once told him to be careful. The mission was always the priority, not the man.

"Sure thing. I'll be fine."

"See you when you get back."

Court tried to think of a reply other than "See you then," but nothing came, so that's what he said.

The two parted at the entrance to the intel building. Julie went back inside, and Court continued on to grab something to drink before returning to the pit.

An hour later Hanley stood with the team as they pored over maps and blueprints. They were in the midst of building a mission plan, but it wasn't long before Redus said, "Boss, this is going to be dicey enough without Johnny Freestyle running around. How about we leave Six behind?"

At this, Court spoke up for the first time. "One, can I make a suggestion?"

Pace muttered, "Hey, look everybody. Six has got a better idea."

Hanley said, "I'm all ears, Gentry."

"What if we go to Lahore, stage in a safe house, and then I go out, on my own, and find a place to recon the site?"

Lennox turned to face him. "Alone?"

"Yeah, give me a couple of days to see if I can get eyes on something actionable. I'll get pictures of the comings and goings."

Hanley glanced at Hightower, but only for an instant. Addressing Court, he said, "We'll talk about that once we know what we're up against at the location."

Five minutes later Hanley had walked Hightower outside, leaving the men to begin sorting their equipment for the trip into denied territory. The sirens had stopped; the vibe around the base was as if nothing happened an hour ago that was, in any way, out of the ordinary.

The two men looked out over the mountain range delineating the border between Afghanistan and Pakistan, just a few miles to the east. The moon was nearly full, and the snow caps glowed.

Hanley said, "It's been a few days since you last called me bitching about Sierra Six. Can I take that to mean he's coming around?"

Hightower spit tobacco juice into the dirt. "He's coming around. He's not there yet, but I give him credit for effort."

"What do you think about using him solo on this one, just to get a good recce of the location?"

"Why are you asking me my opinion? I didn't get any choice at all about whether or not I brought him on the team."

Hanley smiled at this. "Yeah, well now he *is* on your team. It's your circus, so he's your monkey. You make the call."

Hightower shrugged. "The kid joined the task force because he is some sort of secret squirrel, let's let him do some secret squirrel shit. What's the worst that could happen?"

Hanley said, "He goes in alone, gets made, gets killed."

Hightower spit again. "Yeah, but other than that?"

Hanley looked out at the distant mountain range for several seconds.

Hightower said, "He won't go alone. I'll put Lennox in charge of the others, they'll remain at a safe house nearby to act as a QRF. Then Gentry and I will find a layup position to overwatch the factory. That wooded area due south of the loading dock that Marquez suggested. That looks good to me. We'll observe and report from there."

Hanley gave his approval, and then the two men shook hands before Zack turned to head back to the pit, leaving Hanley to head back to the intel building.

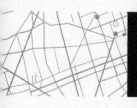

TWENTY-FIVE

PRESENT DAY

Priyanka Bandari knew something was wrong when she heard voices arguing in the hallway outside the storage room she'd been living in for the past day. They were speaking Hindi, but through the wall and through the door, she was unable to make out the words.

Soon the sounds of loud shouts and the pounding of feet filtered through, then the door flew open suddenly, and a B-company henchman rushed in. "We are moving you soon. You will be taken to a car, you will not be tied up or hooded, but if you try anything, you will be killed on the spot. Do you understand this?"

She nodded, and the man shut the door, leaving her alone again.

She asked herself why they weren't going to tie her up, and quickly she worked out that they'd have to move her through a public place and were doing what they could to avoid arousing suspicion about their activities.

This was good news, as far as she could surmise, because Priya had found something inside her in the past few hours. She didn't know exactly what it was. It was not a new strength, not even close. More like a new desperation.

She told herself now she was going to use this opportunity to make a run for it. They would kill her—she believed they had the means, the resolve, and the evil hearts to do so—but she'd told herself she was going to make them work for it.

The discussion outside in the hall continued, louder than before. She picked up some of the conversation now, and the disagreement stemmed from where to take her.

Finally someone banged hard on her door and shouted, "Ten minutes!"

Priya began doing slow deep-breathing exercises, readying herself for what was to come. She told herself her yoga would be her strength.

Until the inevitable end came with a bullet in the back.

She pushed this out of her head and tried to concentrate on her breathing, but her mindfulness took a backseat to her fear and her confusion about what was happening and why a dozen or more armed men seemed suddenly terrified.

A block away Court Gentry handed a wad of rupees to the taxi driver and climbed out of the backseat. Moving quickly up the busy sidewalk, he approached his target location but turned into the alleyway one block to the west of where Priya was being held.

This put him on the far side of the building covered in bamboo scaffolding that he'd noticed late the evening before, and he looked back over his shoulder up the alleyway, making certain he was being neither tailed nor watched, before putting his hand on the first horizontal bamboo rung and pulling himself up. The wooden pole bent as he put all his weight on it, but the cordage lashing it to the vertical poles held as if made of wrought iron.

He climbed up to the next floor, pulling and stepping, swinging when necessary. Court was a practiced climber, and the scaffolding was built to be climbed, so he had little problem with it. More than once he double-checked that no one below was paying attention to him, since even though he was shielded from his target building by the structure the scaffolding was wrapped around, there were cars, rickshaws, bikes, scooters, and pedestrians just seventy-five feet or so off his right shoulder on the main road.

On the second floor he passed a group of construction workers, standing and talking just inside an open window. They saw him, he was only three meters away, but they appeared to think he was part of the work crew here, so comfortable was he with the movement.

They went back to their conversation as if he weren't even there.

He did not scale all the way up the scaffold; instead he entered the hollowed-out construction site through a west-side window on the third floor. Here he moved through the darkened space to the far wall, past more workers who didn't even notice him pass, and he found a window in the southeastern corner facing the building next door. He climbed back outside onto the scaffolding on the eastern wall, made sure no construction crew were close, then drew his heavy knife from its sheath. It was a quality tool, and it cut through one strand of cordage holding the base of a three-story-high vertical length of bamboo with a single drag of its serrated edge. He left the remainder of the cord in place, but his cut weakened the bond where the three-story vertical pole attached to the three-story pole below it.

Back inside the structure, he found the stairs, then went up one more flight, past more workers who paid little attention to him, and then he ran the length of the building's interior to the window just above where he'd exited below. Here, he cut the binding holding the vertical pole to a horizontal pole and spent the next few seconds unwinding the entire cord. While he did this, he peered into the windows of the building across the one-lane street, but he saw no movement. It was unquestionably an apartment building; the men he'd kidnapped confirmed this. He knew many units would be vacant, their occupants at work, but there would still be a bustle in a building that large, Court was certain.

He'd also learned from the two men he'd interrogated that this entire building wasn't a B-Company stronghold, only the sixth floor, but the gang always had ample security posted in the lobby.

He wrapped the two-meter-long hemp cord around his neck several times, then went back inside, climbing the stairs to the next level and exiting another window just next to the vertical pole. He cut the binding here completely, as he'd done below, but this time he didn't keep the cord, he just let it fall to the street.

Now the long piece of bamboo was connected loosely at its origin on the third floor, and directly above Court's position now, at the sixth. Court climbed back inside and moved quickly now through the dark building, knowing that Priyanka could already be long gone from the location he was about to raid.

He also knew he had no other option but to hit the building, hit it hard, and hit it right now.

On the top floor, he went back to the wall facing the target location. He was six stories aboveground, and when he stepped outside onto the scaffold, he eyed the neighboring building yet again. He could see no activity on the sixth floor there, but this was unsurprising. He'd not exactly expected the Indian mafia to operate a safe house with a lot of fanfare. He sliced the cord holding the tip of the bamboo pole to the rest of the scaffold, and the scaffolding rocked slightly. He'd destabilized it by detaching a vertical to the horizontal crossbeams, but there were enough secure vertical beams webbing the construction that he knew he wouldn't crash to the ground.

He took strong hold of the three-story-tall bamboo pole with one hand while he adjusted the two pistols and the knife on his body to make certain they were secure.

Then, just before eleven a.m. on a sunny weekday morning, in plain view of anyone on the busy road who happened to look up six floors above the alleyway between the two tall and narrow buildings, Court leapt off the scaffold, holding tightly with both hands to the top of the bamboo like a pole vaulter.

Instantly the hollow wood bent forward, sending Court over the alleyway in the direction of his push. Five feet, ten feet. If his hands slipped or the bamboo snapped or the cordage he'd loosened holding the vertical beam at the bottom broke completely free, then Court would likely plummet to his death.

But he didn't slip, the beam didn't snap, and the cord didn't unravel, so in just seconds he swung all the way across to the adjacent building. His feet landed adroitly on a balcony railing on the fifth floor. Court held on for dear life to the bamboo while he hooked a toe under the railing; the pole wanted to spring back over the street, but he fought to keep it with him. He dropped down onto the balcony, bending the bamboo even more, fighting its pull as he unraveled the cord he'd wrapped around his neck. He lashed the top of the bamboo to the metal railing of the apartment balcony, leaving the three-story span bent high over the one-lane road, ready for him to use to make an escape.

Then he turned and looked inside the grimy balcony door that led into the apartment.

He knew he was one floor down from where Priya was supposedly being held, so he needed to get in and find the stairs. Looking through the glass, he saw that the apartment appeared empty. He tried the screen door and was pleased that it slid open, though roughly. He moved quietly through the living space; it was kept neat although the building itself was showing signs of neglect. The paint and wallpaper were peeled off, the tile mosaic floor was grimy, and loose wires ran freely across the ceiling, hanging down in places, as if the electricity here had been reworked by the tenants themselves and not an electrician.

He moved out of the flat and into the fifth-floor hallway. Just like the neighboring building, the layout was an atrium in the center, ringed by run-down hallways with waist-high railings and staircases on the north and south sides, and an old rickety elevator on the west side. He saw that the car was stopped at the floor above him, the B-Company lair, and this made him worry that Copper, if she was even still there, could be taken via the elevator to the ground floor at any time. Denying the kidnappers access to a fast exit might just buy him the opportunity he needed, so he found the fire alarm and hoped like hell that it worked. Pulling it down, he was rewarded with a loud clanging bell.

For good measure he pried open the elevator doors, first with his fingertips, then with his hands, and finally with his entire body. He kicked a garbage can closer, then used it to hold open the door.

Court drew his Makarov now, holding it down by his side, and when people began coming out of the apartments around him, he flashed the weapon and ordered them to hurry downstairs.

He looked to the railing above and saw men there, but they weren't looking in his direction, so he moved out of their line of sight.

Just like in the building across the street, anyone using the stairs would have to move in a circular fashion and would necessarily pass all the apartments.

Court made a hasty plan to take advantage of this. He saw a family of three leave their unit, lock their door, and then begin rushing down the stairs, obviously taking the fire alarm seriously. Court pulled out his lock pick set, and in full view of others descending the stairs from above, he quickly picked the simple tumbler lock.

No one paid any attention to him at all, and he was inside the unit quickly. He checked the space to make certain no one had been left behind, then went back to the door and cracked it. Hopeful the kidnappers would descend, his plan was to lie in wait for them, but he knew he didn't have the luxury of standing here indefinitely. He'd give them a minute or two, and then his backup plan was to go upstairs and begin hunting for the woman.

The B-Company thugs would be suspicious of the fire alarm, and more suspicious still that three of their number had disappeared in the past hour, so he knew the men would be on guard every step of the way. But Court saw that as an advantage. He needed to be able to easily discern his targets, and since he had no idea what Copper looked like, he figured a group of especially amped-up mob goons shuffling a lone woman down to the exit would be fairly easy to make out.

He didn't have to wait long at all to see what he needed. In less than a minute he saw a large pack of men, perhaps ten in all, rushing down the stairs. He would have flagged them as suspicious even if they hadn't been carrying pistols and rifles in full view, but they were. Looking carefully, Court picked up a quick image of a smaller, dark-complexioned woman with black hair in the middle of the pack.

They'd be past his position in twenty seconds, so he redrew the Makarov, closed the door a little bit more to hide his view from the approaching enemy, and waited.

The fire alarm continued to clang; everyone out on the floor either was in the process of evacuating or else just stood around talking, no doubt declaring that the damn alarm was broken again or some damn kids had set it off again. Court ignored the noise and tried to anticipate everything that was about to happen.

And then something happened, right in front of his eyes, that he did not anticipate at all.

As the B-Company men and their captive rounded the open hallway across from him, approaching his position, an apartment door opened right in front of the group. A small woman in her sixties stuck her head out, and just as men flashed guns her way to force her back inside, the girl with the dark hair in the center of the mobsters broke free of them and ran into the apartment, pushing the woman out and slamming the door behind her.

And just like that, Copper disappeared. She was still five stories above-ground in a building teeming with armed kidnappers, and he doubted she had a way down available to her, so he didn't see how her predicament had improved very much at all.

As the woman ran for the stairs, the first of the ten Indian B-Company men rushed to the door, tried the latch, and found it locked. They were just thirty-five feet from Court when two of their number stepped back, raised their folded Tantal rifles, aimed at the door, and opened fire. Long volleys from each weapon splintered wood and wrecked eardrums all around while the men behind the front pair readied to pour into the apartment.

Civilians raced for the stairs now, a mad scramble to get away from the danger.

One of the two men kicked at the door, but as Court had noticed from watching them, their gunfire to breach the apartment had been unprofessional and ineffective. They'd failed to do more than poke holes in the wood; the latch and the hinges were untouched.

Another man pushed forward amid the agitated shouts from his mates and lifted his own weapon. He unfolded the stock, and unlike the first pair who'd fired, he actually aimed his rifle at one of the hinges.

This guy knew what he was doing, so while his bursts of rounds boomed throughout the atrium and the door quickly came loose in front of him, Court Gentry reached out with his small pistol and shot the man between his shoulder blades.

TWENTY-SIX

The suppressed Makarov was a decent enough weapon for an assassination up close and personal against one or two unsuspecting victims, but it was an exceedingly poor choice for a tool to deal with this situation. Court was up against at least five rifles as well as the same number of pistols, but although he was outnumbered and outgunned, in the hands of a master, the Russian stalwart did its job.

He hit three men; one dropped to the ground, and the other two spun around to return fire, but subsequent rounds from Court's gun put the men down before they could do so.

Part of the force pushed into the apartment. Copper didn't have a chance in hell of getting away from them, but Court emptied his magazine at the men remaining on the landing, then retreated inside and began running back through the small apartment for the balcony as he reloaded his only other magazine.

Court also had the .25 pocket gun on him, but if it came time to draw that to fight with, Court figured his better option would be diving off the damn building and taking his chances with gravity.

He was certain some of the gangsters would be in pursuit of him now, while the men already in the unit with Copper would work to secure her or to kill her, depending on their orders.

Just then, behind him the door splintered as rounds slammed into it.

He didn't know how many of the mob goons he'd shot, and he didn't know how many more B-Company men were here in the building or close enough to get up here quickly.

He just knew he had to reengage the men going after Copper, to buy her some time and some space to get away. On the balcony, he leapt up onto the railing and looked to the next unit; it was the only balcony between him and where Copper had retreated into the apartment, and it was two balconies away from where his bamboo beam was affixed. He leapt across to the next unit, five stories up; his boots landed on the railing, and then he stumbled to the balcony, where he tried the lock on the door. It was engaged; he could pick it with a little time, but as time was a commodity in short supply, he raised his boot and kicked right at the latch. The latch gave way, and the glass around it cracked, and when Court flung the sliding door open, he found himself standing face-to-face with a woman wearing a shalwar kameez and standing there with two small children.

Shit.

With a wave of his pistol, he got them in the tiny bathroom of their tiny apartment, then ran for the door to the fifth-floor landing around the atrium.

Opening it a crack, he saw no one, but he could hear voices on the landing right where he'd initially engaged the B-Company men.

At the same time, he heard shouting in the apartment on his left.

This told him Copper and a group of B-Company were in there, and many, hopefully most, of the armed gunmen were in the process of checking the apartment on his right that he'd just vacated.

Court ran over to the wall between his unit and the unit where Copper was, and he quickly rapped on the plaster with his fist. The building was one hundred years old if it was a day, and by knocking, he found his way between the vertical wooden studs holding the next floor up.

Holstering his pistol, he looked around the apartment and found a woman's silk scarf. He quickly wrapped it around his left hand, and then, with a force carefully calculated to do the damage he needed without breaking any bones, he punched the wall.

He smashed through the plaster with one hit and found a six-inch space, free of insulation, between his wall and the neighboring one. He tore open a bigger hole, and then he pulled his pistol with his right hand. With his wrapped-up left hand, he punched the interior of the neighboring wall.

His hand went through easily, busting a football-sized hole in the plaster. He reached in with his pistol, brought his head to the plaster, and head-butted it, breaking off more of the ancient material so he could see.

Two men were dragging a woman by the hair just ten feet from where he stood, through an empty room towards the front door of the unit. Both B-Company men had heard the banging, and their weapons were in the process of rising towards the door, but they hadn't yet identified the exact location of the threat since neither had considered the possibility of someone crashing through the wall next to them.

Court fired twice into the face of the first man, dropping him down to the floor next to Copper. The woman yanked away from the second man, pulling him off balance and buying Court the instant he needed to shift his sights.

Just as the man fired a single round with his folded rifle in Court's direction, Court shot him through his windpipe. The young bearded man fell to the ground, gripping the wound, forgetting about his rifle and his mission.

Court fired again and his enemy went still.

He looked down at his body quickly, saw he'd not been hit, but noticed the bullet had hit the plaster wall about six inches from his right hip.

He looked back up now and saw that Copper was in the process of running for the door. He shouted after her.

"Copper! It's Cobalt!"

She stopped suddenly and turned to him.

"Go to the balcony, I have a way down!"

He saw her wild eyes and realized she was on the verge of shock, but he also recognized that she knew who he was and what he wanted.

Court didn't wait. He turned and ran back to his balcony, then leapt again over to hers.

They met on the balcony, but Court just moved past without acknowledging her, entered the living room of the tiny flat, and yanked a pistol off one of the dead men. He then grabbed a rifle, stepped out to the landing, and aimed it, one-handed, towards the apartment two doors down. He waited only a second for a man to come rushing out, pistol in hand, and Court fired a burst into his midsection.

He then sprinted back into the flat, closed the door, and pushed a heavy table up against it. He hoped he'd bought a few seconds for his escape, but he felt certain there would be more B-Company reinforcements already on the way to his position.

Court dropped the rifle next to the dead men in the living room. He would have preferred the firepower of the Tantal to the handgun he'd just grabbed, but he knew he'd need to conceal any weapon once he got down to street level. Looking down at the pistol he'd retrieved, however, he was pleased to find that it was an Indian-made version of the venerable but capable Browning Hi-Power.

Time was of the essence, so he didn't bother fishing around the body for another magazine.

Instead he ran back to the balcony.

Copper was there, kneeling behind the railing so she couldn't be seen. "How do we get down?"

Court pointed to the bamboo pole that was bent across the street and tied to the next balcony over. "With that."

"How do we—"

She stopped talking when Court climbed up on the railing, then put his hands on the exterior of the building, grabbing onto a small hook used to set a clothesline. Quickly he kicked his left boot out, stretched across the distance to the next balcony over a meter and a half away. He said, "Climb onto my back, then I'll get us over."

To their right, gunfire erupted. Court knew the men were making their way into the flat now.

"Do it!" Court shouted. "Hold on to me!"

To his surprise, Copper did not do as he asked. Instead she climbed up onto the balcony railing and put her hand on his back, but only to steady herself a moment. Then she kicked out with her front leg. Her foot stepped on the next balcony rail—she was almost doing the splits—and then she somehow kicked off her hind leg and expertly brought it to her front foot as if she were a gymnast.

Court made it the rest of the way over himself, then fell off the rail down to the balcony, significantly less gracefully than the woman had done. Still, he had the presence of mind to cover Copper's body and put his hand over her mouth.

Next door, on the balcony they'd just vacated, men rushed out, guns high. They looked left and right, up and down, but they couldn't see the pair hiding just feet away behind the balcony rail. Court knew they would come check this apartment, so he hadn't bought himself much time, but he prayed it would be enough.

The men yelled something, and he immediately heard the sound of them running back into the next-door unit, and Court climbed back up and holstered his gun.

"What did they say?" Court asked.

"Something about bamboo."

The pole was tied there, jutting all the way across the street and connected to the other building three stories down. The B-Company men were going to rush over here to check it out, because they'd obviously sussed out that it was the way Court had made it into the building without going through the guards downstairs, and it might also serve as his means of escape.

This told Court he had less than twenty seconds to figure out a way to get down before men would crash out onto this balcony with rifles blazing.

He said, "Grab on to me with everything you've got, and then we can get out of here."

"We are going to slide down?" She didn't get it at all, this he saw.

"Not exactly. I need you to trust me."

She didn't respond as he moved to the bamboo, holding on to it with his right hand with all his might.

Court reached into his waistband with his left hand, pulled out his serrated knife, and began sawing at the cordage holding the pole to the railing.

He looked past Copper into the apartment as he did this. He couldn't reach for his gun now—he had no more hands to do so—so he focused on cutting through the cordage.

He said, "You have to hold on to me, no matter what happens."

"This is crazy."

"Sticking around is crazier."

Copper just nodded with a terrified expression on her face. Court realized he was scared himself, and he did stupid, dangerous shit all the time, so he couldn't even imagine what this was like for someone who hadn't spent their entire adult life doing stupid, dangerous shit.

The bamboo pole came free of the railing, but Court held it firm. He climbed onto the railing, straddled it, and pulled Copper's hand till she came up with him.

"Grab my waist! Hard!"

She grabbed on to him in a death grip; the pole was between them. "Legs, too," he said.

Her legs wrapped around and she hung off him.

Court just stared into Copper's eyes, inches from his.

"Ready?" he asked.

She squeezed her arms and legs tighter as she shut her eyes. "I'm ready."

With a little nod, he kicked off the balcony towards his left, sending the three-story-high bamboo pole dipping wildly in that direction.

They weren't heading back to the first building; there was too much weight between the two of them for the bamboo to spring back to where it came from. Instead they were drooping sideways, heading all the way down to the street, and despite the confidence he displayed to the young woman hanging on to him for dear life, he did *not* know if this was going to work.

They tipped farther over, descending quickly. Copper screamed as a shot rang out above them, but they were moving too fast to worry about their enemy's marksmanship.

No, Court and Copper were too busy contemplating crashing.

At the base of the pole on the third story of the scaffolding, the cut and loosened cord began to give way as they moved through the air, over the street now, passing forty-five degrees, still plunging.

When the bamboo reached the point where Court and Copper were horizontal with the ground, three stories above the one-lane road, the cordage at the base popped, audible over the sounds of the city, but the line kept the end of the pole from simply falling away from the scaffold.

Court realized they were going to hit harder than he'd planned, and they would also land in the middle of the street itself, so he looked, upside down now, at the oncoming traffic. An approaching auto rickshaw seemed like it would be just about in line with their landing zone, so Court locked his eyes on it, ready to release both himself and Copper once it was just below them.

"When I let go, you let go!"

"Don't let go!" she pleaded.

But ten feet above the ground, and five feet above the rickshaw, Court released his hold and the two of them tumbled away from the bamboo. His back slammed into the canvas roof of the tiny covered scooter, slamming hard into the metal beams that held the fabric in place, and Copper's body hit him full-on in the chest.

The roof caved in.

The rickshaw driver careened his vehicle into the sidewalk before coming to a stop; a group of women screamed as they struggled out of the back of the little vehicle, dazed by the impact, and Court and Copper both rolled off the rickshaw and down to their feet.

Without a word to the driver or his passengers, and with only an instant's glance back in the direction of the building where Copper had been held, the two of them staggered, then shuffled, then ran up the street, certain that B-Company men would soon be in hot pursuit.

TWENTY-SEVEN

TWELVE YEARS AGO

The town of Sarai Mughal, Pakistan, sits twenty-five miles southwest of the sprawling metropolis of Lahore and thirty miles due west of the Indian border. It's geographically small, less than three quarters of a mile of development at its widest point, but its high-density population, like much of even rural India, means it is congested with traffic and densely populated.

The buildings are brown and low and walled, back to back and side to side, with electrical wiring running above narrow roads of broken pavement. Dust and smog hangs low in the air when the rains don't keep them away.

A stranger standing in the center of Sarai Mughal among the hundreds of closely packed buildings would find it all but impossible to imagine the verdant countryside that surrounds the town, but farms, fields, hardwood forests, and water sources sprawl away for miles and miles around.

On the southwestern edge of the municipality, the last brown compound before the green begins has a sign in front that reads, "Bismallah and Riaz Chemicals, LTD." The size of three soccer fields, the business consists of a factory, a pair of warehouses, and an administrative office building, all surrounded by chain-link fencing and masonry walls topped with razor wire.

An eight-man team guards the facility; the security force was poorly trained and armed with old pump-action shotguns, but they were sufficient to keep the riffraff and petty thieves away, and Bismallah and Riaz had never had a major incident beyond a warehouse fire a few years back that would have frightened the community had the majority of the townspeople known that potent explosives were among the chemicals manufactured here.

This morning, low, thick, and dark clouds hung over the town, trapping heat and keeping temperatures in the eighties, and a growing warm breeze from the west heralded the approach of rain.

Four hundred yards south of the wall of the compound, Court Gentry swayed gently from side to side along with the breeze. He was thirty feet high in a tree, at the northern edge of a small wood of scrub, pine, and conifer that edged up to a rice field that edged up to the chemical plant. He'd spent much of the previous morning pruning and tying off branches in front of him to give him both maximum line of sight and good concealment from his target location, and now he could see what he needed to see from his perch.

From the ground he wouldn't have been able to look over the wall of the factory, but from here he could view virtually the entire southern side of the facility.

Court had a spotting scope in a pack next to him, but there was no stable place to mount it in a tree, so instead he used a pair of eight-power Zeiss binoculars to scan the main entrance on his right. The sound of thunder approached from the west, and Court imagined that in addition to having a stiff neck and a sore backside from his position here in the woods for much of the past twenty hours, he was about to get soaking wet.

Down below, at the base of the scrub tree and in a small hide formed by the thick vegetation, Zack Hightower lay flat, relaxing after his own four-hour shift above. He and Court had earpieces in and their scrambled frequency-hopping radios turned on, so the two men could easily communicate.

Court was bored, but he was accustomed to this boredom. What he was not accustomed to, however, was a disembodied voice popping into his ear at random intervals.

"We're at twenty hours, kid," Zack said from below.

"Yep."

"I'll call Hanley at noon, see if there's any updates to the intel. We can stick around forty-eight hours max before we really start rolling the dice on getting exposed."

"Agreed," Court said, though he doubted Zack cared if his junior man was in agreement with him or not.

It was quiet save for the rumbling thunder, and then Zack said, "Sierra Two can resupply us, I'm just worried about some dickhead kid or mushroom farmer stepping on my head. I'm sure you encountered Murphy's Law wherever the hell in the Agency you came from."

"Daily." Court didn't feel like conversation, but Zack had proved himself to be a motormouth, and this seemed like something Court was going to have to endure while in Golf Sierra.

Finally Zack's chattiness drifted away, and Court took a break from the glass for a moment, rubbed his eyes, and pulled a long swig from a water bottle out of the pack full of provisions, camera, and radio equipment he'd stowed by buckling a strap around a branch. He took his time adjusting himself so that a different portion of his lower back would be pressed against the trunk of the tall scrub, then raised the Zeiss binos back up and peered through them again.

There were employees milling about the three-bay loading dock in front of him, and more walking through the parking lot between the factory and the warehouse ahead and on his left. Security milled about at the main entrance guard shack; they were clearly just going through the motions and had no idea there would supposedly be some sort of surveillance conducted by a Kashmiri separatist force here at the facility.

He scanned farther to the right, down the road to the east, and here a large mosque, one of many in the area by the sound of it, called the townspeople to prayer five times a day.

Court scanned back to the left, his eyes on a row of barns or woodsheds just outside the main walls of the town but within view of the factory, thinking that if the KRF set up their own layup position, they might do it there. Seeing nothing of note, he swept back to the security gate, planning on taking another moment's break after one more pass at the area to the north, but he stopped panning suddenly, because he detected a change in the guards at the shack. They were more alert now. Not threatened, no, they were still just standing around, but they all seemed to be looking at something up the road in the direction of the mosque. He shifted his view back to the east, farther this time, and he immediately sighted a pair of trucks approaching, moving at a steady but sensible pace on the narrow dusty road.

The vehicles were easy to spot. They'd been named jingle trucks by U.S. military that came across them in Afghanistan, but they were also ubiquitous around Pakistan. Court had seen many on the highway from Lahore, but these were the first he'd sighted since he'd arrived here at Sarai Mughal.

Brightly painted in red, yellow, green, and purple, they were a riot of color, with shiny ornate chains and bells and beads and even fabric tassels hanging off them. They featured arabesque designs or Urdu calligraphy, images of birds and plants and flowers, even portraits of Pakistani pop stars of wildly varying degrees of quality.

As flashy as the jingle trucks were—they were literally mobile works of art—they were just as utilitarian. Court estimated the two vehicles approaching the chemical factory from the east were twenty-five feet long and a dozen feet high, their covered beds capable of hauling several tons of cargo each. The pair weren't riding particularly low on their chassis, so Court wondered if they were here to pick up a shipment.

He triggered his push-to-talk button hooked to the collar of his sweat-and-soil-covered olive drab T-shirt.

"Two trucks approaching."

Zack's voice conveyed his boredom. "Same as yesterday?"

"Negative. Those were commercial vans. These are those goofy jingle trucks."

Court scanned back to the guards. He'd noticed the day before that the security force all but waved vehicles through. But today, in contrast, three guards had left the guard shack and were standing on the drive at the open gate; their shotguns were down, hanging from their chests, but their heads were up and their eyes were most definitely locked onto the approaching vehicles.

Court clicked his transmit button again. "Security was not expecting these guys."

"How do you know that?"

"Because I watch people all day, every day."

After a pause, Zack said, "I'm coming up to take a look."

"Better hurry. Trucks will be at the gate in thirty seconds."

"I can climb a fuckin' tree, Six." Hightower had a decade and a half on his Six, but he was in incredible shape, and he scaled the tree adroitly.

The bright red and yellow trucks stopped at the gate now, and the first guard walked up to the rig in front.

Zack had his own binos around his neck, and he aimed them in on the entrance to Bismallah and Riaz. He said, "Yup. Security were not expecting this. They look halfway switched on, don't they?"

Court was shoulder to shoulder with his team leader, squinting through his glass, trying to see through the windshield of the rig. Just as he did this, however, the side window came down, and he saw the passenger of the vehicle, who seemed to be talking comfortably with the guard below him.

Court's binos were eight-power, but the camera in his pack next to him had an incredible 1,000-millimeter lens attached, giving him more than double the zoom of the binoculars. Knowing he might need to photograph this exchange, he reached for the Nikon and popped off the lens cap, then found the truck through the viewfinder and hurriedly focused the lens.

Now he had a twenty-power view of the man in the front passenger seat as he conversed with facility security.

Zack continued looking through his own glass, but he knew Court had the best view. "What do you see?"

"Unknown subject. Twenties. He's got some papers in his hand, but the guard doesn't seem impressed with them." Court added, "If this *is* the KRF, this is about the shittiest recon I've ever witnessed."

Zack chuckled at this. "Yeah. Knocking on the front door is not the most subtle way to surveil a—"

Court interrupted. "Wait . . . the passenger is getting out."

Just as Court said this, the passenger door flew open, and flashes of light emitted from inside the cabin. The guard lurched back and fell onto his back.

And then the sound of gunfire passed over the trees around them. "Oh, shit," Court said.

Other security men raised their weapons, but the sound of more booming gunfire rolled over the Americans' layup position. Court couldn't identify the source of these gunshots.

"Who the fuck is shooting?" Court asked.

Zack answered the question because he had a wider field of view through his binoculars. "Rear vic. Four gunners. AKs or Tantals, can't tell from here."

Court panned quickly to his right, and now he saw even more men pouring out of the rear of the second vehicle.

"You getting this, Six?"

Court had forgotten he had a camera in his hands. Quickly he began snapping digital images. "Yeah."

While he photographed a gun battle there in the street, Zack said, "I see eight tangos now. Shit, they've got training. Look how they bound."

"Yep," Court said. More security men came out of the warehouse on the left, but they were instantly outclassed and outgunned by the attackers, and they had to retreat to cover as the men from the jingle trucks pushed up the sloped driveway confidently towards their position.

"Security here doesn't have a chance," Court said, then added, "Nobody in that complex does."

Panning back, taking photos with his digital camera as fast as he could, Court saw that now all the security guards near the shack were down. Terrorists shot their still forms, professionally ensuring that the men were no longer threats to them.

"What are we going to do about it?" Court asked.

"You're going to shut up and continue taking pictures. I'm calling in to Hanley now." The fight was already trailing off, the other guards either dead or in flight, and Court watched the two jingle trucks proceed up the drive, finally stopping at the loading docks, as Hightower's call was answered by his group chief.

Court could only hear Zack's side of the call. "Rooster. Golf Sierra One. Target personnel are in sight, time now. This is not a reconnaissance mission. Repeat, *not* a recon. They are hitting the facility. Multiple security forces are KIA. The operation is ongoing."

There was a long pause while Zack listened to Hanley. As Court watched the horrific scene in front of him, he saw a red minibus, also decorated with paint and bells and other accoutrements, enter the factory complex behind the two bigger jingle trucks, then park behind the other vehicles.

Four men exited the minibus; they wore smaller rifles, submachine guns perhaps, and Court took pictures of them in quick succession while Zack continued to talk to Hanley.

Zack said, "Roger. Two truckloads, say about eighteen fighters in all. They are rounding up the civilians."

Court corrected him. "Three vics now, Zack. Twenty guys plus." Zack relayed these details to Hanley.

As Court snapped images, he took note of a bearded man with short black hair who climbed out of the minivan. He appeared to be in his thirties, and Court thought there was something slightly familiar about him. Slowly, he held the camera out for Hightower. "Boss?"

Zack noted the tone of his subordinate. "Wait one, Rooster."

Zack took the camera and handed the phone off to Court to hold. Court said, "The red minibus, just in front of it. One of the guys who got out . . . white shirt. No weapon visible."

"What about him?" Zack said as he looked for the person Court indicated. Court did not answer, and Zack spent ten seconds or so checking him out. The rain picked up a little more, and the tree began to sway more aggressively. Finally, Zack handed the camera back to Court and snatched the phone. "Rooster, be advised, we have eyes on HVT number two, time now."

Court looked back through the camera viewfinder, centered on Omar Mufti, second-in-command of the Kashmiri Resistance Front. The man stood confidently, hands on his hips and erect like the military officer he once was, while in front of him factory workers were led out of the building, down the stairs next to the loading dock and down to the pavement. They were then lined up in a row and ordered facedown on the wet ground. More KRF fighters disappeared inside the warehouse, their guns occasionally barking as they acquired targets.

Court said, "We've got to do something."

Zack ignored his junior team member and concentrated on his call with Hanley. "Understood."

He turned back to Court as he ended the call but kept the phone in his hand. "We take no action here, but we call in Lennox and the others, then follow Mufti when he leaves." Zack reached for the phone, and Court turned to him in disbelief.

"Are you fucking kidding? We're about to witness a mass execution. We can't just sit here."

"We don't know we're about to witness a—"

"C'mon, One. They wasted all the guards, they aren't going to line these people up and just drive away," Court asserted.

"We take no action," Hightower repeated.

"This is bullshit," Court muttered while he peered through the Nikon.

Zack shrugged. "What the hell we gonna do about twenty tangos? Look at us. We're two monkeys in a fucking tree four hundred yards away with a pair of nine-millimeter roscoes under our shirts."

Court knew Zack was right. As hard as it was, he and Sierra One could do nothing more than record the incident for the CIA and then follow the perpetrators after the fact.

He looked back into his Nikon while Zack called Sierra Two. Court watched as Omar Mufti ordered his men around while more and more workers from the factory were led outside. After a couple of minutes a fork-lift appeared, carrying what appeared to Court to be a pallet of large sacks, the size and shape not unlike those that would hold fertilizer or animal feed. The minibus was backed up to the loading dock and the sacks were placed in back, and then the forklift turned and disappeared back inside.

"They are loading the minibus with ammonium nitrate."

"Shit," Zack said.

A lone police car rolled slowly towards the main gate, but after a single burst of fire from one KRF fighter at the guard shack, it backed away violently, crashing through a fence before disappearing up a side street.

Zack hung up on Lennox and said, "I'm vectoring them to the east of the factory in case Mufti leaves in the next couple of minutes. Their ETA is ten mikes."

He then grabbed the binoculars and began watching the scene while Court continued taking pictures with the Nikon. Soon a second load of large bags was brought out by the forklift and again loaded into the big van.

"They mix up that much AN with regular old diesel fuel, and you've got a bomb big enough to blow up a city block."

Court said, "The first load was the same size, and he's heading back for another."

Court and Zack watched for another minute. The rain and thunder were both heavy now, and it only added to the palpable sense of foreboding.

Mufti stood on the loading dock in the rain, surrounded by several of his men, looking down at the cluster of men in work clothes and hard hats, who were still lying facedown. When one of his fighters climbed out of the forklift after a third load was placed in the rear of the bright red minibus, all of the KRF men wearing rifles raised them at the prone civilians, and Court saw smoke and flame erupt from over a dozen weapons.

The crackle of rifle fire, even from four hundred yards away, was ear-pounding.

"Son of a bitch." Court watched two dozen or more innocents die. His hands shook too much to get good images for a moment, but when he recovered enough to survey the carnage, he could make out the blood around the still forms.

Zack began climbing down the tree. "I'm getting the car. You watch them till they go and then we'll head after them."

Court did not respond. He thought he was tough enough to handle anything, but he had never witnessed anything like this in his life. This was death on another scale. He put his head in his hands for a moment.

Zack was halfway down the tree when he tapped his radio. "How copy, Six?"

Court shook his head to snap out of it. He looked back at the factory complex, then tapped his transmit button.

"Solid copy. Better hurry. They're loading up in the vehicles."

TWENTY-EIGHT

PRESENT DAY

Court and Copper had not spoken a word to each other during the long taxi ride through the city. Court knew drivers often served as paid informants for local gangsters—this was a truism the world over—and he didn't want to reveal that he was an American to someone who might very well soon hear from his contacts in the underworld that an American and a local woman were being sought by B-Company.

Before they'd hailed the cab to get out of Andheri East, however, Copper told Court she knew a place where she was certain no one would find them. When he pressed, she said it was the apartment of a friend from college who was out of town in the UK for the semester. A mutual friend had been looking in on the flat from time to time, but no one was living there regularly.

She'd also offered that the location was in Versova, and it was not a high-crime area, and she doubted B-Company had much of a presence there.

Court agreed, principally because he didn't want to go back to a hotel, where there would be myriad opportunities for them to be spotted by staff and other guests.

As they rode, Court looked the woman over surreptitiously, first to see if she had any obvious injuries. He was pleased to see no bleeding, bruising, or other marks on her body, although her hair was disheveled from the man yanking her by it across the floor.

Still, Court thought, a little bedhead wasn't much to complain about after two days as a kidnap victim.

But though he noticed no external wounds, her face was a mask of worry, pain, even dread. He took it to be from the shock of the chaotic and deadly event she'd just been in the center of, and he expected her to snap out of it before long.

And he needed her to do so. Right now, this woman was his one and only link to Arjun, who was, in turn, his one and only link to Murad Khan.

Before they'd jumped into the cab, she'd warned the American that the place she was taking him wasn't much to see, and Court assured her he'd seen everything.

But as it turned out, he was wrong.

The Versova Fish Market would have been an odd choice for Court to establish a safe house on his own. It was busy and dirty and smelly beyond his wildest imagination, but he did appreciate the fact that the woman had her wits about her to the extent that she directed the cabdriver to the main entrance of the market itself, then led Court around the back of the congested two-city-block location before taking a rickety wooden staircase up to a row of doors down a dark hallway. She didn't have a key, but Court picked the lock in thirty seconds, and soon they were inside a small and dark flat, with a single window in the living room affording a view down to the street behind the market.

The smell made its way up here, but Court wasn't about to complain to management.

Once they were inside, he checked over the little one-bedroom unit, using his pistol to do so.

Whoever lived here, Court determined, was young, female, and something of a hippie. Beads hung in doorways, tie-dye art adorned the walls, and a record collection of world music lined the wall of one of the bedrooms.

When he returned to the living room, he noticed the woman standing there, staring into space. Her hands trembled.

She immediately said she would take a shower and change into some of her friend's clothes. Court just nodded and went to the kitchen to look for some coffee, but soon gave up, finding nothing but tea.

His arms were scratched, he was exhausted, and he felt his loose grip on Khan slipping away with each passing minute. Arjun was the key, the one who could put Court and Khan in the same place, but the only way Court knew to make this happen was to use Arjun as bait.

The woman returned minutes later, clean and dressed in a beautiful burgundy and gold shalwar kameez. Her hair was wet and pulled back in a ponytail. She remained sullen, sad, despondent, and this confused him a little. He'd expected her to be in a state of shock, at first anyway, but she seemed incredibly clearheaded considering what she'd been through. But he'd also expected her to be at least somewhat ecstatic about being alive after the danger she'd been in since Algiers. Sure, Court realized, she might just be pissed at him, and that was the darkness he was picking up from her visage, but it seemed like something more was going on here.

She took a pair of soft drink bottles out of her friend's little refrigerator and handed one over to Court. Looking it over, he saw it was called Maaza, and from the picture, he took it to be mango flavored. After popping the top, he took a cold swig. He wasn't impressed, but he needed the sugar and the hydration right now after getting very little food or sleep the last few days.

Court looked out the window, making certain they were safe. B-Company all but ran sections of this town, and even though she'd told him she didn't think this was one of those neighborhoods, he was pretty damn sure they could cobble together a gang of shitheads and climb into a van for a drive. He wouldn't be safe as long as he was in this city, but he wouldn't be leaving this city until he found Murad Khan, so he figured he'd be peeking out of a lot of windows in the coming days.

The woman sat down at a tiny kitchen table. She drank, alone with her thoughts, until Court sat in front of her. He was utterly exhausted, but he had to snap her out of this funk and get on with this operation.

He opened with something light. "The way you made it between those two balconies. You were almost doing the splits, then you kicked over into a handstand. What martial art do you study?"

"It wasn't a handstand, and I don't study martial arts. I practice yoga."

Court chuckled and took another swig. "I didn't know that shit was useful."

"It's kept me alive for the past two days. Mindfulness, relaxation, composure." She shrugged; tears formed in her eyes slowly. "Not that I was really composed."

"Well, you impressed me, and I do this shit for a living."

She said nothing, unappreciative of the compliment.

Court said, "What's your name?"

With a sigh she said, "If the Indian mafia gets to know it, I guess you can, too. My name is Priyanka Bandari."

Court thought about this comment for a second, then said, "Okay, Miss Bandari."

"Call me Priya."

Court nodded and took a pull on the soft drink. "First things first. You were kidnapped because of me. You could have been killed because of me. I know it, and you know it, and an apology is probably worthless, but I *am* sorry."

She answered with a shrug. "I no longer care about my life."

And with that, Court knew he was about to learn the reason she was so sullen right now. "Why is that?"

"I didn't give them your identity because I didn't know it. I still don't. But . . ."

"But you told them about Arjun." Court said it as a matter of fact, but there was no judgment in his voice.

She nodded; tears formed in her eyes.

Court gave her a moment to cry, then said, "Let's just put our cards on the table. Arjun is . . . your dad?"

Priya's face slowly reddened more. The tears dripped from her cheeks. Her voice cracked when she said, "My uncle. He's my uncle."

"Okay."

Then she added, "He is a good man. The best man I know. And . . . and I betrayed him."

Court wanted to console the woman, but he did not reach out to put a hand on her. Instead he just spoke softly. "I've been through all sorts of training to teach me how to keep my mouth shut under extreme stress.

Even during torture. And I've been tortured in real life. Trust me, there was nothing you could have done. Everybody talks if the pain is bad enough."

He thought this would give her some consolation, but he quickly learned it was absolutely the worst thing he could have said.

She looked him in the eyes and shouted back, "I wasn't tortured! They barely laid a hand on me."

He cocked his head. "But—"

"The Pakistani man had me tied up, brought in a car battery and cables and water. He told me what he would do, got ready to do it . . . and then I gave in without so much as a single shock."

Court waited a moment for the young woman to calm down. She cried openly now, and finally he spoke over her sobs. "I'm glad they didn't hurt you. You would have been ruined by it, and you wouldn't have helped your uncle at all, because in the end you would have given them everything you knew anyway.

"And I don't know your uncle, but I promise you, he wouldn't have wanted you to suffer when the outcome would have been the same."

She wiped her eyes with her hands. Court found a kitchen towel hanging at the tiny stove, and he pulled it and handed it over.

Priya said, "We need to call him. Warn him. He is stubborn. He has a secure home, he has security, he won't want to leave, but maybe he still doesn't understand the danger he is—"

"Good idea."

She was surprised the American was going to allow her to make this call. Her uncle had double-crossed him, she knew this, and he had to have known, as well.

When he pulled out his phone, she reached for it hurriedly.

Court held it away from her. "Will you do me a favor and put the call on speaker, and use English when talking to him?"

"Why?"

"I want to hear what is said." He added, "By both of you."

"You don't trust me?"

"I don't know you. I know he gave B-Company my name. He's not *my* uncle, let's just leave it there."

She started to protest some more, but Court was steadfast to the point where she knew she had to drop it or she'd lose the chance to make any call at all.

She took the phone and dialed the number, then placed the call on speaker.

Arjun answered hurriedly. "Yes?"

"Uncle?" Priya began to weep.

Arjun, to Court's mild surprise, sounded much more like an uncle and much less like a corrupt broker of killers and gangsters on the Darknet. Through instant tears of his own, he replied in English, "Chiki! Are you safe? Are you free, my darling?"

"I am safe. Cobalt rescued me. He is here, he has asked me to speak English so he can listen." She continued weeping as she said, "I am so sorry that I told them about you."

"You have nothing to apologize for, Chiki. Nothing at all. Everything is fine. I am safe at home. No one can get me here."

Court didn't believe that for a minute, and he didn't believe Arjun believed it himself. Arjun was a dead man as soon as B-Company and Khan came for him. He wouldn't call the police; the broker was almost certainly a criminal himself, after all. And he wouldn't try to flee the country; he'd probably already calculated that the drive to an airport or to a heliport or a marina would make him a lot more vulnerable than he already was.

No, he'd have to take his chances on private security, and Court was pretty sure private security would be no match for what would be coming Arjun's way.

Court took the phone gently from Priya. "It's Cobalt. What's your personal security situation?"

The voice of the sweet nurturing uncle disappeared while he was talking to his contract employee. "I have four guards here now. The gate stays closed. I have more men on the way." There was a pause. Court realized Arjun was leaving the dead air to convey something about his situation to his employee, something he didn't want to say in front of his niece. "We will be ready for some . . . limited engagement with Khan and his people."

"Right," Court said.

"But . . . anything you can do to protect my niece, I will be forever in your debt. I told Khan about you only to save her. She has done nothing wrong."

"Do you know where Khan is now?"

"I don't have any idea. I didn't know he was alive until you told me." He paused. "But . . . I suspect I know where he's going."

Again, something was unsaid, but Court and Arjun both knew the score. Khan would be coming to Arjun's house. Probably tonight.

"Yeah, I was thinking the same," replied Court, then said, "Priyanka is safe, and I'll keep her that way. You just need to focus on your situation."

"Priya *is* my situation." There was a lightness in his voice when he spoke of her that showed Court that Arjun really did care about his niece more than his own life. "Thank you for what you have done." Then, as before, his voice turned professional. "Anything you can do to stop the aims of Murad Khan . . . you would have the gratitude of a great number of people."

"Yeah," Court said. "I'm not doing this for anyone but me."

Priya took the phone back and spoke another minute with her uncle, they both cried, and then she hung up.

Court evaluated his situation, then looked to Priya. "Despite what he said, your uncle remains in incredible danger."

"I am no fool. I know that."

"I'm going to go there, tonight, once it's dark. I'll try to help him."

To this, she cocked her head in surprise. "You will?"

He didn't want to give the young woman false hope, but he said, "I will try. That's all I can say."

He asked her about her uncle's location, and she told him he lived in a large, secure home in the upscale Malabar Hill neighborhood on the water in south Mumbai. She became more and more animated as she described the building and the security measures there, as if the thin lifeline Court was providing to her uncle was all she needed to have hope that she could save him.

Finally, Court said, "I'll try to get him out of there safely. But not till nightfall. They are probably already surveilling the property. It would be a suicide mission if I went during the day."

Her newfound excitement subsided a little and she looked at him with suspicion. "I don't understand. You are not family, you have no loyalty to me or my uncle. Why would you help him? You were just hired to do a job. Why did you risk your life to help *me*? Why did you even come to India?"

"I am helping you both because I am responsible for what happened to you. And I am in India not just to help you and your uncle but also to find the man I wasn't able to kill in Pakistan."

"The man who interrogated me?"

"Yes."

"Who is this Khan? What did he do?"

Court spent the next five minutes answering this question. Priya didn't interrupt; she hung on every word.

When he was finished, she put her head in her hands. To Court it appeared she now understood exactly what this man was capable of. She said, "I remember, of course. I was thirteen when that happened. All those poor people."

"Yeah," Court said. "The man I saw the other night, the man you met, was the architect of the entire operation. The one who made it all happen. I thought he was dead." Court thought a moment, then amended this. "The entire world thought he was dead, but you and I now know that he is not."

She nodded slowly. "I understand why you did what you did in Algiers. But . . . now . . . Uncle Arjun is in danger. He can't stay safe from B-Company *and* Pakistani intelligence in India."

Court said, "If Khan is planning something here in Mumbai, it must be stopped. Arjun gave me up to B-Company, but that was just to save you. Still . . . he might know something about Khan and his plan."

Priya looked at Court for a long time. "No. He doesn't know anything about Khan. I heard them talk. They had never spoken before."

Court said nothing.

Priya's chin rose as she realized something. "You are lying to me. You don't need my uncle for information. You need my uncle to catch Khan."

She was young, inexperienced in this world, but Court determined she was an incredibly intelligent woman. He also realized that, at this moment anyway, she was smarter than he wanted her to be.

"I will help Arjun if there is any way I can. But if Khan comes after him, that does present me with an opportunity."

Priya nodded at this. "His life is not as important to you as Khan's death. I can see that on your face."

Court looked away. He hated when his true thoughts were so transparent. Finally, he said, "Can you blame me?"

She sat up a little straighter in her chair. "After what happened twelve years ago, I agree Khan needs to be stopped before he acts here in Mumbai." She added, "But my uncle is my uncle. He would die for me, and I would die for him. I am coming with you tonight."

Court shook his head. "Not happening."

"I don't know who you are, and I don't know what you do, other than, obviously, kill people. But whoever you are, I doubt you have the skills to slip into my uncle's home undetected, especially if B-Company is already there, and see what's going on."

He was suddenly confused. "And you *do*?"

With a confidence in her voice she said, "Arjun has been training me for years. Since I was a kid. He was Indian intelligence, and he said I would make a good technical support staffer because of my interest in information technology." She smiled mirthlessly. "He always said it was the safest job in the industry. Anyway, he left R&AW and started his own company, but he said he needed someone with exactly the skills I had learned. And he paid better than the government."

"And you learned how to . . . do what, exactly? Fly drones?"

She said, "The drones . . . that's new. I've done most of my work behind a computer, not in the field. I learned how to break into anything with a computer brain. At first it was a challenge he gave me while I was in college. Hacking, mostly. I used to practice on the camera system at his home. I've been in that system easily twenty times in the past five years."

Court waved away her comment. "If B-Company shows up, with or without Khan, the first thing they'll do is cut the video."

Priya said, "Arjun knows what he's doing, he has a dummy system. *This* they *will* cut. But the main security system is hidden in his house. The cameras are undetectable. He films everything, all the time, and I know how to access it if you can get me into his office. I also know how to get around his neighborhood without being seen. Malabar Hill has a lot of cameras. I've spent years walking those streets, identifying surveillance."

"Why?"

"My uncle was training me."

In talking about her value to Court's operation, Priya had regained some life in the past few minutes, now that she saw an objective in front of her. She said, "You'd be an idiot not to let me go."

He answered this with, "How long since you slept?"

"I didn't sleep, I meditated. It's more cleansing than sleep."

Court was dismissive about this. "Sleep is all the meditation I need. You, too. Let's get four hours, then we can build a plan to try to help your uncle."

"I'm coming with you," she said again.

"I know you are. I need you."

Priya nodded, satisfied finally.

There was only one bed in the flat, but the woman was small, only five-three, so she said she'd take the couch. But Court told her that would not be necessary. He looked around the unit, settled on the closet in the bedroom. He moved boxes and shoes off the floor, then took a pillow from the sofa and climbed in.

Priya just stared at him in confusion. "Are you a house cat?"

Court sniffed the air. "No, but I'll probably dream about fish." He shrugged, then motioned to the bed. "That's all yours. I like closets."

With a bemused look on her face, she lay down on the bed, and both of them fell asleep within minutes.

TWENTY-NINE

TWELVE YEARS AGO

Twenty-five minutes after Zack and Court left their layup position south of the chemical factory where the massacre had just taken place, the two men drove to the northeast through a heavy downpour. They were in a small Suzuki positioned in light traffic a quarter mile behind a blue Toyota Noah minivan that itself was a few hundred yards behind the three vehicles of the Kashmiri Resistance Front. Lennox, Redus, Morgan, and Pace were in the Toyota, and they had the "long eye" on the two jingle trucks and the red minibus as the entire terrorist convoy drove ever closer to Lahore.

The two vehicles full of Americans were in radio contact with each other, and they worried over the net that they might lose their targets in the city of eleven million people, so the Suzuki and the Toyota alternated the eye position every few miles, but the team made certain to never lose sight of their quarry.

Both Omar Mufti and the sacks of material stolen from the chemical plant were in the red minibus, so there was no difficult decision for Zack to make about which vehicle to tail if they split off. No, both his and Lennox's vehicles would stay on Mufti.

. . .

Thirty minutes after leaving the factory, Lennox found himself drifting farther behind the target, indicating that the three vehicles ahead were speeding up. He started to increase his own speed, struggling to keep the big red vehicles in sight through the rain.

As Lennox passed a turnoff, however, Jim Pace in the backseat called out to him. "Hey, Two. Minibus has exited the highway! It turned south, we just passed it."

"Shit," Lennox said. "I didn't see it." He continued on while radioing Zack behind him.

A half minute later, Zack and Court's Suzuki pulled off the highway at the same exit where Pace saw the minibus turn, and they caught sight of the red vehicle as it rolled down a congested road to the north.

The rain fell in sheets now, and both Court and Zack struggled to keep the target vehicle in sight as they made their way down the four-laned avenue filled with motorcycles, scooters, cars, and trucks, many of which were red, and all of which were in the way.

Omar Mufti's minibus was, thankfully, still in view through all the rain on the windshield, so they stayed on it for several blocks, closing to within thirty yards. The weather conditions, while making it harder to see the target vehicle, provided a net benefit to the followers. It would be literally impossible for Mufti and the men with him to pick out a tail through their rearview mirrors, and looking out through the back window to identify a specific car would be nearly as difficult.

After a few minutes of winding travel, they followed Mufti as he turned on Nazaria-e-Pakistan Avenue, and the rain began to slacken considerably. Zack slowed the Suzuki, dropping back a few more car lengths just to be sure he couldn't be sighted.

There were billboards everywhere, an orgy of commercial advertisement. Beautiful women in full makeup modeled clothing of every conceivable color. Furniture, watches, soft drinks, everything was advertised dramatically, sometimes garishly, from huge elevated signs.

This was clearly some sort of shopping district, and people were everywhere, even in the rain.

Up ahead, the minibus slowed and made a left turn into the drive of a three-story building. The gate at the entrance opened, and the minibus rolled through.

Zack continued on past it; fortunately the traffic was such that he had to creep by at a snail's pace. He and Court saw two men, already in the forecourt of the property, sliding the metal gate shut just after the vehicle entered, but the men wore raincoats with hoods, and neither Court nor Zack could make out any facial features at all.

As they passed by, Court read the English-language sign on the building out loud. "Hotel Days Inn. No vacancy."

"Sounds charming," Hightower said, and he radioed Lennox, letting him know where the KRF men had stopped. He continued down the street, looking for a place to observe the location from a safe distance.

Court said, "That hotel looked dead in the parking lot. I don't think it's even open."

They pulled into an ungated lot, parked with their nose facing Nazaria-e-Pakistan Avenue, and Court pulled his binos out of his pack. Looking over the location from fifty yards away, he said, "Definitely shuttered and dark."

Zack surveyed a digital map of the area on his phone. "There's a one-lane street behind it. I'll vector Lennox over there, see if he can get on a rooftop and take a look down over the wall. If he can set up a video feed, we can back off till Hanley tells us what to do."

Court said, "In the meantime, I'll make a pass by the front gate, try to get a shot of anything or anyone visible through the bars. If they start off-loading that AN, that would be good info to have." He began reaching into his pack, looking for something.

Zack grabbed him by the arm. "On foot? You want to just walk by on the sidewalk?"

"Why not?"

"Too easy to get compromised."

Court chuckled. "I got this." He pulled a black poncho out of the pack, began putting it on. "C'mon, Zack. Hanley put me on the team because I can do shit like this in my sleep."

Hightower relented. "Okay. On *this* side of the street, not over there. Keep the hood of that poncho covering your face."

Court opened the door. "Don't worry."

As he climbed out, Zack called after him, "And *don't* do it in your sleep!"

Even in what was now a moderate rain shower, there was significant foot traffic around Court as he headed up the sidewalk in the direction of the hotel. Women in traditional shalwar kameez passed by, umbrellas in hand.

He passed a corner shop offering ice cream and juices, a fabric retailer, and a small cluster of street stalls selling various types of dupattas, the long colorful veils worn by most women in the nation. Men, mostly in modern clothing, walked around or rolled by on scooters and motor bikes, and kids followed their moms into and out of shops on both sides of the street.

This felt like a reasonably upscale and safe area to Court, though he knew that some of the men who'd just killed dozens in a nearby town were now right in the middle of all the peace and tranquility.

Court pulled his cell phone out as he strolled along, looking at it as if checking for a call or text, but he took the opportunity to turn on his camera and zoom it in to the maximum setting. He then lowered the device in his left hand, careful to keep it more or less hidden from view to anyone across the street.

If Mufti had posted sentries in the upper windows of the hotel, they might well spot him taking photos if he was obvious about it, so Court endeavored not to be obvious about it.

A corner barbershop was directly opposite the hotel, and Court slowed to look at the signs on the glass. The writing was in Urdu; he didn't have a clue what any of it said, but he took his time window shopping for a haircut, with his left hand down at his side and his phone filming the location across the street behind him.

After thirty seconds he moved on, past a man standing under a tarp in front of a big metal fire pit grilling sweet potatoes, and he walked a full block to the west. And then, despite Zack's orders that he keep his pass confined to the far side of the street, he crossed to the same side as the target location. The rain had lessened a little more, and he noticed most men weren't wearing raincoats at all now. He took the opportunity to pull off his poncho and drop it on the ground next to a garbage can, where he was certain it would be picked up by a passerby in seconds.

And then he headed back up the street.

He crossed in front of the gate to the hotel with a purposeful stride that matched most everyone else's around him and, in so doing, acquired upside-down video of the hotel and the entrance to it by holding his phone in his left hand and orienting the lens in the right direction. Court didn't even glance into the property as he passed; he just continued on, crossed the street down at the end of the block, and made his way back to the parking lot.

Once Court sat back in the passenger seat of the Suzuki and closed the door, he said, "Did you realize we are parked at a fertility clinic?"

Zack looked over his shoulder, saw that the sign said Sakina Fertility Hospital, and then turned back to Court. "I fucking told you not to cross the street."

"I know what I'm doing, boss."

"So do I, and even if I didn't, I am your TL, so you do what I fucking say. You follow my orders or we are going to have issues, Six. You got that?"

Court looked at Zack, fought a little eye roll. "Got it. Now, how 'bout we look and see if I captured anything?"

Hightower remained angry, but the two of them looked at the video, flipping it upright first, then stopping it and moving frame by frame as it captured the inside of the hotel property through the vertical bars of the metal gate.

There were five people visible inside, but two faces were obscured by raincoats. The images of the others were blurred in most of the frames, and most of the ones that were clear enough didn't reveal any faces. Mufti's white shirt was visible as he stood out of the rain in the covered parking lot that made up the ground floor of the building, which was raised on stanchions, with a staircase in the middle heading up to the hotel.

On video from Court's second pass by the hotel, he again advanced the images frame by frame. About forty-five frames in, shortly before he lost sight of the inside of the property, he'd caught a single image that he thought might prove to be useful.

Omar Mufti stood, his back to the camera, and in front of him were two other men, facing right towards Court's lens. Their attention was on Mufti, and the images were fair. One man was small, with a bushy mustache. He was in his twenties and wore a long brown kurta. There was a slight smile on his face. Next to him, almost shielded by the back of Mufti's head but not quite, was a man in his thirties, with short dark hair parted to the side. He was taller than the man next to him but shorter than Mufti.

Court said, "Any idea who these clowns are?"

"Negative," Zack said, "but I didn't see either at the chemical plant. They might have been waiting back at the hotel."

Court said, "Too important to get their hands dirty on the raid, maybe?"

"We're not analysts, kid." He added, "Vance and his team can get these images cleaned up enough for facial recog. I'm sending them to Rooster right now."

Court said, "What do we do in the meantime?"

"Something you're gonna do a lot of."

"Wait?"

"Yep." Zack pulled out of the fertility clinic to go find a large parking lot someplace where they didn't have to worry about being compromised by the KRF.

THIRTY

Matthew Hanley sat in the ultra-secure Sensitive Compartmented Information Facility in the main CIA building at Camp Chapman, staring at a monitor on a wall and waiting for a video feed to be initiated. He had the images just sent from his Ground Branch assets in Lahore cued up on his laptop, and he could share them with the other participant of the video-conference in real time, as soon as the other attendee arrived on the call.

Hanley was hoping to get lucky, to bypass the time required to send the images back to Langley for evaluation, and to get an answer on who these men were, right here and right now.

From what he knew of the man with whom he was about to speak, it was very possible he might recognize the two unknowns at the hotel where the Kashmiri Resistance Front brought what analysts had determined to be just under two tons of material suspected to be ammonium nitrate. Chief of CIA Station Islamabad Ted Appleton knew a staggering number of players here on the Indian subcontinent. But even if he didn't know either of the men, Appleton and his station could get to work on the images and possibly get him an answer faster than the analysts at Langley could.

Hanley hoped their hunt for the identities of these men would be something of a moot point soon. Omar Mufti and the suspected explosives were both on site, and Hanley had already sent this information to Denny Carmichael at SAD, who would already be on the phone to Greg DeFalco, deputy director for operations for the CIA. DeFalco would, in turn, go to the director, who might or might not need to go to the president for the green light to send in Ground Branch.

Hanley thought it likely that he was going to get the raid he wanted today, but he would need Appleton's help to pull it off. He wasn't sending Zack and the others in with handguns. Non-official cover agents in country would need to deliver weapons and body armor for the lightly equipped American team in Lahore, and Appleton could make that happen easily, or he could slow the process down.

Hanley needed for this to be a good, productive videoconference to grease the wheels in order to make the next few hours go smoothly, but he harbored serious concerns that today's hurriedly arranged meeting would be, instead, somewhat confrontational in nature.

He didn't know the chief of station in Islamabad personally, but everyone at the Agency who had been around since the beginning of the war on terror knew a lot about him. Appleton had risen through the ranks in a twenty-three-year career that had taken him all around the world. He became deputy chief of station in New Delhi, running assets that earned him acclaim and eventually promotion, and then he was bumped up to his current office in Islamabad.

Serving in both India and Pakistan made Appleton a go-to when expertise on the region at large, the conflict between the two nations, or the players involved was needed.

The feed initiated finally, and a graying man in his fifties wearing a suit coat but no tie looked into the camera with a serious face that made no attempt to hide his annoyance. This looked like bad news to Hanley, and any residual hope Hanley had of this convo going better than he expected evaporated just as soon as Appleton spoke.

"I recently heard that I have cowboys running around on my range, and you, I am told, are their trail boss."

Before Hanley could reply, the station chief said, "I understand the need for Ground Branch ops all the way over in the FATA. I don't like it, but I get it. Islamabad station has less influence over there in no-man's-land along the Afghan border. But in fucking *Lahore*? You have your door kickers running around all the way on the eastern side of the country? This is *my* turf, Hanley."

This wasn't the first time Matt and his team had ruffled the feathers of a station chief by running a mission in their area of operations. It didn't really faze the big former Green Beret. He just patiently waited for the chief of station to finish his opening rant.

Appleton added, "I don't blame you, of course. You're doing your job. I just wish Carmichael would keep you guys out of here so *I* can do *my* job."

Now it was Hanley's turn to talk, and Hanley knew how to play the game at CIA. If he acted contrite in any way, Appleton would see it as weakness, and he'd push harder against any further Ground Branch ops in Pakistan.

So instead, Matt Hanley just smiled a little and said, "First, thanks for the meeting, sorry to pull it on you so fast. Second . . . if Lahore is, in fact, *your* turf, you must certainly be aware of the mass execution of dozens of civilians this morning at a chemical plant in Sarai Mughal, twenty-five miles to the southwest of the city."

Appleton showed surprise on his face, and Hanley continued. "A chemical plant that produces ammonium nitrate for fertilizer and for industrial explosives. Approximately four thousand pounds were stolen, we have estimated, and then driven into Lahore in the last hour."

Appleton was speechless.

After a brief pause, Hanley said, "Near as I can tell, Ted, you've got yourself a new terrorist organization nobody had even heard of six months ago, and now they're snatching enough ammonium nitrate to blow up half of downtown Islamabad. *That's* your turf today, so how would you say you guys at Islamabad station are doing right now?"

He imagined Appleton was seething, but to the man's credit, he remained professional. "It was the Kashmiri Resistance Front?"

"Correct. Mufti is on site at a safe house with the explosives right now."

"Send me everything you have."

Hanley said, "I will. I definitely will, because I need your help."

"You aren't taking over control of—"

Hanley ignored the station chief. "First, though, I need to see if you recognize a couple of other personalities at the target location." Without waiting for a response, he clicked the images on his laptop in front of him and sent them to the SCIF in Islamabad.

Appleton put on his eyeglasses, an air of annoyance in the act. Then he clicked on the images and peered closer.

As he did so, Hanley said, "The man with the white shirt, the one with his back to the camera, is Major Omar Mufti. We don't know who the other two are."

Hanley was looking right into the station chief's eyes on the screen as they widened to their full extent. Then the man lurched back in shock.

The Ground Branch group chief immediately questioned the station chief. "Who are they?"

But Appleton did not answer. He just stared.

"You obviously recognize them, Ted. Who . . . are . . . they?"

In an almost hoarse whisper, Appleton said, "I'm going to have to . . . get back to you." There was no denying he saw something that shocked him, but it seemed as if Appleton didn't want Ground Branch to know what he'd seen.

But Matt Hanley wasn't having it. "Stalling now isn't going to do you any good. I've already requested approval for a task force raid on this safe house. We've got the second-in-command of the organization in pocket, along with enough explosives to cause a hell of a lot of misery."

Appleton began shaking his head while Hanley spoke. "No. Absolutely not. You *cannot* send armed Americans into that location. You have to stand down."

"Now why would I do that, Ted?"

"Because . . . because this needs to be handled . . . delicately."

"Trust me. My guys are incredibly delicate when they need to be. Head-shots only. Wouldn't want that AN to go boom, now would we?" Hanley knew that wasn't what Appleton meant, but he was goading him on.

"You can't do this," Appleton stammered. "This is a diplomatic matter, not a—"

"*Diplomatic?*" Hanley barked in surprise. "What, you want to seek UN condemnation? Is that it? Shit, where I come from, there isn't anything terribly diplomatic about a group of terrorists with bomb-making materials."

To Hanley's surprise, the mild-mannered-looking Appleton shouted now. "Those are not terrorists!" His face reddened as he yelled, as if he were on the verge of experiencing a cardiac event.

Hanley leaned forward in his chair. In a measured tone he asked, "Who . . . are . . . they . . . Ted?"

Appleton let out a long sigh, then leaned forward, closer to the camera, his arms on the desk in front of him. Seemingly defeated, he spoke quietly now. "The man on the left, the younger one. I don't know him. We'll run the image."

"But the other?"

"The man on the right . . . His name is Murad Khan."

The name meant nothing to Hanley. "And *what* is Murad Khan, if he's not a terrorist?"

Appleton leaned back in his chair. "He's ISI."

Now Hanley sat back in his chair, as well. "Well, shit."

"He's an officer in FCU, the Foreign Coordination Unit."

"How do you know of him? FCU is pretty covert, from what I understand."

Appleton shrugged. Rubbed his ruby red face. "We have a source. That's all I'm prepared to say." He hesitated, then added, "I also know something else about him."

"Which is?"

"He's Kashmiri. Originally from the Indian side. A Muslim, he was snuck over the border to Pakistan as a boy."

Matt Hanley looked at the image on his laptop now. "A Kashmiri terrorist with ties to the government." Slowly, almost reverently, he said, "Well hello, Pasha. Nice to meet you."

"Wait a second," Appleton said. "That's jumping to one hell of a conclusion. We don't know if he's the leader of anything, much less the KRF. He could be running an op against them. You don't have a clue what the ISI is up to."

"He's not running an op, Ted. He's running the show. We don't know what their plan is, but now we know it involves mass murder and a couple tons of ammonium nitrate."

"We don't know Khan is a terrorist."

Hanley added, "Once my guys get there, he's going to look a lot like a terrorist to them, I can promise you that."

Appleton said, "If the U.S. kills Khan, right there in the middle of the KRF, we will get fallout like you wouldn't even believe."

"You're talking politics, Ted. I'm talking something else entirely."

Appleton was almost begging. "Look, Matt. I've got a source who can find out what Khan's status is currently with ISI. What he's working on. That intel is the clarity we need. I just need a couple days to connect with my source so they can get the intel and get back to me."

Hanley replied, "You don't have a couple of days. I've got a team of Ground Branch shooters a mile away from a terrorist safe house, a dirty intel officer, and bomb-making materials. My guys have real-time images of the location.

"I have everything I need to hit that building and end this bullshit today."

"Matt . . ."

"And I'll get the approval, too. You know I will. Best thing you can do is hunker down and get ready for any diplomatic consequences that come our way after. I know I'm making your tough job tougher, but *you* know this is the right call. If Khan, Mufti, or the AN make it into the wind while I have a team in position to intercept them, then that would be on me, and I'm not going to let that happen."

"Matt, just a day. Give me a day and I can—"

"I'm notifying Carmichael that there is an ISI officer on site, but I'm reasonably sure this will change nothing. We're sending a priority request to your station to provide my men with some small arms and equipment for the hit. I'd appreciate that happening before the sanction comes through. That bus full of explosives can leave at any time and disappear into the second-largest city in Pakistan." Hanley added, "Which is, as you mentioned, your turf."

"Matt. Listen to me. This is bigger than terrorism. This is international relations. You cutthroats in Ground Branch don't get to make policy."

"Watch us," Hanley said, and then he ended the feed with a press of a button.

At the U.S. embassy in Islamabad, Pakistan, fifty-two-year-old Ted Appleton rubbed his hands through his thinning hair, pushing sweat down the back of his neck, then sat up straight and resolute. He left the SCIF, closed the door behind him, retrieved his phone from a locker, and headed up the hall.

He stepped into a restroom, checked to make certain no one else was inside, then locked the door.

He dialed a local number and sat back on the vanity, his eyes skyward as if he blamed the heavens for what he was about to do.

After several rings, a woman with a Pakistani accent answered in English.

"Hello."

"Yes," Appleton said. "Sorry to bother. Is this Majid's phone?"

There was a slight pause. "You must have misdialed, sir."

"My apologies. Did I dial four seven three oh?"

Another brief pause. "You did not."

"Have a good day," Appleton said, and he hung up the phone with a shaking hand.

The woman on the other end of the line was code named Leopard, and she was the source who had given him every bit of intel about the KRF and the inner workings of the ISI.

His call told her that he needed an emergency meeting. The two digits at the beginning of the string of numbers that he'd asked her if he'd dialed indicated where they would meet, a code indicating a park fifteen minutes' drive from the embassy. And the second pair in the number, three-zero, indicated that she had only thirty minutes to get to their prearranged meeting location.

She would be both frightened and furious, this Appleton knew, but he also knew how important it was that she dig into Murad Khan immediately, before Appleton's own organization killed the very source his agent was using to find out about the KRF.

THIRTY-ONE

PRESENT DAY

Court and Priyanka arrived well after sunset in the Malabar Hill neighborhood where her uncle lived. They walked along a leafy street within sight of the ocean back down the hill behind them, and Court marveled at the beautifully landscaped gardens, the large stately homes, and the peace and quiet here, especially considering they were at the southern tip of otherwise chaotic and congested Mumbai.

Seven and a half miles away was the locality of Dharavi, the largest slum in Asia, with a population of over one million. But here . . . looking around, Court saw that these people were living large.

He leaned closer to Priya as they walked. "Your uncle worked for the government?"

She seemed annoyed by the comment and the obvious inference behind it, that he was involved in something illegal. "He used to, then he started his own business, as you already know. Remember, you worked for him?"

"Yeah, but—"

"He did well for himself. There is no law against that." Then she shrugged. "He never told me that he was doing anything underhanded. He knows I wouldn't have worked for him if I knew he did."

Court dropped it. To him, Arjun was just another shady broker in the world of contract agents, hit men, and thieves. But to the woman walking along stiffly now, he was family.

Many of the homes were gated, but many were not, relying on incredibly thick, almost junglelike vegetation to secure the property. Occasionally cars came up or down the lightly traveled two-lane road, and Court and Priya would step behind some piece of foliage in case B-Company gangsters were on their way to, or on their way back from, Arjun's house.

They'd made it most of the way to the location Priya had indicated on a map, and then, without a word to Court, she turned off the road and began walking deeper into vegetation at the edge of the yard of a large yellow house.

Court caught up with her, took her by the arm. "Where are you going?"

"There is a back way." She motioned to the house. "The man who lived here died in May. The home is for sale; I am sure there are still security cameras and motion lights, but I don't think there are guards. We can get to the rear of my uncle's property if you follow me."

This made sense to Court, and he trailed behind her as she began pushing again through leafy palms. He was unaccustomed to having a guide lead him to a target, but his plan to creep up to the front entrance and kick in the door seemed like the much weaker strategy now.

Court first saw the home where Arjun Bandari lived shortly before nine p.m. There were lights on around the property, close to the main house, and lights on inside the building, although sheer blinds made it impossible to see the inside.

Priya started to move closer to the two-story white house now, but Court stopped her. "Give me a second."

"To do what?"

"Look. Listen. Smell."

She remained quiet next to him for the next couple of minutes. He detected no movement inside through the large windows, nor did he hear any noise beyond the natural sounds of a residential neighborhood.

"Something's not right," she said. "There should be movement. He said he had eight guards and more on the way. Where are they?"

Court thought to himself that it was pretty obvious they were too late, but he didn't say this. "I'm going in. I'll text you when it's clear."

"I'll come with you."

"You'll stay right here." When she started to protest, he said, "I promised your uncle I'd keep you out of danger. Just wait for me to check it out, and then I'll text you." Court left her there, then moved across the back garden, slowly, with his pistol low in his right hand.

She watched him disappear, then heard nothing for the next few minutes, other than the sounds of leaves and branches rustling in the breeze from the nearby bay.

Eventually she saw lights being turned off in different rooms, until the entire rear side of the home went dark.

Finally her phone vibrated, and she looked down at the message she'd received.

"Come in." She rose and began moving forward, her legs trembling, terrified of what she would find.

Court was standing at the back door in the darkness when Priya appeared in front of him. Her eyes were wide; it was fear, it was apprehension. He had seen these emotions in enough people over enough years to recognize them easily.

And for her part, the Indian woman seemed to do a good job reading his face.

She asked, "What is it? What did you find?"

Court answered softly, "I'm sorry."

She started to cry, keeping her sobs as quiet as possible. "He's dead?"

Court nodded. He gave her just a moment, then said, "He's in the living room. Members of his guard force, too. It looks like someone disabled the main camera system; I found the computer in the room off the kitchen where the feed was being sent, but it's full of bullet holes and the hard drive is gone. I don't know where the other is located, so I'm going to need you to go inside and check that."

She knelt down in the doorway, her face in her hands; he could tell she was doing her best to be strong, but clearly she held herself responsible for her uncle's death.

He gave her a few more seconds, but only a few. "We've got to move. If there are recordings of tonight somewhere, we need to take a look and then get out of here."

Without a word to Court, she stood and passed him by, wiping her eyes. He looked out over the darkened backyard, made sure he didn't see any movement there in the shadows, then turned and followed her in.

She stepped through the living room, having the presence of mind not to turn on one of the lights that Six had just turned off. She moved slowly, using the light that filtered in through the thin blinds over the floor-to-ceiling window facing the rear garden to make her way over to the dead men on the floor.

Arjun Bandari was in the center of the living room, stripped from the waist up, sitting in a kitchen chair with his hands tied behind his back. His legs were splayed out, his head back, his nose and chin jutting towards the ceiling. Court had placed a kitchen towel over Bandari's face; nevertheless, even in the low light, the blood showing through it and the wounds visible on his bare arms made it obvious he'd been tortured.

Four men, surely hired security officers, lay dead on the floor nearby. Facedown, as if they'd been executed. Court wondered if there were more dead outside on the grounds.

Priya stepped over to her uncle's body. Court moved to stop her from removing the towel, but she just placed her hand on his shoulder, then leaned over and kissed Arjun's forehead through the towel. Court was sympathetic, but his prevailing emotion was one of urgency; they had to get whatever intelligence they could from this location and then go.

He felt bad about the prospect of hurrying her along, so he was glad when she rose back up and began walking again, picking up the pace as she made it to the circular stairs.

Court followed her up to the second floor, then into Arjun's office. He'd flipped a light off here a couple minutes earlier as he cleared the home with his pistol, so he knew the space was empty.

She walked to his desk, sat down like she lived here, and accessed his desktop computer. Within seconds she had the application that controlled the security system open.

After a few seconds more, she said, "The covert system is still operating. They didn't catch it."

She tapped some keys; Court stood behind her while a dozen or more camera feeds appeared.

He saw the live image of the death downstairs and hoped the woman wouldn't focus on this horrific image, because that would only slow them down.

To her credit, Priyanka stayed on mission. She clicked the mouse and began sliding it, drawing the time backwards on the cameras as she did so. Slowly at first, and then more rapidly. Other than their arrival, there was no movement on the camera at all in the last half hour, meaning Arjun had been dead at least that long, but when she started to go back farther, he knelt down next to her.

"Maybe you should wait outside. Let me do this."

"I'm already upset. I'll be fine."

Court said, "I think it might be better if I watch this alone."

"You don't speak Hindi."

"Khan is Pakistani."

"He speaks perfect Hindi. Trust me, I spoke with him." She asked, "Have you?"

It was a rhetorical question, but she definitely had a point. He doubted there would be a lot of intel derived from what was said during the interrogation with Arjun, but he didn't know for sure. He nodded, then steeled himself to witness a young woman watch a close family member die brutally.

She stopped scrolling back and then typed *15:00* into a box on the screen. When she hit enter, the cameras showed the light of day.

Arjun Bandari was alive. He walked around the house, speaking with armed guards, looking out windows. This was well after Priya had escaped, and after she and Court had communicated with him, so at this point the man knew what he was up against.

He spoke on his phone from time to time, but Court didn't want to be here in a house full of dead guys for any longer than he had to be, so he asked her to keep advancing and not to translate his calls. Four p.m., five p.m., everything looked the same. There seemed to be about eight armed guards around the property, and Arjun was clearly paranoid of an attack, but otherwise the scene around the home was unchanged.

And then, around six p.m., a pair of new guards showed up. They wore the same black polo shirts that the other eight or so men Court counted around the property wore. They went and spoke to Arjun briefly, as well as one of the other guards, and then they went back down to the secured iron gate.

Something about them piqued Court's interest. He asked Priya to select the camera showing the front gate; it was apparently positioned high on the front wall of the home, and she advanced in eight times speed. The two men talked to two other guards there for a minute, and then something happened, but it was so quick, neither Priya nor Court could tell exactly what it was.

"Oh my God," she said, and she backed up a minute, then watched the event in normal speed.

All the guards were equipped with submachine guns, but when the first two men's backs were turned, the new guards pulled knives from under their shirts, rushed up behind their unsuspecting prey, grabbed them both by the mouth, and drove the blades, hilt deep, into their backs.

Priya gasped.

Both dead men were dragged quickly into the tiny guard shack and dumped there. Apparently the killers pressed the button to activate the gate, because it soon began to slide open.

Two sleek Mercedes V-Class vans rolled into view and pulled up the driveway, and then the gate was again shut.

Priyanka deftly switched camera views to the front-door feed. This camera was hidden in a light fixture right above the door, and by viewing it, they could see ten men piling out of the two vehicles, suppressed submachine guns at the ready as they charged forward, splitting off into different groups, each with a sector of the property to clear.

Switching to the foyer camera, Court and Priya watched two guards attempt to engage the intruders, then drop dead from silenced subguns before they even fired a shot in their defense.

The attackers flew through the living room; Priya feverishly changed views to try to keep up with the action. Four shooters ran up the stairs, and she switched views to Arjun's office, the room the two of them were now in.

Arjun was here, standing behind the desk exactly where Court now stood. He pulled a pistol out of the drawer, stood up straight, and put the gun to his head. Court himself wouldn't have hesitated; he would have known what was in store for him if he was taken alive, and he would have *much* rather gone out on his own terms than on the terms of Murad Khan.

But for some reason, Arjun tossed the gun to the ground and raised his hands, just as the four attackers filed into the room.

He had to have known he'd just given up the only easy road, and for the life of him, Court couldn't understand why he'd not just put a bullet in his brain and saved himself the pain.

"Why didn't he do it?" Priya asked in a cracked whisper, and Court admitted he had no idea.

There were more engagements on the property, but because of the suppressed weapons and the knives used by the attacking force, the other guards were, without exception, caught unaware and unprepared.

Court didn't see a single gunshot from any of the private security force Arjun Bandari had trusted with his life.

Finally, there were only four guards left—all inside the home—they were surrounded, and they surrendered without firing a shot.

You can't get good help these days, Court thought, but he didn't say it out loud.

Even though Court already knew how this show ended, he cursed at the men for giving up their guns, because now those four men were all facedown on the tile downstairs with holes in the backs of their heads.

Arjun was led down the stairs, his hands lashed behind his back with flexicuffs brought by the attackers. Then he was sat down on a kitchen chair that had been dragged in, the guards were placed on the floor next to him, and then the gunmen just waited.

Finally, Murad Khan entered the room from the front door. Court looked at the digital time readout on the feed and saw that this happened less than ninety minutes before he and Priya arrived at the home.

Court clenched his fists, but he kept his eyes on the screen. Softly to Priya he said, "This . . . this will be more difficult to watch than you can possibly imagine."

To this, she just said, "Trust me. Right now I wish you spoke Hindi."

"Yeah, maybe I can find another translator and we can take the—"

"Stop talking, please," she said, and she turned up the volume.

Over the next several minutes, Priya relayed the conversation to Court. Khan asking Bandari, over and over, about the American who saw him in Algiers, and the identity of the person who hired him for the job.

Arjun kept repeating that he didn't know, but he thought both parties were working for R&AW. This wasn't good enough for Khan, however, and Arjun Bandari was tortured mercilessly, both by Khan and by henchmen ordered into action by Khan. The Indian broker's hands were shattered, his face was pounded by a fist wrapped in a bathroom towel, cigarettes were extinguished on his arms and neck.

Court looked down at Priya while this was going on, and he saw that she had averted her eyes. Still, the wails from her uncle had to be having an incredible psychological impact on her.

Court could hear in Khan's voice, finally, that he was beginning to believe the Indian, and to Court this meant the end was coming soon. One more attempt to elicit a different answer came in the form of a long kitchen knife, its tip turned red hot by putting it on a gas stove, being placed against the side of Arjun's face by one of the B-Company goons.

Bandari's head thrashed from side to side; he screamed over and over. Priya wasn't looking, only listening with her head in her hands.

And when he screamed a final word, she fell to the floor, sobbing.

This was the only word uttered during the interrogation by either man that Court understood.

"Priya!"

Court left her alone while he watched the end. Khan took the long knife, came closer, and knelt down in front of Arjun, who at this point was as beaten and spent as Court had ever seen anyone in his life. Khan spoke, and Priya, though on the floor fighting off hysterics, retained the presence of mind to translate. Through tears she said, "The name of the person who hired you, or we continue. I swear to you, if you give it to me, I will end things fast."

Court saw Arjun's mouth move, but he heard no sound. Neither did Priya, apparently, because she'd translated nothing.

Khan, on the other hand, seemed to cock his head to the side. Hurriedly he moved closer, up to Arjun's ear, but in so doing he covered the view of the camera in the wall to Arjun's face.

Khan shouted, and Priya translated. "Again!"

Khan was demanding Bandari repeat himself.

Whether or not Arjun responded to this, Court couldn't tell; he couldn't hear the man's gasping whispers any longer, and he couldn't see the man's face with Khan in the way.

But then, to Court's astonishment, Khan stumbled back like he'd been poleaxed. He recovered after a minute, though he continued to look unspeakably distressed. Then he lifted the knife higher in his right hand, took a single step forward, and slashed the Indian man's throat without another word.

Blood spurted; Khan turned away, giving Arjun Bandari no more of his attention, and then he began walking out the front door without speaking to anyone. Court got a last glimpse of his face as he did this, and he could see obvious worry, almost panic, in his eyes.

"What the fuck was that all about?" Court muttered to himself.

He stopped the video when everyone left in the two vans.

Priya had regained some control over her faculties, and she sat on the floor now. While wiping her eyes, she said, "He has a safe. Over there, hidden behind a panel in the wall."

"Do you know the combination?"

"Of course not. He kept that very private."

Court didn't think Arjun's safe would contain anything relevant to his mission, but still he went over and popped open the panel. A three-foot-high and very secure-looking combination safe sat there, apparently undisturbed.

Safe cracking was almost impossible without skills, tools, and time, none of which Court possessed. "We've got to get out of here," he said, and he took Priya by the elbow, then started for the door.

She took the hard disk from the computer, securing the record of her uncle's murder as well as the record of her and the man she knew as Cobalt's presence, and slipped it into her bag. She followed him back downstairs, back through the living room past the bodies, and then back outside in the dark.

Court expected that the police wouldn't find this gruesome scene until the next morning, but when they found it, they would look into Arjun's past with the intelligence services and pull out all the stops trying to find out who was responsible.

Ten minutes later he and Priya walked through the dark residential neighborhood down the hill towards Nepeansea Road in hopes of hailing a cab there. They were both alone with their thoughts for a minute or two, and then Priya spoke. "I need a laptop. One better than yours. There is a place open all night near the apartment."

"Good," Court said, and he handed her a wad of cash.

"What will you do?" she asked as she took it.

To her surprise, Cobalt had an answer. "When we get back to the fish market, I have to make a phone call. I know a guy who might be able to point me towards someone who could help us. It's a long shot, but I don't see any other options."

"This is a friend of yours?"

"A colleague I trust. He knows people, and he knows things."

She said, "Well, I need to go shopping. I'll buy a couple of laptops, some other computer equipment. I'm no good with a gun. If I am to be of any help, I'm going to need all my gadgets."

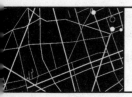

THIRTY-TWO

TWELVE YEARS AGO

Fatima Jinnah Park is a large greenspace in north central Islamabad, just fifteen minutes' drive from the U.S. embassy. CIA station chief Ted Appleton took regular walks in the park, normally during his lunch hour or right after work, flanked by four CIA plainclothed security officers who knew to stay far enough away from their protectee but vigilant to the surroundings nonetheless.

There were playgrounds, mosques, prayer areas, amphitheaters, and other structures in the park, and even a massive cricket ground, but it was also an intercity forest of dozens of acres, intersected by footpaths and little paved roads.

Appleton wasn't here because he liked the exercise or the air. He was purposefully unathletic, and the smog in Islamabad was thick and oppressive. But he had been coming here regularly to establish a baseline pattern of life for anyone who might be interested in his movements. The curiosity of anyone following him would be piqued if the American CIA chief randomly drove to a park and walked deep into the trees—it wouldn't take a master spy catcher to deduce something was afoot. But Appleton had been to Fatima Jinnah Park over one hundred times since he'd arrived in country, so anyone curious about him would have long since lost interest in his regular journeys here.

The four security men had fanned out on the footpath, deep in the woods, listening to the last of the Salat Ui Asr, the afternoon call to prayer, blare from the speakers in the mosque on this cloudy afternoon. Appleton was there, as well, and while this was just a normal day at the office for the armed Agency protection force, for Appleton this was personal, and his hands trembled.

He pulled a tiny radio from his pocket and clicked the transmit key. "Neal. Push your team back another twenty-five yards. I don't want my agent seeing anyone."

"Sir, we won't be much use seventy-five yards away from you."

"Just do it," he snapped, then made himself relax a little. "Please."

"Yes, sir," the leader of the security detail said. In seconds Appleton was, as far as he could see in any direction, the only person here standing on the footpath.

But not for long.

A woman approached from the east. She wore a shalwar kameez with a blue and gold dupatta covering her hair. She was in her forties, beautiful, stunningly so, deep brown complected with dramatic eyes and full lips.

Her eyes locked on his from the moment he saw her, and Appleton knew why. She was searching for any indication that there was some emergency, some trouble that meant she was in imminent danger here.

There were strict protocols established by Appleton to meet with this agent; these protocols had kept them both safe in three cities, in two countries, for well over six years, and Appleton had thrown them all out the window today for this hastily arranged meet.

She was, quite visibly and quite understandably, concerned now, though they had used the established emergency meeting code.

When she was in earshot, he fought the urge to call out and assure her she was fine. Instead he waited until she walked all the way up to him. Her eyes showed fright, and her gait and posture reflected the tension she felt.

He tried to relax her with his soft tone. "I'm so sorry to make you come today, Aimal. I know it is irregular."

She asked the only question he would have expected her to open with. "Have we been compromised?"

"No." Appleton shook his head. "You are safe. I told you I'd never let anything happen to you."

"So . . . then. Why did you—"

Appleton interrupted. "Did you hear about Lahore?"

"The chemical factory? Yes. My office is collecting data on it now, but the camera recordings were erased, and there were no witnesses left alive."

"You told me the KRF was just going to perform reconnaissance on the location."

"That was the information we had. Our intelligence was that they were just going to surveil it for a follow-on force that had not yet been assembled. They weren't supposed to attack it."

When Appleton seemed to be looking for his words, she said, "What is it, Ted?"

Appleton shrugged; he didn't want to reveal this, but he trusted his agent implicitly. "Well, we had a team in position to watch the entire event."

"*What?*" Her voice conveyed anger and panic. "You told the CIA about the factory?"

"Of course I told the CIA. That's how this all works. But that's not even the problem."

"Maybe not a problem for you, you get a feather in your cap for being right. Makes you look like the star that you are to them. But it's a problem for me, isn't it? I was one of a very limited number of people with access to that intelligence. FCU will do a review to see where the leak came from. They might find me."

"You'll be fine. The Agency team wasn't compromised. Nobody knows they were there. Yet."

"Yet? What's happening?"

"The CIA team, they are in Lahore now, and they are about to attack a building where the chemicals were brought from the factory. There are somewhere in the neighborhood of ten KRF personnel inside the location now."

Leopard had known Appleton for many years. She knew there was more he had to say.

"*And?*"

"And . . . there . . . right now at the location, with Omar Mufti and the other KRF fighters, is a man who has been photographed. The photograph has been shared with me, and I presume that by now, it's also been shared with headquarters."

Aimal's eyes narrowed. "*What* man?"

After a look around to the bushes to reassure himself they were alone, he said, "Murad Khan."

Aimal looked at Appleton like he'd suddenly grown a horn on his forehead. "*What?* What are you saying?"

"Khan . . . We think the man you have been working closely with . . . is, in actuality, Pasha the Kashmiri."

"That . . . that's impossible. All the intelligence I've given you for the last six months about Pasha and the Kashmiri Resistance Front was acquired by Director Khan and his agents in the field."

"I know."

"Why would he be giving us—"

"Think about it. What has he given you?"

"Nobody had ever heard of the KRF until Khan's source in Kashmir revealed their existence. ISI implicated them in a series of attacks in Quetta, in the FATA, and even over the border against the Americans in Afghanistan."

"After the fact."

"After the fact, yes. We don't have real-time intelligence on the KRF, not yet anyway."

"Okay, go on."

"Khan's own confidential agents revealed that the organization's second-in-command was a military officer who flew helicopters for the Army Aviation Corps. I was the one who went through dozens and dozens of names before finding out that Major Omar Mufti, a Kashmiri, had been away from his post during two of the attacks in the FATA and one of the attacks over the Afghanistan border."

"What else?"

She thought a moment. "Peshawar. Khan's office found out Mufti would be in that military base south of Peshawar, in advance, and I notified you."

Appleton just nodded. This was another busted mission, and she saw on his face that he felt the intelligence Khan had given her had been tainted.

Aimal had been a Pakistani intelligence agent long before she became a double agent for the Americans. She had been doing this for twenty years, long enough to know what Appleton was thinking now.

"It's not disinformation, Ted. It's good, solid, actionable intelligence."

Appleton nodded distractedly, still thinking. "I've been feeding this to Langley for months. They've been frustrated at every turn, and the KRF is growing stronger and bolder. Now they have a Ground Branch team ready to go in against Khan and the others."

"Khan is not with them! If he is there at the KRF safe house, then he is undercover. He *has* to be."

"A department director who goes undercover?"

Aimal sniffed. "Look at you, Ted. How many station chiefs meet agents in the field? Quite a few, I'd imagine."

Appleton sighed. "Well, if Khan's not dead in the next few hours, I guess I need you to find out what this undercover mission is all about."

She shook her head. "No. No, Teddy. We must warn him."

Appleton cocked his head. "*Warn* him? Are you crazy?"

"Obviously I can't call him up and say, 'Sir, the CIA is outside, run!' But surely there is something we can do that will stop your Agency from going in and making a massive mistake."

"There are two tons of ammonium nitrate and a dozen or so mass murderers in that hotel right now. Going in and ridding the world of the threat of both would *not* be a massive mistake."

Her eyes filled with anger and mistrust. "So you agree . . . Khan should die?"

Appleton had disappointed her, and their interpersonal dynamic meant that he felt the sting of her judgment like a stiletto in his heart. He said, "No . . . I need to know more about him and what he's doing. But it looks bad. It looks *very* bad."

"Then let me find a way to stop this CIA attack. You do nothing, I will take care of it." She put her hand on her heart. "I will make Khan my mission now, find out what is going on."

Appleton softened further. "That's dangerous. If he is Pasha, then you need to be doubly careful."

"I'm a double agent. I'm always doubly careful."

The two of them stood there on the footpath for another moment, just looking at each other. The meeting had already lasted too long, and they both knew it. But still, Ted Appleton could not break away.

"Aimal . . . I need to hold you. To kiss you."

There was fresh emotion on her face; Appleton assumed his face revealed the same. She said, "In public? You are literally violating *all* our protocols, aren't you?"

"We are not in public. My security team is out of the way." He stepped up to her, took her in his arms, and pulled her close. She gave to him willingly, and they kissed. He felt her tears on his cheek. The tears were from fear, or from longing, he didn't know, but he knew he had to protect her, just as he knew that sending her back to the ISI to dig into Murad Khan was essentially throwing her to the wolves.

Softly, he said, "I love you."

She put her head on his chest; the veil covering her hair brushed his chin. "I love you. How much longer?"

Appleton forced a smile. "Not much longer. You and I will leave all this, retire to Mumbai, and you will have your family and your safety, and I will have a cozy teaching job, and we will grow old together."

She sniffed back a sob. "I am growing older already, without *any* of that."

"Patience, my little Leopard. Patience."

She nodded, then pushed away from him gently. "I have to go. Where is this place in Lahore?"

Appleton told her, and he told her that he had officers on their way to deliver weapons and body armor to the small American raiding party. He made her promise to be discreet. Aimal fed him intelligence from Khan, which made Khan, as far as Appleton was concerned, his best asset. He would protect his asset; he would fuck over Matt Hanley and Ground Branch to keep his best asset producing, but if he found out that his best asset was a terrorist, feeding him doctored intelligence to lead him off track . . . well then . . . Appleton knew what he'd do. He'd get Aimal to safety, and he'd rain down hellfire on Murad Khan.

In the meantime, however, Matt Hanley's hellfire was perhaps only moments away from raining down on Khan, and this they had to stop.

With another rushed kiss, Aimal walked off, continuing down the path, and Appleton himself headed off in the direction he'd been traveling.

As he walked, he radioed for his men to close down on him for the movement to the waiting cars, but his thoughts were somewhere else. They weren't on Khan, or on Hanley, or on some nameless, faceless, knuckle-dragging good ole boys from Ground Branch. No . . . his thoughts were on the woman he'd just kissed, the smell of her perfume that lingered on his clothes, the schoolboy-like shivers he got whenever they were together. Even like this, even working, even while discussing life and death and the fate of fucking nations, the thrill of being with her, holding her, staring deeply into her soul, had never subsided in the least.

Appleton had met the woman who had been code named by the CIA as Leopard when she was a midlevel thirty-eight-year-old ISI operative working non-official cover in Mumbai, India. Her work was against the Indian financial sector, making contacts and social-engineering them to provide her with information about economics, the strength of certain nationalized businesses like Air India as well as the petroleum, shipbuilding, banking, and coal industries. She was good at her job, but a senior CIA case officer named Ted Appleton uncovered her.

The Agency decided not to report her existence or activities to the Indian government, but to instead approach her in an attempt to flip her to work for the CIA against her home agency, the ISI.

Appleton himself made the initial contact, and over the next year, she began giving him small tidbits of intel from ISI regarding operations against India.

The CIA, in turn, fed her information about Indian nationalized businesses. Nothing too destructive to the Indian economy, but ultimately the CIA was looking out for America, not for India.

Soon Aimal Viziri, code named Leopard, was promoted to New Delhi, where she worked for ISI developing relationships in diplomatic circles. She flatly refused to work with anyone at CIA other than Appleton himself, so he was promoted to fill the open deputy chief of station position.

Their professional relationship was one year old when their personal relationship developed. One evening during monsoon season, after a stressful ISI operation in New Delhi, Aimal Viziri came to Ted's apartment for a clandestine meet. She needed a shoulder to cry on, and Appleton provided that shoulder.

They slept together that night.

Ted was conflicted about what had happened. He knew it was wrong, but the forty-six-year-old bachelor also knew that he had fallen in love with his agent months before their first kiss, and he was powerless to fight it.

For two years they worked and lived and loved in New Delhi; she received more and more intelligence from the CIA that she used to bolster her position in the ISI, and then she was recalled to Islamabad. Now she was in charge of liaising between the analytical side of Pakistani intelligence and a small but powerful department on the operations side, the Foreign Coordination Unit.

In this position she saw almost everything that had been collected by FCU, and she had some operational details of their activities. She worked closely with a thirty-five-year-old FCU section chief named Murad Khan, a rising star at ISI, much like Viziri herself.

Soon Appleton was moved to exploit his agent in her home country; he was made chief of station in Islamabad, but he still ran Leopard, and he still loved Aimal.

He promised her they would go back to Mumbai someday, walk the haunts they used to walk, and get married. But only after the war on terror, in which her organization had a large part to play.

Leopard had first alerted the Americans to a new Kashmiri separatist group with aims to attack American interests in the region for supporting both the Pakistani government and the Indian government. The separatists were enemies of their own nation as well as India, and soon enough, America was dragged into it.

Leopard's intel put the size of the organization at somewhere around five hundred fighters, but while this was nowhere near the strength of many other terror groups in the region, the fact that the KRF attracted former military personnel to its ranks made it an organization to watch.

Ted Appleton thought about all this on his way back to his office. But mostly he thought about Aimal, the danger he put her in, her intense love for him that caused her to do what he asked, and the risk they were both taking now, knowing that a senior ISI chief was possibly running a terror organization with the means to cause true damage to American interests in the region.

He felt a chill across his body, and he was only able to calm himself by thinking of the plans he and Aimal had, after he retired and after she defected.

That day was coming, he just had to believe.

And now, he just had to find a way to keep Aimal on the inside for a little while longer.

THIRTY-THREE

PRESENT DAY

The Independent State of Papua New Guinea comprises half the island of New Guinea, just north of Australia. It is the most rural nation on planet Earth, with less than fourteen percent of the population living in urban centers, and it is one of the most unexplored parts of the world, with many uncontacted tribes living independently in the western portion of the nation.

The U.S. embassy of Papua New Guinea is, however, right in the middle of a small urban center overlooking Fairfax Harbor in the capital city of Port Moresby.

To call this a backwater posting for a CIA officer would be insulting to backwaters everywhere. It was one of quite a few Agency stations where careers went to die.

If you were a brand-new and shiny twenty-four-year-old CIA case officer and you were stationed in Port Moresby, then everyone knew you had underperformed in your training and were being punished. But you could, potentially, dig out of this hole and work your way back into the CIA's good graces.

If you were a senior officer with the Agency, however, serving in your last decade before retirement, and then you were relocated to Port Moresby, then everyone knew you were fucked, and *most* everyone probably figured that you had it coming.

Fifty-eight-year-old CIA chief of station Matthew Hanley had only been posted here a couple of months ago, sent by the director as retribution for an operation he'd conducted sub rosa, and in the intervening period he had plenty of time to reflect on his sins while swatting bugs and approving cables for transmission to Langley that no one would ever bother to read.

Despite the station's reputation, he came to New Guinea certain this was just a bump in the road in his career, and he'd make it back up the ladder soon enough, but now he wasn't so sure.

He lay in bed at two a.m., wide awake and staring at the ceiling, wiping a sheen of sweat off his thick neck and high forehead every minute or two, because the temps outside, even this late at night, were in the nineties, and the air conditioning here in his home on embassy grounds couldn't handle it.

This was a day like any other for Hanley, or so he thought, until his landline began ringing.

He snatched the phone up, knowing it would be the night duty officer in the station, because no one else used the landline.

"Vaughn?"

"Sir, sorry to wake you."

Hanley hadn't been asleep, but he responded grumpily. "Yeah."

"There's a call for you. It's a blocked number. We can investigate if you want us to, but he said—"

"Send it through." Hanley wasn't expecting a call, but he wasn't sleeping, and his brain wasn't shutting down anytime soon.

He heard a scratchy line, thought the user might be using voice over Internet or some other means of hiding his location.

"This is Hanley," he said, trying not to get his hopes up that this might be something interesting.

He heard a voice he recognized well.

"Hey, Matt."

It had been months since Hanley had spoken to Court Gentry, and there were a lot of reasons for that, not the least of which being that Hanley's organization, the CIA, currently had a kill order out on the former Agency assassin. Gentry had been on the run since the op that got Hanley himself booted out of the deputy director for operations position, and for all Hanley knew, Gentry could be anywhere now and working for anybody.

Hanley looked at his alarm clock quickly. "I was just about to brew some coffee. You got a number I can call you back on?" Hanley wouldn't talk to Gentry on an embassy line, and Gentry would know this, so Gentry would definitely have a secure number set up.

Hanley wrote it down when Gentry gave it, and then he hung up, grabbed his mobile, and headed to change.

Ten minutes later Hanley sat on the front porch of his hillside home, looking out over a dirty strip of water in the marina just fifty yards from the embassy. He pulled out his phone and opened the Signal messaging app. Using the voice calling feature, he tapped in the number Gentry had given him, then waited.

When Gentry answered, Hanley lit into him immediately. "Jesus Christ, Violator. Why the fuck are you calling me at the embassy?"

"I knew your station, but I didn't have your personal number."

Hanley knew this, but he also knew to remonstrate. "Next question. Why the fuck are you calling me at all?"

"I need to tell you something. And I need you to tell *me* something."

Hanley rubbed his tired eyes. The warm, dank air outside here caused him to perspire even more than when he lay in bed. "What do you need to tell me?"

Court spoke softly now. "Murad Khan."

The burly station chief sat up straighter. "That's a name I have not heard in a *very* long time."

"Same here."

"Never wanted to hear it again, actually."

"Same here."

"So . . . why are you calling me up at two in the morning and whispering it into my ear?"

"Because the rumors of his death have been greatly exaggerated."

Hanley looked out over the water. He felt his heart jitter and jolt a little, and he squeezed the phone tighter in an attempt to keep his hand from shaking.

"Don't tell me that."

"I saw him. On a job. Tracked him to Mumbai. He's here now, and he's in play."

"But . . . CIA confirmed his DNA. Back then. He's been dead twelve years." Hanley added, "He needs to stay dead."

"That DNA came from the Pakistanis, right?"

"I . . . I don't recall, but probably so. There wasn't much to work with, as I remember."

"He staged his death. Maybe with help from ISI, maybe not. He's been around this whole time."

Hanley's eyes went glassy. "That's . . . that's not possible."

"Ask yourself, Matt. Would *I*, of all people, make a mistake like this?"

The station chief on his little porch heaved a long sigh. "Not in a million years." He rubbed his meaty face with a hand like a catcher's mitt, then said, "What's he doing in India?"

"Unknown, but he's here working B-Company."

"The Indian mob? That's curious."

"He was in Algiers three days ago; I was told he was working on a way to manufacture counterfeit rupees. Indian intel knew about it, apparently, but they didn't know it was Khan. Just someone from FCU. They thought ISI was doing it to try to destabilize their economy, but again, they didn't know who they were up against."

"Khan wouldn't be currency dumping. Not his style."

"Agreed. Something bigger is going on."

Hanley heaved a heavy sigh. "But why are you calling me? I figured Khan had been taking a dirt nap since back then. How would I know what he's doing now?" He paused. "I can get the local office there in Mumbai working on it, I can say I got an anonymous tip or some bullshit."

"I have a feeling our timeline is shorter than we'd like."

Hanley sighed again. "Always was with that motherfucker."

"Right. I'm calling to ask if you had any back-channel relationships around these parts, here or in Pakistan, someone I could reach out to for more information. I'm not leaving here till I kill Murad Khan, I can promise you that. But I need help finding him."

Hanley answered back in an instant. "Yeah, actually you might be in luck. There's a guy in Mumbai, a guy I wouldn't say I think much of personally; we ran up against each other a lot back in the day, but he's a man who knows the area, and he knows all about Murad Khan and what happened back then."

"He's R&AW?"

"Negative. He's American, actually. Ex-Agency. He was the station chief in Islamabad when all that shit went down right when you joined Golf Sierra."

"What's he doing here?"

"Retired. He'd been out in the field so long, home wasn't home anymore. Happens more than you might guess."

"I'd guess it happens a lot."

"More than a lot, then. He ended up in Mumbai. He'd worked there as an ops officer earlier in his career."

"What does he know?"

"Back then, he knew everybody. A specialist on India as well as Pakistan. I can get you an address. You should pay him a visit, tell him what you know. Trust me, the second you convince him Khan is alive, he'll help you in any way he can."

"Why is that?"

"That whole affair is what forced him into retirement."

"Shit," Court said. "Yeah, we all have our motivations for finishing what we started back then." Court changed gears suddenly. "Hey, Matt. Is there any word about me? Is Langley in hot pursuit, or is it more like lukewarm pursuit, like when you were running the show?"

Hanley sighed. "Kid, I was sent to the hinterlands for what happened in Germany. I don't know anything about what's going on with the hunt for you. I still plan on clawing my way out of this hole I've been tossed down, and when I do, you know I'll have your back, but I don't know when that will be."

"Roger that."

"Did you hear about Brewer?"

Suzanne Brewer had been Court's handler in Hanley's sub rosa unit code named Poison Apple. Court didn't like or trust her, but Hanley kept her around anyway.

Court said, "You think *you* are in the hinterlands. I don't hear anything about anybody."

Matt said, "She got promoted. She works as special assistant to the dep director for ops."

"Damn. You went down, she went up."

"Yeah, well, anyway, if anyone's hunting you aggressively, it's probably gonna be Brewer."

Court said, "She couldn't find me when I worked with her. Doubt she'll find me now."

"Just keep your head down." Matt added, "I'm glad to hear you're working, and I'm not surprised that you are being a hell of a lot more productive than I am."

"Don't know how productive I'm being. I got a guy killed tonight."

Hanley thought this over. "You have the shittiest job in the shittiest industry on Earth. Hang in there, Violator. I'll run this Khan stuff up the flagpole with Langley somehow."

"Don't," Court said. "Right now Khan's freaking out because he knows that someone recognized him in Algiers. But he doesn't know who I am. If he knew he'd been exposed to the CIA—"

Hanley took over. "Then whatever he is planning would happen even faster than it would otherwise. Got it. I'll sit on this till you get back to me."

"Yeah. Let's let him feel like he's still somewhat secure. I'll go meet this ex-COS, see if he knows anything about B-Company and their ties to Pakistani intel."

Hanley said, "Give me a half hour to find him, and I'll text you on this number." He stood up from the chair on his porch and said, "Violator . . . be careful."

"You know me."

To this, Hanley just repeated himself. "Hell yeah, I do. Be careful."

. . .

Court Gentry had been walking the streets of Versova while he talked to Hanley, but he returned to the dark and tiny flat above the fish market now and handed Priyanka Bandari a new burner cell phone he'd purchased in a convenience store. He wrote the number down on his hand, then said he had to go back out to see a man for more information about Khan.

Priya had just made it back to the flat herself, after buying electronics at a twenty-four-hour shop nearby. Twice already she'd almost attached the hard drive she'd taken from Arjun's laptop to her own to watch the dreadful files again, but both times she'd told herself there would be nothing to gain from this other than more pain and torment.

So as Cobalt headed out the back door, she sat on a yoga mat and did her best to meditate.

A half hour after Cobalt left her there alone, however, she climbed off the mat, stepped over to her laptop sitting on a little futon in the tiny living room, pulled the hard drive out of her small backpack, and plugged it in.

She knew what she would see, but at this moment, she only wanted to punish herself for getting her poor sweet uncle killed.

She watched the entire event, only averting her eyes as her uncle was tortured. She listened to him shout and scream, profess that he knew nothing about the man she knew as Cobalt and nothing about who hired him for the job, other than he assumed it was someone with the Research and Analysis Wing. He explained to Khan that the entire operation was brokered over the Darknet, and he therefore had no information to give him.

Over and over he begged Khan to kill him. Priya turned away again before he screamed her name, and she kept her eyes averted until after the Pakistani man slit her uncle's throat.

When it was over she made to get up from the futon, but instead she went back to the beginning of the file and started it again. She was ashamed for turning away from what she had caused. For what she had put her uncle through, she told herself that sitting here comfortably and witnessing it was a pathetically cheap price to pay, but it was the only penance she could think of.

On this third viewing she forced herself to watch the torture; she even zoomed in on Arjun's face, taking in every ounce of abuse he took, even if only through osmosis.

As he screamed and cried, she leaned closer, touched her fingers to the screen, as if wiping away the blood that ran down from above his eye.

She took her hand away slowly, and as she did this, she saw Arjun's head turn and face the camera, staring right into it.

She tapped a key, freezing the video.

At first she wondered how she'd missed this on her earlier viewings, but she realized she'd had her eyes averted at this point of the video. And even now, only by zooming in, could she know for sure that he was purposefully looking into the camera high in the corner.

She pushed the play button again, and just then, he shouted, "Priya!" She'd heard this three times already now, yet still her blood ran cold at the screeching sound of her name.

She went back thirty seconds and watched it again, zoomed in more closely. Now she realized he was looking into the camera for several seconds, right before he shouted her name.

And his mouth moved, though she heard no sound from it.

She zoomed in tighter.

He was mouthing something, something directly to her, and that was why he'd shouted her name.

Of course, she told herself. Of course he knew she would come, and she would know about the covert camera, and she would review the footage.

But what was he saying?

She had no idea, but she *did* know how to find out.

In the end, it took her almost an hour to digitally clean up the footage. She slowed it down even more, zoomed in even tighter, to where she could see only his bloody face.

Priya had learned how to read lips from watching thousands of hours of security camera footage over the years, and now she watched his mouth over and over and over until there could be no doubt as to what he was saying.

It was a string of numbers.

"Fourteen, forty-four, twenty-seven, forty-one."

"What on earth?" she muttered softly in Hindi. This wasn't a phone number. This meant nothing.

But then she realized what her uncle was doing.

He was giving her the combination to his safe.

But why? She solved this riddle quickly, as well. There was something in the safe that she needed to see.

It was her uncle's dying wish for her to go look.

Without giving it a second thought, Priya wrote the combination down, then grabbed her backpack and her keys, and she left the apartment over the fish market, hunting for a taxi.

THIRTY-FOUR

TWELVE YEARS AGO

At a CIA safe house in Lahore, just fifteen minutes' drive to the KRF location at the Hotel Days Inn, the entire six-man Ground Branch team leaned over a laptop with a satellite image of the hotel and the surrounding area displayed. It wasn't in real time, there was too much cloud cover right now, but the shot had been taken the day before.

Hanley had told them that the man they suspected of being Pasha the Kashmiri was at the location, and he indicated which man he was in the photo Gentry had taken just a couple hours earlier. He also notified Zack that the man's actual name was Murad Khan, and he worked for the ISI.

Zack didn't care, and neither did the others standing in the simple home. If the green light for the hit came through, they'd drop him in the dirt with a bullet to the brain just the same as anyone else at the location.

Although they were getting some information about the location from the satellite image, they also *did* have visual coverage on the property. Kendrick Lennox had installed a camera on the roof of the building across the alleyway, and it beamed images of the parking lot and rear walls of the three-story structure through another laptop they had open.

Since the hotel was up on stanchions, effectively making the ground floor an open but covered parking lot with a staircase in the middle, the camera's view showed most of the front side of the hotel lot, as well.

And now, as when the team left an hour earlier, the parking lot contained the red minibus and three Toyota Hilux pickup trucks. To the best of anyone's knowledge, the AN had not been offloaded from the minibus, and the CIA analysts back at Camp Chapman said there was, indeed, something heavy enough inside it to push the frame low on the chassis.

On the live feed the men could see that the rain had stopped, and now four men milled around the parking lot, rifles on their backs. Another man was on the roof, observing the busy city outside the walls of the property.

Zack said, "Okay, the exterior of the property is protected by five pax. The rest seem to be inside. We are working under the assumption that the AN is still on the minibus, and there's no way they've mixed it with diesel yet to make a proper bomb."

Lennox said, "But that shit will still go up with a detonator."

"That's right," Zack agreed. "There's enough ammonium nitrate in there to take out a city block."

Court asked, "Do we think they are just going to lay up there till nightfall, then go to another location?"

Zack shrugged. "It's possible, but they could also move out at any time. We need that green light from Hanley, and we need the guns and gear from Islamabad station."

Court told Zack he wanted to return to the parking lot across the street, just to have a physical, human intelligence asset there in case there was something else that could be learned before the raid.

A couple of the other men rolled their eyes at this. Morgan said, "Boy wonder wants to hit this bitch by himself."

"I'm not going to hit it, I'm going to reconnoiter it."

Zack wasn't opposed to the idea, but he didn't like Court going alone.

This was still under discussion when Zack's sat phone rang, and he put it on speaker.

"Go for Golf Sierra One."

"Golf Sierra One, this is Rooster. Green light. Say again, green light."

Hanley continued. "A vehicle will arrive at your poz within sixty mikes with rifles and body armor. You are cleared hot to hit the Hotel Days Inn as soon as able. It's got to be a hasty plan, Sierra One, there is no way to track them if they try to leave."

"Understood. We've got it figured out."

"Your primary target is Murad Khan, your secondary is the ammonium nitrate. Tertiary is Mufti. How copy?"

"Good copy."

When he hung up, Zack said, "Me and Six will go back to the south side of the location now to get a better view. When the equipment comes, you four kit up. Pace, take the Suzuki and bring our shit to us. We'll slap on our gear, and we'll all hit from both sides. Three and three."

The men rogered up, Court included, and then Zack and Court climbed into the Toyota and not the Suzuki because they didn't want to loiter in the same vehicle they'd brought to the fertility clinic before, in case the man on the roof of the hotel was extraordinarily skilled in counter-surveillance.

Court and Zack took off, carrying only their Glock pistols and some extra magazines.

Fifteen minutes later they were in the parking lot of the fertility clinic. Looking across the street for only a moment, the men realized something was different. The security men were not visible through the gate, nor was the one on the roof of the hotel.

Zack looked at the image from the other side of the street on his iPad, and there was no movement back there, either.

Soon enough, through the metal gate, they watched as men began filing out of the stairwell carrying large duffel bags, walking through the parking lot and then loading the bags into the back of the minibus.

Zack said, "Is that thing a fucking clown car? It's got three forklift loads of AN in there, and now they are putting in . . . six, seven big duffels?"

Court said, "They might have offloaded the AN."

Zack replied, "We would have seen them do it."

Court disagreed. "They were here a good five minutes before we had visual through the gate on this side, and we can't see the minibus from here. And Sierra Two didn't mount that camera on the east side for another twenty. Eight or ten guys could have carried those sacks into the hotel."

"Yeah," Zack admitted. "The hotel might *be* the bomb."

Zack reported what they saw both to the rest of the team and then to Hanley at the tactical operations center back at Chapman. While he did this, the Kashmiri Resistance Fighters continued loading items into the minibus.

While Zack talked to Hanley, Court said, "Something's got them spooked."

"Wait one, Rooster." Zack looked at the iPad, and then across the street through the gate. "Yeah, I think you're right."

Hanley asked, "What's going on?"

"These fuckers are loading up, boss. They're rushing it, too. Like they're agitated."

"Shit," Hanley said. "We need to end this today."

"Understood."

Court said, "What are we going to do?"

Zack replied, "If they unass that hotel before the rest of the team gets here, then we just do our best to tail them."

"They drive that thing up to the front of the U.S. embassy and—"

"The embassy is in Islamabad. If the target is in Lahore, then it's the consulate. Or something else."

Hanley asked, "What's the ETA on the rest of your team?"

Zack said, "About seven mikes now. I can change the play here. Bring the entire team to my side when they get here and we ram the gate. We can stop that bus from moving out of here, at least."

The group chief said, "Those aren't great odds."

"Higher stakes, lower odds, boss. Same as ever."

"Copy," Hanley replied.

Just then, the gate across the street slid open.

Court said, "Shit. They're leaving, but we don't know how many guys and how much shit is still in that building."

Zack was thinking quickly now. "Kid, can you tail that minibus on your own?"

"Of course I can," Gentry said with all the swagger of a young man.

Zack started the engine, then opened his driver-side door, but only a little. Court started to get out on his side, but Zack called to him. "Hold . . . hold . . . hold."

Across the street, the red minibus pulled out of the hotel property and turned in their direction. It passed them by, gaining speed and heading to the north. They saw two men in the front seats, but they didn't recognize either of them.

"Now," Zack said, and Court launched out of the minivan, running to the other side. Zack remained there next to the driver-side door. He said, "I'm going to lead the assault on the hotel, then you can vector us to wherever that vic is when we're done."

"Got it," Court said as he sat down behind the wheel.

Zack added, "Stay in comms and good luck," but Court was already shutting his door. He lurched forward, then turned onto Nazaria-e-Pakistan Avenue and headed off in the direction of the red vehicle.

As soon as Court drove out of the fertility clinic, Zack clicked his radio transmitter. "Sierra Two, Sierra One. You up on this net?"

"Affirmative, One. We are about six minutes out."

"Then you are seven minutes too late. The minibus is rolling, unknown who is inside, but Six is tailing it."

"Want us to link with him?"

"Negative. We don't know what's in the hotel. I'll wait here for you; we'll hit this location from the main gate and clear it. Link up with Six after that."

"Copy that. We're hauling ass."

Inside the Hotel Days Inn, the director of the Foreign Coordination Unit of the ISI, thirty-five-year-old Murad Khan, looked out a third-story window with Omar Mufti, his second-in-command, standing at his side. Together they watched the street, looked up and down it for the CIA men they'd been warned were now getting ready to strike the location.

Mufti was agitated, but Khan was calm. Softly, with no small amount of reverence, he said, "The sacrifice our brothers will make today will long be remembered."

"Did we have to send so many?"

"Yes. There will be questions about the size of the explosion. An eight-man force along with the material should cause enough havoc to reassure our enemies that this was the true objective."

"You've had this planned all along, haven't you, brother?"

Khan smiled a little. "A backup plan. In case we were discovered before we had time to enact our true mission. All those men in that bus knew this day might come."

Mufti nodded, still looking out the window. His leader's voice was the epitome of calm, but Mufti himself was still nervous. "The Americans will be here soon. I trust you have a plan for us, too?"

"A plan for us, a plan for the material downstairs, and a plan for our brothers on their way to martyrdom." He smiled and put his hand on Mufti's shoulder. "I have a plan for everything, Major."

THIRTY-FIVE

Five minutes later Court found himself moving along in the Toyota at a snail's pace. The minibus was up ahead, still well in sight, but the choking traffic on the big avenue made it next to impossible for him to close any ground on the vehicle.

He watched his target turn off on a service road a minute later, and there was little traffic on it, so the KRF terrorists began racing off to the northeast. Court felt panic wash over him; he couldn't go forward or backwards, nor could he simply exit until he hit the service road, which, at this pace, would take him several minutes to get to.

So he did the only thing he could think to do. He put the minivan in park, leapt out, and began running through traffic.

Cars honked behind him in protest of his leaving a vehicle in the middle of the congested road, but Court ran on, as fast as his legs would take him. He felt the comforting pressure of the Glock 19 he had secured in an inside-the-waistband retention holster in his pants on the right side, its grip covered by his light gray T-shirt, along with the comforting pressure of the magazine holder, IWB on his left side, which carried two more fifteen-round mags.

He made it one block to the north, still sprinting with everything he had. Here he saw a raised footbridge that ran parallel to the service road over a culvert, and he took the stairs up, two and three at a time.

Once above the culvert, he peered into the distance. The red minibus was just visible in the haze and smog and dim evening's light, but he was able to see it make another turn for the north.

Court ran on. He was nearly half a mile behind the vehicle now, and he was on foot. It seemed like a hopeless endeavor at first, but then he saw a young man climbing onto a scooter just off the sidewalk ahead of him. Court slowed, drew his pistol, and stuck it in the man's ribs when he made it to within contact distance.

"Sorry, brother. I need this more than you do right now."

The man was stunned into immediate compliance. He climbed off, Court climbed on, and he fired the engine and raced to the east. He turned sharply to the north when he came to a small road that bisected the one the minibus had just turned off on.

He had no visual on his target now, and hadn't for the past minute. He sped as fast as he could on the little scooter, his head scanning left and right into parking lots and side roads.

But when Court made it to the road he had seen the vehicle turn onto, he realized it was, in actuality, a long driveway that led to a massive shopping center. He raced along it, passed a sign that said "Gulberg Galleria," and he thought there was a fair chance this was the destination of the terrorists.

His blood ran cold.

He kept his scooter racing at top speed through the parking lot, standing on the footrest at times to look for the red minibus. There were cars everywhere, people moving to and from them, to and from the entrances of the mall. If the terrorists were targeting this location, Court knew it would be a bloodbath.

Finally, after making it halfway around the massive structure, he called Hightower on his radio.

"Sierra Six for Sierra One, how copy?"

Zack came over the net, though his voice was scratchy due to the distance between them. "Sierra One copies. The team is pulling up in one mike. Say your status and poz and make it quick, over."

"I'm at the Gulberg Galleria, about five klicks from you. The target vehicle entered the parking lot, I've lost viz but I'm hunting for them. They could be here, or they could have gone out another exit."

"You *can't* lose that vic, Six."

Court had, without question, lost the vic, but he wasn't ready to admit defeat to Sierra One. "Scanning now. If they are here at the mall, then you know what that means, right?"

Zack wasn't so sure. "Ammonium nitrate by itself isn't enough of a bang for this group. And attacking a soft target in Pakistan . . . that doesn't seem like their big play here."

"They've done it before, though, right?"

"Yeah, little hit-and-runs. But if Pasha and Mufti are personally involved . . ." Zack sounded rushed. "Look, Six, find them, stay on their asses, but get off this net. The team is here and we are rolling as soon as I get my gear on."

Sierra Two pulled his van up next to Sierra One, who was standing alone in the parking lot of the fertility clinic, around the corner from the street so he couldn't be seen by anyone in the hotel. The side door of the green vehicle slid open, and Zack climbed inside, and he was instantly handed a load-bearing vest.

The weapons the team had been provided were folding-stocked AKs that looked like they'd been in use since the seventies, but Zack knew local assets hadn't had much time to cobble together an armory full of equipment for the Ground Branch team, and he and the four men with him now had all been well trained on the Kalashnikov platform. Zack did a quick function check on the weapon handed to him by Morgan and found it to be in fair condition. More magazines were already stuck in the chest rig he wore, as were heavy steel ballistic plates to absorb rounds should he be shot in the torso.

As soon as he Velcroed the cummerbund of his vest tight across his midsection and racked the bolt of the AK, Zack crawled past Morgan and Redus in the back of the van and stuck his head between the front seats. Here, Kendrick Lennox was behind the wheel on the left, and Jim Pace was riding shotgun on the right.

"How we doing this?" Lennox asked.

Zack was unequivocal. "Ram the gate. We'll debus and stack up, move to the stairwell and ascend. Stay together."

Kendrick Lennox replied, "Got it."

Zack slapped him on the back. "Go!"

Lennox put the van in gear and started to roll forward, pulled out of the fertility clinic parking lot, made a right, and picked up speed as he closed on the metal gate of the darkened hotel building across the street.

But just as he spun the steering wheel to force the van hard to the left to hit the gate from a right angle, a Lahore city police vehicle passing in oncoming traffic slammed on its brakes, blocking the gate.

Lennox had committed to the turn, however, so he shot towards the hotel and slammed into the police car, knocking it sideways into the gate, simultaneously slamming the Americans around in the van.

Zack looked out the window and saw a second, then a third, police car skid to a stop around them, effectively boxing in the van except for the rear.

"Reverse! Reverse!" Zack shouted.

Lennox jammed the van's transmission into reverse to get out of there; he stomped on the gas, but he instantly impacted with a fourth police car that was sliding to a stop behind the van.

The Americans were surrounded; cops poured out of the four vehicles, and the men heard sirens approaching, indicating there were a lot more cops on the way.

"Son of a bitch!" Hightower shouted.

The men put their hands up as guns were pointed at them through the windshield. There was no scenario that involved killing local cops, so turning this into a gun battle wasn't an option.

Zack looked through the windshield now and saw men looking out of the stairwell at the ground floor of the hotel. He wondered how many terrorists were standing about fifty feet from him right now, and he felt helpless to do anything about it.

And then he thought of Gentry. Alone, up against a second unknown number of terrorists, armed only with a pistol.

But there was nothing Zack and Golf Sierra could do to help him now.

Court Gentry found the target vehicle two minutes after entering the parking lot, illegally parked in a loading zone just outside the main entrance at the northernmost portion of the mall. Even from a distance he could see that the minibus looked lighter on its chassis than it had before, and this told him that some or all of the men, or some or all of the equipment, were no longer inside it.

Quickly his head shot to the right, towards the row of doors leading into the multi-level shopping center. There he saw what appeared to be about eight men, all carrying large backpacks, heading towards the front door.

Court sped in their direction and watched them disappear inside the entrance before he got to them. He parked his scooter next to the minibus and called Zack on the radio. Zack had ordered him to stay off the net, but this development, in Court's estimation, warranted the communication.

"Sierra Six for Sierra One."

There was no reply.

He tried again as he climbed off the scooter, and once more as he approached the minibus on foot, but he received no response from Hightower. Attempting to look inside, he found that the back windows had been covered with black paper. He moved around to the front but he couldn't see what was in back because a tarp hung from the headliner down to the floor behind the two front seats.

Court gave up on reaching Zack and on getting a look inside the locked vehicle. Instead he began running towards the mall entrance, past men and women who looked at him curiously.

He had just pulled the door open, forty-five seconds behind the group of men with backpacks, though he couldn't see them near the entrance, when he heard the first echoing booms of gunshots coming from inside the building.

Murad Khan stood with his arms crossed at the bottom of the hotel staircase, five kilometers away from where the terrorist event he'd ordered began, but he wasn't thinking about the Gulberg Galleria. Instead he watched while a group of five Westerners—he'd been told they were from the CIA—were pulled out of the van that sat damaged, sideways, and smoking in the street in front of him. The armor-clad men were thrown up against the hood and trunk of the wrecked-out police car pressed up against the gate. Khan smiled as he made eye contact with a tall, bearded, blond-haired man, who quickly disappeared from view as he was yanked with the others down to the ground, just as a large armored police van pulled up and stopped in the fading light.

The men were handcuffed and loaded into the windowless and secure back cabin, along with two Pakistani police officers, and the heavy steel door was slammed shut.

Omar Mufti still stood at his leader's right shoulder. "When they take the Americans away, will the police come in here to check what they were after?"

"No," Khan said with confidence. "In moments they will have something else on their mind. We'll transport the chemicals as soon as they leave."

"Then . . . that's it? Everything stays the same with the plan?"

"No," Khan said again. "We will have to speed up the attack."

"We can't," Mufti replied. He was subordinate to Murad Khan, Pasha the Kashmiri, but he was also an army officer and knew how to assert himself, even to his superiors. "We need a week to do it properly."

Khan did not reply to Mufti; he instead turned to another man in the room, standing back from the doorway. "Nassir. What about your end of the operation? Can it be sped up?"

Nassir Rasool was in his twenties, bespectacled, and he wore Western clothes. "The team from China requires time to set up and test their equipment on site, and weather conditions can't be relied upon. We *have* to move under cloud cover on the night of the attack to have any chance for success. Heavy clouds are predicted by the weekend."

Khan then turned back to Mufti. "We will act in five days, then."

Khan put a hand on the shoulder of Mufti, and another on the shoulder of Rasool. "Relax. Both of you." With his head he motioned at the police vehicles out on the street. The Americans were already rolling off to the north in the back of the black paddy wagon. "I know what the CIA is going to do as soon as they do. Look at them. They are flailing. We are moving ever closer to our goal. Our endeavor will be met with glorious success, I promise you both."

THIRTY-SIX

At the Gulberg Galleria, a mall security officer armed with a revolver on his hip stood near the front doors, staring at the sounds coming from somewhere in the mall but out of his line of sight. He was slow to understand what was happening, so Court grabbed the man by the arm to get his attention. "Do you speak English?"

The man nodded.

"Get on your radio! Move everybody out of here and call the police! Tell them there are eight terrorists, and there might be a bomb in the red bus out there." He pointed back through the doors, then took off in a run, delaying drawing his pistol because he didn't want the rent-a-cop to see the weapon and then reflexively shoot him in the back.

More gunfire rang out; it was coming from different vectors, and this told Court the men had probably split into smaller groups.

Court had never dealt with terrorism; this all felt like someone else's war, stuff he'd been watching on TV for the last decade. But even though this shit was like nothing he'd ever experienced, he knew he'd have to figure out his enemy's tactics on the fly.

He came to a T intersection in the center of the galleria; men and women and children by the dozens sprinted past him, rushing for the exits. He heard sustained shooting from both the left and the right, so he quickly scanned both directions. He saw nothing on his right but a long concourse of shops, open to three levels of stores above it. He knew there hadn't been enough time for anyone to ascend to another level, so he wondered if the attackers who'd moved this way were already inside a store here on the ground floor.

When he looked to his left, however, he immediately saw two armed men on an escalator heading up, backpacks slung over their shoulders and AK-47 rifles raised to fire.

Civilians ran in all directions on the main floor of the mall, and he saw blood and bodies among them.

The two men on the escalator gunned down a security guard who looked over the second-floor railing, and then an older couple who were caught in the open on the escalator heading down.

Court took off in this direction, fought his way through fleeing mall patrons, and finally drew his weapon when he was at the bottom of the escalator. The two men continued shooting as they reached the top, concentrating their attention, and their fire, at targets they could see on the second floor.

Court aimed as he jumped onto the escalator and fired a single shot, hitting the first man above him in the small of his back. The terrorist pitched forward into his partner, knocking the other man onto the second floor at the top of the escalator and out of Court's line of fire.

Court ascended at a run, but when he lost sight of the second man he realized all the KRF fighter would have to do was reach his weapon over the top of the escalator and fire down, and Court would have no way to avoid being raked with rounds. So he kicked his legs over the side and dropped ten feet back to the ground floor and into the middle of a group of panicked civilians.

He collapsed his body to absorb the impact, then rolled on the floor up to a kneeling position.

Gunfire ripped the escalator above where he'd been an instant earlier, validating his decision about remaining there in the open.

Court climbed off the floor of the galleria now, and he was instantly met by more gunfire, coming from somewhere down the mall on his right. AK rounds sprayed into the masses around him; he saw a woman fall, and he hit the ground again to avoid getting shot.

Looking back up, he noticed a young boy standing alone in the center of the concourse, some fifty feet away from him.

Court leapt to his feet and went for the kid through the crowd. He had no idea if the parents had been killed or just pushed away in the frenzied jumble. He heard gunfire now from three different locations, confirming his assumption that the terrorists had split into groups, probably into groups of two, so that one man could cover while his partner reloaded.

Court ran in a crouch all the way to the kid; the boy couldn't have been older than four, and he scooped him up with his left arm while his right shifted the Glock around, hunting for a target.

He burst into the first refuge he could find, a clothing store called Alkaram Studio. With echoing gunfire outside in the mall, he put the boy down next to an employee who was crouched behind her counter. "Take care of him."

She just stared in shock.

"Do you speak English?"

"Ye- yes."

"You have a back door?"

"It . . . it leads to a rear employee hallway."

"Go! These guys are looking for a big kill, they won't worry about the employee access areas for a while."

Court turned and ran back out the door, and as soon as he looked to the left, he saw just a glimpse of one of the terrorists as he ambled along at a comfortable pace, disappearing into a Nike store.

Quickly Court scanned the little he could see of the three levels of the mall above him, afraid that the man he'd left alive from the escalator, or one of the other Kashmiris, would start taking potshots over the railing down at those on the ground floor. Upstairs, to his left and to his right, Kashmiri separatists were indiscriminately gunning down everyone they saw, focusing first on the several poorly armed security men who died valiantly, but died nonetheless.

But he only heard this by reading the sound of the gunfire, he didn't see any oppo close to the upstairs railing, so he took a chance. He ran out into the mall concourse, sprinting closer to the Nike store.

He stopped before he reached the door, instead looking through the glass window, past a display of mannequins in fitness gear, and he saw two armed men pushing several customers and staff up against a wall. They raised their AKs to fire, and Court realized he had to act now.

He aimed and pressed his trigger over and over, through the glass, shattering it. The first terrorist took a round to the arm, and then the second pitched over, but Court couldn't tell where he'd hit the man.

With the first man still on his feet but focusing on his wound, Court crashed through the now-broken glass, made it into the store, and found some cover behind a sales counter.

He rose up from behind the counter and fired again at the KRF fighter, this time hitting him twice in the chest as he searched in vain for a target.

Court dropped to his butt behind the counter again, ejected the nearly empty magazine from his gun, and stuck it in his back pocket. He pounded in a fresh mag, then crawled around the side of the counter to peek out at a different angle.

But before he'd made it around the side, he heard a single gunshot in the back of the store where the civilians had been lined up. He leapt to his feet, aimed in again, hunting for a target, and saw a middle-aged man in a white dress shirt holding an AK, pointing it down.

This was not one of the terrorists, Court realized just as his finger began pressing on the Glock's trigger, so he let off the pressure and yelled at the man. "Drop it!"

The man did as ordered, letting the weapon clank on the tile floor and then raising his hands high in the air in terror. Court moved around a display and was able to see what had happened. The second man Court had shot through the glass had fallen to the floor, but he'd survived. He'd dropped his rifle and tried to crawl away, but a civilian had picked it up and finished the man off.

Court ordered the middle-aged civilian to put his hands down and guide the rest of the people out of the mall via the back hallway, then raced forward, holstered his pistol, and picked up a blood-covered Kalashnikov. He did a mag change off the vest worn by the dead guy who was lying faceup, and he noticed the weapon had a high-end red-dot optic sight, as well as a flashlight mounted to the side that could be activated with a pressure switch. It was a quality gun, and money had been spent to upgrade it.

He grabbed a second full rifle mag out of the man's chest rack and turned to run back towards the mezzanine. By his count, three of the terrorists were down now, but there were at least five more, and he could still hear AKs rattling somewhere in the mall.

In the back of the police truck, the five Americans of Ground Branch team Golf Sierra sat on benches along the walls, their bodies swaying with the driver's turns. The men in back were accompanied by a pair of Pakistani SWAT officers wearing Heckler & Koch MP5 submachine guns around their necks, sitting by the rear door of the vehicle and watching the prisoners to make sure they didn't get any bright ideas about an escape.

It was silent other than sporadic but routine-sounding broadcasts on the cops' radios hanging from their chests, broadcasts the Americans didn't understand because they were spoken in Urdu.

Finally Zack leaned back against the thick wall of the vehicle and looked around to the rest of his team. "Does it seem odd to anybody else that the local five-oh just happened to get this paddy wagon on scene in under two minutes?"

Lennox said, "And when they pulled us out of the van, they immediately yanked our earpieces. They didn't just stumble onto them."

Pace added, "They didn't just stumble onto *us*, either."

Redus said directly what Sierra One, Two, and Four were inferring. "Somebody told the cops not just that we were here, but who we were."

The two police officers sat across from each other on the two benches, looking at the handcuffed group. They said nothing, just eyed the tough-looking Americans who somehow still managed to look tough with their hands secured behind their backs.

It went silent again for a moment, Zack spending the quiet thinking about how the hell the embassy in Islamabad was going to react when they learned the Ground Branch team got popped by the local po-po and was being taken to some shit-hole prison in Lahore, when suddenly a new burst of radio traffic came over the two cops' radios. Again, Zack and his team couldn't understand a word, but there was shouting, a quick barking of indecipherable words, and unmistakable panic in the voice of the broadcaster.

The Golf Sierra men looked around at one another.

"*That* don't sound good," Morgan said.

One of the cops radioed back, the net came alive with near-constant radio traffic, and soon the van, which had been rolling along at a normal pace, began speeding up, forcing the handcuffed men in the back to brace themselves with their feet.

Zack looked to the cop on the opposite bench from him. "What's going on?"

The man appeared dialed in, focused, even more so than when he was guarding over a team of American gunmen. He said, "Terror attack at galleria. We go there now. You stay locked in here."

Zack knew Court was in the middle of whatever was going on, and he pulled against his cuffs behind his back in frustration. He looked to the others, then back to the cop. "How far?"

"Not far. We will help with perimeter, and then when it is over, we will take you to jail."

Hightower rolled his eyes. "You don't need to worry about a fucking *perimeter.* This is what me and my guys are trained for. You need to let us go in there."

The man shook his head, looked at his partner, and they both laughed a little, though nervously. "You go nowhere but jail, American."

Zack eyed the man, then said, "At least tell your driver that if he sees a red minibus outside the mall, he might want to think about not parking next to it."

Now the cop cocked his head. "Why not?"

"Because it's a fucking bomb, dipshit!"

The cop looked at Zack angrily for a few seconds, and then the young man reached down for his radio. He broadcast something in Urdu, then received a reply, possibly from the driver of the paddy wagon. The police officer then looked back to Zack. "No more talking."

Court Gentry raced towards the sound of gunfire, past the lifeless forms of civilians strewn around the first-floor concourse as he kept his eyes scanning the mezzanines above him, still terrified he'd see a rifle poke over a railing and then aim down at him, like he was a fish in a barrel.

Observing the dead, he realized he'd never seen carnage like this in his life. He'd killed—he was still a teenager the first time he took a life—but he'd never seen innocents targeted until earlier that day, and it simultaneously sickened, frightened, and angered him to his core.

There was a new burst of automatic gunfire one level up; he took a quick glance at a sign near an escalator and thought the shooting might be coming from the mall's food court.

Court bypassed the escalator and continued running. Though it would be the fastest way up to the second level, he also knew it could remain a fatal funnel of fire if an armed man was up there and looking down. Instead he ran through a doorway marked with an exit sign, raced through a narrow and poorly lit employee access hallway, and finally found a set of concrete stairs that he thought might take him upstairs to the southern side of the food court.

Gunfire around the mall had lessened considerably, but it had not stopped. Court imagined that the terrorists no longer had the target-rich environment of an unsuspecting mall filled to the brim with potential victims, and now they were simply going from store to store, looking for anyone who had hidden in hopes of weathering this attack in safety.

On the second level he left the employee stairwell on the south side but immediately heard fresh shooting and determined it was still above him and not, in fact, at the food court. He ran back to the stairs, his AK up and trained, and ascended another floor.

He burst out the third-floor employee access door, his heart pounding from the exertion and the terror and the utter panic that came from the realization that every time he heard a gunshot—and he'd heard hundreds—another innocent man, woman, or child might have been killed.

It was less than twenty seconds before he caught a glimpse of someone stepping into the Tag Heuer store. The man was armed with a black AK, he was no longer carrying a backpack, and he moved at an angle to where Court couldn't be sure the man hadn't seen him.

Slowly Court advanced, trying to get an angle on the man fifty feet away inside the high-end watch store. He caught himself hoping to hear gunfire inside, indicating the man was directing his attention somewhere else, but he also knew that would mean more dead innocents, so he pushed the thought out of his mind and kept moving.

He looked off the mezzanine, down to his right, and saw the mall's entrance, and while it was nearly dark outside now, he could see flashing lights pouring off the highway and coming this way. He figured the cops would need several minutes to form en masse to come in here and help, so he wondered if Zack and the guys would get here and bail his ass out of this mess first.

But he couldn't sit here and wait. The fight was going on right now, and he was on his own.

The Lahore Police van with the five American prisoners slowed, and inside the armored and windowless back space, Zack could hear sirens all around. He figured he and his team were approaching the perimeter being set up around the mall, and he figured he would be sitting here inside this tin can while his Sierra Six was fighting for his life just a couple hundred yards away.

The distant boom of gunshots confirmed this. They were barely audible but unmistakable, and Zack, in desperation, looked across to Jim Pace, Sierra Four. The men made eye contact, and then Zack flashed his eyes to the cop on Pace's left. He was giving his man the order to take the cop out, though it was going to be tough to do with Pace's hands behind his back.

Sierra Three was on Zack's right, and also next to a police officer. Sierra One figured Morgan would pick up on the cue that he needed to overpower the man next to him as soon as Pace went for his target.

Zack himself planned on launching off his bench and slamming a shoulder into the cop across from him, giving Pace a little support in his endeavor.

This was a low-probability move all around, but Zack was desperate. The chattering AK fire in the distance and the fact that one of the men he was responsible for was in a life-or-death gunfight meant he had to act, no matter the odds.

. . .

Court lay prone behind a concrete garbage can on the third-floor mezzanine, firing his bloody AK towards the man in the Tag Heuer store. The enemy returned fire proficiently, conserving ammo but keeping Court's head down, making sure he was unable to move from the weak concealment of the garbage can and towards more cover.

Court had the tactical expertise to know that this shooter was well trained. There were several more armed enemy in this building, and they could approach Court from any direction, even shoot up at him from the mezzanine below, and there wasn't a hell of a lot he could do about it while the guy in the watch store had him pinned in the open. He concentrated on the target before him, telling himself if he could eliminate this asshole, then maybe he could advance and get some cover for when the rest of the assholes started showing up.

Court looked quickly to his left and saw movement inside Punjab Optics. An armed man peeked around a wall. The young bearded fighter saw Court as well, almost out in the open on the third-floor mezzanine. Court threw himself up to his knees and slung his rifle around, turning attention away from the Tag Heuer terrorist and focusing on the optical store terrorist, but before he could press the trigger on the AK, he saw a flash reflected off all the glass and metal surfaces of the mall around him.

And then he launched into the air.

He was flung forward as if he'd been slammed in the back by a truck. He crashed to the tile, slid halfway across the mezzanine, and an incredible noise enveloped him while he was still airborne.

A shock wave blasted his eardrums, and then the lights went out.

THIRTY-SEVEN

Zack Hightower lay on his side, shaking his head, trying to get his brain to clear. He didn't know what the hell had happened, but he was reasonably certain he and his team had not even begun their planned attack on the cops in the paddy wagon before everything went black. Shaking his head again, he slowly became aware that the van was now on its side, and he was lying on top of Jim Pace, next to an unconscious Pakistani police officer. The interior lighting had gone out, but the rear hatch of the paddy wagon was bent and partially open, letting a shaft of dusky light into the space.

Men around him groaned.

The faint light illuminated a smoky haze, but not much else in the back of the metal box. Zack looked around, struggling to do so because he was twisted and tangled among others with his hands behind his back.

He focused on the man closest to him as the haze cleared. Pace had a broken nose; blood poured from it, but he was unable to wipe it, letting it instead drip down on the interior wall of the truck.

Zack looked around for the other cop now. He was conscious but dazed, lying on top of Morgan, who himself didn't seem so clearheaded. Morgan tried to push himself up with his legs, but his limbs looked heavy and uncooperative.

Zack knew there had been an explosion, but he didn't know if it had been the minibus itself, or else an extremely powerful bomb placed inside the mall. He also knew he wouldn't have his answer until he got the hell out of this tin can packed full of prostrate bodies.

He couldn't see the driver or front-seat passengers of this vehicle because he was in the back of the paddy wagon, but with the obvious proximity of the explosion, he could imagine them injured or dead. Only the steel box he sat in had saved the lives of himself and his men.

He spit dust to clear his mouth and shouted now, "Who's up?"

Lennox was to his right. "Two's good." From the sound of his voice, he was no more and no less disoriented than Zack.

"Three is up," Morgan said with a cough. He was next to the barely conscious cop, so Zack didn't wait for the others to sound off.

"Three, get that dude's handcuff key."

"On it." Morgan grunted and groaned as he struggled with the weight of the man, searching his utility belt for his key with his hands held behind his back.

Pace's face was pressed up against Zack's face in the cramped space. Still, he said, "I'm good, boss."

"Your nose is broken," Zack corrected without emotion, then called out to Redus. "Five, you alive?"

"Over here, boss." He was behind Zack, close to the forward end of the vehicle. "That sure as shit rang my bell, but I'm good to go."

"Got the keys," Morgan said, then used his forehead to smack the cop in the face to stop him from trying to fight back.

Morgan uncuffed himself, then began crawling around the paddy wagon, freeing his teammates. This done, the men relieved the two Lahore cops of their MP5 submachine guns, their soft body armor, and their Browning pistols, and then they forced open the door of the paddy wagon and fell out into the parking lot.

Smoke was everywhere, vehicles burned, police sirens mixed with car alarms, and Zack could hear coughing and moaning in every direction.

When he climbed to his feet, he sent Redus and Morgan to the front of the vehicle to check the driver and anyone else up there for usable weapons, and he looked through the smoke and impending darkness at the mall in front of him.

The building was still standing, but all the glass was blown in at the entrance. Following the scatter path of debris and damage back into the parking lot, Zack had no trouble identifying ground zero. There was a large smoking, burning pile of cars not far from the entrance, and even though he didn't see any trace of the minibus among them, he was certain that had been the source of the blast, its sacks of ammonium nitrate, along with some kind of a detonator, making a reasonably efficient bomb.

There was no shooting in the mall at the moment, but Zack imagined that if Six had been anywhere near the entrance when that bus exploded, he might not be in a position to do much fighting at present.

Morgan and Redus returned to the others armed with MP5s. The five Ground Branch officers stood in the haze, saw dead, injured, or just disoriented cops everywhere they looked, and then Zack strapped his subgun over his neck.

"What's our play, boss?" Morgan asked as he put on Kevlar taken from one of the drivers.

Zack finished donning his own soft body armor. "We're going into that mall to find Six, or to recover his body. Understood?"

"Understood," Redus said, then checked his MP5 and put the sling around his own neck. He didn't think much of Sierra Six, but his team leader had given an order, and he was going to carry it out or die trying.

Court awoke in a panic because he'd lost all situational awareness in the three-way gunfight he had been involved in. He lay facedown on a cold tile floor; some sort of ceiling light had fallen on top of him, but it was plastic and cheap aluminum and hadn't seemed to cause him any damage.

But the smoke and the low light in the building made getting his bearings all but impossible.

His only prayer was that his enemies were as disoriented as he was, because if they *did* have all their faculties, then he was fucked.

The red jingle minibus had exploded outside, that much was obvious, but as to the disposition of the rest of the KRF fighters here in the mall, he didn't have a clue. He was relieved, however, when he realized he was lying on top of the Kalashnikov he'd gotten off the dead dude in the Nike store downstairs, so he fumbled with it a moment and brought it up to his shoulder.

He pushed off the ground, back up to his knees, and tried to scan for threats. It was late dusk outside, and the power was off in the mall now, so there was little illumination beyond that which came from burning cars at the entrance.

He pressed the switch to turn on the weapon light and scanned around quickly to hunt for targets and to get his bearings before turning it off again.

Court rose awkwardly to his feet, spit a trickle of blood from his lips, then headed for the Tag Heuer store on weakened legs, telling himself this fight was still on, no matter what the hell had occurred outside.

He was halfway to the store when a rifle cracked behind him, and he threw himself back down to the ground. The guy in the optical store was still making trouble, but the poor lighting had obviously saved Court from catching a 7.62-millimeter round to the back of his head.

The man turned on the light of his AK, hunting for a better shot, and this gave Court the man's exact location.

Court fired back, giving away his own location in the form of muzzle flashes, but he raked the area where he'd seen the terrorist's weapon light, desperate to force the man's head down if nothing else.

Zack was third in the stack behind Redus and Pace, and in front of Morgan and Lennox, as they entered an employee access door and began moving up a darkened hallway. There was no emergency lighting here in the mall, or at least none that was working, so the men activated the lights on the two MP5s that had them, and they pressed on.

Gunfire above them—it was muted enough for Zack to surmise it was at least two floors up—gave them an idea of where they were heading first. They found a staircase and began moving that way, then both lights quickly flipped off when the unmistakable sound of a metal door opening on the floor above them echoed in the tight space.

Hightower and Redus had weapon lights; they waited to turn them back on, listening to the sound of multiple rushing footsteps enter the metal stairwell and begin descending.

Only when the footsteps told the Americans the people approaching were on the landing, not ten feet away, did Redus, who was still the point man, actuate his flashlight.

A group of five civilians, all covered with dust and sweat, and one man covered with blood from a wound above his eye, lurched back in surprise and began moving in the other direction.

Hightower called out to them. "Police! Police! Move past us and get out of here."

The group slowed and stopped, spoke to one another in Urdu, and then did as they were told, though Zack was highly confident he and his men did not look like any local cops these civilians had ever seen.

Zack and his team continued ascending, bypassing the second floor and heading up to the third, as more gunfire pounded around them in the mall.

THIRTY-EIGHT

Court Gentry was most of the way through his last magazine of Kalash-nikov ammo, but the weapon remained on his shoulder as he scanned the darkness for a target. He'd managed to move away from the garbage can he'd been using for cover, concealing his retreat in the darkness and lin-gering smoke from both his rifle and the burning cars in the parking lot down two floors and off to his right, and now he was crouched behind a counter in a bakery. All around him, pies and cakes sat under glass display cases, while he wiped blood from his face with the shoulder of his T-shirt and then put his eye back in the red dot sight of his AK.

Through the darkness of the blacked-out mall, and through the haze from the dust and smoke that enveloped it, Court recognized the move-ment, identified the form as being a person, and then squinted through dust and through the display case he hid behind, searching to see if the man held a weapon.

Finally, the shooter in the Tag Heuer shop made a mistake. Court had moved to the terrorist's left; he was across the mezzanine from him now and not down from it, but after a moment he heard the crunching of shoes on glass. Just as he was about to turn on his light, confident that he would have a target to shoot, his enemy switched on his own light but swung it around to the location where Court had been earlier.

Court Gentry did not hesitate. He fired a single round from his weapon, hitting the man in the right side of his head, and the terrorist who'd had Court pinned for the past few minutes dropped where he'd stood.

Court himself rose and began running out of the bakery, using the darkness and the smoke and the dust for cover while he made his way towards a slow but rather steady series of AKs booming somewhere off to his left. He told himself he'd go down the stairs in the employee access hall on the opposite side, then head up to the fourth level, listening for gunfire to guide him on.

Hightower and his team moved as a single entity out of a women's clothing store on the third floor that was far enough away from the explosion to where the dust hung in the air but the smoke had not reached. They avoided using their weapon lights as they entered the mezzanine, relying on any light that reached into this dark mall, plus their ears, listening for the telltale crunching of steps over broken glass, the rattle of sling swivels on a weapon, the whispered orders of one enemy to another.

In the end it wasn't the faint crunching of glass or the hushed whisper of the enemy but a burst of gunfire off to their left. Redus was point, and he knew to move in that direction; the rest followed, and once they came around the T intersection of the mall, he saw a muzzle flash out on the mezzanine in front of them.

Hightower actuated the light on his MP5 now; the target was identified as a terrorist, and the five Americans cut the man down, but not before he executed a wounded shopkeeper in front of his store.

Golf Sierra Five rushed forward, kicked away the dead man's weapon, and then Four shot the man once more in the chest for good measure.

More gunfire erupted, but it wasn't coming from out in the mall. Instead the booming echoed to their left, inside the employee access hall that ran behind every store here on the third level. The volume of fire indicated more than one shooter, and all five of the men recognized the sound of AKs.

Hightower called to his point man in front of him. "Dino."

Redus turned and began moving quickly, his weapon still to his shoulder, its stock pressed against the shoulder strap of his body armor. He rushed through a shoe store, found the back room, and moved carefully through this space, using his light here because he had no choice.

He found the rear exit and entered the hallway, turned off his light, and began moving slowly and blindly back for the stairs.

Court expended the last round in his AK at muzzle flashes across the open atrium here on the fourth floor of the mall. He'd taken fire and found cover in a cosmetics shop, diving behind a display just as hot rounds zipped inches from him.

With his rifle empty, he drew his Glock again. He didn't want to get into a long-range gunfight with a guy wielding a rifle when he was armed with only a pistol, so he crawled along the floor until he got to the back room of the establishment. Here he launched to his feet and ran to the exit, planning on racing back to the stairs to head back down. There was shooting there, sporadically, and Court thought that here he might be able to get the drop on one of the enemy and score himself another long gun.

Once in the hallway, however, he realized he should have kept the rifle, if only for the light on its rail. It was near pitch-black darkness here, but he put his empty left hand on the wall and moved along as fast as he could, knowing the stairs were just ahead.

He found them and began descending as quietly as possible, but a noise below him made him stop in his tracks. He had no doubts there were still civilians scrambling around here and there, so he wasn't sure he'd encountered the enemy, but the sound was unmistakably footsteps on the stairs themselves.

He descended some more, and right when he began to turn for the landing, a brilliant light shone from just feet away.

Court reached out with his free hand at the light, then put his hand around the steel barrel and polymer forestock of a Kalashnikov rifle, just behind the light. He ducked down to his right and shoved the weapon up and to his left, the gun cracked off, and Court felt the heat of the barrel scorch his fingers.

He threw his body against the man on the landing, slamming him into the cinder-block wall, though Court couldn't see his attacker at all after the light had shone right in his eyes.

He jabbed his Glock hard against the man's gut; the rifle fired again, further burning Court's hand, and he pulled the trigger on his pistol, sending round after round after round into the terrorist's midsection.

The man dropped his rifle and fell. Court stumbled over his falling body on the landing, bounced a shoulder against a wall, and turned towards the darkness where the stairwell continued down to the third floor.

These terrorists had been moving in groups of two, so he was worried another man would be coming up the stairs.

Just then, a new white light blinded him from the hallway below, just twenty-five feet away, and Court instinctively fired two rounds at it. The light spun to the ground and extinguished, and he lined up to shoot where the man behind the light had probably fallen.

But as he began pressing his trigger a third time, he heard a voice boom in the hall.

"Friendlies! Cease fire!" It was Zack.

Oh my God, Court thought. He'd just killed one of his teammates.

He lowered his weapon quickly.

Keith Morgan's voice rang out in the echoing hallway. "Five is down!"

Court stood there on the landing twenty-five feet from the men he'd taken for terrorists. Hightower shined his weapon light on the ceiling now, using its reflection against concrete to illuminate the entire section of the stairwell and hallway.

Court holstered, then hurried to aid Dino Redus, who was on the ground on his back and surrounded by his team, but Pace stepped forward, blocking him, using a submachine gun as a shield.

"Get the fuck back!" he shouted.

Court had engaged five men in five incidents in the last five minutes. He'd been blown across a mezzanine by a bomb, he'd witnessed more death and horror than ever before in his life, and he'd been hit in the eyes with a powerful light just seconds before, killing a man at contact distance.

He had been in the process of rushing to aid yet more innocents under fire, and in the middle of this frenzy, he instinctively fired at a weapon light that clicked on in pitch-black darkness twenty-five feet away.

Still, he knew the circumstances didn't matter. He'd shot a teammate. He knew he was in deep shit.

To his relief, however, a groaning Dino Redus spoke from the floor. "Both rounds caught my soft armor. Fuck! That hurt."

Zack felt under the man's armor quickly. "No blood, ribs don't feel broken. Guys, get him up."

Sierra Five was pulled to his feet by Morgan and Lennox, and he looked at Court in the low light as he himself rubbed his hand under the soft body armor he'd taken from the Pakistani cop. "You motherfucker."

Court said nothing.

Morgan shouted, "I told you this prick would fuck up and someone would—"

Zack moved forward now, pushing past Lennox. "Everybody calm the fuck down! Redus, you're fine. Morgan, we've got work to do. You, too, Six. We'll deal with this after."

"Copy," Court said softly.

Just then, another rattling of gunfire erupted back on the level above them. Zack grabbed Court by the shoulder and pushed him forward.

Zack said, "Six, you're on point with your Glock. We clean the last of the fuckers out of here and then slip the cops outside."

"Easy day," Court said. He was being sarcastic, but Zack didn't seem to pick up on it.

He said, "Easy day."

The Golf Sierra team shot at an armed man on the fourth level; a single round from Lennox hit him low, in either the pelvis or the leg, but the man's partner was across the mezzanine, and he engaged the Americans, forcing them into a tea shop. Both terrorists disengaged, the wounded man no doubt crawling off to hide, and the ambulatory fighter racing south in the mall, surely on the hunt for easier prey.

The Americans found the ambulatory man a couple of minutes later. They were down on the second floor, but they followed the booms and flashes of gunfire to locate the man by the escalator Court had leapt off minutes before. He was in the process of shooting dead bodies, having no more living targets in sight. To Court, the man seemed to be biding his time, waiting for someone to come up here and fight him.

Golf Sierra obliged, cutting the young man down with a fusillade from a half dozen weapons.

But in the end it was the local cops who finally attacked the mall and found the last terrorist wounded in a McDonald's in the food court. He'd been shot through both legs by Lennox minutes earlier, and he'd then re-treated up here in the dark to make his last stand. As the poorly trained police moved on him, he managed to injure two with his AK before a dozen pistols and rifles sprayed into the McDonald's, finally finishing the KRF fighter at close range with a shotgun blast to the chest.

Golf Sierra used the cacophony of gunfire as a distraction to leave the mall via a back door. There was a police cordon around the place, but it was full of holes, and the men crouched between parked cars on the opposite side of the wrecked main entrance, making their way through the lot between a pair of Lahore city police vehicles and men crouched behind them, until they were out of sight of the cops and could stand up and move normally.

The men hot-wired an old delivery truck in a strip mall next door. Pace climbed behind the wheel, his bloody nose now stanched with a couple of torn pieces of his T-shirt that he'd crammed into his nostrils.

They drove off, melting into traffic on Nazaria-e-Pakistan Avenue, which had not been altogether affected by the explosion or the attack at a mall a half mile to the east.

It was only after another line of Pakistani police vehicles raced past them, indicating finally that they had not been spotted during their escape, that Pace asked his TL the question the whole team must have been asking themselves. "Where to, boss?"

"Straight to the airport. If Hanley doesn't already have extraction wait-ing for us, then he will by the time we get there."

Redus was seated next to Gentry in the back of the van. "Yo, Six. If it took me catching a double-tap from your gun to get your ass out of our lives, then I'm cool with that."

"You took one for the team, Dino," Morgan quipped from the back of the van.

"Two, actually." And then, to Court, he said, "You're outta here."

Court said nothing, and Hightower looked back from the front passenger seat at his Six. "Your mouth is bleeding. You hurt anywhere else?"

"No. I don't think so. What did you find at the hotel?"

"We didn't get in. Somebody called five-oh on us."

"I didn't get compromised."

"I know. I'm going to have a talk with Hanley. My bet is ISI got word we were operating, and they weren't going to let that happen."

Zack continued looking at Court in the low light. The younger man's eyes were distant, the veins in his neck throbbed, and he trembled.

Zack said, "You're okay, Six. It's over. You did good."

Redus said, "*Good?* Are you kidding?"

Zack silenced his man with a hard stare.

Softly, almost to himself, Court said, "I've never seen anything like that."

Lennox spoke from the driver's seat. "You don't really get used to it, but you kinda do. Just concentrate on breathing. Think about getting the hell out of Pakistan, because that's what matters now. We'll save everything else for later."

Redus said, "But—"

Lennox's voice boomed, every bit as loud as Hightower's. "I said *later!*"

The men drove on, the sound of sirens fading into the distance behind them.

THIRTY-NINE

PRESENT DAY

It was just past twelve forty-five in the morning when a lone figure appeared in the dark in the central Mumbai residential and industrial development of Bandra Kurla Complex. He had walked the length of the wall outside the American School of Bombay, but then he turned around and began heading back, avoiding bored-looking security guards at a gatehouse by climbing a fence just south of their position.

He then moved across several tennis courts, remaining in the shadows, towards a row of small buildings.

Court had learned from Matt Hanley that the ex-CIA man he was coming to meet, Ted Appleton, was now a teacher here at the school and benefited from this chiefly by living in a bungalow on campus along the banks of the Mithi River, which snaked through central Mumbai from north to south.

He found the unit he was looking for; it was as still and quiet as all the other bungalows running up and down both sides of the little road, and then he moved through thick palms to make his way to a narrow corridor between the home itself and a wooden fence. He stepped onto the porch, where he saw a small sign on a stake stuck into a rock garden by the front door proudly announcing that the property was protected by a security system. Noting the company of the system on the stake itself, he determined he could disable it simply by finding the electronic junction box that would likely be on the wall of the home somewhere around back. He moved between the eastern side of the bungalow and the old, rickety wooden fence that partitioned the property from the next one, ducked under a ground-floor air-conditioning unit, then made his way to the back, where he found not only the box to the security system that he'd hoped to find but also a rear entrance to the home and a view to the west.

The rear of the property ended abruptly, falling down a steeply sloped riverbank that looked over the Mithi, although this was not a selling point of the property. The reed-filled and murky body of water was no great sight to see, and on the far bank, some fifty yards away, Court saw electric lighting illuminating some sort of a massive car junkyard, an apocalyptic view from the back windows of Appleton's bungalow.

He turned away from the tiny backyard and the water and focused his attention on the box. He used a multi-tool to open it, then looked the wires over carefully with a small penlight. Determining which one to cut to remove main power and which one to cut to extinguish the backup battery, he pushed through the dummy wires that would set off the alarm and made two quick snips.

This done, he retraced his steps in the dark, back around the side of the building, returning to the air-conditioning unit. Court climbed up on top of the warm box, placed his hand on the beams holding the AC unit directly above in a second-floor window, and pulled himself up, using his deeply treaded hiking boots against the wall to help him with his climb.

Standing on the upstairs AC, he tried the window next to it and found it locked. Taking his time to pry it open carefully with his multi-tool, he entered a cluttered little office.

A minute later he found a man asleep in the next room. He was alone, which made this easier, but Court had no idea what Appleton looked like, so he wasn't about to start complimenting himself yet on a job well done.

Court pulled a chair up next to the man's bed, then quietly opened the man's side table, double-checking that there was no weapon there.

There was nothing on or in the nightstand other than an asthma inhaler, more books and magazines, a pair of reading glasses, and a glass of water.

Already Court was getting the idea that coming to talk to this old professor was going to be a dry hole. He'd been a CIA station chief twelve years ago, but now he looked exactly like what he was: an academic pushing back against impending retirement.

Annoyed that he'd likely wasted his time, he pulled out his Browning Hi-Power pistol, reached over to the sleeping man, and tapped him once on the forehead roughly. The man stirred, took a few seconds to open his eyes, and then looked around the room to determine what had awakened him.

He saw a man in a black hoodie sitting three feet away, a gun held between his knees.

The older man lurched back but said nothing.

Court said, "If you have a weapon stashed under a pillow, reaching for it is going to work out exactly the opposite way you'd always dreamed it would."

The man blinked a few times. But still, he said nothing.

"I need to talk to you."

Now he spoke, his voice raspy with age and sleep. "Who . . . who are you?"

"The question is, who are *you*?"

Still hoarsely, the man said, "I'm Appleton."

"Good." Court slid his gun back into his waistband.

The man sat up in bed. He seemed nervous, but not overly so. "Do we know one another?"

"No. Matt Hanley sent me."

At this, the man sat up straighter. "Hanley? *That* bastard?"

Court gave a tired smile. "That bastard."

"Can I . . . can I put on my glasses?"

"Be my guest."

Appleton put them on, smoothed out the thin wisps of hair on his head as best he could, then pushed the covers off him. "I heard Hanley got the boot from the seventh floor. Sent down to be the station chief of . . . Papua, was it?"

"I'm not here to talk about New Guinea."

Appleton shrugged. "What does Hanley want from me?"

"It's not like that. I need some information about activities here in Mumbai. He says you are the man to talk to."

The older man raised both eyebrows, then looked around at his tiny little room in his small home. "Does it look like I've been keeping my finger on the pulse of Mumbai? Hanley knows I've been retired for a long time. In the old days, sure. The Indian subcontinent was my beat for over a decade. But now . . ."

His voice trailed off, but Court said, "What I want to talk about . . . is the old days."

Appleton cracked a little smile. "Ah. If it's ancient history you want, then maybe I *am* your man. Go on."

"Twelve years ago. Pakistan."

Appleton's smile disappeared. "What about it?"

"I was there. I was Ground Branch."

Now the man in bed blinked hard. "You look too young to have been in Golf Sierra back then."

"Trust me, I got that a lot."

The former station chief shook his head. "I don't believe you."

"The Gulberg Galleria."

"What about it?"

"There was one Agency asset who wasn't captured at the KRF safe house. One guy who made it to the galleria before the bomb went off."

Appleton cocked his head. "I remember all that. So?"

Court just said, "Me."

"What was your call sign? Be careful, because I remember from the after-action report."

"Golf Sierra Six."

"Oh my God," Appleton muttered softly. "Sierra Six. You?"

"Me."

The man in the bed took a long time before speaking. Finally he said, "Are you here to kill me?"

Court cocked his head. *This* he hadn't expected. "Why? What did you do?"

The older man hesitated, then said, "I don't know how you see things that happened back then."

"Was it your fault? Everything that happened?"

"I could have made some different decisions. Would that have changed the outcome? I don't know." He sniffed. "It's what I do with my free time now. Try to determine where I went wrong back then." After a moment he added, "Those poor people."

"Yeah," Court said. "Except . . . it's not over."

Now Appleton was the one who cocked his head. "What's that supposed to mean?"

Court said, "Murad Khan is still alive."

When Court told this to Arjun, and when Court told this to Hanley, both men had clearly been astonished and doubtful, at least at first. But Appleton said nothing, and he made no reaction.

"You don't seem surprised," Court said.

"Nothing surprises me anymore. Did I know? No. But did I suspect ISI was lying to us back then when they offered up some trace DNA as proof of his death? Yes. I've always harbored doubts." He shrugged. "It's what led to the fast track for my early retirement."

"Meaning?"

"Meaning I wouldn't shut up about it, and I got the axe." He shrugged. "That, and other things. Again, I could have handled myself differently."

Court didn't care about this old guy's shitty career. Instead he said, "Why are you in India?"

"I took a teaching job here at—"

"Not what I'm asking."

Appleton sighed. "I could brew us some coffee."

"You could answer my question."

The older man took his time before speaking. Finally he said, "I fell in love with a girl from Mumbai, it seems like forever ago now. It didn't last . . . nothing lasts forever . . . but there was never anyone else for me.

"Being here makes me feel as if we're still together, I guess. I doubt that makes much sense to a young man like you."

Court replied, "It makes more sense than you could possibly know."

"Well, then. I'm sorry to hear that."

Court shook a thought away, then said, "Hanley told me you'd still have contacts here in Indian intelligence. He said you were doing some consulting."

Appleton nodded. "Consulting, yes, but not with R&AW. I worked with the Department of Atomic Energy here, just assisting them with security protocols, making sure they are up to date on their safety methods to protect nuclear material from proliferation."

"How's that going?"

Appleton gave a big shrug to his bony shoulders. "Not particularly well. Their controls are . . . subpar. I've been let go from that position, as well. I'm just a professor now."

Court switched gears. "What do you know about B-Company?"

Appleton seemed to think over how to answer this. "India's largest criminal enterprise. Founded by Palak Bari back in the eighties. The man grew up as a Mumbai slum dog, a kid of the ghettos. He hates Hindu-majority India with every fiber of his being. Rumor is he is living in Karachi under the protection of the ISI."

He then looked to Court quizzically. "What does B-Company have to do with Khan?"

"Khan is using B-Company here. I don't understand what they get out of it."

Now Appleton spoke like a college professor. "Bari has ordered attacks on Indian government offices over the past three decades. Bombs, shootings, things like that. He is an enemy of the government. His foot soldiers are in it for the money, but Bari would burn this nation to the ground if he could. Khan is a Kashmiri Muslim separatist. Indian by birth but an immigrant to Pakistan. Twelve years ago his sights were set on America for offering support to Pakistan, but Khan himself truly has no greater enemy than the Indian government."

Court understood now that if Khan's target was here in India, and his target involved the national regime, then B-Company would be natural allies to him.

"If Khan was working with B-Company, where could I find him?"

"If I were Khan and I needed a place to hide out, I'd do it right in the middle of the group I was working with that could offer me protection. Wouldn't you?"

"Where would that be?"

"B-Company is strongest here in Mumbai. In the slums but also in the neighborhoods around the slums. There are skyscrapers there, lots of money. Lots of criminal money."

"So you are telling me, basically, that in a city of eleven million people, Khan could be just about anywhere."

Ted Appleton shrugged. "I'll reach out to my contacts in the police, in R&AW, even in other departments around Mumbai. I'll see if anyone knows anything, or even just suspects anything."

Court said, "By tomorrow morning, there is going to be news of a B-Company massacre in Malabar Hill. A dozen dead or so."

"Christ," Appleton muttered. "Like the thing in Andheri East. A whole building got shot up. Nearly a dozen dead or wounded gang members."

Court said, "This time it was B-Company who was doing the killing."

Now the ex–station chief looked Court over with a keen eye. "Son . . . if you were Ground Branch, then you will have some skills. If you see Murad Khan . . . kill him for me."

"I'll kill him for both of us."

Appleton just nodded. "Right. You said you were there." He regarded Court for a long time, then said, "I can give you the number to my burner phone."

"You have end-to-end encryption on it?" Court asked.

Appleton looked at him with disappointment. "I was following security protocols before you were in grade school, son."

"No offense, but you weren't using Signal on your smartphone when I was in grade school."

Appleton nodded with a smile. "Touché." He climbed out of bed. "I'll grab it, we can set up contact protocols."

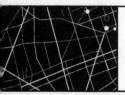

FORTY

TWELVE YEARS AGO

The Golf Sierra Ground Branch team didn't know what had gone on behind the scenes to get them out of Pakistan. That had been coordinated by Hanley back at FOB Chapman and, presumably, CIA Station Islamabad. They were taken from their safe house by local NOC officers and driven under cover of darkness to the airport in Faisalabad. Here they changed into fresh clothing to be loaded on an early morning Gulf Air flight to Bahrain International Airport, where, upon landing, they waited, sitting on a concrete floor of a hangar in 120-degree heat.

Court wore a bandage on the fingers of his left hand where he'd been singed by the AK barrel in the stairwell, and Pace's nose was taped and gauzed, but everyone was in good shape considering what they'd been through.

There wasn't much talk during the journey among the men. Even the normally loquacious Hightower was more subdued than normal.

He checked in on his youngest team member from time to time; Gentry had seen the most action, after all, but the other guys treated him as if he weren't even there.

Court had felt cold-shouldered by the team before Lahore; *now* he felt like a pariah.

They were put aboard an American Air Force C-17 Globemaster transport flight to Jalalabad, where they landed just after dark. Here they staggered down the ramp, battling stiff muscles and their heavy backpacks, walked a quarter mile to another part of the airport, and climbed aboard one of the red and white helicopters Court had noticed flying around Camp Chapman.

They put on headsets and immediately took off.

Court saw that the pilot was an overweight man in his fifties who looked like any military experience he might have had been most of a lifetime ago. The copilot appeared younger, but no more like a military man than his pilot.

Court leaned to Hightower as the helo began climbing and heading to the south.

Court said, "These are CIA Chinooks?"

"Boeing-Vertol 107s. It's the civilian version of the Chinook CH-46. They're flown by private contractors. A U.S. company called Chesapeake Air. They ferry troops and other personnel, like us, around Afghanistan. If you see a red and white BV-107, it's Chesapeake."

Court nodded.

Zack added, "They're the bus drivers around here for us. No combat ops."

Redus had been listening in to the conversation, but now he turned to Gentry. "You'll be climbing back on one of these helos tomorrow when they send your ass stateside."

Court turned away from him and looked out the portal into darkness.

They landed at midnight and climbed out of the Chesapeake helicopter into a cool night wind that blew the grit of the desert into Court's face.

The men were picked up by a van—it seemed to Court like it was his tenth conveyance of the past day—and then driven back to the tactical operations center.

Though it was midnight and the men were beyond beat, Matt Hanley, intelligence chief Terry Vance, and a team of analysts were there, all working and waiting to receive the Ground Branch team for the joint after-action review of the events in Lahore.

Court found a chair in the middle of the darkened room, lit mainly by wall monitors and glowing computer screens. The rest of his team headed straight for the coffee, but Court hadn't been able to eat or drink much since the day before.

The instant he sat down, he felt a presence standing over him. Looking up, he found himself happy to see it was Julie Marquez.

"How are you?" she asked.

Court shrugged a little. "How do I look?"

With her arms crossed in front of her chest, she said, "Terrible."

"Yeah."

She asked, "Have you heard the numbers at the mall in Lahore? Sixty-one dead, not including the KRF fighters. Most in the bombing. Lots more injured."

Court just shook his head in disbelief. "It was a fucking mess."

"All day on the news they've been talking about a hero at the mall who fought the terrorists until the police arrived. A Westerner."

He shrugged now. "Not a hero. You're read in on everything we do, so you probably already know it was just me."

She sat down in the folding chair next to him. "Yeah. I also heard you shot one of your guys."

Court shrugged. "Once in a while," he said, "a little coating of sugar isn't a bad thing." He then motioned with his head towards Redus, who was pouring himself a cup of coffee. "That one."

Julie regarded Redus, then turned back to Court. "Well . . . he looks in better shape than you do, so I wouldn't worry about it too much."

Court smiled a little. He was fucked. He and everyone in the room knew it, Marquez included, but at least she wasn't treating him any differently than she had before.

His smile went away quickly, though. "I am getting sent home."

She nodded slightly, her characteristic gaze changing a little, as if she were sad to hear this news. "They told you?"

"Not officially. Not yet. I just doubt they let you shoot a teammate in the chest around here." He shrugged. "It was a crazy situation, but I'm responsible for every bullet that comes out of my gun."

"I'm sure it was an accident."

Court shook his head. "It was negligent. I shot into the photonic barrier."

She cocked her head. "The what?"

"I was blinded by a light. I fired anyway, without identifying my target as a threat."

"But—"

"But nothing. Nothing else matters." Court caught himself feeling sorry for himself. He just looked down at the floor.

Julie said, "It would be too bad if you got sent home. Your job isn't finished."

"What does that mean?"

"You didn't get the AN away from the KRF."

"Yeah, we did. I know because I still have a pounding headache. That shit blew up fifty yards from me."

Julie Marquez shook her head. "Maybe a thousand pounds did. That's all. That means as much as three thousand pounds are still missing."

"How do you know? And don't tell me the ISI told you."

She waved a dismissive hand. "I don't listen to the ISI. I saw the explosion. Did some bomb damage assessment, compared the scatter path to known ammonium nitrate VBIEDs where fuel oil wasn't added, because we know Khan and his people didn't have time to do that."

"VBIED?"

"Vehicle-borne improvised explosive device. You really *are* new at this, aren't you?"

"So . . . you saw the explosion?"

"Not in real time, but via some traffic camera data our team broke into after the fact. There was, at most, a half ton of AN that went up. The rest, another one and a half tons or more, must have been back at the KRF safe house still."

Court thought it over, rubbing the fatigue from his eyes. "I'm sorry we didn't get it all, but I guess I should be glad. If that was a fourth of the material, I wouldn't have survived the full monty."

Julie spoke matter-of-factly to this. "Your body would probably never be identified."

"Well," Court said, "when they send me home, they'll probably recall

Golf Sierra until they can get back to full strength. That means the KRF is going to be Lima Foxtrot's problem, at least till Hightower gets back with his crew."

Julie smiled a little, uncharacteristic for her.

"What?" Court asked, suddenly intrigued.

"One of the guys in SIGINT came up with a nickname for Lima Foxtrot, since all their assignments seem to go so smoothly and they don't meet much resistance. He started calling them the Lucky Fuckers, and the name has stuck around the TOC."

Court emitted an exhausted laugh. "I like it. What about us? Did he come up with a nickname for the dumb bastards that walk into every nest of terrorists there is?"

She smiled a little more now. "He didn't. *I* did."

"Do I want to know?"

"It's not bad. You guys have such a high body count, I started calling you the Goon Squad. I don't know if it will stick like the Lucky Fuckers, but it would be cool if it did."

"The Goon Squad," Court muttered to himself. "Honestly, I'd rather be lucky than a goon."

She shrugged. "You *are* pretty lucky that the KRF split up that ammonium nitrate."

"You got a point."

"I'm sure you'd rather sleep in, but would you like to meet me for lunch tomorrow at the DFAC? If you're heading home, I want to say goodbye."

"I don't know what the DFAC is," he admitted.

"The dining facility."

"Right." Court was too tired to feel socially awkward at the moment. "Let's make it breakfast. Doubt I'll still be around by lunchtime."

"Breakfast works," she replied. "I've got a meeting at oh eight hundred. How about oh seven fifteen?"

"You mean a quarter after seven o'clock?"

She sighed. "Get with the program, Six."

Just then, Vance called for everyone's attention. Julie stepped back over to her workstation, leaving Court with the rest of the Ground Branch men, who now sat around him in the middle of the room.

The meeting lasted an hour, and the hour went pretty much the way Court had expected. Hightower explained everything the men had done in Lahore; Redus brought up the fact that Court shot him, *twice*; and while Zack didn't dwell on it in front of Hanley, neither did he put up any defense of his Six when Redus complained.

Court was asked about his actions in the mall; he told the group everything he remembered, including the hand-to-hand interaction with the terrorist with a weapon light and then, seconds later, the shooting of Redus behind another weapon light.

But he didn't have a lot to add.

Court didn't expect Hanley to fire him on the spot, in front of everyone, but as soon as he finished, he turned and looked to the big group chief.

Hanley did not address Court or his situation. Instead he said, "Vance is saying there is more ammonium nitrate in the hands of the KRF."

Vance looked to Julie, who stood and told the group what she'd already told Court.

When she was finished with her delivery, Hanley said, "So now they have around three thousand pounds of the material left. Mix it with fuel oil and it's six thousand pounds. A lot of explosive left for us to deal with. Any idea where the material was taken?"

Vance said, "I have everybody looking into that now. Islamabad station is pressing their contacts, as well. SIGINT, HUMINT, OSINT, GEOINT, you name it. If we or Islamabad station get some hard targeting data, through any means at all, we'll send Lima Foxtrot or Golf Sierra back out."

Both Redus and Court looked around the room, waiting for someone to mention that Golf Sierra was about to be depleted by a man and would have to stand down until the man was replaced. But none of the brass said anything of the kind, and the meeting was adjourned.

Court saw Redus and Morgan both give Zack a "what the fuck" look, but Zack just told everyone to return to the pit to get some sleep as he stood from his chair.

Court started to head over to Julie's workstation; she seemed like the only person who wasn't looking at him like he was a dead man walking, but he was cut off halfway across the TOC by Hanley and Hightower.

"Sierra Six. On me," Hightower said, and then the three men walked out into the night.

Court shuffled along behind the two older men, fully expecting to get his ticket back to the States, along with a lecture about how it's not kosher to shoot one of your own dudes. He didn't want to listen, but trailed them until they stopped a hundred feet or so away from the TOC, standing under a halogen light outside a storage shed.

Court spoke first. "What time's my flight to the States?"

Hanley's arms were crossed in front of his chest. "When you get back stateside, you'll be dismissed from Ground Branch."

Court nodded. It hurt, but he got it.

"But that's for back home. For now, anyway, you are still on the team, and you are still operational."

"But I—"

"*But* you double-tapped Sierra Five, center mass. I know, I know. We're all lucky he was Kevlared up, but he was, and we still have work to do. In any normal situation, both in the military and paramilitary intelligence realms, you'd be cashiered from your place in the stack immediately and sent packing, put on some desk for the rest of your career. But I most definitely don't have to tell you that these are *not* normal times."

Court did not respond. He was in a state of shock. He turned to Hightower, expecting him to argue with Hanley.

But Hightower seemed to be on the same page. "You've lost the confidence of the team, so you have to leave Golf Sierra when we're back. But let's be honest. That was some crazy 'fog of war' shit you had to deal with. It's bad, could have been worse, but any one of us could have done what you did considering what you were in the middle of when we crossed your sight picture behind a thousand-lumen light."

"If you're trying to make me feel better about it, you—"

"Yeah, I am. Because you aren't going anywhere until the KRF is dealt with, and I need you emotionally fit for that. We *need* six guys. I vouched for you. You pulled off some epic stuff back in Lahore; I want you with us when we go back out."

Still fighting disbelief, Court said, "Roger that."

"Now, that's not to say you're off the hook. Starting at oh eight hundred we are going to begin intensive training here at Chapman; I'm damn well going to integrate you tighter into the team than you've been so far, because if we *do* get to go out again into the badlands, you'll be at the front of my stack, not free-running through a mall full of tangos, you read me?"

"I read you. But . . . what about Redus?"

"Redus is pissed, and he'll probably stay pissed." Zack shrugged. "Whatcha gonna do?"

Hanley softened now. "What you went through, kid . . ." The words didn't come to him, so he said, "Get your ass on a cot and get some sleep. Sierra One is going to run your ass ragged till you go back outside the wire, and that's when the hard part *really* begins."

Court nodded, turned, and headed for the pit, still amazed to be given a reprieve, if only a temporary one.

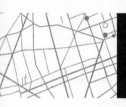

FORTY-ONE

PRESENT DAY

Priya Bandari climbed out of a taxi at one fifteen a.m., and for the second time in the past five hours, she began walking with trepidation up the hill to her uncle's house. She had no idea if police had arrived yet, so she took the same route as before, moving through the thick bushes of an unoccupied home, making her way slowly through the darkness as branches scratched into her jeans and black cotton shirt. She finally arrived at the same place where she and Cobalt had gone earlier to survey the area, and she was both happy and terrified to see that the entire home remained blacked out.

The police weren't here, which was good, but she'd have to move again through the dark and scary place, past the dead, past her uncle, and this was definitely *not* good.

She steeled herself for what she had to do, told herself it was her uncle's last wish that she see what he had in the safe, and then she moved forward.

She'd not told Cobalt where she was going. He was off on a quest of his own right now, and she didn't want to hear him tell her that she should wait until they could go together. The police could come at any time, she knew, and then any chance she had to get into the safe would be lost.

Back inside the home, she could smell the death now. She covered her face as she passed through the living room; she did not stop to kiss her uncle's shrouded forehead as she'd done before, because now it was all about getting in and getting back out.

She took the stairs two at a time, stepped into the office, and made a beeline to the panel hiding the safe, popping it open.

She knelt in front of the safe, hyperaware of the death downstairs and of the fact that, unlike when she was here a few hours earlier, she did not have Cobalt and his pistol here to save her if anything went wrong.

She dialed the combination with a quivering hand. Fourteen, forty-four, twenty-seven, forty-one. She took a long, slow, cleansing breath, whispered a yoga mantra to calm herself, and then turned the handle on the safe.

It opened with a muted *click*.

Inside it she found reams of papers, stacks of cash, gold jewelry, and a Rolex watch. There were family photos; her uncle had been a bachelor his entire life and had no children of his own, so most of the pictures she saw were of her.

She bit her lip, thinking about the good times, and then she pushed every item in the safe aside, and her hand clutched a small foldable thumb drive.

The answers, whatever they were, would lie not in the paperwork but on the drive, she had no doubt of this.

She took the little device, launched to her feet, and then raced for the door.

But then she stopped. She had to know what was on the drive.

She moved back to the desktop computer and slipped the drive into the machine, then clicked on the icon for it as soon as it appeared.

But the thumb drive was encrypted. She stared at the monitor; it demanded a password she did not have, and she had no idea what to do now.

How could her uncle give her the combination to the safe but forget to give her the password to the drive?

And then, finally, she realized he would not have done this. If he'd not given her the password, it was only because he'd know that she could guess it.

She typed in her name, both *Priya* and *Priyanka*, and both times the screen informed her that her access was denied.

It also told her she had one more chance to type in the correct password before she would be locked out of the drive for twenty-four hours.

She closed her eyes slowly; a new supply of tears dripped down onto the keys. She tried to channel her uncle's thoughts, remember their conversations, and push out the smell of the fetid death wafting up from downstairs.

What could it be?

And then, as if a light beamed down on her from above, she had a sudden clarity, and she knew.

Slowly her eyes opened, and she typed *Chiki.*

It was the pet name Arjun had used for Priya ever since she was a little girl. It meant "Chicken." Until the day he began calling her Copper for operational purposes, she'd almost never heard him call her anything but Chiki.

She hit enter, and the screen loaded with files. She rubbed tears from her eyes, scanned what was in front of her, and determined that each file corresponded to a certain date, and each date signified a particular operation.

She understood that what she saw on the screen before her represented every single job Arjun Bandari had conducted in the private sector. He'd kept secret records of it all, and now she had access to them.

She clicked a date at random and saw that it was a contract he'd picked up off the Darknet three months earlier, something about planting a bug in the phone of a politician in Bangladesh. The hirer of the contract was unknown to Arjun, but he speculated in his notes that it was an R&AW proxy operation. Another file she opened was also a Darknet contract, this one six months back, and here he wrote that he was certain the British government, or an intermediary thereof, was hiring him to steal banking records from an auction house in New Delhi.

On each file Arjun recorded the resources he used, the price he charged, and the people he contracted to do the actual footwork.

Most of the contractees were code named.

She scanned quickly for a specific date, her first job with her uncle. It had been in Dubai; she'd run a drone over the home of a wealthy shipbuilder to get photos of who was on his property. It was easy work; clearly there was a domestic element to it, because Priya had been ordered to get images and video of any young women present.

A wife catching her billionaire husband philandering. *This* was the kind of work she thought her uncle did.

Not any of the madness that had happened since.

She finally traced her cursor over to the last job on the list, but it was something in Bangladesh that wasn't scheduled to begin until the following month. She knew nothing about this, but she didn't dwell on that. She moved the cursor down to the next file.

September 11. This was the night she had been in Algiers with Cobalt. The night everything went to hell.

She double-clicked, then scrolled over to the notes, looking to see if her uncle had any idea who hired him for the job, despite what he'd told Khan.

But instead of speculation, there was a name. It was clear to Priya that Arjun did not receive this contract via the Darknet, where identities could be protected, but rather he actually communicated with this person.

She read the name to herself. She'd expected it to be a Hindu name. It was, after all, presumably the Research and Analysis Wing that had sent them after the ISI operative in Algiers.

But she was surprised to see that it was not.

She read the name, and then she read it again out loud.

"Theodore Appleton."

This name meant nothing to her at all.

Scrolling down now, she looked at the resources and personnel Arjun used for the job. The drones, the IMSI-catcher, the trackers, all the gadgetry was listed under resources. Under personnel, however, she saw something curious.

She was listed as Copper only; he did not use her true name. But Cobalt, listed just under her, had a long string of numbers next to his name. There was a small tag on the number; she clicked it, and it opened a small comment box. As she read it, her blood ran cold.

Appleton personally requested this asset be hired. A Darknet contract agent. Hired him September 6 and notified Appleton that day.

Appleton, whoever he was, not only hired Arjun for the job in Algiers, but he'd also stipulated that Arjun hire Cobalt.

She was certain Cobalt would want to know this, as soon as possible.

She pocketed the thumb drive and powered down the machine. Retracing her steps out of the darkened home, she told herself she'd wait and call Cobalt when she was somewhere safe. He needed to know that it wasn't R&AW who'd hired him in the first place, though she had no idea what this all meant.

FORTY-TWO

The killers came from the river by rigid-hull inflatable boat. Eight men, part of the crew that had attacked Arjun Bandari's house earlier the previous evening, approached the small two-story bungalow of Ted Appleton through the darkness and the mist. These were B-Company regulars, foot soldiers with blood on their hands—in many cases literally, because they'd not cleaned up after the knife attack in Malabar Hill.

The driver of the boat throttled back his engine when he was still one hundred meters or so from Appleton's neighborhood, which was nestled behind the walls around the American School but open to the water. He steered the boat towards the shore almost silently; the men in front of him pushed themselves down to the deck to make themselves as small a silhouette as possible, and then the motor was cut fully and the prop lifted because of the thick reeds and other vegetation at the water's edge.

Men climbed out of the RIB and waded through waist-deep water as they pulled it to land among trash and more wild growth unattended by either the university or the city. Looking up at the incredibly steep slope, the leader of the group of killers realized it was impossible to tell which home was his target's from the backside, so they pulled the RIB along with them as they began heading north, wading parallel to the shore, remaining stealthy in black shirts and brown pants.

They finally beached the boat when they found a wooden staircase that led from the river up to the road where Appleton lived, and then they climbed quickly.

The B-Company men had orders to do this quietly, if possible, so while they all carried pistols on their bodies, just like in Malabar Hill, it was the black-sheathed knives on their belts that would serve as the principal weapons for tonight's operation.

Appleton was the target because, according to Arjun Bandari, Appleton had been the man who ordered the operation in Algiers. Khan didn't know what the old man's game was, but he knew the old man from back in the American's days in Pakistan. Appleton would have a very personal reason for wanting Khan dead, again, and if he was living here in Mumbai and somehow got word that Khan was here, too, there was no telling the lengths the former CIA man might go to.

Court wrote Appleton's Signal number down, then stood to leave. The former station chief quickly threw on some khakis and followed him downstairs. He said, "I will make some calls as soon as people start waking up this morning."

"This has to happen fast," Court replied. "Khan is feeling the heat I put him under. He's not going to sit around."

"Agreed."

Court went to the front door, looked out the small pane of glass in the window, and saw nothing but the other bungalows and the moonlight. He considered leaving via the river, but it had looked pretty dank and nasty when he was out back, so he decided to just retrace his steps by the tennis courts and jump the wall again. He took a few more seconds to survey his surroundings, put his hand on the latch, and pushed it down.

And then he froze.

Appleton stood behind him, but he noticed the younger man's hesitation. "What are you doing?" Appleton asked.

"Something's wrong."

"Wrong?"

Court peered deep into the shadows across the street. There was movement in the bushes in front of the home there, and it was slightly out of sync from the breeze blowing.

Finally Court made out a brief silhouette of a head in front of the lighter-colored wall of the home.

Someone was crouched in the foliage, looking at Ted Appleton's house.

Court didn't wait around to pick out others in the darkness. He *knew* there would be others.

"Company. Out front. Probably out back, too."

Appleton's voice cracked when he spoke. "What? Why?"

"They're here for me, I guess. Like flies to shit, I attract them. I didn't get comped, so somebody must be watching your place."

"Why would somebody—"

"That's a question for later."

"How many are there?"

"More than we can handle." Court looked back towards the rear of the house. "We're going to make a play for the river."

"The river? You can't get down to it except from a staircase a block away."

"We're not taking the stairs, Ted. You got a little run in you?"

"I . . . I ride my bike a lot. I am healthy enough for a man of my—"

"Where's your bike? Didn't see it outside."

"I keep it in the kitchen by the back door. Why?"

"Let's go," Court said, and he started moving for the kitchen.

"Go where?"

Court went back and got him. "It won't be fun, but I've seen what those dudes out there can do to a man, and a little tumble and then a swim is much better than the alternative."

"A swim?" Appleton croaked, but he followed the younger man into the kitchen.

Court found the bike against the wall between the refrigerator and the back door, and he flipped it and began removing the front tire.

"What the hell are you going to do with that?" Appleton asked.

"I'll carry this till we hit the water, then you find me and grab onto it. We'll both hold on to this to stay oriented below the surface, and I'll pull you along if you can't keep up. We stay submerged, all the way to the other side. They'll know which way the water's going, and they'll be off hunting in that direction."

Appleton couldn't believe what he was hearing. "That's fifty meters to the other side. How will we breathe?"

Court unscrewed the valve on the big tire. "You can get air from this. When you need a breath, pull on the tire, and I'll slow down. You can push the valve to the side and suck in a breath of air. You can get five, maybe seven breaths out of this thing. It'll taste like old rubber, but it will work."

"That's crazy."

"Beats getting your throat slit."

The attackers would break in simultaneously from different parts of the home, Court assumed, and that would give him and Appleton an advantage. The force would be split apart with probably no more than two or three men out back.

When they made it to the door, Court drew his Browning pistol with his right hand and held the tire in his left.

Court cracked open the back door quietly and saw nothing between himself and the edge of the garden where it fell away suddenly towards the river. He peeked out to the left and saw a man struggling to open the sliding glass door that connected to the dining room off Court's left, and he assumed there would be someone else to his right, coming this way.

He felt the door he was holding pull open, and he realized someone was right there on the other side.

Court fired from the hip, his Browning Hi-Power blasting a hole straight through the door. Quickly he brought the weapon to eye level and spun on the balls of his feet, shooting the man at the sliding glass door, who was only now in the process of pulling his pistol.

He came out the door at speed, shot the man on the ground behind it again, and then ran towards the cliff above the water. Appleton held on to the other side of the wheel, and Court all but pulled the slower man along.

Several pistols cracked back at the house just as Court and the former CIA station chief leapt out into the darkness and began falling. Both men slammed into the brush as they rolled and tumbled, Appleton lost his hold on the wheel, and then both men splashed into the reedy water.

Court leapt to his feet and found Appleton standing up and sucking in a lungful of air, but Court yanked on him, forcing both himself and the man he was trying to protect under the water, just as another gunshot came from above.

As soon as they went deeper, Court kicked along, but he also took Appleton by the back of his head, then brought it gently to the bike tire. As he pushed in the valve, air shot onto the older CIA man's face and he sucked the bubbles, then swallowed them along with dirty river water.

They swam on, farther out into the river, Court half fighting the current and half allowing it to carry him to the west. He wanted to get to the other bank where he'd seen the car junkyard, because he knew there would be lots of places to hide there if the men who'd attacked Appleton's house came looking.

They remained underwater for over two minutes, with Court only taking a single breath from the tire, leaving the rest to Appleton. They finally broke the surface within ten yards of the northern bank. Appleton wheezed in a huge lungful of air, and he kept hold of the tire so that the former Ground Branch man could pull him along the rest of the way.

Court crawled through the reeds and onto the muddy and rocky bank, finally dropping the now-flat bicycle tire; he was exhausted from the effort, but he made sure the older man was still on his heels as he climbed up, then found a broken portion of the wire fence that was put in to protect the junkyard from looters coming from the water.

As they walked through the early morning, their bodies soaked to the bone, Court said, "There's no reason B-Company would have monitoring equipment in your house, is there?"

"Why would they?"

"I don't know. I *do* know that it's not often some second-rate mob organization compromises me, and I did *not* get tailed to your place, so I have to wonder if they had some other way of knowing I'd be here."

Appleton shook his head. "No idea. None at all."

Court pulled out his phone and saw it was dead. It hadn't been sealed in anything before he'd leapt into the river. He thought for a moment.

"You can't go back home, not until this is over. We walk until we find a taxi, although we're going to have to dry out first. We'll go to a place I have in Versova. We'll figure out our next steps from there."

Appleton nodded. "When I get a new phone, I'll get to work reaching out to contacts in R&AW to see if we can learn more about the FCU/B-Company relationship."

The two men walked on through the night, their shoes squishing water out with each exhausted step.

FORTY-THREE

TWELVE YEARS AGO

Court had been told the previous evening by Hightower that he and the team needed to be at the armory by oh eight hundred, so he climbed off his cot at oh seven hundred, took his first shower in two days, and brushed his teeth. He changed into a nondescript tan flight suit in his hooch and then laced up his boots.

This done, he headed for the DFAC, the CIA base's dining facility.

Julie was already waiting for him there, seated at a table, thumbing through a magazine. Court stepped up behind her quietly and looked over her shoulder to see what she was reading.

With surprise he said, "*People*? Really?"

She closed it quickly, tense. Then she stood up, leaving the magazine there. "I study pop culture when I can. I saw this lying here, I didn't buy it."

"Why do you study pop culture?"

"It's supposed to make me relatable to the rest of the world."

Court cocked his head. "How's that working out for you?"

Without smiling, she said, "That's a joke, isn't it?"

"An attempt."

"You are hilarious."

"Pretty sure nobody's ever told me that before. Was that sarcasm?"

"An attempt."

Court told Julie he'd been given a temporary reprieve by Hanley, and he would *not*, in fact, be on the first red and white helo out of FOB Chapman. She nodded at this, characteristically showing no great emotion, and then together they walked through the line, where both of them ordered healthy amounts of pancakes, eggs, and sausage. Court took a ladle full of cheese grits, but Julie admitted she didn't see the appeal.

"I'm from New Mexico. I thought only southerners ate grits, and you don't sound southern."

"I'm from northern Florida. It's like weird southern. We don't have strong accents, but we like grits and country music."

"Not sure I'd fit in," she said, with no judgment in her voice.

"I sure as hell didn't."

They both ordered large coffees and orange juice, then sat to eat, far away from any of the other CIA and military personnel in a sparsely populated mess hall the size of a high school gymnasium.

As they ate, Julie talked about the foods she liked but never learned to cook, saying she preferred to spend her time reading or studying on her computer while her mom and grandmother made authentic Mexican meals.

"I'm not your typical Latina," she admitted.

"That's okay, I'm not your typical redneck," Court responded.

She nodded at this, didn't correct him and tell him he was not, in fact, a redneck, but instead asked him, "How did you end up in the Agency?"

When Court didn't immediately answer, Julie said, "I might be new here, but I *do* know they don't classify how you came to join."

Court was part of a program that was, in fact, classified, as was his induction into it. He didn't want to obfuscate and draw more attention to his recruitment, so he just said, "I worked at my dad's law enforcement firearms training school. Some Agency guys came in, they liked what they saw in me, and a couple years later they came knocking."

This was mostly true, although no one actually came knocking because, when they showed up to talk to him, Court was in a prison cell in Florida, serving a life sentence for the murder of three Colombian assassins at Opa-locka Airport in Miami.

Meeting with the Agency guys had been pretty much mandatory, and it happened in a holding cell that had all its cameras removed.

But Julie didn't need to know any of this. She told Court about how she worked her way up through the Army, then into DIA, and from there into CIA.

"You told me you tend to ruffle a lot of feathers wherever you go." He said it with no judgment in his voice.

"Yeah, I don't last anywhere for long. But that's okay. I like the challenge of something new. I actually love what I do." She then asked, "How about you?"

Court took a bite of his eggs while he thought it over a moment. He'd never been asked this question. Finally, he said, "I'm pretty sure I'm not supposed to love what I do."

"But . . . saving all those people in that mall. That must make you feel good."

Court shrugged. "Saved some, didn't save others. I can't really remember the faces of anybody I saw who got out of there safely. I remember the dead bodies, the injured, the screams. I can't say that feels too good."

Julie just looked at him a moment, then said, "Will you go back out into the field when we find Murad Khan?"

"I didn't come this far just to come this far."

"What does that mean?"

"It means if you and your team find us a target, then me and my team will be there to take it down."

"Well then, whether you like your job or not, you are, at least, committed to it."

They ate for another minute, and then Julie looked up at him. "I'm committed as well, maybe too much so."

"I don't think that's possible, considering the stakes."

"Well," she said, "that's part of the problem. I'm not sure everyone around here actually understands the stakes."

"Meaning?"

"Hanley, Vance, the rest of my team, they keep talking about the KRF using that amount of ammonium nitrate to build one hundred IEDs, each able to destroy American armor, a roadblock, the front gate to an embassy, something like that. But I keep wondering if something even worse is in the works."

"What could be worse than one hundred IEDs?" Court asked in surprise.

"A lot, actually." She finished her orange juice in a gulp. "I've looked into every single operation we've tied to Pasha the Kashmiri, aka Murad Khan. His force has been growing, and his attacks have been increasing in both size and scale. The event at the mall in Lahore was his biggest so far."

"So?"

"One hundred IEDs would make one hundred small to medium-sized statements. That won't serve him as well as one, two, or five large statements."

Court realized she was beating around the bush, not saying what she wanted to say. He leaned forward across the table, closing on her face with his. "What are we talking about, Julie?"

"I am concerned that the ammonium nitrate that was stolen could be used to build several RDDs."

"What the hell's an RDD?"

"A radioactive dispersal device."

Court cocked his head. "You're talking about a dirty bomb."

"Most people refer to it as a dirty bomb, yes."

"Holy shit. You're serious?"

"I don't know. But it's possible."

Court said, "I don't know much about them. Maybe you can give me some pointers in case I come face-to-face with one."

She took a bite of her eggs before speaking. "First lesson: it's much better if you *don't* come face-to-face with one."

She was being serious, but Court laughed nonetheless. "That I knew *without* your expertise. Got anything else?"

"The thing to remember is that in most dirty bomb scenarios in the developed world, where people have access to good healthcare, more people will be killed in car wrecks fleeing the area than would die from radiation poisoning. It's primarily an area denial device. A weapon of mass disruption, actually, not destruction." Julie spoke with authority; she sounded like she was reading a manual out loud, though the words were her own. She added, "But the area affected will be dangerous to live and work in."

"For how long?"

"Depends on a lot of factors. Concentration, material used, the size of the conventional explosion. At the minimum . . . generations."

Court's eyes widened. "Whoa."

"A dirty bomb going off in a small place"—she waved her hand over her head—"over a forward operating base like Camp Chapman, for example, would contaminate virtually everyone there. Would they all die? Not at all. Most of the fatalities would happen in the conventional blast, the explosion of the mixture of ammonium nitrate and fuel oil. Some unlucky ones extremely close to the blast might die from radiation poisoning, but the rest of us might have just a few years shaved off our lives."

Court slowly reached for his coffee, his eyes locked on Julie's. "Well, *that's* encouraging."

"But the base itself would have to shut down, be rebuilt somewhere else, and that would take a lot of time and money. A man like Khan, who obviously wants the U.S. to cease meddling in affairs around here, might bargain that the U.S. wouldn't go to the trouble, especially if two or three or four bases were attacked."

"So . . . how do you make a dirty bomb?"

Julie obviously had been thinking about this for some time already. "If he's going to do this right, he needs long-lived radionuclide concentrations, meaning they have significant thermal power."

Court pushed his plate away from him. "I like how you throw out the word 'meaning' as if what you're about to say next is gonna make any more sense to me than what you said before."

She nodded. "Sorry . . . I am trying to say that for an effective RDD, you need significant amounts of HLW."

Court appreciated Julie's intelligence, but not her ability to put things in the layman's terms that he needed.

Court said, "HLW?"

"High-level waste. Makes the best dirty bomb."

"Where do you go to get high-level waste around here?"

Julie shrugged, as if the answer were obvious. "At a nuclear processing plant."

Court shook his head. "But, surely to God, all the nuclear processing plants in Pakistan are incredibly well guarded. I know the KRF is grow-ing, and they have some trained fighters, but there are a shit-ton of terror-ists in this part of the world, and so far none of them have managed to get into a nuclear facility. It wouldn't be like raiding the chemical plant out-side Lahore. It would be like hitting a military installation."

"You're right. The two nuclear processing plants in Pakistan have really good security. I've actually been evaluating them on sat images in the past couple of days." She gave a little shrug. "I've been thinking about this since learning the KRF was after the AN."

"So," Court asked, "is there some other way they could get the mate-rial? Make it, buy it from another country, dig it up out of the ground?"

Julie now looked at Court in a way that conveyed he'd said something that struck her. She thought for a moment; her eyes went distant. "They could . . ." Her voice trailed off.

"They could *what*?" Court asked.

"Dig it up," she said softly, marveling at the thought. She explained, "Well, not really dig it up. But HLW can also be obtained at a geological disposal facility, a place where they bury the material in concrete."

"And Pakistan has one of these places?"

"The Chashma reprocessing plant, in Punjab. The Chinese helped them build it."

Court drained the rest of his coffee and looked at his Luminox watch. "Have you talked to Hanley about this?"

"I haven't even talked to Vance about it. I don't know that any of this is happening. We don't get to evaluate any raw intelligence from Islamabad station, so I don't know if it's credible or not."

"Yeah, well, what does your gut tell you?"

"I don't work with my gut. I work with my head, it's just the way I'm wired. And I don't know. I didn't find any evidence or RUMINT about thefts at the processing facilities, but thanks to you, I'll look into the dis-posal facility angle." She added, "You've been helpful."

Court stood. "You're the smart one, I just asked you a bunch of dumb questions. You might be on to something; you really need to talk to Vance."

She nodded. "I'll have to. If I'm going to get geointelligence from Pun-jab, where the disposal facility is located, he's going to want to know why."

FORTY-FOUR

PRESENT DAY

Court Gentry and Ted Appleton made it back to the neighborhood around the fish market shortly after seven a.m. Their clothes had dried, mostly, in the past hour, but their phones stayed dead, so Court picked up a couple of burners in a twenty-four-hour electronics stall a block away, fanning out soaking-wet rupees to a cashier who either didn't notice or else just didn't care.

They'd also bought clothing from a street vendor. Polyester slacks and a button-down for Appleton and black denim work pants and a black T-shirt for Court. Appleton bought a bag of chai, milk, and sugar, and they both purchased bottled water and food because there wasn't much to eat or drink around the safe house.

With their shopping complete, they headed to the stairs behind the market and then to the little flat.

Court entered to find Priya Bandari on the floor of the living room, her legs in the lotus position, meditating. When her eyes opened, to his surprise, she leapt quickly to her feet and raced over to him.

Gone was her peaceful and mindful state; now she just looked pissed off.

"I've been calling you for hours!"

"Ran into some more B-Company assholes." He shrugged. "Or the same B-Company assholes, I don't know. Anyway, I lost my phone. We've spent the last few hours making sure we didn't have a tail before we came back here."

She looked at his disheveled appearance, then to the older man who'd entered the flat with him. Back to Cobalt, she asked, "Are you all right?"

"That depends. How clean is the Mithi River?"

Her eyes widened now. "Not at all."

"Yeah, then we're probably not all right."

Priya looked out the door nervously before shutting it and locking it, then turned to the gray-haired American who'd entered with Cobalt.

"Hello." She said it with a hint of suspicion.

Court said, "Priya, this is Ted. He's American, he knows a lot about things in this part of the world, and he's offered to help us."

She shook his hand. "Nice to meet you, Ted."

"Likewise, Priyanka. Beautiful name." He beamed at her when he spoke, enough to make her uncomfortable.

Priya looked back to the man she knew as Cobalt. "We have to talk, I—"

Court said, "We'll all sit down and talk after Ted and I get a shower. We are crawling with microbes. I'll go first."

Appleton said, "That works for me." He looked to Priya, holding up his bag of groceries. "I brought chai and cookies. I've had a long night, I'd love to share with you."

"Sure," she said distractedly, and she took the bag to go into the kitchen. In truth, she wanted to talk with Cobalt and not drink tea with an old American she didn't even know, but Cobalt had already disappeared into the bedroom on his way to the shower.

A few minutes later Priya returned from the kitchen with two cups of tea, and Appleton thanked her and took a sip. She opened the tin of butter cookies Ted had brought as well, and she put them on the table between them.

Curious, she said, "How did B-Company find you?"

Ted said, "They didn't find me, they found him. The problem was, for me anyway, that they found *him* at *my* house."

"I see."

"I teach at the American School of Bombay. He and I were talking, he was about to leave . . ." Appleton shrugged. "And they showed up." He added, "It was terrifying, but he kept me safe."

Priya sipped her tea now, and she kept looking at the door to the bedroom, wishing Cobalt would hurry up washing the dirty river off himself so she could tell him about last night.

And then, as if from nowhere, it came to her. Slowly, her head turned back to the older American. In a measured tone, she said, "'Ted.' Is that a name that is short for something?"

"Teddy is what my parents called me. Of course, it's actually short for Theodore."

Priya blinked, took several seconds before speaking again. "That's . . . nice."

Ted ate cookies while Priya just stared at the door to the bedroom.

Finally Court came out dressed in all black. His feet were bare because his boots and socks weren't yet dry, but he looked sufficiently cleaned up after his early morning escapades.

Appleton finished his tea in a few gulps, then grabbed three of the cookies and the bag holding his fresh clothes. "I won't be but a minute." He smiled at Priya. "We'll need more tea for our talk, but allow me to make it. You'll find that, for a Westerner, I can manage a pretty tasty cup of chai."

She nodded distractedly, her wide eyes locked on Cobalt.

Ted didn't notice; he stepped into the bedroom and closed the door, but Cobalt *did* notice, and he moved close to the Indian woman.

"What's wrong?" he asked.

She waited to hear the shower start running before answering him. Still, she spoke softly. "What is Ted's last name?"

Surprised at the question, he said, "Appleton. He's a former CIA station chief. Why do you ask?"

Priya appeared suddenly panic-stricken. She opened her mouth to speak.

"What the hell's the matter?" he demanded.

She sat down on the sofa. "I went back to Uncle Arjun's house, early this morning."

Court's voice raised. "You did *what*?"

"He gave me a clue, on the video. Told me to check his safe."

Now Court was the confused one. "On the same video *I* watched?"

"Yes. It was subtle. That doesn't matter. In his safe I found a computer file, with all his operations laid out, step by step."

Court sat down on the sofa as well. He said, "He recorded his Darknet operations, too?"

"He did."

"And . . . what did you find?"

"That you were hired for the job in Algiers because the client requested you specifically."

Court looked around the room, thinking about this. Finally, he said, "That's impossible. My name isn't—"

"He didn't request your name. It was a string of numbers, must be how you operate on the Darknet."

To this, Court nodded. "And he reached out to Arjun and said, 'Get this guy'?"

"Exactly."

"Any idea who the client is?"

"I know *exactly* who the client is." She paused, biting her lip, then pointed towards the bedroom. "Right now, he's taking a shower in the next room."

Court's head swiveled to the door. "You've got to be kidding me."

"Theodore Appleton contracted the entire Algiers operation and insisted you be hired to carry it out."

It was all but silent in the room for several seconds, the barking calls of fish market hawkers downstairs the only sound audible.

And then, softly, Court said, "That motherfucker."

He rose, drawing his pistol from under his shirt as he did so.

Priya grabbed him by the arm. "Wait."

"For what?"

"For him to get out of the shower, at least."

Court looked at the door, then back at Priya. He shook her hand off his arm and marched on. "Fuck him."

Court Gentry kicked in the locked bathroom door, his pistol high. He grabbed a towel and threw it over the shower curtain, obviously surprising the older man. The water turned off a moment later. "Hey! Can I have some privacy?"

Court ripped the curtain off its hooks, jabbed his Browning under Ted Appleton's chin, and shoved him, naked, up against the wall. The towel was on the older man's shoulder; Court pulled it off and put it in his shaking hands.

"Cover yourself up, then come with me into the bedroom. You and I are going to talk again, and I'm going to find out if you left anything relevant out of our earlier discussion."

Appleton did not speak. Court detected shock but no surprise, as if the older man was terrified but had expected that this would happen all along. The former station chief complied, wrapping himself in the towel, then exited the bathroom with the pistol still pressed against him.

"Sit on the bed," Court ordered.

"Any chance you'd let me put on my—"

"Sit on the bed!"

Appleton sat; Priya looked in from the living room. Court went to the door and spoke softly to her. "I need to do this part without you."

"Why?"

"Trust me, you won't want to see what I have in store for him."

Priya reached for the door handle. With her eyes locked on Court's and a grave expression on her face, she pulled it shut, leaving the two men alone.

Court dragged the only rickety wicker chair in the room to a place on the floor right in front of Appleton and spun it around. Sitting backwards on the chair, his pistol remained in his hand, dangling over the chair back, only three feet from Appleton's face.

The older man was soaking wet still, but he had, at least, covered his privates.

Appleton said, "Somewhere along the way . . . I take it you learned that I was the one who hired Arjun Bandari for the job in Algiers. Hired you, as well."

Court nodded. "Why?"

"Because of Murad Khan. I knew he would be there, I knew you were Golf Sierra, and I know you are the Gray Man."

Slowly, Court Gentry thumbed back the hammer on the pistol until it made a loud click in the little room.

India for you." He shrugged. "You were either never here, or else you were invisible."

"I was never here."

Appleton took this at face value. "When I realized Khan was heading to Algiers, I went onto the Darknet. I looked for a contract killer who came highly recommended. I found several, but I know about your languages, I know about areas of operation you've spent time in . . . all things that led me to your profile.

"From there it was a simple thing to go to Arjun Bandari. He even told me he'd tried to hire you for other jobs in the past."

"You did all that just to get me?"

"I did, because I knew you'd take the job."

Court slowly shook his head. "This isn't about you losing your job at CIA. This isn't about dead people you probably didn't even know." He shook his head harder now. "No. Murad Khan took something from you. Something personal."

At first, Appleton just looked at the floor in front of him, shaking his head. He held his position there for a few seconds; the fishmongers' barking downstairs continued.

Then his face grew a slow, rueful smile, his teeth just visible in the low light of the room. "I suppose you were trained in interrogation, which means you've read every deception cue that just flashed across my face."

"Yep," Court said flatly. He repeated, "Khan took something personal."

Now the former station chief looked up at the former paramilitary officer. "For you to determine this, the way you just did . . . then you must have your own history of loss. Of pain. Of that cloying crush in your heart that tells you that you must personally seek vengeance."

Appleton's smile was gone now. "You are a young man still, but you have seen too much."

"We aren't talking about me. We're talking about you."

The older man shook his head. "No, we're not talking about me. This isn't about Teddy Appleton. We are talking about Aimal Viziri."

"Who?"

The older man spoke more softly now. "Her code name was Leopard. She was ISI."

FORTY-FIVE

Court said, "So, the entire operation was a setup. You manipulated me from the start."

Appleton shrugged his bare shoulders. "I got you involved. You did the rest." He smiled a little. "Like I knew you would."

"Why shouldn't I just kill you now?"

"Because you aren't even thinking about me. You love the fact that you are here, you love the fact that you have a chance to fix what went so wrong twelve years ago."

Court shook his head. "There is no fixing what happened."

"We can't bring those lives back, no, but we can get some closure." Appleton shrugged. "If you were at Gulberg Galleria, if you were there with your team a few days later . . . I *know* you think about Murad Khan and what he did every single day. If you have any sort of a soul, you have to be holding on to all that.

"I've got to trust that you *do* have a soul, Mr. Gentry, and you'll see this through to the end. Just like I will."

"How do you know who I am?"

"I'm not connected to the Agency, but five years ago, they were looking for you, and they came to me. Showed me your file. Told me about some things you had done in the private sector. I agreed to put feelers out in

Court sat up straighter on the chair, his shoulders rolled back. But he did not interrupt.

"I turned her myself, here in Mumbai. Sixteen, seventeen years ago now. She was a Pakistani intelligence officer. A good one, bright, dedicated. But she didn't have a stomach for the game. She wanted a life beyond espionage, dead drops, surveillance vans. I identified this and I approached her. Within six weeks she'd flipped."

He looked up at Court now and held his rapt gaze. "Within a year we were in love."

Court dropped his head. "Jesus Christ." A CIA officer romantically involved with an ISI asset during the war on terror sounded, to him, like a shit show in the making.

Appleton saw what the younger man was thinking. He shrugged. "I knew it was wrong. She did, too. But we got swept up in it. You can't even imagine. Those were heady times. We were young." He corrected himself with another shrug. "Younger, anyway.

"She was recalled to Islamabad, so I followed. Continued running her while she worked at headquarters. She was made an HQ liaison to the Foreign Coordination Unit; she provided us with incredible product for years. We kept up our affair. We had to be damn careful about it, of course, but we managed.

"She told me about a Kashmiri FCU officer named Murad Khan. He was shooting up the ranks, operating against India, or so she thought. He wasn't getting in the U.S.'s way in our fight at the time, so I wasn't focused on him, but I knew about him. Then . . . your group chief at SAD sent me a photo one day, taken by a Ground Branch cell in Lahore."

Court said, "Taken by me."

Appleton raised his eyebrows. "Then you know the rest. Khan was with the Kashmiri Resistance Front, stealing explosives. Aimal . . . Leopard, didn't believe Khan was KRF; she insisted his office provided much of the intel we'd been using to fight the KRF in the months prior. She convinced me to buy her some time to find out more."

Court let out a long sigh. "You told ISI that Ground Branch was about to hit the Lahore safe house."

"I didn't. *She* did. But I okayed it."

Court's grip on the pistol stiffened. Appleton looked at the hand, the gun, then back up to the younger man. "She called in an anonymous tip to the police; she didn't tell Khan anything. It would have compromised her to do so. I suspect the police reached out to Khan."

"I know what happened in Lahore," Court said. "What happened in Islamabad?"

Appleton shrugged. Suddenly he looked like he'd aged decades in the past five seconds. He said, "I waited for contact from her to find out what she'd learned about the situation. Contact never came."

"She disappeared when she went looking into Murad Khan?"

Again, Appleton looked down to the floor. He nodded without speaking. Court sensed the answer was genuinely true, though the older man was holding on to some personal details.

Some pain.

Finally Appleton said, "When ISI informed us that Khan was dead, I didn't believe it. They had remains, they said, but no body. The DNA proof they gave us could have come from a fucking nasal swab.

"But in typical CIA fashion, they wanted to make up with ISI, they wanted to paper over Langley's own responsibility in the debacle, and they sure as hell didn't want to hear that the KRF and Murad Khan were still out there."

"But . . ." Court said, "you wouldn't give it up?"

Appleton smiled. "I was recalled by Langley from Islamabad station in under a month, and I was out of the Agency in under a year.

"I moved here after retirement, consulting in the nuclear security field. Easy work, overall, but I always had an eye to Pakistan. My job put me back in touch with old contacts in R&AW, and I could poke my nose in different offices, make it look like I was interested in nuclear proliferation, when in truth I was looking for the latest news from the enemy camp, the ISI.

"A few years into it, I started to hear about someone who sounded a lot like Khan. I went to work, confirmed that he was alive six months ago. Then I learned he was here, connected with Palak Bari's B-Company. I've been working on a plan to make him pay ever since."

"What was your plan?"

Appleton looked up at Gentry. "The plan *was* to put you and Khan in the same place in Algiers. I figured nature would do the rest. You would kill him."

"Yeah, well, that plan failed."

Appleton's eyes narrowed. "Because you failed."

Court said, "Ted . . . one thing I've learned. I can't undo the past."

Appleton nodded, wiping tears away. "You can't undo it. This is true. But what better man than you to make the culprits pay for it?"

"There's more. About Khan, here in India." Court's eyes narrowed. "You know what he's up to, don't you?"

"I am worried that I do."

Court stood suddenly, startling Appleton. "The woman in the other room. She's Arjun's niece."

The older man nodded. "I know."

"She's helping me find Khan."

"Because he killed her uncle?"

"More than that. She feels responsible. She thinks she gave Khan information about Arjun that got him killed."

Appleton nodded understandingly. "Guilt is driving her forward, then." He flashed another rueful smile. "So much of that going around these days."

"Yeah."

"Nothing quite fuels the flames of retribution like personal blame."

"She knows me as Cobalt. Understood?"

Appleton nodded.

"Get dressed and come out. I want her to hear the rest of this."

Court opened the door that led to the little living room. Priya was there on the couch, watching television news about a spate of mob-related murders across Mumbai.

Court said to her, "Appleton knew Khan from the old days, discovered him here in Mumbai, tried to trick me into killing him." He shrugged now. "He's going to work with us to find him."

Priya was amazed. "You *trust* him, after what he did?"

"In my line of work, it's not about trust. It's about recognizing people's motivations. The three of us: me, you, him. Our motivations coincide at this moment. That's good enough for me."

"So . . . you *don't* trust me, you just know I want to get the bastard who killed my uncle."

Court began to nod, but he stopped himself. After a moment he said, "Appleton, in any other circumstance, I wouldn't trust him to watch my cat. But you . . . I have no reason not to trust you."

Priya missed the point of the metaphor. "*You* have a cat?"

FORTY-SIX

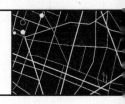

Terry Vance knocked on the door to Matthew Hanley's small living quarters in the intelligence house at FOB Chapman. It was nearly midnight and there were no Ground Branch ops outside the wire this evening, so Vance fully expected to find Hanley catching up on the significant sleep he'd lost since returning to Khost. But Hanley opened the door quickly, appearing disheveled but awake, wearing cargo pants and a black polo that strained against his frame.

He invited his intel chief in, though he raised an eyebrow when Julie Marquez stepped through the doorway behind her boss. Still, he said nothing as both sat down on metal chairs in front of Hanley's desk.

For the past three days there had been no word on the KRF, no word on Khan or Mufti, and no new relevant leads produced by Vance and his team, by CIA headquarters back in Langley, Virginia, or by Ted Appleton's CIA Station Islamabad.

He knew that Vance and his people were trying their best, working around the clock, and he knew that both of the Ground Branch teams, Golf Sierra and Lima Foxtrot, had been training nearly nonstop. But Hanley himself felt adrift, purposeless, a leader of men and women with nowhere to lead them.

"Whatcha got?" he finally asked Vance as he pulled up another chair to sit down.

"It's what Marquez found, Matt, and you ain't gonna like it."

Hanley turned to his youngest employee.

Julie Marquez had a tablet computer in her hand, and she held it up to him.

"Sir, are you familiar with the term 'high-level waste'?"

Hanley looked at her a long moment. Then he slowly closed his eyes and let out a long audible sigh. "*Please* tell me you're kidding."

"I think that means you are aware of it. Radioactive material that comes from reprocessing spent nuclear fuel."

Hanley opened his eyes slowly. "Used, theoretically speaking, in a dirty bomb."

"Precisely."

"And what do you have there on your iPad that I am so sure I do *not* want to see?"

She held a satellite image of a sprawling complex of concrete structures in low rolling hills. "Chashma. A geological disposal facility in Punjab. It's where waste from the nearby Kundian Nuclear Fuel Complex is secured."

Hanley nodded. "So, it's basically a hole in the ground."

"Lots of holes, actually. With thousands of tons of cement, steel, and the like."

"Are you saying Murad Khan, aka Pasha the Kashmiri, is going to dig up buried radioactive materials?"

"I am saying there is intelligence to indicate he already did. In actuality, I believe he stole the material before it was buried."

"When?"

"Four and a half weeks ago." She thumbed through her iPad till she found the page she was looking for. "This document is in Urdu, but our translators tell us it is a police report that has since been removed from the servers of the Punjab CPO—that's their Central Police Office."

"Why was it removed?" Hanley asked, his interest only somewhat piqued.

"I need to tell you about the report first."

Hanley waved a hand Julie's way. She didn't have the ability to humor him by answering his question, so he settled in to hear her entire spiel.

"Go ahead."

"The initial report, now removed from their database, detailed the theft of two trucks at the intersection of I-95 and Pishin Road, just two and a half kilometers west of the geological disposal facility. The trucks were traveling north, which means in the direction of the facility, and they were in the process of turning onto Pishin, which definitely means they were heading to the Chashma disposal site."

Hanley said, "Somebody stole a couple of trucks. That doesn't mean—"

Julie interrupted. "Not *somebody*. An armed force of two dozen men. Not exactly typical highway banditry. And this information didn't come from the drivers of the trucks, they haven't been seen or heard from, but it came from other cars passing by. Blood was found at the scene. It's possible the drivers were killed and their bodies removed."

"And you think this was the KRF."

"Ammonium nitrate/fuel oil and high-level nuclear waste are exactly what one needs to build a dirty bomb. We know the KRF has the ability to produce a few tons of ANFO. All you have to add are containment devices, detonation systems, and a bombmaker who can put it all together. You do that, and you have multiple dirty bombs."

Hanley took it all in. "The only intel we have about the truck heist near the nuclear facility is from the local cops?"

"Correct," Vance answered. "No chatter from our sources, nothing official from ISI channels, no corroboration from our assets. It's like the cops filed this report, because that's what cops do, and then the report was quietly pulled, because that's what governments do when they're trying to cover up something embarrassing or uncomfortable."

"Dicks," Hanley said after another sigh. He rubbed his tired eyes. "How many dirty bombs could be assembled with the material we know was taken from the chemical plant?"

Julie said, "To do it right, I estimate they could make three to four devices, each about the size of a four-door car."

"And the nuclear waste stolen? How many bombs could that fuel?"

"We don't know how much material was in the trucks, assuming it was nuclear material at all . . . but the size of the trucks as described here could easily carry a half dozen devices' worth of radioactive waste. We postulate that the explosion of the AN at the mall was a diversion to make us think the chemicals had been expended. That diversion is the only reason they don't have the explosives necessary to make one or two more bombs. As it stands, three to four is our best estimation."

"Four dirty bombs," Hanley almost whispered to himself. "This is getting into worst-case-scenario territory."

Vance agreed. "The targets could be in Pakistan, India, Afghanistan. Hell, they might find a way to sneak them into the U.S."

Julie Marquez cleared her throat now, and Hanley turned to her. "What?"

"I don't believe the KRF is targeting India, Pakistan, or the U.S. mainland."

"And why is that?"

Julie said, "Since I discovered this police report this morning, I began to wonder where they would take the devices once constructed. I had a lot of theories, but then I thought again about Ismail Zai."

Hanley was surprised. "The old UAV base in Khyber? The one near Peshawar?"

"Correct. The location Golf Sierra hit last month, where their previous Sierra Six was killed. Remember, you had me look at the data when you hired me."

Hanley was impatient. "Yeah, Marquez. I remember."

"Well . . . Ismail Zai base has a lot going for it as far as a place to stage for a significant operation into Afghanistan, and maybe more importantly, no one has ever figured out why the KRF was even there last month."

Vance said, "Our best guess was, just as you said, that they were prepping it to become a staging area for cross-border attacks. The Khyber Pass isn't far away. A large enough force could potentially punch through that border crossing en masse. Ismail Zai base was remote enough and large enough to provide a perfect place to assemble before the attack.

"Plus," Vance added, "it has a massive underground hardened bunker there; it had been used to store American UAVs in the first couple years of the war on terror, before the Pakistani government figured out U.S. troops in the FATA was a singularly bad idea for them politically. A bunker that size could house all five hundred KRF men and keep them invisible to satellites."

Hanley turned to Julie to see if she would dare take issue with her boss. And it was absolutely no surprise to him when she did exactly that.

"No. I think they were readying the location for something else."

Hanley cocked his head. "You found something?"

"I did, in fact. We haven't been looking at Ismail Zai since that operation. Supposedly the military was, but they missed this completely."

"Missed what?"

"Remember, there weren't many men there, and intelligence never proved Omar Mufti was present at all. I was, however, able to cobble together relevant sat photos taken to the north, over Peshawar, that happened to catch images of Ismail Zai outpost over the past couple of weeks."

Hanley leaned forward. He was completely engaged with Marquez's report now.

"What did you find?"

"Not a mass assembly of men, maybe a couple dozen or so. And I've seen tracks after rainfall that indicate heavy trucks have traveled into the outpost grounds. The trucks have either left or else they are still there, parked under one of the structures."

"If you can't see into the structures, how can you say you know there aren't more men there?"

"Because of the shit."

Hanley cocked his head. "I'm sorry?"

"The lack of shit, I should say."

Hanley rubbed his eyes again. "I'm begging you to make some sense."

Vance added, "Marquez. It's late."

She didn't acknowledge him. "You can hide the men, but you can't hide their waste. Yes, they can burn it or bury it, but if there were one hundred, three hundred, five hundred troops at this site, we'd see obvious latrines. You can't put those in a warehouse and live under that roof for long." She added, "Trust me, I grew up with two brothers."

Julie wasn't intending to be funny, and that only made it funnier to Hanley, but he was in no mood to laugh. Instead he said, "So a smaller KRF force is staging in a location just over the border from us, and they have multiple dirty bombs?"

Vance turned to Julie. With an admonishing tone, he said, "Marquez. A lot of speculation going on there."

Now Julie shrugged a little, something Hanley didn't often see her do. "Eighty percent probability on the first, sixty percent on the second."

Hanley frowned. "And what is the probability that coalition forces in Afghanistan are fucked if you are right about both?"

She looked to Vance. She answered this as if it were patently obvious, which it was, but she was unaware Hanley was being rhetorical. "One hundred percent."

Hanley turned to Vance, who begrudgingly nodded his agreement with Julie.

The group chief said, "*That's* the stat that's important to me.

"I'm going to Carmichael with this; I'll try to get a raid back into Khyber approved. He'll go to DeFalco, who will go to the director, who will go to POTUS, and they will *all* go ape shit for trying this again after we failed the first time."

He held up a finger. "But if we get a green light, it needs to come in the next day or so. I don't like the thought of radioactive bombs sitting there, fifty miles from Jalalabad, one hundred from Kabul."

Hanley stood in his little room and opened the door for the two intelligence officers. "I've got to call Langley. I also have to call Islamabad station and tell Appleton about the nuclear waste theft." He thought for a moment. "Maybe I don't tell him about Khyber. Not just yet."

Vance cocked his head. "Why would you keep the station chief out of the loop on that?"

"Because somebody who knew about our raid in Lahore told the local police about our raid in Lahore. They prevented it at the last minute."

"You don't think—"

Hanley shrugged. "This is Appleton's fiefdom. He might have spoken to someone who blew the whistle. If you ask me, he's been in country too long."

Julie spoke now with surprising emotion in her voice. "You have twelve operators, Mr. Hanley. Only *twelve*. If there are a dozen defenders at Ismail Zai, or maybe two dozen, then an attack on that compound will be very dangerous for them."

Hanley said, "I'm going to push to get some SEALs folded into this op. Maybe some conventional military, as well. The Rangers stationed at Salerno. We'll need UAVs, comms, a joint operation plan. It will take time, but I need you guys working around the clock to give us the best intelligence picture you can find." He pointed to Vance. "Better than the last go-around at this base."

Vance headed out into the hall, followed by Julie Marquez. "We'll get everything we have on the compound and forces there to you within a few hours."

FORTY-SEVEN

Two hundred twenty miles from Camp Chapman in Afghanistan, Fatima Jinnah Park in Islamabad, Pakistan, was quiet, dark, and empty at five a.m. As Ted Appleton strolled along a leafy footpath, he felt as if he were the only person for miles around, though he was in the center of a metropolis with one million inhabitants.

Still, a cold shiver of fear tingled in his body.

He had been slipped out of the U.S. embassy in the trunk of a car ninety minutes earlier, then dropped off by himself to run a sixty-minute surveillance detection route. His meeting this morning absolutely could *not* be disrupted by the ISI watchers who pestered him much of the time, so special measures and utmost discretion had been mandatory.

He walked alone through the darkness now, felt the cool wind that rustled leaves and branches on either side of him, and then, when he arrived at a park bench below a Himalayan cedar, he sat down. Checking his phone, he saw he'd received no new texts or calls, so he waited, far away from the smoky light of gas lamps closer to the street at the edge of the park.

His agent arrived right on time, as he knew she would. They had a long history together, after all, and this experience meant Appleton also knew she would be scared. But *she* had called for this meeting, the stakes were the highest they'd ever been since the two had been together, and running a CIA station, Appleton knew, was all about deciding when to avoid risks and when to take them.

Managing risk. Intelligence work was, he had decided while working with Aimal Viziri, very much like love.

Leopard sat down next to him and he smelled her perfume, but he couldn't tell if she'd put it on just for him or if she'd been wearing it anyway. He chastised himself for thinking about such things at a time like this and resolved to stick to the business at hand as much as he possibly could.

He was about to say something when Leopard spoke, with strength in her voice. "They are watching the embassy, you know."

"Of course they are, darling," Appleton replied. "I took steps."

"What steps?"

"What steps? First, a ride in a trunk, then I was dropped off at Nur Railway Station, then I took a taxi to a safe house we have. From there I climbed on a bicycle and made my way to the park. Locked my bike up at a lamppost and walked for ten minutes." He added, "We're safe."

Aimal Viziri nodded, her relief evident, and then she slowly unwrapped the dupatta from her face. She looked at Appleton; he read it as a cue for a kiss, but before he had the chance to lean in and part his lips, she said, "Director Khan has disappeared. Leadership says he's gone rogue. Reaching out to assets at home and abroad for his own aims, not sanctioned by ISI."

Appleton sighed, for a number of reasons, and then he recovered quickly. He said, "Can there be any doubt now? He *is* Pasha the Kashmiri, and he is in play."

He told her about the news he'd just received regarding the possibility that nuclear fuel had been stolen at Chashma, and she put her face in her hands.

When she lifted her head, she said, "I have been providing intelligence to the Americans about a terrorist organization that works out of my own fucking organization. How could I be such a fool?"

He put his arm around her, damning protocol once again because of his affection for his agent. "You *aren't* a fool. Your intelligence product has been valuable. Khan gave you no indication whatsoever that he was the enemy."

"Just as long as you don't think that I had anything to do with any of—"

Appleton put a finger to her lips. "Of course not. You are the best asset America has in this part of the world." He smiled. "And I love you."

She let it go, but he could see the pain on her face. "I love you," she said, rubbing a single tear from her eye.

He fought the urge to kiss her again, and he said, "Is that why you called me here tonight? To tell me Khan had disappeared?"

"That . . . and something else. Something unrelated to the KRF."

"If it's unrelated to the KRF, then it will have to take a backseat for the time being. All we care about right now are—"

"This is about China," Leopard interjected. "Does America care about China?"

Appleton cocked his head. "What about China?"

"Our military has purchased two orbital jammers from the People's Republic of China. Chinese technicians are in Pakistan with the equipment right now to teach our officers. In Quetta, I believe.

"The equipment is supposedly state of the art. They have the ability to disrupt satellite transmissions."

Appleton was utterly confused by this information. "I know what orbital jammers are. What the hell does Pakistan need them for?"

"I don't know. I don't have sources in the military. But I know China uses them to block transmissions of satellite programming in nations whose sat feeds would be embarrassing to China. Maybe the government wants to use them to disrupt Indian broadcasting."

Appleton understood the larger abilities of orbital jamming equipment. Much of what he knew was theoretical, and he hadn't seen them used in the field in any large capacity anywhere in the world.

The news was perplexing, but he didn't see it as related to his main focus. He knew there was a terrorist organization trying to put together dirty bombs, on his turf, and that was where his concerns lay at present.

He was about to give Aimal new instructions when she said, "I want out, Teddy. I need to get out. Now. I know the product I'm giving you is important, but am *I* not important, as well?"

"You are the most important thing in the world to me, darling." He grabbed her, hugged her, kissed her, then said, "You *know* that. I would do anything to take you with me right now and put you on a transport back to the USA."

She pulled away from his embrace. "But?"

Appleton sighed. "But we have to take Khan off the table first. We have to find him, we have to find the material he stole, or the devices if he has already constructed them." Off a look from her, he said, "It's not me. It's my masters. We all have masters. We need their help to get you out of the country. I swear to you that I will take you out of here just as soon as this is all over."

She folded her hands in front of her, looked down at them. "Khan is gone. I told you."

"But the ISI will be looking for him and for the rest of the KRF. You are safe from him, but you can still feed me information about his organization.

"You listen for anything out there that we will want to know about. The Chinese jammers is good intelligence, thank you, but help us find out exactly what was taken at Chashma, or who has the expertise in Pakistan to assemble a dirty bomb. Check with immigration. Has a known bombmaker from Iraq or Syria or Saudi shown up in your nation?"

She nodded at all this, but she wrote nothing down.

They kissed again; he felt her tremble, and it sickened him to his stomach. Then she stood, wrapped her head in her veil, and began walking off into the darkness.

Appleton watched her leave; the cold fear of what he was asking her to do was almost unbearable, but he shook it off, stood, and began walking back to his bicycle.

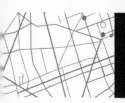

FORTY-EIGHT

PRESENT DAY

The dark hippie apartment over the Versova Fish Market was an unusual location for three people to discuss the fate of India, but Ted Appleton, Priyanka Bandari, and Court Gentry were doing just that.

Appleton said, "What I'm about to tell you is known by the government in New Delhi, but it has not been released to the public.

"Two months ago, here in Mumbai, a container of nuclear fuel rods was stolen from Dhruva reactor in Trombay. Some one hundred kilos in all went missing. It was an inside job, that much is known."

Court's head rose slowly, his tired eyes wide. "You've got to be kidding." When Appleton said nothing, Court added, "Khan is going to try to do it again, isn't he?"

Priya tried to ask how Appleton knew of the theft, but the two American men were too absorbed by their mutual past to hear her.

Appleton said, "You're damn right, he's going to try again. *That* I know. What I *don't* know is his target or where he's getting his expertise or the other materials he needs for a dirty bomb."

"Or his physical location now," Court added. "Which is what matters most."

Priya asked, "Does the Indian government have any leads about the theft?"

Appleton turned to her. "I've talked to my sources." Then he shrugged a little. "My *former* sources—now they are just a few old friends who still like to gossip over drinks. Anyway, they say the government thinks B-Company was behind the theft. That said, it is their opinion that whoever stole the fuel rods planned on selling them on the international black market. It's a containment threat, a proliferation threat, but it's not a terrorist threat to the nation."

Priya's voice grew louder. "But if they know Khan is alive and here, and that he did something like this in the past, then the terrorist threat is obvious."

Appleton said nothing.

"Isn't it?" she pressed.

Still, the older American did not respond. Priya looked at him, then to Cobalt, then back to Appleton.

Turning again to Cobalt, she saw something register on his face. "*What?*"

Cobalt said, "I think this is where Ted tells us that he hasn't notified the Indian government that Khan is alive, is in India, and is in play."

Priya's mouth dropped open.

Appleton just shrugged. "I learned long ago, young lady, that voicing your greatest fears is the best way to get you put on the outside looking in."

She stared at the older man in disbelief. "That's madness." Then her eyes sharpened. She understood. "No. That's not what this is about at all. You didn't tell India because you want to be the one to kill Khan. *That's* why you hired Cobalt, my uncle, and me in the first place instead of going to R&AW. You wanted to be the hero."

Appleton gave Priya a tired smile, with no light behind it in his eyes. "I'll never be a hero, not if I killed Khan and ten more men just as wicked. My die is cast for what I've already done. But R&AW will only help me if I have put the puzzle together myself. Trust me, I've worked with them long enough to know. My job in the security sector was exclusively to fill out papers no one would read, about scenarios no one believed would ever happen."

"But they're *happening*!" She all but shouted this, and then she turned back to Cobalt. "Why aren't you saying anything?"

The younger American replied, "Because I get it." He turned to Ted. "Dropping a dime on Khan to the cops in Mumbai won't exorcise your demons. Killing him just might."

The older man shrugged, a confirmation of Court's statement without admitting it outright.

"I get it," Court repeated, softly. Then, when Priya was about to grab him by the arm and yell at him, he spoke again, just as softly as before. "But if a nuclear-laced explosive goes off, you'll meet an entirely new set of demons, won't you? And we can't let that happen. You *have* to tell your contacts in the government every single thing you know about what's going on."

Priya heaved a dramatic sigh of relief. She obviously thought both these men were nuts, but at least one of them was beginning to come around.

"I will," Appleton relented. "But . . . what *do* we know?"

Court said, "We know Khan is in Mumbai, working with B-Company, and we *think* we know he's acquired spent fuel rods."

Priya said, "Why would he work with B-Company? Isn't he still ISI?"

Court turned to Appleton. "You sent us to Algiers because R&AW learned an officer with the Foreign Coordination Unit was going to be there that particular night. You figured out they were talking about Khan." And then Court sat up straighter, a look of doubt on his face. "Or that was your story, anyway."

Appleton said, "Just a story. I was reasonably certain Khan was here, in Mumbai. I identified a known associate of his, a Pakistani security specialist named Nassir Rasool. He was, no doubt, the one who tracked Priya's drone back to her hotel room. Brilliant man. Trained and equipped by the Chinese. He's been with Khan from the beginning, they were in ISI together, they were in KRF together. And now he's here."

"How did you find him?" Priya asked.

"There was a computer breach of the Nuclear Command Authority, the department I consulted for. That's how Khan and his people found out about the transport of fuel rods. I had some of the best minds in the private sector in India retrace the intrusion, and it led them to a location in

Andheri East. I hired locals to watch the building, and I caught images of Rasool, the Pakistani technician who used to be ISI but who disappeared, along with Khan, after the events twelve years ago.

"I'd always thought Khan was alive, but then when his colleague appeared in the middle of the theft of nuclear fuel . . . well, I knew.

"I had private detectives tail Rasool, found an associate of his, an Indian in B-Company, and bugged the man's phone. He spoke of going with Rasool and the other Pakistanis to Algiers on a mission at the Turkish embassy, and I knew Khan would be there, too."

Court said, "So it's possible Khan is just working with B-Company and not ISI?"

Priya shook her head. "There were several Pakistanis there in East Andheri, when I was kidnapped. They weren't mob goons. They were sharper."

Court said, "Could be ex-ISI. Men who made the jump with him into terrorism."

Appleton nodded. "And I don't think we should assume B-Company is on board with the plan, either. Palak Bari, the leader of the organization, lives in Karachi. He's seventy-five years old, and at this stage of his life, he hates India more than he loves money. He's bombed this nation's government buildings before. Blew up an Air India office. He has no compunction about destroying whatever he wants. His foot soldiers still on the ground here in Mumbai are in the gang for the money and power, but Bari has wanted revenge on this nation's Hindus his entire life."

Priya nodded at this. "The B-Company man in charge of my kidnapping. His name was Jai. He told me he didn't understand why his boss would work with the Pakistanis."

Court said, "Well then, that tracks with what Ted just said. Bari, Khan, and Khan's men from back home . . . they are in on the plot. The Indian gangsters, they're just following their nutjob boss's wishes from over the border in Pakistan. Who knows if they are even aware of what they're involved with."

Priya asked, "What's our next step?"

Court had an answer. "Ted gets on the phone with whoever he can. He tells them about Khan, about Rasool, and B-Company, and also tries to find out where Khan is. I'll be ready to go check out any location he learns about from these discussions."

Appleton nodded. Priya, on the other hand, said, "Well, I'm not just going to sit here at the fish market. We need more information. We know Khan was at that building where I was being held. Two nights ago. I wish there were some way to get back into that building and try to look at their security footage."

Court shook his head. "Forget about it. We aren't going back in there."

But Appleton had an idea. "Traffic camera recordings from that time and that location. If we can see the vehicle he used, maybe get a shot of him entering or exiting, we can try to get a plate number. Assuming it's not a rental, that might provide us information about the entity he's working with here in the city."

"He's working with B-Company," Court said. "Haven't you been paying attention?"

"B-Company doesn't register their vehicles as B-Company." The older man rolled his eyes. "Shooters." It was said as a pejorative. "Again, assuming it's not a rental, it will be registered to a corporation or an individual here, and that is the best lead we may get."

Court understood. He said, "Murad Khan didn't go to Hertz at the airport to rent a car."

"I agree. He's being ferried around by whoever is supporting him."

Court looked to Priya. "Can you get into those cameras?"

She shook her head. "No. I can do a little hacking, but not on a government-entity scale. I'd need a back door into the system. Credentials of someone with access."

Appleton smiled. "I know a guy. For the right price, he'll give up his password so you can get in and take a look."

Court said, "I'll break one of his legs to show him I'm serious, then ask him if the right price is me not breaking the other."

Appleton rolled his eyes, not for the first time in the conversation. "Won't be necessary. Violence isn't always the answer."

"It's often the quickest answer."

"I'll convince him. Don't worry."

Court was on board with the plan. To Priya he said, "If Ted got you through the back door of the software, could you take it from there?"

She nodded with certainty. "With the right credentials, of course I could."

Appleton stood. "Give me an hour." And he headed for the door.

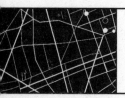

FORTY-NINE

TWELVE YEARS AGO

For the past few days Court hadn't seen Julie around Camp Chapman at all. Not that he'd had much time to look for her. Hightower was keeping his men busy, pushing the entire team with day and night training. Fast-roping, close-quarters battle, radio protocol lessons, low-light training, weight lifting, and running, as well as blade and unarmed fighting evolutions.

Court excelled with a gun, with a knife, with hand-to-hand combat, and so on. Individually he was the best on the team in these disciplines. But he remained the straggler when it came to team tactics as well as other skills one learns in military special operations.

Lennox for one had chided Six's fast-roping abilities, asking if he could, at least, learn how to "slow-rope" so that he could show up on the X to share in a little of the fighting by the end of their next hit.

But Court worked hard, he improved, and his need to do things his own way was slowly being trained out of him.

Even with all the work, he had some downtime in the early evenings after drills at the shoot house or on the range and before low-light training, and he'd spent a portion of this time, each night, walking around, hoping to run into Julie. He didn't want to go into the task force intelligence building—a Ground Branch officer had no business there unless he was invited—but he hadn't seen her outside the building, nor had he seen her in or around the TOC or in the DFAC.

He also kept his eye on the bonfire, a nightly occurrence at the CIA base and the de facto meeting place for socializing here at Chapman, but he hadn't seen any sign of the quirky but friendly junior intel analyst.

He *had* overheard Redus and Pace talking to Morgan in the pit the day before, mentioning that they ran into Marquez in line at the base coffee shop, where, according to Pace, Redus made an unsuccessful pass at her.

Redus just muttered to Morgan that he thought Marquez was a weirdo.

Court remained out of the conversation and kept up with his work.

He assumed that the fact she wasn't around meant the theory she'd put forth the last time they talked, that Khan and his people were working on a dirty bomb, was taking all of her energies and her time.

It was six p.m. now; he'd just finished cleaning his rifle after some intermediate carbine practice at the range with Lennox and Hightower, and was about to head out alone to grab some dinner before returning for night op training.

He stood in his cage with all his weaponry, armor, and other gear, and looked at two sheets of paper zip-tied to the wire at eye level. One was the official Pakistan Army photo of Major Omar Mufti, a stern-faced, clean-shaven man in his early thirties.

And the other was the image of Murad Khan that Court himself had taken in Lahore. He looked at the images multiple times a day, both from these photos and on two laminated cards that he carried with him at all times.

These men were the two jackpots on his team's mission here on the other side of the world, and he wanted to be damn sure he recognized these guys if he ever came across them in the field.

He broke away from his staring contest with the photo of Khan and walked over to his tiny hooch, where he took off his dirty and smelly brown T-shirt to replace it with a clean green one. Hightower was meeting with Hanley, but Redus, Pace, Lennox, and Morgan were all here, all in their cages or sitting on their bunks. A stereo played some rap that Redus had put on. Court didn't much care for it, and Lennox declared it "white boy bullshit," but Redus protected the stereo from anyone with designs on changing the music.

The door opened and Court looked up, thinking this might be Hightower with news from Vance or Hanley, but instead he saw Julie Marquez peering into the room, still somewhat blinded by the sun outside. She wore a helmet and armor, khaki pants, and a white long-sleeve T-shirt.

The other men hadn't noticed her yet, but he imagined his luck wouldn't hold in that regard.

He quickly slipped on his shirt and hurried across the space to her, knowing the rest of the guys would need about five seconds before they focused their attention on the interaction between the female analyst and the young Ground Branch officer.

Her eyes had just adjusted to the light when Court stepped up to her.

He said, "Don't take this the wrong way, but you look like you've been working your ass off."

Julie looked him in the eye. "I don't take *anything* the wrong way. Yeah, I've been working. You, too, I guess."

He waved a thumb at the men behind him. "They are trying to whip me into shape. Or they're just whipping me, I can never tell the difference."

He invited her into the room; they made it no more than four or five steps closer to his bunk area when Dino Redus's head poked up from behind the low shelves of his hooch.

"What's she doing here?"

Court passed by the large table in the center of the room. "She's talking to me."

Now Morgan stood up from his bunk. "Yet another rule you don't know, then. 'No tits in the pits.'"

Julie said nothing, but Court squared off to Redus.

"Are you in high school?" Court asked. He redirected her over to his cage, farther away from the other men on the team.

Jim Pace, whose nose was still packed with gauze after breaking it in the back of the paddy wagon in Lahore, chimed in now to Morgan and Redus. "It's just Marquez. She's cool."

Redus stepped out from his sleeping area and walked towards Gentry. "Six is fucking up enough around here to where we don't need to be changing the policies just for him." To Court he said, "We have procedures. Ways of doing things. Lots of rules, but good rules.

"One, we don't let women in the pit, and two, we don't shoot our fucking teammates. Why are both of those things so hard for you to understand?"

Court stood between Redus and Julie now. "I feel bad about double-tapping you in the chest, but I have to say, if I *had* to shoot one mother-fucker in this room . . . it *would* be you."

Redus closed the distance quickly, but Julie moved between them now, turned her back on Redus, and looked up at Court. "Do you have dinner plans?"

Court heard Pace chuckle behind him.

Recovering from the mind-spinning twist of thought, Court quipped, "Tried to get a reservation. But you have to know the maître d' to get in anywhere good at this FOB."

She didn't seem to get his joke. "I was thinking about the DFAC."

"That works, too," Court said, and then he threw on his armor and helmet, closed his cage, threaded the padlock through the clasp, and pocketed the key. Julie noticed that Court didn't close the padlock in the process.

"You didn't—"

"I know," he said with a shrug. "There's a lot of security around here. I trust them more than I trust myself not to lose the key and get locked out of access to my weps."

Soon the two of them began heading for the door.

Dino Redus, however, wanted the last word. He called across the room to them both. "You're a prick, Gentry. And you're a fucking nerd, Marquez, you know that?"

Court's jaw muscles just flexed in anger, but Julie spoke without breaking stride. "Actually, I prefer the term 'smarter than you.'"

All the men, with the exception of Redus, broke into laughter.

When it subsided, Morgan said, "Gentry, we've got low-light training at twenty-one hundred. You're gonna have to be switched on, so don't come back here with your bullshit."

Court reached the door behind Julie. He looked back over his shoulder and said, "I'm going to dinner, then I'll be right back with my bullshit."

Marquez and Gentry sat at a table in the middle of the DFAC, surrounded by others, but none close enough to hear. Court ate meatloaf that was filling if not particularly satisfying, while Julie ate a salad with a chicken breast thrown on top as an afterthought. She consumed her meal much more slowly than he did, principally because she was doing most of the talking.

"Back there, in your building. Thanks for sticking up for me like that."

Court shrugged as he ate. "I didn't do anything."

"You did, and I've never had anyone do that for me. I mean, my brothers, back in high school, they were always getting into fights with guys who said rude things. But not since."

"Well . . . you're welcome. Redus is an asshole."

"And . . ." Julie added with a shrug, "can you blame him? You shot him."

Court laughed. "Yeah, but *you* didn't."

She took a bite of salad, then said, "What do the men in Ground Branch say about me?"

Court tried to think of a measured response. He said, "Not much. Everybody's pretty busy. Pace said Redus hit on you in line for coffee. That's probably why he was being an ass back there."

Julie cocked her head. "I didn't notice if he did. I'm not good at stuff like that."

"Me, either," Court confided.

"You're not good with what? Flirting with girls?"

Court shrugged. "Didn't date in high school. Didn't go to college. Didn't exactly land a job with a lot of eligible females around."

"Sounds like an excuse to be alone."

Court didn't necessarily agree with her, but he was uncomfortable with the focus on himself, so he didn't argue.

He ate a moment, then looked up to Julie and said, "Hanley likes you, says you're smart as hell." Then he added, "He did say you were an odd duck."

She sipped bottled water, then said, "I don't know if I should be offended or if all the ducks of the world should."

"I think you just shrug and say, 'That's just Hanley.'"

"That's just Hanley."

"Feel better?"

"You are assuming I was bothered by what he said in the first place. That's not really how my mind operates."

"I'm gonna figure you out, Julie."

"It won't be easy."

"Neither is finding, fixing, and finishing Murad Khan, but we are totally nailing that fucker. *You* should be a piece of cake."

Suddenly she turned even more serious. "Has Hanley told you what we found?"

Court chewed while he answered. "He hasn't told us anything."

"Well, I expect you'll be hearing from him tonight."

Court put his fork down and sat up straighter. "I *knew* it. You were right, weren't you? Khan is making dirty bombs."

She clarified. "We *think* he is. We have a line on a location for a portion of his force, as well, but I don't think I can say more than that. If Chief Hanley gets authorization to send you out, I'll give you all the full briefing."

Court nodded, took a sip of his iced tea as he thought.

Julie put her fork down. Suddenly she appeared emotional, stressed. "I've been looking at all this raw intel for the past seventy hours. There is a good chance they are going to send you, along with the rest, into a very dangerous place, based, in part, on my analysis."

Court waited for what was to come next.

"Vance and the rest of the analysis shop . . . they respect my abilities. But they treat me like I'm some kind of a computer. Infallible. I'm a human being, and I make mistakes."

Court sensed something in her tone. "You *did* make a mistake once."

"More than once, of course, but one time was different."

"What happened?"

She looked off across the room a moment. "It was when I was in JSOC. I underestimated the size of a quick reaction force in a nearby village. I had the information for a better assessment, but I was rushed, the op was green-lit before I had everything I needed analyzed. I went with what I had. A team of Delta working with Afghan special forces raided a compound." She waved a hand in the air. "No big deal, they do that every night. But then one of the analysts monitoring the nearby village spotted truckloads of fighting-aged males heading towards the contact.

"A hasty extraction was sent in, and they got all coalition forces out of the compound thirty-seven seconds before forty armed Al Qaeda fighters pulled up."

The pain on her face was obvious. "We would have been wiped out if someone else didn't step in to fix my mistake."

Court gave her a little smile. "Like you said, we're only human. We're all just out here trying our best." He hesitated, then said, "Is that why you left JSOC?"

She shook her head. "No. Nobody blamed me but me." She looked at her plate and said, "Where Hanley wants to send you now. It's the same thing. I don't have access to the information I need to make a complete threat assessment."

"What's your concern?"

"The Agency hasn't been looking at this location. It's the responsibility of the Air Force. But I can't get any imagery they have. Presumably they've had UAVs overhead for weeks, but I can only see what's gone on since the day before yesterday."

"Which is?"

"Which is significant activity, but not a lot of personnel. I have no idea of the enemy's size on site."

"You've done your best. That's all anyone can ask for." Court added, "I know you've been working on this with everything you've got. I haven't seen you in three days."

She blinked her eyes once, surprised by this. "Were you looking?"

Court stared at his meatloaf and ate for a moment. Finally he said, "Yeah."

An awkward silence overtook both of them.

Julie finally broke the stillness. "Everyone is talking about what you did at the mall. Nobody knows which member of Golf Sierra went in alone . . . they all think it was Lennox or Hightower." She flashed a conspiratorial look across the table. "I haven't said anything."

"Good."

"But everyone is saying what you did was incredible. One of the targeting officers started calling you 'the One.'"

"The one *what*?"

She cocked her head. "The *One*. Like Neo. In *The Matrix*."

"The *what*?"

She appeared crestfallen. "You haven't seen *The Matrix*, you haven't seen *Big Bang Theory*. What rock have you been living under?"

Maurice's rock, he thought but did not say. "I don't watch much TV."

Julie sighed. "It's a movie, *The Matrix*. Keanu Reeves."

"Okay."

She waved her hand in front of her face. "Never mind. They are just saying you are special."

"I'm good at what I do. Am I good enough? I don't know."

"I'm having the same thoughts about myself. Am I good enough?"

Court lifted his iced tea and tapped her bottle of water with his. "Well, from what you're telling me, we're *both* about to find out how good we are."

They finished their dinner, then left the dining facility. The sun was low, but Court knew he didn't have to be back in the pit until sundown.

Julie said, "I've got a meeting in forty-five minutes. Want to go for a walk first?"

"Why not?"

They strolled all the way to the fence that ran along East Perimeter Road, then walked along it with the mountains in the near distance. Gray clouds were building around the white tips of Spin Ghar, reflecting the setting sun in the west.

Julie said, "I'm sorry I haven't been around much the last few days."

Court said, "I get it. All this trying to stop a terrorist from detonating a dirty bomb is really getting in the way of your social life."

She smiled at this. "I like it when you joke. I might not think it's that funny, but I can tell you do, and that's good."

"You're a bundle of laughs yourself, Julie."

"You did it again."

"What?"

Julie stopped walking and Court followed suit. "You don't smile with your mouth when you joke. You think you're too cool for that. But you smile with your eyes."

Court looked away. "I doubt that."

"You *do*."

He felt like she could see into him in ways no one ever had. Except Maurice. Maurice had once stripped his psyche so bare that Court had shown everything deep on the inside.

He had an aversion to such vulnerability now, but Julie wasn't Maurice. She wasn't going to hurt him.

He looked up at the sky. "Getting dark. I'd better be heading back."

Julie looked at the sky herself, focusing on the east over the mountains. "If you are sent over there tonight, is it okay if I come to the flight line to wish you luck?"

There was a softness in her voice that he hadn't heard before, and emotions welling inside him that he was wholly unaccustomed to. He lived a life thinking that no one gave a shit if he lived or died save for those who merely benefited from his ability to kill. But this was different; this was someone who seemed to care about him as a human being, and he couldn't remember experiencing this before.

Ever.

"I'd like that," he said.

Julie just stared a moment longer, still and quiet, but it seemed to Court she was deep in thought. Finally, she said, "You and I have a lot in common. And one of those things is we don't really know what we're doing here."

"In Afghanistan?"

"No. I mean . . . alone with a member of the opposite sex."

Defensively, Court said, "I'm twenty-five. You're acting like I'm some kid."

Julie said, "I'm twenty-seven. You *are*."

He didn't know how to respond.

"If you are attracted to me," Julie said nonchalantly, "then now would be the time to kiss me. If you aren't attracted to me, now would be when you say let's just be friends. I get it, either way. It's totally your decis—"

Court leaned forward and kissed her hard on the lips. She kissed him back, put her hand behind his neck, and he followed her lead, doing the same to her.

It was awkward with the body armor and helmets, but it didn't slow them down, and neither noticed the added weight or bulk.

They stood there by the fence, in front of the backdrop of the impossibly rugged Spin Ghar mountains, for several minutes, kissing, being comfortable in each other's silence. Court was certain his nerves were showing, but for the first time he could remember, he didn't give a damn.

Julie finally took a half step back, and she started to say something with a smile, but then, at exactly the same moment, both of their walkie-talkies beeped on their hips.

They answered their radios, and an instant later the two of them were running across the base as fast as they could, their romantic interlude behind them now, because the green light for the task force mission outside the wire had just come down.

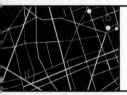

FIFTY

It was standing room only in the TOC at nine p.m. Golf Sierra was in attendance, as well as Lima Foxtrot. A sixteen-man contingent of SEAL Team 10 operators from Forward Operating Base Salerno, just three miles to the northwest, were also present, many of the men in shorts and flip-flops along with their body armor and rifles hanging haphazardly from slings around their necks or shoulders. Three junior officers from the 75th Ranger Regiment who'd also come over from Salerno stood in the back, their forty-eight-man platoon having been tasked to assist with this hasty hit, as well.

A dozen CIA paramilitary officers, sixteen U.S. Navy SEALs, and three Army officers, as well as pilots, copilots, and crew chiefs for ten Blackhawk helicopters, crowded around, all facing a dozen workstations with analysts and techs seated in front of computers. Beyond the analysts, Hanley, Hightower, and Duane Anderson, team leader of Lima Foxtrot, stood on a low riser in front of a 120-inch monitor showing alternating views of Ismail Zai base.

A UAV flew thirty thousand feet over the site now, and even to Court, who had zero experience evaluating top-down real-time images of targets, it was obvious there was a lot of activity at the location. Through breaks in the cloud cover, trucks and men could be seen moving about, most around a large building labeled "HAS" on the screen.

Court had no idea what a HAS was, and he was too proud to ask, but Lennox leaned over to him after a few minutes and answered the unasked question.

"Hardened aircraft shelter. Basically a big bombproof bunker. A concrete structure buried under tons of dirt." He added, "That's a big one, you could park a 747 in there."

As Court looked at it, he could tell it was the size of a couple of football fields. Lennox said underneath the hill was a hardened concrete and steel structure able to withstand multiple salvos of missiles. He explained it had been built by the Americans to house Global Hawk UAVs ten years earlier, but now, as far as the intel went, it lay abandoned by the Pakistani military.

It was clear from the overhead feed, however, that the structure was in use tonight. Men moved around in front of the HAS, and trucks were parked out front.

The three-story-tall blast doors on the south side of the bunker were closed at the moment, but a small garage-type door was open, and light could be seen shining from inside.

The HAS stood in front of a large tarmac, which gave way to a grassy area and a taxiway that led to a runway, splayed out east to west, running across virtually the entire southern end of the base.

And across the runway from the bunker, a row of six old and disused-looking aircraft hangars sat close to the wire fence there. Lennox said these had housed Predators long ago, before the Pakistani army used the shelters for Mi-17 helicopters when they briefly occupied this remote base in the Federally Administered Tribal Area.

A Dishka crew-served gun in the control tower was manned by three men, and a small armed security presence, perhaps six men in all, stood around the front gate. Several pickup trucks rolled patrols around the perimeter, obviously more security for Ismail Zai.

The operation to raid the location had been orchestrated over the past several hours, in large part by Hightower from Golf Sierra and Anderson from Lima Foxtrot, with consultation from the SEALs and, less so, by the officers and NCOs of the Ranger platoon.

The first person to speak to the audience was a CIA meteorologist, who informed the group that the site would be completely covered in heavy clouds beginning at roughly ten p.m., and the clouds would linger until the morning sun burned them away. The UAV overhead would be useless other than to provide thermal images of activity at the site, and the helicopters flying into Pakistan would have to deal with the heavy cloud cover, as well.

Hightower spoke next, and he discussed the insertion itself. The low clouds made a high-altitude jump too risky, and the fact that the target location might possibly contain multiple radioactive devices meant a helicopter fast-rope insertion into the compound would be ill-advised. The enemy would hear the helos coming for several minutes before they appeared, and the enemy could simply detonate a device and kill the entire raiding party.

That only left one viable option. The men would load up into eight Blackhawk helicopters with two more flying as backup, then fly across the border, nap-of-the-earth over the Spin Ghar mountains to avoid Pakistani air-defense radars, and land in multiple locations, none closer than five miles away from the compound. The terrain worked in the Americans' favor, Hightower explained, as Ismail Zai base was surrounded by hills that would baffle some of the helicopters' noise, but the terrain to the east of the mountains and to the west of the base was easily passable, even at night.

Hightower said he anticipated the trek from the LZs to Ismail Zai to take no more than three hours.

All eight helos that delivered troops, as well as another pair of empty Blackhawks sent in case any of the helos were shot down, would leave the LZ and return to Afghanistan, where they would refuel from a bladder at a forward fueling station erected by Army Pathfinders.

Matt Hanley took the floor next and explained that it would be the Army's mission to control the perimeter. The platoon from the 75th Ranger Regiment would dominate and eliminate existing base security, then form a defensive perimeter around Ismail Zai to ward off any quick reaction force the KRF might be able to call upon from Peshawar.

The SEALs would go over the wall from the south, behind the hangars across the runway, and then they would cross the runway and attack the main entrance of the HAS via the garage door on the western side.

Lima Foxtrot would enter through the main gate and then hit the command building on the northern end of the base, the same building Golf Sierra parachuted onto a month earlier.

The two Reaper UAVs flying thirty thousand feet above the scene were each armed with a pair of Hellfire missiles, and though they would only be able to see heat registers through their thermal cameras, they could be employed in the fight if a target was identified.

One of the Rangers asked about the Reaper's ability to tell friend from foe when using thermal cameras exclusively. Hanley admitted that a friendly-fire incident was a real danger in this scenario and stressed the need for good communications back to Chapman to avoid any fratricide.

Julie Marquez took the floor without being invited, and she stressed that the latrines at Ismail Zai, while still only indicating that a couple dozen men were present, could be some sort of misdirection if the KRF had other ways of containing their human waste.

The chief petty officer with the SEALs spoke up to this. "You mean, like, burying it?"

"Possibly, though that would be difficult to remain undetected. They aren't burying anything outside."

The bearded man asked, "Then . . . how could they hide all that shit?"

Some men laughed, but Julie said, "A truckload of chemical toilets kept inside one of the buildings could be used to conceal the true number of enemy personnel at this location."

Vance, standing at the monitor showing the real-time image of Ismail Zai base, pushed back on this, asking Julie if she'd ever witnessed chemical toilets being used for such purposes by any of the organizations she'd conducted intelligence against. She admitted she had not. Vance then echoed and amplified this, saying that his career was three times that of his junior analyst, and he'd never heard of this, either.

Vance pointed out that two dozen KRF fighters plus another ten or so security was the estimated force size, and the joint operation against the base would consist of seventy-six men, with air support from armed UAVs.

If anything, Vance said, this appeared to be overkill.

Finally, Hanley addressed the force. "Anything else?"

Julie just looked back blankly, neither agreeing nor disagreeing verbally, but Court could tell she wasn't sold. They made eye contact across the room, and he saw a grave expression on her face, as if she now felt she and her team were leading the men seated and standing in the center of the room into a buzz saw.

Back in the pit minutes later, the six men of Golf Sierra worked on their own portion of tonight's raid. Hightower listened to the ideas and observations of all his men, jotting down notes, and then he stood over the map table and gave his instructions. Golf Sierra would hump overland from the LZ to the cluster of buildings just north of the wall of the base, where they would clear the area of any hostiles before entering the small dwelling where Julie Marquez had found evidence that the tunnel from the base led. If possible, the team would access the tunnel and then use it to move into Ismail Zai to support whichever force there most needed the help.

Hightower didn't love his team's assignment. It was clear they had what all existing intelligence suggested to be the easiest job out of any of the four forces being sent to the target. He knew Hanley had assigned this mission to Golf Sierra because they had been run so hard and they were operating with a new man, but still . . . he felt like he was on the outside looking in.

He kept his opinion of his team's assignment to himself, however, and outlined the plan for the others.

Hightower said, "If those buildings to the north are housing personnel, you can consider them hostile. Intelligence is showing no innocents in the area, no normal patterns of life for families, and we know of no hostages on location.

"No reason to be discriminatory with our weapons systems. We can apply lethal power liberally in the village."

Court said, "What does that mean?"

Redus said, "Shoot anything that moves. Except me."

Court replied, "Marquez said coverage of the area has been spotty until today. Some issues with the weather, and with the NSA not passing on their intel in time. The fact is, we don't know everything going on at that site. There *could* be civs."

"We're green-lit," Hightower said. "We'll avoid CIVCAS where possible, but our mission continues, and our mission is to clear the residential buildings, then haul ass to Ismail Zai to support forces there. That's it."

Court didn't like the idea of shooting indiscriminately in a little village full of unknowns. "But—"

"I don't want to hear another word about it, Six." Hightower looked at Lennox, his number Two. "Anything I left out, Kendrick?"

Lennox flashed his eyes at Sierra Six. "Yeah. Gentry. Shoot the bad guys, not the good guys, hoo-yah?"

"Hoo-yah!" belted Redus.

"Hoo-yah," Court replied meekly.

"All right," Hightower said, "we are wheels up in two hours. Get water and food, then jock up. Full battle rattle. A transport vic will move us from the pit to the flight line together."

Court felt butterflies in his stomach, a rare occurrence, and he told himself he was still a little nervy because of all that had happened in Lahore.

But it was more than that. He had been trained as a singleton, a lone operator, and now he was one man on a force of over one hundred in the air and on the ground, and even with the training he'd received in Golf Sierra in the past three weeks, he still felt very much out of his element.

Hightower stepped up to him. "Six, we're taking a walk."

The two men exited the pit, just out of earshot of the rest of the team, and then Zack turned around to him. "Do we have a problem?"

"I'm good to go, Zack. I just have a thing against civilian casualties."

"CIVCAS can be a problem in any fight around dwellings. Just do your best."

Court just looked at him.

"You can't catch devils with angels," Hightower said. "We don't get to be the good guys all the time. We are here to execute U.S. foreign policy as determined by officials elected by places in America you and I wouldn't want to take a shit in. There are some real pricks in government calling the shots, and we're the ones who have to *take* the shots. Sometimes they get it right. I've done shit in DEVGRU and here at Ground Branch that I'll be proud of for the rest of my life, whether that's twenty-four hours or fifty years.

"Also, as you can guess, there is some shit I've done that I don't feel that great about. But I process it all like this. I'm a hammer. You're a hammer. You have to accept that. Sometimes the hammer is going to be wielded by a person who wants to fix something; sometimes it'll be some asshole who wants to break something. I'd rather it was always the former and never the latter, but wishing it doesn't make it so.

"Our country needs dudes like us. I love my country, so I give myself over to the powers that be and hope, when all is said and done, I did a hell of a lot more good than I did bad."

Court nodded. He got it. When he was in Russia working for AAP, he didn't always know much about his operations beyond what he needed at ground level. His targets were his targets because he was told to target them. Full stop. He didn't get a vote.

"Copy all, One. I'll do my best."

Zack slapped him on the shoulder and then went back inside the pit. Court stood there, just outside the door, and tried to control the doubt he was feeling about all this.

He kept his misgivings to himself; he knew there were enough misgivings about him around the FOB to where he didn't need to add to them, and then he headed back inside to his cage, planning to check and recheck every piece of gear he'd be taking into battle tonight.

A low mist covered Islamabad's Fatima Jinnah Park at a quarter after ten p.m., and four CIA security officers stood far from the gas lamps, surveilling the empty greenspace in the center of Pakistan's capital, looking for indications of threats. The three men and one woman of the detail had been here many times, doing exactly the same thing in exactly the same way, and they never much cared for the assignment. Their chief of station insisted on running an agent personally, here in the city, and this created a host of concerns for the men and women tasked with protecting him.

No, they'd always approached these in-person agent meets at the park with caution and concern, but tonight their collective stress level was growing by the minute, because for the first time any of these officers could remember, Leopard was late to the meet.

They scanned footpaths and nearby roads and apartment balconies and the rooftops of office buildings, searching both for the person they wanted to see—the agent—and for people they did *not* want to see, namely Pakistani counterintelligence officers.

Ted Appleton sat alone on a park bench, and just like his four officers standing at least fifty meters away, he gaped into the mist, hoping in vain to see movement.

Any movement.

And if the Agency security officers around the park protecting him were concerned, chief of CIA Station Islamabad Ted Appleton was approaching full-on panic.

Aimal had never been late without notification, and she'd been the one to call for this meeting earlier in the day. He knew she'd have urgent news for him, and he knew that if she was late, it was due to some sort of personal or operational security threat.

And if she ended up being a no-show, with no text or call . . . then that could only mean one thing.

That he'd left her in the field one damn day too long, and she had been compromised by a very dangerous enemy.

He shuddered thinking of this possibility, and then he told himself everything would be fine, because that was all he could do.

The earpiece that connected him to his security team crackled in his ear.

"Boss, this is Bodnar. It's seventeen past the hour. Recommend we call it."

Appleton knew what time it was; he'd checked his watch every other minute since he'd arrived.

He clicked a transmit button under the cuff of his shirt to respond to the chief of his detail. "We wait. A few more minutes. No more."

There was a pause just long enough to let the station chief know that his lead close-protection officer did not agree at all with his decision. And then the man said, "Copy."

Appleton fought the urge to simply call Aimal's mobile phone now. He wanted to hear her voice, to find out if she needed help, but he knew better than to actually pull out his cell and make the call. If she had been compromised somehow, then a cryptic phone conversation with an American would only put her in exponentially more danger. So he sat, waited, worried, and continued to check his watch every other minute.

At the twenty-two-minute mark, he knew his own PERSEC was now very much in danger. If he had an agent who had been picked up by the opposition, especially on the way to a clandestine meeting, then there was no way to be certain that the enemy didn't know about the location of this meeting, as well.

Just as he was about to click his transmit button to tell the team they would be leaving, he saw movement in the mist, approaching up the footpath. He stood, looking into the darkness, as the form of a woman appeared.

He began walking towards her; his heart soared.

But only for a moment.

When the figure came out of the mist, he realized it was Caroline, a CIA security officer on his protection detail. She was still fifty feet from him when he heard her voice through his earpiece.

"Sir . . . Bodnar sent me to collect you. It's time to go."

With an incredible weight in his heart, he acknowledged the transmission and began walking back towards the car they had parked nearby as his security closed on him from all directions. He kept his chin up, put on a brave face for the team around him, but inside he felt like he was dying.

All he could do now, he realized, was return to the embassy, monitor his phone and his email, and seek out any chatter from ISI sources.

And wait.

He'd do whatever he could for his agent, as soon as there *was* something he could do, because that was his job.

And also because, he knew without question, the missing agent just happened to be the love of his life, and he'd sent her into the jaws of an enemy that had likely swallowed her whole.

FIFTY-ONE

The last thing on Court Gentry's mind had been the weather, but Priya changed that in an instant, calling across the apartment over the fish market from where she sat at her computer to where he sat on a bean bag chair.

Court was trying to get Appleton on the phone to check his progress with local and national authorities. He'd left hours earlier, promising to get Priya the intel she needed about the back door into the nation's security camera database. Court was impatient; he knew they were all operating on borrowed time, and he'd been calling every twenty minutes or so for an update.

"Cobalt," Priya said, "have you heard about the storm?"

Court hung up the phone. Without much concern, he asked, "What storm?"

"A monsoon is coming. Moving up from the southwest. Should hit this afternoon. It's been on the news for days."

"I've been a little busy."

"Really? Me, too," she snapped back.

Court ignored her tone. "How bad?"

"Thirty-five centimeters are predicted. Winds of eighty kilometers per hour."

"Awesome," he said, dryly. Court converted the numbers quickly. A foot of rain and fifty-mile-an-hour winds were nothing to ignore, but there wasn't a damn thing he could do about the weather.

The city was accustomed to monsoons, flooding, power outages, and the like, Priya explained, but she also said it would bring the city to a standstill until after it passed. "No taxis, no trains, impassable streets. Believe me, a monsoon this big will be bad."

Court wasn't worried about Mumbai washing away; he was worried about Mumbai becoming uninhabitable due to nuclear fallout. The storm would be a hassle to his operation, of course. But if he got word of Khan's location, he'd go in whatever conditions he had to do it in, even if he had to backstroke across the massive city.

Priya brought Court some chai, and she sat down on the sofa across from him without looking his way.

More to pass the time than anything else, Court said, "Can you help me understand why Bari would go into business with Khan to damage the nation of his birth?"

Priya shrugged. "I am Hindu, but I understand the oppression the Muslims feel."

"How so?"

"The government in India has pursued a Hindu nationalist agenda for many years. The rights of Muslims are all but ignored. Poverty in that community is everywhere, and police don't go into Muslim areas to fight crime." She turned to Court. "And I am talking about what is going on now. Don't get me started on partition."

"Partition?"

"Nineteen forty-seven. The British Empire, what was left of it anyway, carved British India up into two nations. The Dominion of India and the Islamic Republic of Pakistan. This decision led to the forced uprooting of tens of millions. As many as two million were killed during the partition.

"I am an unapologetic Hindu, proud of my nation, but that doesn't mean I can't acknowledge how we got here." When Court said nothing, she added, "Your nation displaced millions so that your ancestors could have land, as well, did they not?"

"They did."

The door opened. Court went for his gun but relaxed when he saw Ted Appleton. The former station chief had a sack of burner phones and he looked as energized as Court had ever seen him. He immediately followed Priya over to her computer, where he gave her an access code to the national traffic camera database.

"What did you have to do to get this?" she asked.

Appleton shrugged. "Not everyone knows I'm no longer working with the Nuclear Command Authority."

In minutes, Priya was inside the database, pulling footage of various cameras that had been recording near the building where she'd been held two nights earlier. She warned the two Americans this could be a lengthy process, so Appleton and Court went across the living room to sit and talk things over.

Court said, "Say you were Murad Khan. Knowing what you know about him, his history, his affiliations, what would your target be?"

"India is the target, obviously. More specifically, it's anyone's guess."

"Where would you put a dirty bomb that would cause the most damage to India?"

Appleton had obviously been thinking about this. "I'd hit New Delhi. It's the capital."

Priya, still working on her computer across the room, said, "New Delhi isn't the heart of India. It's Mumbai. This is the financial hub of the entire nation."

Appleton said, "True, but both Murad Khan and Palak Bari are from Mumbai. Why would they destroy their own home to hurt the Indian regime?"

"They are both Muslim," Priyanka said. "Maybe they would locate the blast in an area away from large Muslim concentrations."

Court pulled up a map of the city on Priya's other laptop, positioning it between himself and Appleton on the little table in front of the sofa. The two Americans looked at it for a moment. Finally Court said, "Priya, take a look. What do you think?"

She remained fixated on the camera footage she was scanning, but she answered, "I live here. I don't need to look at a map. The most likely target is one of the two main financial centers."

"How do you mean?"

"Bandra Kurla Complex and Nariman Point. An attack against either one of these would have an impact that would last generations."

Appleton said, "She's right about that."

"Show me," Court said.

Appleton scrolled the satellite map over. "Here's Bandra Kurla. I live there, you were there last night," he said. "It's one of the big centers for banking and the economy."

Priya pulled herself away from her screen now, moved over to the computer on the table in front of the sofa, and sat down between the two Americans. She scrolled down to the south of the city, near the water. "This is Nariman Point. It used to be the only main financial hub, until Bandra Kurla grew."

Appleton said, "Which would Khan pick?"

Priya thought this over. Then she pointed to the southern tip of Mumbai. "He'd pick Nariman."

"Why?" asked Court.

"Bandra Kurla is much closer to the slums. It has more Muslims there and around there. Nariman, it's on the water, it's the main business district, and it's sort of closed off from the Muslim parts of the city. There are mostly Hindus here. Rendering this entire district uninhabitable, killing a few thousand people who live and work there, destroying the existing financial hub for years and years . . . *this* would do more to hurt India than a dozen wars in the north for Kashmir."

Appleton looked at her and then at Court. "The young lady is absolutely right."

Court zoomed in on the satellite image. "He'd want to detonate it somewhere high."

Priya sighed. "There are a lot of tall buildings there."

"A rooftop, maybe," Court said.

"And certainly," Appleton added, "he'll wait for the monsoon to pass. Blowing a dirty bomb in fifty-mile-an-hour winds would contaminate the entire city."

"Well then," Court said, "we might have a little time yet to look for his location, and we've narrowed it down from hundreds to . . . dozens, maybe."

"That's progress," Appleton said, hopefully.

Priya went back to her workstation and spent another twenty-five minutes looking at video feeds until she froze an image.

"I might have something."

Court and Ted rushed over to her.

"A side employee entrance to a restaurant on the ground floor of the building I was held in. Eleven fifty-four p.m. Three Volvo SUVs, all black, just pulled up."

The men looked over her shoulder at the three vehicles in the lighting of the alleyway. Court realized this was just minutes after he'd left the area, having reconnoitered the building the night before he assaulted it. He'd walked down this very alley at one point, and he would have remembered these three vehicles if they had been there at that time.

After less than a minute parked there, men in casual clothing began filing out of all three Volvos. With the drivers still behind the wheel, eight men went to the side entrance, which was opened for them by someone on the inside.

Court and Ted both looked the men over. The angle wasn't great and the light was bad, but when the fifth man arrived under the light at the door, the two Americans both spoke in unison.

"Khan."

"Yes," Priya agreed. "That's him. Now, we have to see the plates on these vehicles."

Court looked at the screen. "That's impossible. You're twenty meters away, and you can't even see the rear of the SUVs from this angle."

"From here, no, you can't. But we just have to follow these cars when they leave until they pass a camera that *does* get a look at them. If we can do that, I can use software to clean up the images, and we can find out who these Volvos belong to."

"How long will that take?" he asked, impatiently.

Priya said, "Not as long as it would take you to find Khan while sitting on the couch making guesses."

Court looked at Appleton but said nothing.

In the end, Priya Bandari had a clean tag image in under thirty minutes. When the motorcade left the building, it passed under a high-definition street camera. Priya barely had to enhance the image at all before putting it in a paid database her uncle subscribed to that matched car tags to their owners.

It took just seconds for a result.

She said, "The Volvo is owned by Church Square Holdings and Investments."

Court looked to Appleton. "Mean anything to you?"

"To *me*? No, but let me make some calls."

Over an hour later Appleton was the one with the information, while Court and Priya waited impatiently, both looking out the window at the darkening clouds and increasing wind. He said, "My sources in the local police confirm that Church Square is a B-Company money-laundering front."

"If the police know about it, why don't they shut it down?" Priya asked.

Appleton and Court looked at each other and then back to the young woman.

"You think I'm naïve," she said. "I can see it in your faces."

"Nothing wrong with not knowing the inner workings of corrupt practices," Court said. "That's not naïveté, that's a virtue. I assume, and it looks like Ted here agrees, that some B-Company enterprises are tolerated by the government."

"More than tolerated," Ted said. "Palak Bari's organization funds a lot of politicians and other leaders around this area."

Priya said, "We need to find out about any physical locations this Church Square Holdings and Investments owns. They have cars, obviously. So, where do the cars park at night?"

There was an open-source avenue for this information, and it was basic corporate intelligence and private investigative work Priya had been training on for years that got the job done. She plugged in the company, as well as other companies held by Church Square, and came up with a list of seventy-seven offices, buildings, apartments, and physical storefronts across greater Mumbai.

"Shit," Court said, and then, "Any of them at Nariman Point?"

"Yes," Priya confirmed. "Eight. They own two buildings, a penthouse apartment in another building, plus they have the physical location of Church Square Holdings' offices, as well as four private companies owned by them."

Court and Ted thought for a moment. Finally Ted asked, "The buildings owned by the holding company? How tall are they?"

Priya focused on her laptop for a minute, then said, "One is twelve stories, the other is sixteen."

"And the penthouse apartment?" Court asked.

"Twenty-fifth floor. It's in a building called Express Tower. On Marine Drive, overlooking the bay at the southern tip of Nariman Point."

Appleton looked at the map on Priya's computer and saw the building in question. "Could be the place. Worth a look." He then asked, "What about the other locations?"

Priya pulled up each of the businesses, as well as the main offices of Church Square. They were all on ground floors or very low floors of buildings in the area, so they were discounted as potential sites to position the bomb.

Priya wasn't as sold as the other two. "Why does he have to detonate the bomb on a building? Why can't he use a helicopter or an airplane?"

Court said, "These devices are big, and the bigger they are, the more dangerous they are. If he had one hundred kilos of nuclear fuel, he's going to need tons and tons of explosive material. Sure, he could get a cargo plane and fly low over the city, but why bother if he has a skyscraper at his disposal?"

Court added, "Still, we don't know for sure, and we won't know till we see Khan or the device."

He launched to his feet. "The guy who trained me used to always say,

'The map is not the territory.' We aren't going to be able to find anything sitting here." He was excited that he finally had a mission. "I'm going down to Nariman Point to see what I can see around this building." He looked to Appleton. "In the meantime, tell your contacts in R&AW and the police what we've found. Even if we don't find the bomb, Khan might very well be working from this location."

Appleton nodded distractedly, and only after a moment, but Court didn't pick up on this. Instead he slipped his pistol in the small of his back and headed for the door.

Priya closed her laptop and began packing it as well as a charger into a backpack. "Wait. I'm going with you. If I can get in the building, I can hack into their security system."

Court said, "We're going to need a car, I'm going to have to steal one."

Priya shrugged. "Is that supposed to scare me off?"

"Just testing."

She looked out the window again. "In a couple of hours, we won't need a car, we'll need a boat."

"Let's go then," Court said, and they headed out the door.

Appleton called out to them as they left. "I'll make contact with an old colleague in R&AW, then I'll meet you down at Nariman Point."

FIFTY-TWO

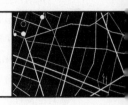

TWELVE YEARS AGO

Ten sleek and advanced EH-60 helicopters sat tip to tail on the flight line, their rotors spinning. Powerful electric lighting cast a sharp tinge to the scene, and long shadows danced in multiple directions as seventy-six men in combat gear congregated near the big aircraft.

The different forces were divided by uniform, load-out, position on the tarmac, even age and disposition.

The Rangers were both the most plentiful and the youngest, some teenagers, most in their early twenties, and they wore conventional military uniforms, carried M4 rifles, and sat on the tarmac in neat rows, their backs resting against their packs. Their dual-tube night observation devices propped high on their helmets differentiated them even more from the rest of the combat-ready men at the scene.

Next to them, the sixteen-man SEAL contingent were older, in their twenties and early thirties, and they donned better uniforms, better armor, and better gear, and they wielded high-end HK416 rifles and quad-tube NODs.

And next to the SEALs, a dozen more men, all at least thirty-four years old save for one, wore flame-resistant and moisture-wicking cold-weather adventure-wear clothing, knee and elbow pads, and body armor with loaded ammo pouches attached. They carried 416s, same as the SEALs, and similar helmets and NODs, but they looked nothing like the Navy men, who themselves looked nothing like the Rangers.

Six of the twelve CIA paramilitaries had been SEALs themselves, including Zack Hightower, TL of Golf Sierra, and Duane Anderson, TL of Lima Foxtrot. The others had been members of Delta Force or Green Berets, with the one unique exception being the twenty-five-year-old brown-haired man standing in the center of Golf Sierra, who was now looking up at the heavy cloud cover and wondering how the hell ten helicopters were going to fly through that soup and through a rugged mountain range.

Court wasn't even thinking about the danger at the target; his worry right now was focused on getting there.

Like the others on his team, he was strapped with sixty pounds of armor and equipment, and his gloved hand rested on his rifle, hanging on his chest by a two-point sling. His nervousness had only increased in the past two hours, and having recently noticed the impenetrable clouds hanging just over the base, he now realized he had something new to worry about.

Redus looked over at him, the taller American's face visible in the electric lighting but partially obscured by a thatchy beard, goggles, and the radio microphone that curved in from the left. He wore ear protection and a helmet, same as Court and the others, and his night vision goggles jutted above his head like a crown.

All the men carried gas masks in pouches on their hips, opposite their pistols, and each man had at least two knives on his belt.

Court turned away and looked off down the flight line in time to see a pair of red and white Chesapeake Aviation BV-107s lift off a quarter mile to the east, no doubt taking personnel to another FOB or, if they were lucky, back to Bagram to catch a flight to the States.

Court watched their blinking lights until they disappeared in the clouds heading north, barely four or five hundred feet above the tarmac.

"Look at you," a woman's voice said from just behind him. He turned to find Julie standing among the dozens of jocked-up men on the flight line. She was wearing a gray sweatshirt with camel-colored body armor over it, a helmet on her head, and a radio clipped into a front pants pocket of her jeans. "You look ready for anything."

Court waved a hand up and down his body, motioning to the fifty thousand dollars' worth of equipment strapped to him. "Unfortunately none of this shit is going to help me if the helicopter corkscrews into a mountainside."

Julie looked over at the flight line. She said, "One Hundred Sixtieth. From FOB Salerno. They're the best pilots in the world. You'll have to find something else to worry about tonight."

Court found himself comforted by her words. He stepped closer. "I'll think of something. Didn't think you'd actually drop by."

"Why not?"

Court shrugged. "I don't know."

"Here I am," she said, looking around. "Even more testosterone than I'd expected."

"Dudes getting their game faces on."

"Right." She shrugged. "I wanted to see you off. Plus, nothing for me to do back at the TOC. Nobody's listening to me, anyway."

"About the oppo?"

She bit her lower lip, and Court realized he'd seen her do this before they'd kissed earlier. She said, "I keep telling everyone that we don't know the size of the force. Don't let them tell you there are two or three dozen pax on site; we really have no clue."

"Okay. We'll deal with whatever we find." He was trying to convince Julie all would be fine, which was difficult because he'd yet to convince himself of the same.

"I'm serious," she implored. "Be careful. This is going to be very dangerous."

"If it's not very dangerous, I'm not usually involved."

In Court's headset he heard Hightower's voice; the man was less than thirty feet away, but all the helos' engines made conversation at that distance impossible without shouting.

"Golf Sierra One to all call signs. Our aircraft is Thunder Six Four. We will load up in two mikes. Skids up in five."

Court had no idea how to tell one helicopter from the next, but he figured he'd just follow the rest of the group to the right helo when the time came, and if he got into the wrong helo, he'd sure as hell hear about it from Hightower before they took off.

He turned his attention back to Julie Marquez. They were two feet apart; Court wanted to kiss her, but he was in view of the rest of his team, so he held back.

She said, "I'll be watching from above." She looked up at the clouds. "On thermal, anyway. Right now the cloud cover over the target is even worse than it is here. Almost totally obscured. It won't clear till daybreak."

"I'll be sure to wave."

She rolled her eyes. "I still don't think your jokes are funny, but I respect you making one at a time like this."

"Gallows humor. When you're off to the gallows as much as I am, then that's pretty much all you've got."

"Are you scared?" she asked. "It's okay if you are."

In truth he was fucking terrified, but he shook his head. "Nah."

Julie gave him a look of disbelief. "Why not?" Then she motioned to the men around. "They're all scared. They're hiding it. They're controlling it. But they're feeling it. It's the natural human emotion at a time like this."

Court had no response to this. Instead he stepped forward, moved his microphone out of the way of his mouth, took Julie's head in his gloved hands, and kissed her. His goggles and his helmet pressed against her face and forehead, but she kissed him back hard.

This was a natural human emotion at a time like this, he realized.

He couldn't hear the men around him, and at this moment, he didn't care what they were saying.

When their lips parted, he remained close to Julie. "I'm good. Ready to get the job done and get back."

She held him, their armor tight against each other, and then she stepped back.

Court nodded, his heart pounding from fear and excitement and desire; there were almost too many emotions for him to process at the moment.

Quickly, Julie leaned forward, kissed him on the cheek, and said, "Come back."

Court nodded. "I will."

She backed away a few feet, bumping into kitted-up men who looked at her with annoyance, and then, after a quick nod to Court, she turned away, heading back to the hangars at the edge of the flight line.

Court watched her leave, then turned away to find Zack Hightower looming over him. The former SEAL Team 6 member had a big wad of dip under his lip, and he spit on the tarmac. Looking at Gentry, he said, "Fuckin' horny-assed kids," and the men around laughed at this.

And then, just like that, Hightower switched on. He triggered his push-to-talk button and said, "Everybody load up!"

Up and down this portion of the flight line, men lumbered towards the helicopters. Court lagged back a couple of steps, following Hightower as they neared one of the Blackhawks. Behind Court, Jim Pace leaned in close, speaking directly into his ear.

"Bad luck, dude."

"What's bad luck?"

"Makin' out with your old lady right before an op. Don't you ever watch any movies? Those are the dudes that don't make it back."

Court sighed and kept walking. He wasn't superstitious in the least, but he dreaded the shit he was in for about this, on top of everything else.

"You guys have any side bets on whether or not I make it tonight?" he asked Pace as he walked.

The forty-year-old operator just shook his head. "I'm rootin' for you, man, but I'm not risking any cash on it."

"Right," Court said, and he followed Lennox and Hightower through the large side hatch of a Blackhawk, then attached a multi-point harness around his chest and midsection and leaned back against the bench with his rifle pointing down between his feet, his body facing the front of the helo.

He looked ahead in the low light, past Morgan, Pace, and Redus, who faced the rear, past a crew chief behind them who knelt by a minigun that jutted out of the port side of the aircraft. Through the soft green lighting in the cabin, he could just make out the shoulders and helmets of the pilots between their seats at the front of the aircraft. Looking around at the array of screens, buttons, and knobs up there, Court found himself bewildered by the technology. He knew helicopters; he'd been trained to fly both rotary-wing and fixed-wing aircraft in Virginia and North Carolina during his two years of intense daily one-on-one training years earlier, but he'd certainly never piloted anything one tenth as sophisticated as a Blackhawk.

He'd flown Bell Rangers and two-seater Robinsons. Though he could understand the basic controls in the cockpit in front of him, he was like a crop duster sitting in a 747; this was a completely different animal.

The ten EH-60s took off more or less in unison. Court looked at the tritium-lit watch face on the underside of his left wrist as they jolted into the air and saw that it was midnight. He knew he was in for a whipping, dipping, stomach-lurching half-hour flight, followed by a three-hour walk through ragged trails, before arriving on target sometime around three thirty a.m.

In seconds the ground below disappeared out the portal in the closed hatch next to Court's head, and the lights below went dark, replaced by the impenetrable cloud cover.

He closed his eyes, an attempt to calm himself, but quickly Hightower came over the interteam radio. "Pilot says he's going lights out. It will be NODs from here on. Thirty-five minutes to target."

The blinking lights on the outside of the helo turned off, the lights in the cabin around Court did the same, and they flew through blackness towards the unknown.

FIFTY-THREE

Three hours later and one hundred seventy kilometers away, a different helicopter tracked over terrain with its own lights off, its pilot and copilot navigating the way through their windscreen with the aid of their single-tube helmet-mounted night vision monocles.

The Bell 412 flew just three meters over Ismail Zai Agency Road, following every turn of the blacktop as it ventured to the west. The pilot kept his airspeed around one hundred kilometers an hour, about the same ground speed a wheeled vehicle would travel around here, so any satellite or drone flying above would assume the helo to be just another car or truck on the road.

The pilot of the single-rotor Huey variant was Omar Mufti, a former major in the Pakistan Army Aviation Corps and second-in-command of the Kashmiri Resistance Front. In the army, Mufti had normally flown the larger and more advanced Mi-17, a Russian transport and gunship helo, but his nation had many other aircraft, and Mufti had procured this Huey for this evening's work because of its small size, its nimble maneuvering, and the fact that he had no equipment to carry.

He and his copilot did have one passenger, however. Thirty-five-year-old Murad Khan, formerly of the Inter-Services Intelligence agency and now the leader of the KRF, sat in back looking out at complete darkness because he wasn't wearing NODs like the pilots.

Khan worked hard to keep himself calm, but it became harder to do so when he received word through his headset that everything at his destination was ready, and they were only waiting on his arrival to begin tonight's operation.

Khan was certain his actions early this morning would be the greatest achievement any Pakistani had made to his nation's national security since another émigré from India had single-handedly delivered nuclear technology and then nuclear weapons into the nation's arsenal.

A. Q. Khan was no relative of Murad Khan—it was a common surname for Muslims in the region—but the younger man felt that after tonight, he would go down in history along with the now-seventy-two-year-old hero of the nation.

Not that he did any of this for Pakistan. The government in power, as far as he was concerned, was weak and useless; they, along with previous administrations, had refused to fight India for Khan's territorial homeland, refused to lift a finger for any of the Muslims on the other side of the border. He'd committed attacks against Pakistan in an attempt to weaken the government and sow terror, but by tonight's action, he hoped to, in one fell swoop, push America's assistance away from Pakistan and wound them deeply.

Then, God willing, he would have the freedom to go after an even bigger threat to his people, to his religion.

India.

But India was for another day. *Now* the target was the American coalition.

This mission of Khan's was in no way sanctioned by the ISI, but through years of building contacts, he'd determined that he could use his Kashmiri roots to found a new organization, one that pretended to be nothing more than a relatively unsophisticated ideologically motivated terror faction, remaining on the low end of the spectrum behind other Pakistani militant groups, like Lashkar-e-Taiba and Tehreek-e-Taliban.

Until the day Murad Khan painted his masterpiece.

And *that* day was *this* day.

Murad Khan shuddered with anticipation of what was to come in the next few hours.

. . .

Omar Mufti piloted his Bell helicopter through the western front gates of
Ismail Zai at three a.m., right on time, flying now just a single meter over
the ground at a speed of only thirty kilometers per hour. They continued
on, proceeding along a broken and weed-strewn asphalt runway that ran the
length of the property, appearing to anyone watching the heat signature
through the clouds above to be a small truck, similar to a dozen more that
had arrived in the past day. He flew this way through the base, past the command building on his left, past the tower above the runway on his right, past
the barracks and the storage building, and then on to the massive bunker on
the far eastern side. Mufti finally put his skids down just short of the huge
aircraft hangar doors of the largest structure in the property. He shut the
helicopter down and left his copilot behind to refuel it and ready it for
another flight, because they planned on leaving with Khan within the next
thirty minutes.

The former Aviation Corps major climbed out of the pilot's door while
the rotors slowed above him. Khan opened the rear hatch simultaneously,
and the men met on the concrete tarmac in front of the hardened bunker
just as a smaller double garage door opened closer to them, right next to
the three-story blast doors.

Kahn looked up to the sky, and then, with a wide grin, he turned his
attention to Mufti. Shouting over the still-spooling-down engine, Khan
said, "We have been blessed tonight with the weather, my brother."

"Truly, we have," Mufti said. "It will be difficult where the men have to
go with these low clouds, but the clouds ensure they will at least have a
chance."

Khan grabbed him on both shoulders and embraced him tightly.

"Confidence, my friend. The men you have chosen for the job will be
successful. I know it."

Together they walked through the garage doors and into the well-lit
bunker, and they both quickly noticed the contrast. Other than the still-
spooling-down helo, it was quiet and still and dark outside. Inside, in a
space the size of a small sports stadium, generators powered dozens of
light towers, and nearly one hundred men moved around, making last-

minute preparations. Most of the men were fighters, the best soldiers of the Kashmiri Resistance Front, already dressed in full battle gear and carrying AK-47s or PKM light machine guns, along with the steely-eyed looks of men who knew they were likely going to be in a fight before the night was through.

But most of these men had other tasks, as well. They were mechanics, technicians, logistics, transportation.

The men had arrived here, one vehicle at a time, over the space of a week and a half. Never more than four vehicles in a day, and never separated by less than five hours. By this bit of subterfuge, they'd been able to amass a large presence here in the hardened bunker and remain hidden from American drones and satellites, but this had not been easy.

Food, tea, and water had come from the village of Kayala, eight kilometers to the northeast, handed over by women to the men in each car as it passed the village, where it was then taken into the bunker and consumed.

The men at Ismail Zai had even used a tunnel that led from a tiny postage stamp of a village to the north into the command building to store their human waste. It was known that the Americans had discovered the tunnel and its access in the command building when they'd raided this base the previous month, so the tunnel had been sealed at the northern end, outside the base, and since then, it had become a place to store bucket after bucket of shit, so that the Americans wouldn't spot a massive latrine or burning waste from the air.

Instead the men erected a smaller latrine outside, subterfuge to fool the coalition over the border of their numbers.

Khan was so fearful of American drones and satellites that he'd even planned this mission for the cloud cover that came inevitably over the area most every night in October, and he'd made certain that movement around the facility outside the hardened aircraft structure would be kept to a minimum. That was until early the previous morning, when twelve large trucks had arrived, nine of which pulled a flatbed trailer and a payload covered by a thick canopy to make identification of the contents impossible. The arrival of the trucks had been spaced apart so as not to be noticed as a convoy on the road, and they were out of sight just moments after entering the base at Ismail Zai, having pulled straight into the bunker.

But the trucks had made it into the hardened shelter unmolested, and then the covers had been removed from the flatbeds and the contents organized. These nine vehicles then left, one by one, and eventually the contents were assembled by Kashmiri separatist mechanics who had worked for the Army Aviation Corps under Omar Mufti before themselves going AWOL to serve in the KRF.

And now, just inside the protection of the hardened bunker, Murad Khan put his hands on his hips and stared at the glorious sight in front of him. There, under the light of several high floodlamps, he gazed upon his entire mission, the components for tonight's action that would elevate his plan and Khan himself into the ranks of legend.

There were four of them, and to Khan, they were beautiful. Large, dual-rotor helicopters sat one in front of the other, the first aircraft's front rotor just ten meters from the inside of the blast doors. All their noses pointed forward, as if they were horses at the starting gate, ready to launch.

The aircraft were dark and still but massive and foreboding; each rotor was fifty feet in diameter, and the fuselages of the helicopters were forty-five feet in length.

These were Boeing-Vertol models, old but reliable variants of the American Chinook, and they had been purchased in secret by Pakistani intelligence agents from the Royal Thai Army under Khan's instruction, then dismantled and secretly transported by container ship to Pakistan months earlier.

In a chop shop in Karachi, the Thai tiger-stripe pattern on the fuselage had been painted over, and now all four reassembled helicopters in front of Murad Khan were red and white in color, and they bore the insignia of Chesapeake Aviation, Inc., an American civilian transport company ubiquitous just over the border.

These BV-107s were, in every outward appearance, identical to the Chesapeake helos that ferried troops and other coalition personnel throughout Afghanistan, and they would serve as Murad Khan's Trojan horses tonight.

Khan could not see inside any of the aircraft from his vantage point, but he knew what they contained. Each of the first three large transports was loaded with a single two-thousand-kilo ammonium nitrate/fuel oil bomb roughly the size of a full-sized car, and each of these ANFO devices was lined and packed with dozens of kilograms of high-level radioactive waste.

Khan smiled as he looked upon the helicopters, because this was a scene that he had imagined in his mind's eye for over a year now.

All three targets tonight had been selected by Khan personally. The first helicopter to take off would fly to the northwest, and it would also have the longest distance to travel. It would then detonate over Bagram, the largest U.S. military base in Afghanistan. Hundreds of Americans would die, and the base and much of its equipment would be rendered untouchable for one hundred years or more.

The second BV-107 in the air would head half the distance of the first flight, to the large U.S. military base at Jalalabad. Its detonation was designed to kill hundreds more, and similarly contaminate all the territory and equipment there.

And the third helo in line would head west to just over the border in Kunar Province, where it would, near simultaneously with the others, detonate over Forward Operating Base Bostick, a small but important U.S. military outpost from where many attacks into Pakistan had originated.

The lead housing surrounding each weapon kept the pilots and crew safe, at least until they neared their destinations. When they were within fifteen minutes of their targets, a technician on board each of the aircraft would attach the detonator and hold it in his hand until the order came from the pilot to trigger it.

It would be a trifecta of blows to America, all in a single night; it would kill thousands, render billions of dollars of military hardware inoperable, deny valuable territory to the Americans, and, hopefully, spell the end for the presence of the meddling infidels here in the region.

There was a fourth helicopter, and initially Khan had intended for it, too, to be carrying an identical radioactive dispersal device. The plan was to fly due west to Khost and detonate over U.S. Special Forces base Salerno.

But he found himself one bomb short and with a helicopter all dressed up with nowhere to go.

Utterly destroying this military base to the south of the others, with a dirty bomb, no less, would have been grand, and Murad Khan was bothered that Salerno had been granted a reprieve from his massive attack.

But he had seen no alternative. Fully a fourth of his ammonium nitrate had been sacrificed in Lahore to lead the CIA away from the rest of the stolen chemicals, hopefully to buy some time to move into the execution phase of the operation. And his organization's theft of radioactive waste at the disposal site at Chashma the previous month had yielded only enough material for three dirty bombs of the yield he felt was necessary to send the right message to the coalition.

So Khan had three enormous radioactive dispersal devices built, ensuring maximum impact at Bagram, Jalalabad, and Bostick, but that was not to say he had no plan for the fourth helo in the line.

The last of the four helicopters had been loaded with ten 125-millimeter high-explosive tank shells stolen by the KRF from stores used by T-80 battle tanks at a base in Abbottabad, then all wired together by the same Egyptian bombmaker who'd created the RDDs.

The fourth helo was a conventional vehicle-borne improvised explosive device—other than the fact it was being flown in a helicopter, it was similar to any massive VBIED employed by any one of numerous insurgent organizations in the region—but it would still cause impressive damage to U.S. special operations forces in Afghanistan.

Salerno wouldn't be destroyed, but it would be suitably punished.

The seventy armed men here in the bunker who would not be boarding a helicopter tonight had one job only: to ensure that the four helicopters made it safely into the air if the Americans attacked Ismail Zai before takeoff.

As soon as the helos were safely launched, Khan and Mufti would climb back into the Huey to fly to nearby Peshawar, where they planned to disappear into the metropolis around the time the unspeakable carnage in the west was being carried out. They'd lay low there for a while and then slip out of Peshawar, back east into Kashmir, where they could simply melt away among their people.

If all went to plan, Khan told himself now as he looked at the fruit of all his labors inside the bunker, one week from today, this part of the world could be a very different place, and he could find himself in a very different station in life, as well.

As he stood there admiring all he had accomplished so far, Nassir Rasool stepped up to him, and Khan embraced the younger man. "As salaam aleikum."

"Wa aleikum as salaam," came the reply.

Rasool was, simply put, Murad Khan's ace in the hole. He was a Kashmiri but not particularly zealous, a young technical specialist in the Pakistani army who had been sent to China to learn from some of the best military information technology specialists in the world. He was taught techniques and tactics that he then brought back to the ISI to bolster his home nation's countersecurity apparatus.

ISI officer Murad Khan had worked with Rasool on an operation in Germany a few years prior, and he'd found the young man invaluable and brilliant.

Khan immediately handpicked him out of the army to work for the Foreign Coordination Unit.

When Rasool wanted a new piece of equipment, Khan made certain he acquired it for him, be it from China or France or Russia. Rasool protected Khan's operations, he counseled Khan on ways to employ technology to achieve his aims, and he ran counterintelligence for all of Khan's dealings, professional and personal.

While all this was happening, Khan was working Nassir Rasool, indoctrinating him to the fact that they had to go against the stated wishes of their nation in order to rid his people of one of their greatest threats: American intervention.

The younger man was not interested in politics, but after years of Khan showing him the effects of U.S. drone strikes that killed civilians, Rasool was converted into his zealotry.

Rasool worshipped the ground upon which Khan walked. He'd joined his organization, leaving the ISI behind, because Khan promised they would all be considered heroes by the nation of Pakistan, and by the people of Kashmir, when tonight's mission was complete.

"The men in the command building are ready to begin, sir," Nassir said now, pride evident on his face and in his tone.

Khan had no need to go to the command building to check for himself. Nassir had a team of eight Chinese technicians he'd hired, along with the jamming equipment that came to the Pakistan Army a month before and was then reappropriated to the Foreign Coordination Unit. These men knew nothing about radioactive waste attacks against America; they only knew their own role tonight.

Khan patted his young technician on the shoulder to calm him. "So, Nassir, my friend. You are saying we are ready?"

"Ready, sir. When you give the order, we will begin thermal spoofing, the satellite jamming will commence, and then the delivery vehicles can be safely brought out of the bunker for fueling and takeoff."

"Excellent," Khan said. "Let us begin."

FIFTY-FOUR

PRESENT DAY

Forty-seven-year-old Murad Khan stood on the twenty-fifth floor of the Express Tower on Nariman Point, taking in the view. The other side of the large office had floor-to-ceiling windows that displayed the beautiful vista of the harbor, but Khan stood on the northern side of the building and looked out over the city of twelve million souls.

The decision the Pakistani national wrestled with now was truly the hardest of his life. His bomb was ready and it was nearby. Today was the day he'd planned on detonating it to cripple his archenemy, the nation of his birth.

But the storm had disrupted his plans.

On the one hand, he could stand down, wait for better weather conditions, and then achieve his objective.

But on the other hand, he could feel the authorities closing in on him; he knew that B-Company's feeble attempts to protect his mission here, their failure to kill Appleton and the henchman working for him who had caused him so much trouble, and even their inability to hold on to a young and untrained girl told him that he couldn't trust the dozens of Indians at his disposal to protect his mission for another day.

He trusted only the twelve security men he'd brought along from Pakistan, and most of all, he trusted Nassir Rasool.

The Indian gangsters were just fools. They didn't even know what his true mission was here in Mumbai; only their leader, Palak Bari, knew that. B-Company had served their purpose; they stole fuel rods from Trombay, they'd purchased and taken delivery of black-market RDX explosives from Algiers and detonators from a Swiss manufacturer. They'd provided Khan with a warehouse where a Syrian bombmaker, paid for by Bari himself, had come to assemble the device, using his education as an electrical engineer in Germany to combine the nuclear fuel rods with the explosives, wiring everything up with a high-tech remote detonation system that only Khan had access to.

B-Company goons had even transported the device, though they had no idea what it was. A forty-foot shipping container weighing eight tons was moved by crane onto a heavy-duty flatbed truck, then brought to the building construction site right next door to where Khan now stood. Another crane removed the shipping container and placed it on a construction hoist attached to the side of a thirty-three-floor skyscraper three fourths of the way through its construction process, then lifted it to the thirty-second floor, where a hydraulic loader was waiting to move it through the building, placing it where it would be most effective.

Now, one hundred meters north of where Khan stood, and seven floors above him, the project he'd been planning for twelve years now waited for his signal.

But the damn monsoon presented a problem. The wind blew hard from the southwest now; it would blow harder still through the afternoon and evening, and the rain was still several hours off.

Wind wasn't necessarily a bad thing for a man intent on detonating a dirty bomb on a high floor of an open building. Obviously the intent was exposure. But Murad Khan's plan was to irradiate Nariman Point and the southern quadrant of the city, and leave the slums to the north intact and safe.

Eighty-kilometer winds blowing from the water towards the northeast would ensure that the entire city, all twelve million residents, would be subjected to exposure.

The death toll of Muslims, who were poor and had little access to medical care and no ability to simply move their families and their lives out of the city, would be catastrophic.

And Murad Khan was trying to wrap his head around this.

Delaying until tomorrow gave his enemies more time to stop him. Going forward today—now even—meant, quite literally, overkill.

Nassir Rasool stepped up to him. The thirty-eight-year-old had a lot of worry on his face, but Khan was accustomed to this look.

"What is it?"

"Work is halted next door, the crews have been sent home, so our men there will stand out if they're spotted. The cranes and heavy equipment are pinned down, so there is no quick escape. Plastic sheeting has been erected on the higher floors where the windows will go . . . but eighty-kilometer winds will tear that out."

"Your point, my friend?"

"We have to wait until tomorrow."

Khan looked at his young protégé. "This isn't about a threat to our security. This is your concern about the fallout."

Rasool shrugged.

"You are Kashmiri. Why do you care about the people of Mumbai?"

"The Muslims, sir."

Khan looked back out the window. The winds were already high, the air cloudy and wet. In the distance he could see Dharavi, the slum where Palak Bari himself had grown up. Bari had helped orchestrate today's attack from his home in Karachi—as a paymaster, as a benefactor to Khan, and as an arranger for local assets—but Bari had made one stipulation.

Dharavi was not to be affected by the blast.

Khan had readily made that promise and positioned his device in the financial center on Nariman Point so that the fallout wouldn't move too far inland.

But the monsoon had come like a curse, and the monsoon assured that if Khan did go through with the attack today, then Palak Bari and his henchmen would hunt him down to the ends of the earth.

Before Khan could speak, Rasool said, "If we detonate in monsoon winds, Bari will hold us personally responsible for the devastation." Imploringly, he said, "We must wait till the weather passes. We *must* wait until tomorrow."

"Do you think Theodore Appleton is waiting until tomorrow to notify the authorities about what he knows?"

Rasool countered, "B-Company has multiple contacts in the local and federal police. They have reported no indication that anyone is aware of our activities."

"That can change at any time. And when it does change? When the B-Company lieutenants working for us under Jai learn what we have in store for their city? What then? Then it won't be Appleton we have to worry about, it won't be the police. It won't even be Bari back in Karachi. It will be our benefactors here.

"Every hour we wait, every *minute* we wait . . . we come closer to losing everything."

Rasool wasn't giving up. "Fifteen hours, tomorrow morning, the winds will be calm, twenty kilometers or less. *Then* we detonate the device."

Khan looked back out the window at the city. He was unsure, and he was seldom unsure.

Finally, however, he said, "We keep security around the bomb. B-Company on the outer ring, our men in the inner ring. They will just have to weather the storm in the construction site. You and I will stay here in the penthouse tonight, ready to initiate the detonation sequence if B-Company sources alert us to any problems. We watch the weather closely, and as soon as the monsoon passes us and heads to the northeast, we initiate the device right behind it."

Rasool nodded, relieved. "I think that is very wise."

"Of course you do," Khan said with a little smile. "It was your idea."

Court Gentry and Priyanka Bandari arrived in Nariman Point in a stolen Ford Econoline van, pulled into an empty taxi stand a block south of the building with the B-Company-owned penthouse, and parked along the tree-lined promenade that ringed the swelling and choppy waters of Back

Bay. From here they had a view not only of the tower to the northeast but also, looking southwest, of the apocalyptic-looking clouds still out to sea but rolling ominously in this direction.

There was still some traffic on the roads, and this had made Court confident enough to drive here and to park here, but he didn't plan on staying long. He'd hoped to reconnoiter the area on foot, to get an idea of the security presence, if any, at the location, and to make a judgment as to whether this building was, in fact, where Khan was hiding out.

He liked it as a potential target location because while B-Company owned the penthouse on the top floor, they did not own or control the rest of the building. If Khan was here, he was protected, but he was protected in the penthouse.

Court started to climb out of the van, but Priya took him by his arm. "One white man, walking alone, down here as a monsoon blows ashore? Does that make sense to you?"

"What do you suggest?"

"Express Tower One is a residential and office building. Let me do a little research on who lives and works there. If we can find someone who will invite us in, we can get inside the building itself, and then I can hack into their closed-circuit camera."

"Don't you need to do that from their security office?"

Priya shook her head. "Access to the CCTV data will be shared not only with building security but also with large offices inside the building. Private companies want to see the cameras on their floors, so the main system will be accessible from any number of workstations in that high-rise. I just have to get into a terminal, then swim upriver with some tools I have right here." She held up a thumb drive.

Court shook his head. "I like your thinking, but you can't go in that building. You spent two days in the hands of the assholes I'm hunting. They don't know what I look like, but they sure as hell know you. If the wrong guy happens to be walking through the lobby, someone who saw you in Andheri East, then we're screwed." He repeated himself with authority. "You can't go in."

Priya reached into her purse and pulled out a long veil. Wrapping it around her face and head, she tied it and tucked it into her top.

Court just nodded, impressed. "Nevermind, then. You can come with me."

She rolled her eyes, pulled out her laptop, linked it to the wireless radio on her phone, and went to work.

Minutes later Priya was talking, having an animated phone conversation with someone she had not yet identified to Cobalt.

When she hung up, she said, "I called a real estate management company that owns some condos on the lower floors of the building. They are closed today because of the storm, but I told them I was your translator, and you had come all the way from America, and wanted to look at one or two more properties before you left tomorrow."

"But if they're closed . . ."

"I was persistent. I told him you were worried about living so close to the water, considering the possibility of monsoons. He took that as a challenge. He told me he'd have someone unlock a furnished model, and we could ride out the storm in it for a couple of hours."

Court was more than impressed.

They climbed out of the Econoline on Marine Drive, leaning into a wind that seemed to be growing by the minute. There were still quite a few people on the street, even entering and exiting the twenty-five-story tower in front of them, but Court knew that this area so close to the water would be all but impassable when the rains came.

A man at the security desk in the lobby called the name given to Priya by the real estate broker, and a few minutes later a woman came down the elevator and brought Priya and Court inside. Her English was good; she was chatty, mostly about the impending weather, as they took the elevator up to the sixth floor.

Here she unlocked the door to a condo and told the couple to make themselves at home to watch the storm roll in. She said she'd be back to check on them later, and then she left them alone.

Priya looked around. "I need an office, not an apartment. Someplace large. A call center. Looking at the floor plan in the van, I saw one on the ninth floor that looks like it will be big enough."

"Why does it have to be big?"

"Because I need access to a computer hardwired into the security system. And to get that access, I need to find someone's login credentials."

"How do you—"

"Can we just go?"

Court laughed a little. "Listen. You and I have to sell the fact that we're a couple."

She cocked her head a little. "Meaning?"

"There are security cameras all over this place. I guarantee B-Company has access to the feeds. We can't look like we're snooping around."

"We'll have to break into the office. I'm sure they're closed because of the storm."

Court said, "I'll get us in, but on the way there, we need to act naturally."

The two of them headed back outside the condo and into the elevator. Court was painfully aware of the security cameras here in the hallways of the building, so he portrayed himself as exactly the opposite of a man who was about to break into anything.

For her part, Priya played her role well. They chatted lightly, even as they left the elevator on the ninth floor and began looking for a suitable office.

There was no door to pick because the entire floor belonged to a call center: hundreds of desks with computers were situated in a large room, with executive offices, many with their doors left open, along the wall. Court and Priya walked back to a corner that gave them a view to the north and to the west, and here Priya went from terminal to terminal. Court looked on but didn't interrupt her. At each desk she pulled open the top drawer to the right of the chair, fumbled around through paperwork a moment, and then moved on to the next.

On her ninth try she found what she was looking for. Triumphantly, she waved a single handwritten note in the air. "Studies show that workers often leave their login info somewhere easily accessible. Nobody's too worried about someone sneaking in and doing their job for them, I guess."

Court's own knowledge of social engineering confirmed this. People tended to freely or easily give up information about themselves in many ways, but laziness and braggadocio were the two most common.

It took her a moment to boot up the computer and get inside. Once there, she quickly looked over the applications installed. "Perfect. Their computers are already tied into the building's system so they can have access to the cameras at the elevator bank. They are locked out of the rest of the feeds, but that's no problem for me." She added, "This is almost too easy."

Court stood thirty feet away, looking out the window towards the bay. "This is going to be one hell of a storm."

Without looking up, she said, "That's what I've been telling you."

"Yeah." He glanced to his right, facing the north in the corner office, and was surprised to see an even taller building next door to Express Tower. It was positioned slightly to the northeast, and he hadn't been able to see it from the street on the other side of the building he was in now. It was still under construction, however, and surrounded by cranes and building materials, fenced in all around. No one was working at the site at the moment, obviously because of the approaching monsoon.

Court said, "What's that?"

Priya looked out the window. "The building? I don't know."

Court looked at the area around it. "It's on the same property as this one. Looks similar in style, too."

Priya pulled up the area on Google Maps, but there was nothing there on the satellite image. "This sat photo is from a year ago. It was just an empty site then, but yeah, it looks like the land belongs to the same people who own Express Tower."

She spent the next few seconds performing a Google search. "Here it is. Express Tower Two. It's eight stories taller. Thirty-three floors in all. Supposed to be ready in a year and a half." She went back to accessing the CCTV system.

After a moment, however, the man she knew as Cobalt spoke. "If the bomb is in this building, in the penthouse or on the roof at the top of this building, like we thought . . . how did it get there?"

"B-Company brought it."

"Right. But . . . if it's going to be effective, it will need to weigh several tons."

Priya looked up at Cobalt now. "You could bring it up one piece at a time."

"If you had to, maybe, you could haul the component parts and build the device on site. But what if you didn't have to?"

"What are you getting at?"

"Right there." He pointed.

Priya stood and walked over to the corner window. Cobalt was indicating the construction to the north.

He said, "Hammerhead tower cranes that size can lift ten tons. Hydraulic wenches, pneumatic hoists. All that equipment over there could easily transport a massive bomb to the top floor of that structure."

"How do you know so much about heavy construction?"

"A past life," he said cryptically. In truth he'd spent a lot of time working in cover around shipyards, and much of the equipment for moving shipping containers was similar to that used in construction.

Court looked higher on the building and saw that the top several floors were open to the elements, though plastic sheeting blew in the heavy winds.

He said, "A perfect scenario."

"What do you mean?"

"You wouldn't have to put the bomb on the roof, where it could be detected by aircraft, or exposed to the weather. You could put it on one of the top floors that are open. Blow it, the radioactive cloud goes in all directions."

Priya said, "But Khan wouldn't do that in the middle of a monsoon, would he? With these winds it would blow inland for tens of kilometers, infect millions. Millions who couldn't be decontaminated, because India doesn't have the infrastructure to deal with that."

Court thought it over. "I learned a long time ago not to underestimate Murad Khan's capacity to do *anything* really bad." He turned to Priya. "Can you find out who owns that building?"

She said, "It doesn't matter who owns it. It's not occupied yet."

"But—"

"B-Company has a stranglehold on the construction industry in Mumbai. They could easily use that building for their own designs, and the owners wouldn't know about it."

Court kept looking out the window. The high jibs of the cranes swiveled slightly, back and forth in the wind.

"What do you want to do?" she asked.

"We call Ted. Tell him to get the police to Tower Two, now. I *know* that bomb is up there. I *don't* know when they plan on detonating it."

"And after we call Ted?"

"I'm going over there. Alone."

Priya squinted into the dimming light outside as the black clouds rolled over. "There's nothing going on over there right now. Even if the device is there, I don't see anybody around."

"If the device is there," Court said, "then Khan has posted security. We just can't see them from here."

"What can I do?"

"You can stay here, get into the camera system at this location. I want to see anyone coming or going in this storm. Anyone coming or going up in the penthouse. Be careful." He slipped in an earpiece. "You can alert me if you see anything."

Priya said, "How will you get into that construction site?"

"I'll jump a fence and go through the front door if I don't see any security. Otherwise . . . I'll wing it."

As he walked out the door, she said, "You be careful."

He sniffed out a laugh and left the room.

FIFTY-FIVE

TWELVE YEARS AGO

At three a.m., Court Gentry walked in silence and in darkness, first in line of his six-man unit as they made their way through a pine forest on a rocky hill.

They'd been humping for over two and a half hours now, bypassing any buildings or signs of human activity, which had thankfully been few and far between.

The helicopters that had dropped them in this rugged terrain had returned back through the mountains and over the border into Afghanistan, and both the Rangers and the SEALs had been dropped off to the south, so it was just Lima Foxtrot and Golf Sierra walking together here, single file and spaced over a few dozen meters, through a dark and misty night.

Court thought about the nicknames for the two teams Julie had mentioned: the Lucky Fuckers and the Goon Squad. It made him smile a little.

They used no lights; only their NODs showed them the way, and although everyone had said the terrain here made for an easy five-mile walk, to Court this seemed pretty damned difficult. They'd negotiated rocky paths, crossed a shallow but fast-moving stream, climbed hills, and descended into rutted valleys as they'd made their way in nearly complete blackness.

He was in peak physical condition, and he was fifteen years younger than many of the men around him, but he could feel the weight of his gear and the ache in his calves as he neared their target.

As they entered the last half mile before they would have visual on Ismail Zai, he heard Zack Hightower's voice in his headset, transmitting back to the TOC at Chapman.

"Golf Sierra Actual for Homeplate."

"Homeplate. Send your traffic, Sierra Actual."

"Be advised. Golf Sierra and Lima Foxtrot are at phase-line Echo. Lima Foxtrot separating at this time, over."

The response came from the TOC at Camp Chapman seconds later. "Understood, Sierra Actual. All forces have reported in. Still heavy cloud cover at the target, but thermal imagery showing increased activity. Personnel and unidentified vehicles present. How copy?"

"Good copy, Homeplate. We will advise at phase-line Omega."

"Roger that. Happy hunting. Homeplate out."

Court watched while Hightower and Anderson shook hands, and then the two Ground Branch teams went their separate ways, Golf Sierra continuing north through the piney hillside, and Lima Foxtrot south towards a stream that ran east to west through lower ground.

Just inside the colossal blast doors of the hardened aircraft shelter, Murad Khan stood with Omar Mufti and Nassir Rasool. The younger man grabbed a walkie-talkie from his hip and gave an order, speaking in Arabic and then repeating himself in Urdu. Within seconds, four Toyota pickups rolled by on their way out the smaller exit near the three-story blast doors, each one carrying several men in the truck bed.

The trucks peeled off in different directions and began driving around the several acres of paved and grassy space between the northern side of the bunker and the north wall of the compound. A dozen large metal dumpsters had been filled with old truck tires, and the men in back of the trucks used burning torches to light them, one by one.

Several large grassy spaces in front of the hardened bunker and alongside the apron and taxiway were waist high and unmaintained, and they'd also been soaked with gasoline, so when the men in the pickups lit them, it created billowing smoke that mixed with the smoke coming from the tire fires assembled in the past few days and only doused with gas after dark this evening, and it took the vehicles some minutes to set it all alight.

The last to be set on fire were piles and piles of tires just outside the bunker, and as their flames grew and their black smoke rose, further obscuring any view from above, the eight rotors of the four big helicopters behind the blast doors began to spin.

The plan was to have the two fuel trucks roll out of the blast doors first, then the first of the Chinooks. All four of the aircraft had been loaded with enough fuel for their taxi out to the apron, but no more, because Mufti declared it too dangerous to fully fuel the helicopters in an enclosed space.

The first helo would finish fueling and then take to the air ten minutes after the blast doors opened. It would fly immediately to Bagram, arriving over the airfield in under one hour. Then the Jalalabad aircraft would leave ten minutes after that, hitting at the same time as the first flight, and then the third aircraft, this one targeting Camp Bostick, would leave ten minutes later.

The fourth flight, heading to Camp Salerno, would leave as soon as the helicopter going to Bostick cleared the sky above the base.

Khan didn't like any bit of this operation being seen from the air, even with the thermal spoofing, even with the jamming, even with the cloud cover. He knew it wouldn't take the coalition over the border in Afghanistan long to work around the jamming, and he wanted to have a fail-safe, so the burning tires and smoke in addition to the cloud cover would serve to further blind overhead eyes.

Mufti appeared in front of him, a radio in his hand. "I will let the smoke build over the base for a few more minutes, then call for the doors to be opened." He smiled. "We will be triumphant."

"I have no doubt. And I also have no doubt that we will someday soon see all your valiant pilots in paradise."

Mufti nodded with purpose, checked his watch, then spoke into his radio. "Ten minutes until taxi."

Khan looked to Nassir. "Tell the Chinese in the command building to initiate satellite jamming."

Nassir did so via his walkie-talkie, speaking English to the hired technicians. A response came in English.

"Jamming initiated."

Khan could feel the nerves of the younger man standing next to him, so he said, "It was inevitable the Americans would see that something was happening here tonight. I knew better than to underestimate them. Now they won't know what is going on until it is far too late."

Nassir said, "They'll send men. Tonight even. They'll have to know we have an operation imminent."

"I am sure you are right. By then, however, you and I will be gone."

Nassir nodded, smiled nervously, then went back to his radio to check with his guests from China.

Back at the TOC, a state of pandemonium erupted. All monitors showing real-time images at Ismail Zai from the pair of Reaper UAVs were blacked out, and efforts to reach the four forces converging on the target had been unsuccessful.

Hanley shouted over the loud clamor in the room. "Who the fuck can jam our Reapers?"

"The Chinese," Vance said, then added, "in theory. Sat jamming can be defeated, it will just take some time to retask equipment in geosynchronous orbit."

Hanley had read the cable from Appleton two days before about the purchase of Chinese satellite jamming equipment by the Pakistani army. Vance had read it, too.

"It's the Pak Army," Vance declared.

But Hanley shook his head. "This isn't the Pak Army. This is Khan. He must have gotten the jamming equipment from the army." He looked to Vance now. "We have to get an Air Force overflight. We need eyeballs on that site."

Vance was against this. "Surface-to-air missiles in Peshawar. SA-7s. A C-130 flying over into Khyber, even an F-16, wouldn't stand a chance. The Reapers are programmed to return to base if they lose comms. They'll be back here in thirty minutes."

"How long to reestablish comms over Ismail Zai?" Hanley demanded.

Vance picked up a phone. "I've got to call Langley, get all traffic sent to another sat. This will take twenty to thirty minutes minimum."

"Shit," Hanley said, and behind him, Julie Marquez looked down at her blank screen. She'd been afraid the KRF was more prepared for whatever they had planned tonight than the coalition was, and now she feared all she could do was simply wait to react to their next move.

Hanley turned around and faced her now, gave her a look that told her she'd been right all along.

Softly, she said, "They were ready for us."

Hanley nodded, turned away. To the room he said, "We have seventy-six troops converging on that target. They are on their own until we get back online. Be ready to support them as soon as we have some means of doing so!"

FIFTY-SIX

PRESENT DAY

Ted Appleton had spent the day forcing himself to conduct the tradecraft that had been a part of his life since his midtwenties. It got harder as one got older: the SDRs, the aimlessly moving around nowhere for hours, looking for any evidence of a tail.

But he was a man on autopilot, even if every fiber of his being told him he didn't have time for this shit, he had to rush, and he had to act now.

He'd contacted an old Indian acquaintance, a respected Tamil case officer in R&AW named Daruk Raja, and he asked him for a clandestine call on Signal. Raja complied immediately, asked what he could do for his old friend, and then Appleton told him he'd picked up intelligence chatter that Murad Khan was alive and operating with B-Company, here in the city.

His contact was taken aback for two reasons. One, Appleton had communicated with Raja a dozen times in the past few months, ostensibly to get unclassified background information or even random scuttlebutt that might help him with his job working in nuclear nonproliferation, and he'd never mentioned Khan. And two . . . well, R&AW, Raja claimed, had no information whatsoever to corroborate the fact that Khan was alive and well *anywhere*, much less here in Mumbai.

He was interested in whatever Appleton had on the subject, that much was clear, because he immediately asked for an in-person meeting, a rare occurrence for an intelligence transaction between the two men.

Ted didn't like the risk and the delay of a face-to-face meeting, but his contact at R&AW was old-school, older than Appleton himself but still very much in the game, and he was a trusted friend.

Daruk Raja let Appleton choose the time and the place of the meet to ease the American's mind about the situation, and now, at four p.m., the American had finished his SDR, and he stood in a camel raincoat, an umbrella under his arm, and under the semiprotection of the roof over the entrance to Mumba Devi Temple. It was in the center of a large market area, and the men had met here before for clandestine communications, but today all the stalls were shuttered or tarped over or otherwise broken down to weather the storm.

Normally this would be an incredibly lively place, but the weather had turned it into a virtual ghost town, something Appleton had expected somewhat, but not to this degree.

His phone rang and he saw it was Priya. When he answered, she told him Cobalt now suspected that Khan's device was at the top of Express Tower Two. He assured her he was moments away from speaking with the right person, and he would get authorities on the way to the construction site.

As he hung up the call, an SUV pulled up in front of the temple, the driver's window rolled down, and Daruk Raja waved to Appleton and bade him forward into the car.

The window immediately rose back up.

The American headed for the SUV, fighting the wind for control of his balance. He finally made it to the vehicle, opening the front passenger-side door and climbing in.

He was unaware of the second SUV that had pulled up behind him.

He reached for the door to pull it closed, but as he began to do so, he saw that Raja had climbed out of the driver's side and walked around to Ted's door. The man leaned over, close to Appleton, his wispy thin hair blowing wildly in the wind.

He said, "I'm sorry, old friend. You know how it is. How they can get to you, wear you down, over time."

A big Indian man entered the driver-side door and sat down, and a second man sat in the back, directly behind him.

Appleton *did* understand. He recognized the rough fit and finish of B-Company thugs, and he knew he'd been double-crossed.

The SUV lurched forward; the R&AW man was left behind in the wind, and the man in the back behind Appleton placed a coarse black bag over his head.

The goon behind the wheel pulled out a lead-filled leather blackjack and slammed it hard into the American's midsection, doubling him over in pain.

The one in back reached forward, handcuffed Appleton's compliant hands behind his back, and then pulled him upright in his seat.

The B-Company driver said nothing, but the thug in the backseat now said, "Yesterday, our job was to kill you. Today it is to take you to see the boss. Your stock must be going up, old man."

Appleton said nothing. He was fucked, he knew it, but that was not all of it.

He'd not said a word to anyone but the man who'd just betrayed him about Khan, and he hadn't even told him about the construction site or the dirty bomb.

No one would be coming to help the Gray Man and the girl now, not even Appleton himself.

Priyanka Bandari hacked into the wireless relay of the closed-circuit camera system in Express Tower One in a matter of minutes. Once in, she brought up all 105 cameras in and around the building, then individually selected the ones that looked the most interesting. She wanted a view outside, in the front of Tower One, looking over towards Tower Two, any view that might help if she needed to alert Cobalt to danger.

She looked outside through the ocean spray now wetting the windows, then hurriedly flipped through the cameras until she found the one she was looking for, on perhaps her twentieth try.

She accessed the cam positioned over a north-side service exit of Tower One. To her pleasure, she found that the device was motorized, and by using her mouse, she could pan it higher, giving her a view of the construction site next door.

She was able to zoom the camera, then tighten up the focus, centering it on the covered entry of Tower Two, identical in style and size to the one downstairs here in Tower One.

She leaned close to the screen, squinted, then went to work to improve the image because she was beginning to pick out objects there on the drive that she needed to evaluate.

Court exited the main door of Tower One, zipping his raincoat up to his chin and tightening the hood before doing so. He passed a couple of bored security guards in the covered driveway and headed out into the open air.

The wind was easily thirty-five miles an hour now, and the sea spray made it feel like his eyeballs were under fire from a BB gun when he faced towards the bay. He shoved his hands in his pockets and trudged to the north, planning on making his way into the seemingly abandoned garage alongside the thirty-three-story building undergoing construction.

He was halfway there when a voice came through his earpiece, barely audible over a driving gust. "Cobalt. Hold."

He wasn't in an ideal location to "hold." He was walking along a churning bay on the street in a monsoon.

"What is it?"

"I have a long eye on the ground-floor entrance into Tower Two."

"What do you see?"

"I see multiple men standing just inside the door. I see vehicles under the covered entrance that have no business at a construction site. Expensive-looking SUVs."

Court said, "B-Company is guarding the location."

"That's what it looks like from here."

Court started walking again. "Okay. I'll have to find another way to get inside the building."

"What other way is there?" Priya asked, confused.

Court looked up. Just west of the Tower Two construction, the five-story parking garage looked new but complete. On the top level of the garage was a massive construction crane. At its summit, the shorter, weighted counter-jib faced the wind, and its long-arm jib jutted out, parallel to the ground, and swung left and right, shifting in the direction of the wind.

This was called weathervaning in the industry, and it meant the turntable of the crane had been unlocked so the long vertical jib, high above the ground, could blow with the wind. If the jib had been locked, on the other hand, the force of a crosswind could literally blow the entire 265-foot tower down to the ground.

The far end of the tower crane's jib, some two hundred feet long and extending over the parking garage and the ground between the garage and Tower Two, ended right above the new building's roofline.

There were other cranes around the building, but this was the only one that seemed to reach all the way to the top of the structure.

Court realized the best way up was to ascend in the parking garage, then climb the massive tower of the crane, *then* shimmy out onto the long jib and make his way to the tall building. From there he'd have to swing from the hook hanging from the bottom of the trolley, until he could, hopefully, drop onto the roof.

It was, in his estimation, just slightly less dangerous than walking into the lobby of the construction site and pulling out his pistol, then taking on all comers with gunfire.

But it *was* at least somewhat less dangerous. He committed himself to this course of action and walked up the street, leaning to his left to combat the punishing wind coming from that direction.

He had forgotten he was still connected to Priya.

"Cobalt?"

"Sorry. Yeah, I've got another way in. I'm going to be outside for a while, and where I'm going, I'm not going to be able to hear you, so I'll put my earpiece in my pocket till I get inside."

"Okay," she said.

"Have you reached Appleton yet?" Court asked.

"Yes, right when you left. He is aware about Tower Two. He says he'll alert the proper authorities immediately. They should be on the way soon."

"Good. I'm going to try to get to that bomb before the cops get here, just in case Khan decides to blow it."

"Do you know how to dismantle a bomb?"

"I'll Google it."

"You'll *what*?"

"One thing at a time, Priya."

"Okay," she said nervously. "Good luck to you."

"You, too. Keep monitoring."

Court hung up the call and put his earpiece in the pocket of his jacket, zipping it closed just before climbing the chain-link fence around the construction site.

He entered the garage and found it empty of cars and equipment; it had the new-construction smell of concrete dust, and the wind made a loud whistling effect throughout the structure.

Court pressed on towards the stairwell at the center of the garage, but he remained on the lookout for security even here, inside the fence and still fifty yards away from the tower.

He was glad he'd remained vigilant, because just as he came to the entrance to the stairwell, he smelled fresh tobacco.

Someone was smoking, likely on the other side of the wall in the center of the garage, near the entrance to the stairs. If they were any good at their job, they would have an eye on the stairwell, so Court figured there was a second stairwell entrance for people who parked on that side of the ground floor.

Court decided to bypass the stairs, and he jogged up the ramp of the parking garage up to the next level.

A minute later he approached the eastern stairwell entrance, ducked his head inside, and again smelled cigarette smoke. The man or men were below him somewhere, so Court moved silently as he began climbing the stairs.

On the roof he stepped back out into the crazy wind; he fought to make it to the foundation of the crane, which he climbed up on, and then he slipped inside the skeletonized mast.

If it were not for the wind and the spray from the bay, this would have been an arduous but relatively safe means of climbing; the metal beams had a ladder attached that ran all the way up to the operator's cab, barely visible in the heavy weather.

But with the weather this was extremely dicey, even for a man with Court's training and dexterity. Each time he stepped on a new rung of the ladder he made sure he had three points of contact, and though he ascended impressively fast, it wasn't one third as fast as he would have liked.

He climbed and climbed, worried about the fight he might find himself in after all the exertion he'd have to undergo over the next several minutes.

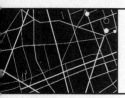

FIFTY-SEVEN

TWELVE YEARS AGO

The six men of Golf Sierra crawled on their bellies, their rifles shifted to their backs as they moved through pine trees, only feet from the crest of the last hill before arriving just northwest of the cluster of dwellings on the northern side of the fence line of Ismail Zai.

They crested the rise and saw the tiny village—maybe a dozen little stone structures in all—on the leeward side of the hill just to the north of the compound wall. Looking into the old military base, they had eyes on the command building, but this shielded them from seeing anything beyond it other than the top of a control tower in the center of the base and a smaller guard tower at the front, still partially destroyed and blackened by the Hellfire missile Hightower had called onto it a month earlier.

Hightower rolled onto his backpack now, pulled his sat radio, and pressed the button for the TOC. "Sierra Actual for Homeplate. Over?"

It was quiet on the hillside; perspiration formed on Court's face as he waited to hear the TOC's response in his own headset. After several seconds Zack called again. "Golf Sierra One for Homeplate. How do you read?"

There was no response.

Zack looked down at the radio, then made a third and then a fourth call.

Kendrick Lennox checked his watch. "Boss, we've got to be on target in four mikes."

Zack tried the TOC one more time, and then he switched to the short-range VHF/UHF radio, hoping to reach Lima Foxtrot, a kilometer or so to the south.

"Sierra One for Foxtrot One."

The response came quickly, though the distance between the two men was evident in the scratchy reception.

"Go for Lima Foxtrot Actual."

Zack said, "I'm reading you two by five. How me, over?"

"Two-five."

"Are you guys hearing from the TOC? I tried to raise them but got nothing."

"Same. Dead air."

"Understood. Somebody's jamming the satellite."

Anderson's voice seemed fainter each time he spoke. "Last intel I got says the Paks don't have sat-jamming equipment."

"You and me might be the lucky ones who find out otherwise."

"Yeah, the hard way."

Zack said, "Op continues, we are on schedule. How copy?"

Duane Anderson, somewhere to the south, replied, "Solid copy. The Rangers should hit in three mikes, then we are heading for the main gate. Foxtrot One out."

Zack rolled back over onto his stomach, where he pushed himself up to his knee pads. "Let's hit those dwellings."

The six operators of Golf Sierra fanned out on the southern side of the darkened hillside as they exited the tree line, approaching the cluster of single-story structures just outside Ismail Zai base. There was no movement visible in the men's NODs, and all was quiet other than an occasional barking dog in the distance.

Court had his rifle to his shoulder, his finger flat across the trigger guard and his safety off. Every step of his boots was measured to land as gently as possible; even his breathing was slow, silent, and controlled. He'd skulked into harm's way many times in his career, and he knew how to be quieter than a cat when the situation called for it.

Then, with a suddenness that surprised him, all need for stealth melted away.

Gunfire to the south, dozens of rifles and machine guns all kicking off at the same time, told him the Rangers and perhaps even the SEALs were engaging KRF personnel at the base. As soon as the sustained fighting commenced, Zack spoke into his mic for the five other men stretched along twenty meters of hillside. "Step it up," he said, and all men increased their advance down the hill.

Approaching the first building, Court took the lead, but Redus moved to the left, finding an angle on a side door to the little structure. He almost instantly fired a controlled pair of suppressed shots from his 416. Court couldn't see the target, he just advanced on an open window in front of him. Once there, he began to push a burlap curtain out of the way to scan inside, but Jim Pace stepped up to the window next to him.

"Banger," he said softly, and he dropped a canister inside onto the floor.

Court just had time to roll his body away from the window and press it against the wall when a flash bang grenade began popping off multiple flares and booms inside the little building.

As Court swung back into the window, Pace yanked the burlap away, and Court found a pair of men in front of him, both with Kalashnikovs in their hands. They were disoriented from the concussion but had clearly been in the act of getting their weapons up after the suppressed shots dropped their partner in the side doorway.

Gentry and Pace both fired on the men, sending them down to their backs.

Pace fired another round into each man's head from a distance of five paces; their bodies jolted and then went still.

Zack's voice came through their headset. "What you got, Four?"

Pace replied, "Two dudes in man jammies and AKs. They're EKIA."

Redus spoke up now. "Five has one EKIA at the side door."

The team moved on to the next building as the constant noise of gunfire made it clear that a massive battle was raging inside the base.

Golf Sierra found nothing in the second structure, and the third was empty as well. In the fourth dwelling, Court was again the first man through the door, and with the aid of his night vision goggles, he saw a group of women and children, all huddled together in the corner.

The rest of Golf Sierra moved in behind him an instant later. Court dropped his rifle to his chest and raised his arms. Yelling at his team behind him, he said, "Hold fire! Hold fire!"

A woman stood up in the center of the group in front of him.

A single gunshot cracked from behind; he saw the flash bounce off the walls around him and he felt the pressure of a hot rifle round whizzing by his head.

The standing woman's head snapped back, blood splattered the wall, and she dropped dead to the ground in front of the group.

A black automatic pistol fell from her clutches and tumbled down onto the floor in front of her.

All the other women's hands went high. The kids followed soon after.

Court turned around to face Hightower, who had just killed the armed woman. "How did you know she was armed?"

Hightower looked past Court, at the pistol on the ground. He stepped over and picked it up, shoving it into a dump pouch on his belt. "Didn't. I just didn't care for the way she stood up like that." He shrugged. "Your lucky day."

Redus grabbed Court by the back of his neck now, brought his face so close the men's night vision equipment smacked into each other. "Toughen the fuck *up*, Six! Right now! Got it?"

Court just moved past the others and back out of the building, while Pace and Morgan hurriedly began zip-tying the noncombatants.

Soon the stack set up to hit the next dwelling. Gunfire began cracking out of one of the windows, causing the Americans to rush wide of the line of fire, and then they hit it from the opposite side. Here they kicked in a burlap door to find a dark room, where two teenagers wielded folded-stock AKs and fired outside to the north without even aiming.

Zack Hightower shot them both before either one ever saw the Americans.

Finally Court was first through the door in the building where the tunnel into the base originated, and he swept the small area with his rifle.

"Clear," he said, and Zack moved past him, up to a metal door at a forty-five-degree angle above the floor.

Morgan said, "Looks like a storm cellar."

"Entrance to the tunnel," Zack declared. "I'm opening it."

Court aimed his rifle along with the other four operators standing there, while Zack tried the latch.

It did not give.

"Dino. Blow it."

"Roger that." Redus hurried forward, but before he put a breaching charge on the door, he tapped it with the suppressor at the end of his rifle's barrel. He turned back to Hightower. "They hardened it. Something's behind the door. They might have filled in the tunnel."

"Can you blow through it?" Hightower asked.

Redus said, "I can blow through *anything*. Can't say this building won't fall down in the process, though."

He set a strip of sticky explosives at the tunnel entrance, then looked back to Hightower. "We're gonna need a big bang."

Zack was listening to the incredible battle happening just a few hundred yards away. A battle he was missing.

"Make it happen."

"Copy."

Redus pulled another strip, and then a third, and he put them around the hinges of the welded door.

"Clear out," he instructed, and the other men left the building, taking cover behind the low wall of a nearby sheep pen.

Redus joined them seconds later and made himself small behind the wall. In his hand he held the detonator.

Hightower squeezed Court's shoulder now. "Don't wait for the dust to settle. Get your ass into that tunnel and start moving. We're on your six."

"Roger that."

Hightower looked at Redus and nodded.

"Breach, breach, breach," Redus said. Then he turned the dial on the detonator in his hands and plunged it in.

Court's hearing protection saved him from blown eardrums, but the sound from the explosion fifty feet away was still deafening.

As soon as the larger pieces of stone fell back to earth, Court climbed onto his feet and ran around the wall, charging to the building with his weapon raised, encountering smoke, dust, and still-falling bits of debris.

Inside he found the door off its hinges and a wooden staircase leading down, half destroyed by Sierra Five's explosion.

He knew his night vision equipment would be worthless in a tunnel with zero ambient light, so he flicked it up higher on his head as he descended. The bright light on his rifle would be similarly useless until he got past all the dust and smoke, so he didn't thumb the pressure switch to turn it on.

He was halfway down the stairs in pitch-black darkness, still feeling bits of debris floating back to earth and landing on his face, when the most rank smell he'd ever encountered filled his nostrils, so overpowering it made him stop in his tracks.

Men began to pile up behind him on the stairs, so he called for them to hold where they were, then forced himself forward.

Still waiting for the dust down here to clear so his light would illuminate something more than the dirty air in front of him, he took in another lungful of breath and immediately gagged.

"What the fuck?" he whispered.

At the bottom of the stairs the dust began to settle. He walked forward, kicked what felt like a large, full, plastic bucket in front of him, and he stopped again.

The rest of the men held positions on the stairs behind him.

Court flashed his light ahead.

There, as far as he could see through the narrow path, were rows of buckets lining both walls of the tunnel.

He couldn't see what was inside, but he didn't have to see, because he could smell.

Court transmitted on his headset. "Boss?"

Zack was twenty feet behind now. "Jesus, what *is* that?"

"I have, like, I don't know, maybe two hundred five-liter containers full of human shit down here."

Jim Pace muttered, "Fuck me."

Morgan said, "This is their latrine?"

Gagging, Court said, "I think they were just storing it here to hide it from us."

Hightower didn't respond; he just clicked his radio. "Mask up! That's pure methane you're breathing."

Court fumbled with his gas mask for several seconds, rushing to get it on before he passed out. Once on his face, he took a few breaths, each a little clearer than the last.

Behind him the others quickly donned their masks.

Zack called to Court. "Can we pass through the tunnel?"

"I mean," Court said, "we *can*, it's just not gonna be fun."

"No factor," Zack said. "Continue."

"This is nasty, boss," said Redus.

"Never promised you a rose garden."

Court had to squat to move through the roughly five-foot-high tunnel, and as it was only three feet or so wide, he had to work to avoid the two rows of pails on his right and left as he headed south, closer to Ismail Zai.

Behind him, the other men struggled along, muttering curses as they advanced.

Lennox said, "This isn't the latrine for a couple dozen dudes. This is enough shit for a hundred guys or more. They could have been here for weeks."

Hightower said, "Yeah. That chatty Mexican chick in analysis that Six is boning called it. They've been hiding the number of pax on site here."

Court wasn't "boning" Julie, but he didn't argue the point. He was too busy trying to come up with a tactic to breathe less foul air to risk speaking any more than he absolutely had to. The god-awful stench made it through his mask's filter, and it made him feel like he was going to pass out halfway through the tunnel. But he pressed on, kept his weapon high and his light beaming ahead, working hard to keep from putting a boot into a bucket and then spending the rest of the night with some Kashmiri separatists' waste halfway up to his knee pad.

Mercifully, Court found the terminus of the tunnel, and he climbed the steps to get him the hell out of there. This metal hatch was flush against the ceiling, not angled as the door at the origin had been, and it hadn't been barricaded, either.

The hatch was also unlocked, so he pushed it open by pressing his helmet against it, and he kept both hands on his weapon as he swept a small and dark storeroom. He still was using his SureFire flashlight on his rifle; there wasn't enough ambient light yet for his PVS-24s.

The room was clear, but he noticed a massive splatter of dried blood on the cinder-block wall in front of him. He swept the light on his barrel back towards the door, used his nondominant hand to pull the hatch all the way up and lock it into place as he climbed out, and held his position so the rest of the team could leave the tunnel, and the smell, behind them.

Zack was the third man out. He took off his mask and took a deep breath; it smelled like shit in this storeroom, as well, but it wasn't one tenth as bad as it had been in the tunnel.

Court had just taken his own mask off when Hightower flashed his light on the bloodstain.

Holding it there, he whispered, "Six."

"Yeah?"

"That's where your predecessor bought it."

Court looked back to the stain, a feeling of unspeakable despair overtaking him. He just headed for the door and cracked it open as he crammed his mask back in its pouch.

Seeing a hallway with a little bit of ambient light shining through, he aggressively nodded his head down, and his PVS-24s fell back over his eyes.

The path ahead formed into a hazy green but easily discernible focus. He waited for a squeeze on his shoulder from Redus, and when it came, he headed out into the hall.

To the immediate left was a chained door, presumably leading outside to the parade ground.

Behind him, Hightower said, "All hold."

Court dropped to his knee pads, kept forward security with his rifle in the darkness, and listened as Zack tried to raise the other Ground Branch team, speaking in a whisper as he did so.

"Sierra Actual for Foxtrot Actual."

Court could hear both sides of the transmission through his headset. Duane Anderson's own whispered voice came back in response to Hightower. "Read you five-five, Sierra."

"What's your location?"

"Command building. Second floor. There's a sealed door here we're trying to get through, then we'll clear up to the third and then the roof. Negative contact so far. Where you guys at?"

"Below you. First floor of the command building. We just exited the tunnel."

"Get outside, then over to the bunker to support Ten and the Seventy-Fifth. Sounds like they're heavily engaged there."

"Copy that," Hightower said. "We'll hightail it towards the HAS and try to raise Team Ten on the radio."

"Roger that. Good luck."

Zack ended the transmission by wishing Anderson luck as well, and then he spoke to Court. "Six. Through this door, across the parade ground, and over to the warehouse. On the far side of that, we should enter the action at the bunker."

"Roger that." Court took a large pair of bolt cutters from Morgan, then went to work on the chain lock holding the door.

FIFTY-EIGHT

PRESENT DAY

Priya Bandari sat in the office on the ninth floor of Express Tower One and continued cycling through the various camera views on her borrowed terminal. She was looking for evidence of B-Company men in this building, and it took her only moments to find two men standing in front of a door in the twenty-fifth-floor hallway outside the penthouse. They were shoulder to shoulder, facing the hall and the elevators.

Looking them over, she decided these were not, in fact, B-Company, but they were most definitely providing security for the door at the far end of the hall.

She didn't recognize either of them from the distant camera angle, but she thought they could have been from the group of Pakistanis she'd seen around Khan that night in East Andheri.

All the pieces fit together. *This*, she told herself, could very well be where Khan was staying now. He wouldn't be over in a construction site waiting out a storm. He'd be close, in view of the location, but comfortable and out of the rain.

If these were Pakistani security men, then it was, to Priya, a good indication that Khan was here now, as well. She assumed he would want to be long gone when the bomb detonated, so she took this as a good sign that she wasn't about to be blown to bits or irradiated in the next few minutes.

She didn't bother trying to reach Cobalt; she only told herself she had to remain vigilant until he came back online.

She continued watching the twenty-fifth floor, only occasionally checking the other cameras. She was working under the assumption that if Khan was in the penthouse, he would stay hunkered down in Tower One, but she couldn't be sure he wouldn't go somewhere else in the building.

After almost fifteen minutes of climbing the tower crane in what now felt like sustained forty-mile-per-hour winds, Court pulled his way up to the last few rungs below the operator's cab, just behind the operator's seat, and yanked it open, desperate to get a moment's respite from the weather.

But instead of a moment's rest, he found a man sitting there, looking back over his shoulder at him in surprise.

At first, Court thought the man to be a crane operator—a reasonable enough assumption considering the circumstances. But quickly the man shifted around, put his knee on the seat and faced the rear, and reached inside his raincoat towards his waistband.

Court knew the tell of a man going for the gun in his pants.

This was a B-Company security man, given the supremely shitty job of watching the construction site from up here, and with the arrival of the Gray Man, this dude's job just got exponentially worse.

Court executed his own draw stroke, but the B-Company goon kicked his foot against the slew handle of the big crane, which turned the entire horizontal jib, including the cab attached to it.

Court was outside the cabin still, and the sudden movement to his right had him spinning away, losing his footing on the wet railing of the tower.

He dropped his gun, used both hands to grab onto a horizontal handle outside the cabin door, and swung back around as hard as he could, leading with his boots as he propelled himself into the cabin, striking the man there in the face and chest just as he got out his gun.

The weapon clanked to the floor, bounced once, and flew out past

Court, meeting the same fate as his own weapon: a two-hundred-fifty-foot drop to the roof of a parking garage.

Court had a folding knife in his pants, but no time to reach for it. He was on top of the Indian, and the man was still slewing the crane with his foot, turning it to the left.

The heavy winds buffeted the cabin up here over three hundred feet above the ground, and with the two-hundred-foot jib no longer freely weathervaning, the wind had more and more effect on the structure.

This man might not have been much of a gunfighter, but he was a fighter, and he threw his body weight into Court, knocking him back through the open door, where again Court reached for the horizontal handle. He caught it with his left hand but had to settle for grabbing the open door latch with his right, and with these holds, he pulled himself up a few inches.

The man inside the operator's cab swung a wrench he'd picked up from a shelf at Court's hand on the latch, but the American let go, then let go with the other hand and dropped out of view.

The B-Company security man hustled back into the cab, searching for his walkie-talkie, which had fallen somewhere on the floor during the fight.

Court had fallen just feet before he caught a horizontal bar on the tower just behind the motor that turned the crane to the left and to the right, and he climbed back up as his enemy turned away from the door.

Just as the man grabbed his handheld radio, Court dove back in on him, grabbed him in a headlock, smashed the radio with his fist, and swung the man around like a rag doll in the small space.

The B-Company soldier's right hand slammed into the control panel of the crane, and the motor room below them began to rumble.

Court's first inclination was to push the man out the door to his death, but he decided on a more covert option. He held the man in a choke hold till he passed out, then cruelly snapped his neck.

He let the body fall to the floor of the cab, then spun around and hit a red master-stop button to turn off the motor. He didn't know what had happened, but immediately the jib began gently weathervaning again, its long arm facing to the northeast over Tower Two.

He sat down, exhausted from the climb and the fight, but his mind was still working. He told himself the fact that security had been posted all the way up here to protect the building meant his assumption that the bomb was here at the construction site was a safe one.

He thought he had time to call Copper and check in—he was protected from the wind here and could probably communicate—but then a squawking sound grabbed his attention. There was a walkie-talkie on the floor next to him, and voices on it sounded to him like the Hindi-speaking men were performing a radio check.

Shit. He had to move.

Court opened the top hatch of the cab, then climbed back out yet again into the hard-driven sea spray and looked down the length of the long jib, now swiveling back and forth in the shifting easterly-northeasterly winds.

"Here we go," he said to himself, and he began creeping forward, more than thirty stories above the ground, as the wind slammed into his back.

FIFTY-NINE

TWELVE YEARS AGO

As soon as the American force had been detected to the south of Ismail Zai, Murad Khan had sent dozens of fighters out to meet them, where they took positions behind sandbagged bunkers, in trenches dug into the hillside that covered the bunker itself, and even prone on the tarmac.

The fight kicked off instantly and had been raging for nearly ten minutes now, while all four of the red and white helicopters remained behind the closed blast doors, still nose to tail in a straight line from the front of the huge space to the back.

Omar Mufti had ordered the vehicles to be fully fueled inside the bunker, despite the risk the fumes posed, but this had been a time-consuming process.

The only helicopter outside the hardened structure now was the Bell 412 that Mufti had flown in to the base with Murad Khan. The copilot was inside the Huey variant now, trying to find cover while pressed down against the seats. He'd started the ignition of the helo, and the rotor spun above him, but he remained on the ground, because he knew if he took to the air, he would likely be shot down, as enemy fighters were positioned by the hangars on the other side of the runway, just three hundred meters or so from him.

He also knew that if he left Khan and Mufti behind, he'd be hunted down and killed by the KRF as punishment.

So he lay there, waiting for the fighting to stop, waiting for his people to finish off the Americans.

In the meantime, he held a pistol in his hand and prayed he wouldn't get caught in the crossfire.

Back inside the bunker, Khan ran over to Mufti, who had just climbed down from the side of the first helicopter, where he'd been conferring with the pilot through the window.

"How much more time do you need?" Khan demanded.

"The aircraft have enough fuel to get to their destinations. What's the situation outside?"

"We are holding them back from overrunning the bunker, but we won't defeat them. They sent a company or more. Probably Special Forces, SEALs, or Delta."

Mufti said, "From Salerno."

Khan nodded.

Mufti seemed to think a moment; he looked like he wasn't sure what to do.

Khan said, "We have twenty-five men still in reserve here in the bunker. When we open the blast doors, they will suppress the attack. The pilots will have to taxi out of the bunker under fire and then take off quickly."

Mufti looked up at the ceiling, then at the blast doors in front of him. "My pilots aren't taxiing anywhere. Rolling takes too long. They're going to *fly* out of here. It's the only way to get out of the line of fire from those machine guns."

Khan himself looked up at the ceiling and at the doors. "Your men. They can do this?"

Major Omar Mufti looked at the four spinning helicopters, one in front of the other. It seemed he was evaluating the pilots, one by one. "The first three pilots have the skill. But the fourth aircraft . . ." He just shook his head. "He's just too inexperienced."

Khan said, "Put one of the copilots from another flight into that seat. We have to try to get them all out of here."

Mufti pulled his shoulders back and stood tall. "No. The last helo will be the hardest to pilot. The Americans will be ready, since three helicopters will have already performed the same maneuver. There is only one pilot here with the skill to fly that mission."

"Who?"

"Me."

Khan looked at his second-in-command in astonishment. "Where will you fly it?"

Mufti was absolutely resolute now. "You will come with me. There is no way you can get out of here in the army chopper outside in the middle of the firefight. We will escape from the base in the last BV-107. I will take you north, some kilometers away, land and let you out, and then I will continue on to FOB Salerno." With pride in his voice he said, "I will detonate the conventional explosives right over the operations center of the base, and kill all the leadership commanding the Americans' attack."

Khan looked around the bunker. From the sound of the intense battle outside, there was no other way out of here.

"You will protect me to fight another day, and you will martyr yourself." Khan said it with reverence.

"It will be my honor to do both, sir."

The two men began running for the rear helicopter. On the way there Khan passed Nassir Rasool. The young technical specialist had put up his walkie-talkie, and now he held an AK in his hand as he moved towards the blast doors.

Khan lurched to a stop. "Nassir? What are you doing?"

The young man looked resolute. "I am going to fight the Americans! The helicopters must make it to their targets!"

Khan grabbed him by the arm. "You are too important, brother." Khan told him what he wanted him to do, and then Rasool lowered the rifle and lifted his radio again. Into it he said, "Cut all lights! All mujahedin to the blast doors! Open them and go out and fight the Americans! God willing we will be victorious!"

A moment later the entire bunker went dark.

"Follow me," Khan said, and then he and Rasool ran to the rear of the last Boeing-Vertol and leapt up onto the rear hatch. Mufti himself was already climbing into the copilot's seat in the cockpit, explaining to the young pilot there that he was now the copilot, and Mufti himself would fly the helicopter out of the tight bunker and through the gunfire.

The young man was visibly relieved.

Khan made it up to the cockpit, and he looked through the windscreen as men ran past on both sides through the darkness, Kalashnikovs, RPGs, and PKMs at their shoulders, desperate to buy time for the four Trojan horses.

Hightower and the rest of Golf Sierra moved quickly but carefully through the darkness, south across a parade ground on Ismail Zai base, and towards the cacophony of gunfire on the far side of the large metal warehouse building. They could see flashes in the sky beyond, and Court thought he could also hear the *thump-thump* of a single-rotored helicopter in the brief spaces when the *clack-clack-clack* of gunfire waned for a moment.

Hightower was desperately trying to raise the chief petty officer leading the SEAL team engaging the KRF on the south side of the bunker.

"Golf Sierra Actual for Dodger Actual. Come in."

He'd called over the radio multiple times as he'd advanced, before a man with a southern accent finally responded.

"Dodger Oh-Eight for inbound traffic. Repeat your last?"

"Dodger Oh-Eight, this is Golf Sierra Actual. How copy?"

"I copy. Good to hear from you boys."

"Where's your actual, over?"

"He's WIA. Being treated at this time. We've got one KIA and two more WIA. We're engaging hostiles from the aircraft hangar with the Ranger element."

"Copy all, we're heading to you. Six operators."

"What's your ETA on our poz, over?"

"We'll bypass the warehouse and approach the northwest side of the HAS, swing around and engage from the west, how copy?"

"Solid copy. Be advised. We estimate fifty-plus enemy. PKMs, RPGs, and battle rifles. Some are dug in, some have hasty fighting positions, but they sure as hell are protecting that bunker. Lots of burning tires over here, viz is bad and NODs are useless.

"Also, be advised, there's a Huey spinning at idle on the tarmac, just west of the entrance to the HAS. Appears to be unoccupied."

Zack was about to confirm receipt of this information, but Dodger Oh-Eight spoke again. "Wait one!" Court heard a shuffling through his headset, then the SEAL's voice as he spoke to others around him. "Blast doors are opening! Blast doors opening!"

Court was in tune with Hightower now; he knew it was his job to pick up the speed of the stack as they progressed through the dark. He broke into a full run now, still sweeping his weapon left and right as the other five men stayed with him, and they ran along the side of the metal warehouse and came out just one hundred yards or so from the side of the bunker where all the fighting was taking place.

The SEAL-enlisted man came back over the radio. "More enemy coming out of the bunker! It's dark in there, but I can make out a large vehicle inside. Could be a tractor-trailer."

Court heard a voice near the SEAL doing the talking. "Ya hear that shit? Those are rotors! Fuckin' rotors!"

"Fuck me," the radio man mumbled. And then, "Dodger Oh-Eight to Golf Sierra Actual. We've got a twin-rotor helicopter flying out of the bunker at this time! It appears . . . What the *fuck*?"

Court could hear Zack's voice, labored from the sprint, straining to get information out of the SEAL. "What do you see, Dodger?"

"It's a Chesapeake! What the fuck's he doing in Pakistan?"

The man from SEAL Team 10 didn't get it, but Zack understood. He transmitted, "Trojan horses! That's how they are delivering the dirty bombs into Afghanistan!"

"Say again, Sierra Actual?"

Hightower barked into his radio. "Listen up, Dodger Oh-Eight. That is a hostile aircraft!"

The SEAL enlisted man said, "We're clear to fire on the helicopter?"

"Affirmative, Dodger!"

The young man remained unsure, even in the middle of all the combat. "Say again, Sierra One. You are confirming the red and white Chesapeake helicopters as hostile?"

"*That* one is, *goddammit!* Light that motherfucker up!"

SIXTY

PRESENT DAY

Priyanka Bandari had been alternating the image on her monitor between a pair of camera views: the two men standing around the hallway on the twenty-fifth floor of this building and the view of the entrance to the building under construction next door.

She had neglected to check the other cameras for the past several minutes, so as she flipped from the construction site view to the twenty-fifth-floor view, she was startled to see the elevator door open.

Three men stepped out; she saw only their backs now, and she chastised herself for not noticing them when they were on another floor, or being aware if they came in through the lobby. Looking them over as they passed down the hall, she decided two of them were Indian, one big and burly and the other shorter but no less burly. The third man, however, was slight; he wore a tan raincoat, he had disheveled graying hair, and his hands seemed to be secured behind his back.

Her heart sank when she realized she was looking at Ted Appleton.

Appleton was escorted past the guards, then the door to the penthouse was opened, and he was led inside by a third man.

There could be no doubt now. B-Company and the Pakistanis were here, in Tower One.

This, to her, meant Khan was here, as well. And now he had Appleton.

The Indians on twenty-five headed back towards the elevator, and the door to the penthouse slammed shut.

Priya tried in vain to raise Cobalt on the phone, but he did not answer.

She took a moment to slow her breathing, and while she did so, she also did her best to process the situation before her. She had told Ted that Cobalt was on his way over to Tower Two. She knew how easily Khan had extracted information from her. Appleton would be better; it might take some time for him to tell all he knew, like Priya had done without receiving so much as a scratch, but still, he would talk, and Cobalt would be in danger.

She sat there, looking at her computer monitor in the darkened office, and she realized she couldn't be sure if Appleton had had the time to alert the authorities before he was taken.

Quickly, she picked up the phone on the desk.

The elevator door dinged and then opened on the other side of the office behind her, and she spun around towards the sound. Men filed out; they were still some distance from her, so she turned to dial 100 on the phone, the Mumbai police emergency number, but before she could do this, she heard the sound of a stairwell door opening on her left, just feet away.

She punched the three numbers, then crouched down under the desk to hide while she made the call.

The phone rang, rang again, and then it stopped ringing.

A voice just on the other side of the workstation, near the window, said, "You won't be contacting the police, Miss Bandari."

She reached into her pants pocket for her phone, then realized it was up on the desk above her.

"Come out, please."

She did so, and stood up to find five men: four with squat submachine guns and one standing closer, his finger still on the telephone desk unit, pressing down on the disconnect button.

The men with guns kept them up and sweeping back and forth around the large room. Two more men, the ones who came out of the elevator, had done a sweep of the space, and they approached with heads shaking.

She realized they were searching for others here with her.

Looking back at the man who'd hung up the phone, she realized she knew him. She had seen him two days earlier in Andheri East. He'd stood out at the time because he was the one man in the room who refused to watch when Murad Khan was about to torture her.

He smiled at her now, and spoke in Hindi with a Pakistani accent. "I ran a check of the building security system, and I could see that this terminal, on this floor, was watching the camera feed of the hall on the penthouse level. From there it was easy to deduce you were in the building."

He looked around now. "Where is your friend?"

"My friend?"

"The American assassin you work for."

Priya said nothing.

He forced her to unlock her phone, and he scrolled through her calls quickly, trying to ascertain if she had contacted the police, R&AW, the CIA, or any other entity. Satisfied she had not, he nodded, then spoke in Urdu to the others. "Take her upstairs. Stay vigilant. The killer is somewhere close."

In the penthouse on the twenty-fifth floor, Murad Khan stood in a study in front of a floor-to-ceiling window that gave a perfect view to the construction site next door, although it was as dark as dusk outside now at four thirty p.m. He faced the glass, his telephone to his ear. Former CIA station chief Ted Appleton was brought into the room behind him, then shoved down onto a chair to wait.

After several seconds, Khan spoke into his phone. "Hasan." It was Arabic, and Appleton knew it meant *good*.

He put his phone back in his pocket, then sat down on the sofa, eyeing the American with derision, while three other armed security men stood close.

"We meet at last," the Pakistani said, but Appleton did not immediately reply. The American was too busy looking into the eyes of the man who had ripped his heart out so many years ago.

He wasn't afraid, he wasn't even angry; he just felt an unceasing weight of failure. Of being bested by the man in front of him.

Not once. But twice.

Finally, after mustering up the energy to speak, Appleton said, "You won't get away with it."

"By *it*, you mean . . ."

Appleton did not try to be coy. "I am talking about the bomb you have positioned somewhere high in that building right behind you. The one with the fuel rods from Trombay and the detonators from Switzerland. I'm guessing the RDX came from Algeria."

Khan shrugged. "I'm impressed you know as much as you do. Why is it that my misdirections have fooled everyone but an old college professor, a former CIA station chief who couldn't even protect his greatest asset?"

Appleton bristled now. "People believe what they want to believe. Me . . . when I found out you were alive and working with B-Company, I *wanted* to believe you were here planning new crimes. From there it was simply a matter of hard work."

Khan nodded, impressed. "You say I won't get away with it, but, Theodore, the difficult part is already achieved," Khan said. "It will be the easiest thing in the world to simply detonate the device. I won't wait for the wind to stop, but I will wait for the rain that should be here soon, and it will help contain the radiation to this section of the city. By my act I will single-handedly carve out the financial heart of India." He shrugged. "Other than you and your friends, things could not be going more perfectly."

Appleton said, "Why are you doing this?"

Khan nodded again, appreciative of the question. "Palak Bari has been my benefactor for over a decade. We share a mutual hatred of the Hindus, a mutual hatred of the government in power here. It transcends all the other differences between us. I was slipped into India one year ago, along with other men I recruited back home, with this mission in mind." He waved a hand around him. "I've barely left this flat in all that time." With an added shrug, he said, "I've barely left this office."

"And B-Company?"

"The local gangsters did what I asked because Bari told them to."

Appleton raised an eyebrow. "The local gangsters don't know what your plan is, do they?"

To this, Khan smiled. "The leader of the cell does. He's been promised riches in Pakistan when this is all over. The other men in the gang helping me? They don't know, and they *won't* know, until it's too late for them to do anything about it."

Appleton nodded, looked at the floor a moment. The wind thrashed against the glass of the floor-to-ceiling windows.

Finally the American said, "Tell me."

"Tell you?"

After biting his lip, Appleton said, "Tell me what you did to her."

Appleton did not say Aimal Viziri's name, but he didn't have to. Murad Khan understood what the American was asking of him.

The Kashmiri shrugged. "I liked Aimal. She was talented. Professional. Not terribly intellectual, but she did her job. When I started the Kashmiri Resistance Front, I knew I could use my position in the ISI to lead people off the track of me and my plans. Someone in my office got a tip from the military about Major Mufti being a part of the organization, and I tried to keep a lid on this within the ISI, but somehow the Americans found out.

"*That's* when I knew we had a leak.

"From then on, it was simple counterintelligence, made more complicated by the fact that I was holding two jobs at the same time. I would leak a little information to different members of our staff in Islamabad, then wait and see if the Americans reacted.

"It was a few months before I homed in on Aimal. She was a liaison with the executive offices, not a member of the Foreign Coordination Unit itself. I didn't know for sure until I told her, and her alone, that we'd picked up chatter about Major Mufti's visit to the base in Peshawar. When the CIA sent a strike force in parachutes right on top of the place I indicated to Aimal, I knew she was the one."

Appleton swallowed hard, but he did not speak. He only waited.

"After that, it was only disinformation that I passed her. If you ever harbored apprehensions that I tripled her, that she was actually working for me against you, let me allay you of those concerns. She was your agent. *You* used her." He shrugged. "*I* used her."

"And then?" Appleton's voice cracked when he asked.

Khan shrugged. "After Lahore . . . you should have pulled her from the field. You should have gotten her far away from me and the ISI."

The American's face showed so much anger that two of the Pakistani security men moved closer, lest he try to attack Khan with his hands tied behind him.

But he did not attack, and Khan continued. "I had her kidnapped from her apartment. I had her killed." He raised his hands to the former CIA man. "What else could I do?"

Through tears, Ted Appleton said, "Piece of shit."

"I believe in my cause, Theodore. More than you believe in anything in the world, I swear that to you. I believed in it then, and I believe in it now."

He stood and motioned out the window, towards the second tower. "My plan here, it's the culmination of my life's work. Even when I targeted America, it was to get them out of the region, to stop their support for Pakistan so I could have the ISI resources and the freedom to target India."

Appleton's eyes had misted over. "I don't believe you. I think your mission twelve years ago was sanctioned by the ISI, just as your mission now is sanctioned by Palak Bari."

Khan smiled but did not answer.

Appleton sniffed, then gave an exaggerated shrug. "You can tell me, because obviously you are about to kill me."

Khan looked out to the ever-darkening sky, then back up to the retired American spy. "Yes, I am going to kill you." Again, he raised his hands. "What else can I do? But no, you don't get the answer to all life's mysteries as a consolation prize for your failure to stop me today."

Appleton brought his shoulders back. "I told the police."

Khan just shook his head. "You told Raja at R&AW. And Raja told B-Company. And B-Company told me. If you had notified the police, B-Company would tell me that. They *have* not, so that means you *did* not."

"I also told—"

Khan shook his head. "Just stop, Theodore. Keep some shred of your dignity intact until the end. When I die, whenever that may be, that is what I will do. You failed twelve years ago, and you got your agent killed. You have failed here, and you have gotten another one of your agents killed."

"What are you talking about? I don't have agents."

Priyanka Bandari was led into the study; she was not bound, but Nassir Rasool walked close to her, ready to grab her if she made trouble.

Appleton could not hide the expression of shock and pain on his face.

Priya, however, kept her head up, her eyes strong and fixed on the face of Murad Khan. When she was pushed up next to Appleton, she said, "You killed my uncle."

Khan held his hands up to her face. "With these very same hands."

She lunged at him. Gone was the panicked girl who'd trembled and wept under his stare. She was made of fury now, and he was the focus of all of it.

Nassir Rasool recoiled in surprise; she slipped away from him before he could grab her, but Khan just smiled as she got within inches before the men watching over Appleton yanked her back.

Khan motioned for her to be shoved down onto the sofa. Appleton was still on her right, and Khan stood above them both.

To Priyanka he said, "I needed your uncle to tell me who hired him. He did, and by catching Theodore here, I have also caught you." He smiled. "I can only assume you were here to assist the American assassin, who is lurking somewhere close by."

Priya shrugged. "I was here to identify your location, and the location of the bomb, and then to notify the police."

Rasool said, "I prevented this. She did not call the authorities; I checked the phone at her terminal and her mobile."

Satisfied, Khan said, "My only question to both of you now is . . . where is this American assassin?"

Rasool's phone buzzed in his pocket. He turned away quickly to answer the call.

With wide eyes he looked up to Murad Khan. "It's Jai. B-Company can't get in touch with one of their perimeter team next door. It might just be the wind, or some technical problem, but—"

Khan looked startled. "He's here. We have to go over there."

Rasool shook his head. "We have four of our best men protecting the device."

"And that American over there has killed a dozen men so far!" Khan stood. "We are all moving to the device. We'll wait for the rain over there."

One of the security men said, "What about these two? Should I kill them?"

Khan looked at them both. "No. They are coming with us. Appleton employs Mr. Cobalt, and this woman . . . she has some influence on him, as well. He's risked his life to save her already; we might be able to draw him out by getting him to try again."

Rasool said, "He might already be inside the construction site!"

Khan had begun moving to the door. "We have six security with us! You and I are both armed! If he *is* there, and if the B-Company men on the ground floor don't stop him from getting upstairs, then *we* will. We can take the elevator directly to the thirty-third floor."

He added, "We will protect the device until we use the device."

To this, Rasool said, "We *can't* use it till the rain comes. That could be another two or three hours."

Khan didn't answer this directly; instead he shouted at the American man and the Indian woman as the entire entourage headed to the elevator bank. "If your American continues to interfere, then I will blow the damn bomb and all of us up with it, to hell with the fallout. *He* will be responsible for the death of millions."

SIXTY-ONE

TWELVE YEARS AGO

The six men of Golf Sierra ran around the side of the warehouse, where they could then get eyes on the western side of the bunker. When they made their turn, guns high, they saw a huge mound of dirt the size of a couple of city blocks surrounded by concrete. The fight was to the south, around the corner ahead, but Court saw movement coming out a side door, just forty yards or so in front of him. He'd barely had time to register the three-man RPG team when Sierra Two opened fire, shooting the grenadier at fifty yards. Gentry and Pace also began shooting, dropping the two riflemen who had been accompanying the grenadier.

And then the men heard it. In a slight lull in the battle, the roar of a dual-rotor helicopter straining for altitude passed over them. Looking up, they saw the red and white Chesapeake helo rise over the bunker, then bank hard to the left and dive back towards the deck.

The Golf Sierra men opened fire on it, but only for an instant before it disappeared on the far side of the massive building, heading due east.

"One away," Lennox said, frustration in his voice.

The SEAL came over the radio again. "There's another helo coming out. We're engaging!"

Court reloaded his magazine as he continued to move, then clicked his transmit button. "You want to access the bunker from that door, One?"

Zack said, "Negative. We stay outside the bunker. We've got God knows how many friendlies firing into that building, I don't want to walk into that."

"Copy," Court said, and he continued running forward, closing on the battle from the northwest.

The gunfire had picked up again by the time Golf Sierra arrived at the side and took a position behind a low blast wall that jutted from the hill that covered the bunker, and the sound of another helicopter flying away could be heard on the other side of the wall. They couldn't see this helo from their vantage point, and it must have been flying without its lights because there was no glow in the sky above them.

Zack got back on the radio, raised the captain of the Ranger platoon now, and told them his location. The young captain allowed that he'd lost a dozen men, killed and wounded, and was with the SEALs and engaging from positions behind the hangars on the far side of the airfield from the bunker, some three hundred yards from the now-open blast doors.

The captain said, "Be advised, there is a Pak Army Huey spinning at idle outside a smaller door to the bunker. It's about seventy-five feet from the other side of the wall you're behind. The aircraft appears empty. Do we destroy it?"

Zack said, "Negative. Do not fire in this direction. We'll knock it out so that no squirters fly away."

The Ranger said, "Copy. Oh shit, there's a third helo in the HAS!"

The six men of Golf Sierra came out from around the wall now; they saw the flashes of gunfire over several acres of concrete and smoldering grasses in front of them, men hidden behind vehicles, burning piles of tires, discarded equipment of all kinds. The Bell 412 was less than one hundred feet away, alongside a smaller garage-style door that was open to the bunker. The massive blast doors, also wide open now, were just beyond it.

As Zack and his team watched, a third red and white dual-rotor helicopter flew out of the darkened bunker with surprising speed, its wheels just a meter or so over the ground, and it immediately banked hard to the left, away from their position, as it struggled to climb.

By now, however, the SEALs and the Rangers were ready. Light machine guns from six different locations concentrated their fire on the aircraft. Sparks and fires flickered from the lumbering beast when it was less than one hundred feet in the air.

The red and white helicopter dipped back down, as had the others, but the withering fire had eviscerated the control surfaces and the hydraulics, and soon the big helicopter went nose down, heading straight for the flat earth to the southeast of the bunker.

Court watched from several hundred yards away, but he knew there was likely a radioactive bomb on board, and he told himself there was nowhere he could hide to minimize the fallout.

He just stood there, next to the wall, watching the unreal spectacle before him.

Kendrick Lennox, however, had not been stunned into passivity. He grabbed the drag handle on Court's body armor and yanked him back around the wall and onto his ass, just as a shuddering explosion rocked the entire battleground, knocking everyone else to the ground, as well.

Flames shot high into the air, and smoke boiled from the wreckage.

The six men climbed back to their feet and regarded the scene. The new fire burning four hundred yards away gave an ethereal glow to the entire area, and bodies lay everywhere; it appeared the crash had killed many of the KRF fighters trying to defend the launch of the helicopters.

Hightower quipped quietly, almost to himself, "Guess we all got nut sack cancer now."

But Lennox said, "That wasn't tons of ANFO going up, so I don't think the dirty bomb went off. The plan must have been to wire the detonator while in the air to avoid an accident on the ground."

And then, without warning, yet a fourth helicopter screamed out of the darkened bunker, its own wheels no more than a meter off the tarmac. It flew directly through the fire and smoke there, moving more than twice as fast as the previous Chinooks.

Machine guns opened up in the direction of the helo, but it banked hard, the pilot clearly a master at moving his aircraft in ways that seemed to defy physics, and in seconds it disappeared over the eastern wall, lost in the darkness.

Hightower said, "Son of a bitch. Three of those bastards got away." Then he turned his attention to the smaller helicopter spinning nearby, and he reached into a pouch to retrieve a hand grenade.

"I'm fragging this Huey." He pulled out the baseball-sized grenade, and Jim Pace did the same next to him.

Court didn't have a hand grenade, so he aimed in on the right side of a distant KRF fighter crouched behind a burning pickup truck. He fired a few rounds; the man dropped, then Court quickly lowered his rifle and looked to the helicopter ahead on his right. Its main rotor and vertical tail rotor spun, but the lights were off inside and it appeared to be empty.

Hightower and Pace were about to pull the pins on their frag grenades.

Court said, "Wait!"

Hightower turned to him. Angrily, he shouted, "What?"

"If *our* comms are out, does that mean the Reaper feed to the TOC is dead, as well?"

Zack thought quickly. "If somebody is jamming the satellites, then the Reapers could be blind." He looked up. In addition to the clouds, the smoke from all the fires had blackened the sky. "Even if they were back online, they sure as shit didn't see those helos take off. Why?"

Court took a deep breath before he spoke. "Zack, don't blow the Huey. Get the team into the cabin and strap in tight."

"What the fuck are you talking about?"

"We're going after those helicopters."

Redus turned around and looked at the younger man. "Who's gonna fuckin' fly us, dumbass?"

"Me."

Court didn't wait for anyone to say anything else, he just broke across open ground, running as fast as he could for the Bell helicopter.

In his headset he heard Zack transmit, though all of the Golf Sierra men were close together now. "Everybody board that Huey!"

Court was less than halfway to the helicopter when the copilot's door opened, and a man in a Pakistani army flight suit appeared, raising a pistol in Court's direction. Court's rifle had been aimed towards the garage doors to cover his run from anyone lurking there, but he dove for the ground and rolled onto his right shoulder as the pistol cracked. He came up in a combat crouch, pressed the trigger of his rifle twice in impossibly quick succession, and the copilot slammed back against the fuselage of the helicopter, then slid down to the concrete and onto his face.

Court arrived at the aircraft, shot the fallen pilot again in the back, and then kicked his pistol away, and while doing so, he heard Hightower on the radio trying to raise the other American forces present.

"Dodger, Ranger, Lima Foxtrot. This is Golf Sierra Actual. Be advised. Golf Sierra is taking the Pakistani Air Corps Huey and going in pursuit of the three Chesapeake transport ships at this time. Do *not . . . fucking . . . shoot . . . at . . . us!* How copy?"

To Court's relief, just as he climbed into the copilot's seat, both the Rangers and the SEALs rogered up, while still engaging KRF fighters in sandbagged positions in front of the bunker. Someone on Lima Foxtrot rogered, as well, though it wasn't Foxtrot One.

Zack ran around the front of the 412 and climbed into the seat next to Court. "You sure about this?"

Court wouldn't have considered this course of action if the helo had been sitting there still and dark, but the fact that it was running at idle rotor RPM now told him the aircraft was ready to take to the air, and he wouldn't have to fire it up from a cold start and wait for the oil and hydraulics to reach the right temperature, a process that could take ten minutes or more, if he even knew how to make it happen.

He'd never flown the Bell 412, could only guess at the startup procedures based on the helicopters he *had* flown, and he most assuredly hadn't mentioned this to Sierra One yet.

But, he told himself, he'd get to it eventually.

Right now he was only thinking about the third helicopter that took off, catching up to it, and putting his team in position to shoot it down with their rifles.

Hightower called again over the radio to the SEALs and Rangers. They were several hundred meters away and had had a better view of the fleeing Boeing-Vertols. "Anybody see where they went?"

"Affirmative," replied the Ranger captain. "The first departed to the east but then banked around to the northwest, flying low. The second helo followed the same course as the first, about thirty seconds behind it. The third that got away . . . I didn't see. He was lower, faster. I think he went north."

Camp Chapman and Camp Salerno were due west; if the armed helicopters were heading to the northwest, they were likely going after Bagram or Jalalabad.

Court opened the throttle and pulled back on the collective, and the Huey went light on its skids, then rose into the air. He pressed on the left foot pedal, countering the main rotor's torque, but he severely overcorrected and turned the aircraft hard to the left. He lightened up the touch on his left foot; the 412 rotated back around to the east on its axis, and he continued pulling back on the collective as he held the cyclic in his right hand.

When he was only twenty or thirty feet in the air, he pushed the cyclic forward, tilting the rotor disk above him, and he began moving forward as he continued to climb.

Despite assurances from the men on the radio, Court half expected some nineteen-year-old Ranger or some hot-shit SEAL with a squad automatic weapon to rake fire at his little helicopter, but he climbed into the thick smoke without getting shot at by either the good guys or the bad.

They banked over the wreckage of the downed Boeing-Vertol, increasing speed, and Court struggled to manage the helicopter's simple but stiff controls.

In the back, the men flew with both doors locked open. They were strapped in, and Court could communicate with the men without using the helicopter intercom system because everyone was still up on the team radios.

Just as they entered the thick soup of low clouds, however, Zack leaned close to him and shouted into his ear without hitting the transmit button.

"What's the plan?"

Court joked as he picked up more and more speed, staying just below the low cloud layer. He answered over the whine of the engine and the thump of the blades above. "The *plan*? I was supposed to have a plan?"

"Seriously."

"If I can get us to within rifle range, then there's a chance we can shoot them down. That's as far as I've gotten with a strategy."

"Good enough. How long till we're in range?"

Court looked around at the panels and gauges in front of him. There was a simple radar, which he thought he'd have no trouble operating, and a radar altimeter along with an HTAWS, a sophisticated Helicopter Terrain Awareness and Warning System that might, if he could figure the damn thing out, help keep him from crashing into a mountainside.

On the radar he saw three blips. One flew due north, towards Peshawar, not even in the direction of Afghanistan. The second and third, however, were farther away, and they seemed to be heading in the general direction of the U.S. military base at Jalalabad, just a thirty-minute flight from here, over the mountain range separating Pakistan from Afghanistan. Bagram was in the same direction, well past J-Bad, so he couldn't rule out that one or both of them might be headed there.

It occurred to Court that the Americans over the border in Afghanistan wouldn't be able to see the inbound helicopters on radar yet, due to the mountains themselves obstructing any radar echo of aircraft flying this low.

He ignored the lone flight heading north towards Peshawar; it didn't seem to be a threat to American forces, and instead he oriented his helicopter to go after the two heading to Afghanistan.

Hightower repeated himself, again leaning close and shouting in his ear. "How long till we catch them, Six?"

Court concentrated on his controls and instruments because he could still see nothing outside the windshield. He decided now was the time to come clean. "I've got to be honest about something, boss."

"Shit, here it comes."

"I don't know anything about the operating ceiling of a Huey, or the weight limits. It's very aircraft specific, and I'm not trained on it. The air is going to be thin going over those mountains, and I don't know if I'll be able to make it over the top of the range."

"Can you catch them *before* the mountains?"

"Maybe. Our speed isn't that fast, but those big Chinooks are going to be carrying a lot of weight." Court looked back over his shoulder at the four men there, two on each side of the helo, strapped in with their legs hanging out the doors. "I'm carrying some weight myself." He just shrugged. "This was kind of a spur-of-the-moment thing, no idea if this shit is gonna work."

Zack flipped up his NODs, then reloaded his rifle in the tight confines of the pilot's seat. "Well, kid, I like your style, and we're gonna give it a try. We've got to stop them or at least get line of sight on somewhere with a coalition radio so we can report the Chesapeake transports as hostile."

Court said, "Roger that."

Zack added, "Maybe avoid mentioning to the guys that you don't know what the fuck you are doing right now."

"Yeah, that'll be our secret."

Zack nodded his head, and the PVS-24s slipped back over his eyes. "Don't you fuckin' crash us, Six."

"Copy." Court looked ahead and saw nothing but clouds pressed tight to his windscreen, but he nevertheless increased to full power.

SIXTY-TWO

PRESENT DAY

Priyanka Bandari moved through the lobby of Tower One surrounded by men, guns, and what she felt to be an intense, almost evil energy. Appleton was in front of her, and they had not spoken; she hadn't seen the point, and he had a look of despondency and defeat that meant he wasn't about to start chatting with her.

She stepped outside, again in the center of the entourage, and was immediately slammed in the face by the high winds. The air was wet though the driveway was covered and the rain had not yet begun to fall, and the only thing keeping her from tipping over was the men pressed tight up against her as they ushered her into the back of one of three big SUVs.

Khan and Rasool climbed into the same vehicle as Priya, along with a driver and security man, and Appleton was shoved into the SUV behind them with four more men. The rest of the Pakistani gunmen took the last vehicle, and the motorcade immediately raced off, out from under the covered entrance and into the incredible wind for the sixty-second drive next door.

Priya felt gales buffet the vehicle. She watched the driver struggle to negotiate this as well as a heavy mist from the nearby bay that hit the windshield faster than his wipers could clear it.

Khan turned to her from the front seat, though he almost seemed lost in thought. He said, "My plan was to live. I was going to have a helicopter pick me up after I initiated the detonation sequence." He waved a hand around the car. "Then the monsoon. No helicopter. Still . . . managing setbacks has been a huge component of my profession." He pulled an iPhone out of his pocket. "I have the weapon set with a sixty-minute countdown timer. That was the plan." He shrugged. "But with my phone I can override that and detonate it immediately. Anytime I want. If we get your man, then the plan continues, we wait for the rain, I activate the bomb, and I leave. But if your man causes any more trouble for me . . . I'll just go down with the ship." He smiled, genuinely, it seemed to Priya. "You'll go with me, of course. The damage to India . . . just the same if I live or die."

Priya said, "I heard you were adept at faking your death. I have no doubt you're still trying to find a way out of this for you personally, no matter what you say now." She looked at Rasool, at the driver, at the other man in the back with her. "These men are as good as dead. More fools for you to use."

Khan looked to Rasool, sitting next to her. "Gag her."

She fought back as both the big security man and the smaller Pakistani struggled to get the veil off her head, which they then tied tightly in her mouth. They finally accomplished this just as the SUV skidded to a halt under the covered drive at Tower Two.

The driver and the other security man climbed out and immediately drew pistols.

They looked around a moment; armed Pakistanis filed out of the other vehicles, and soon the all clear was given.

Khan and Rasool stepped out, while Priya and Appleton were led from their respective SUVs. Priya saw that Appleton had been gagged, as well.

All ten entered through the glass front doors of the tower.

Building materials, forklifts, generators, and other equipment were positioned and stacked all around the space. Easily fifteen men were already present here in the poorly lit and still unfurnished lobby. These were B-Company regulars, Priya knew instantly. She recognized a couple of them from Andheri East, and she could also discern that they were extremely agitated.

Jai was here, the commander of the force supporting Khan, and he shouted into a radio, demanding an update from someone who did not reply.

Rasool marched up to him. "What floor is the American on?"

"We don't know if he's in the building. Our guy in one of the tower cranes on the southwest side hasn't responded. We're sending two men up the tower to check him out, could be a radio issue." He looked to Khan now. "You told us to stay at the perimeter, but we have enough men to search this entire—"

Khan said, "You and your men remain on the ground floor or outside. My men are up there, and we are going up, as well."

Jai looked at him with suspicion. "Why can't we, at least—"

"If you have a problem, you know who you can call, and you know what he will say."

Priya thought Khan was talking about Palak Bari, and Jai immediately backed down, making her more confident she was right.

She and the rest of the group from Tower One then walked to the center of the lobby, where a massive bank of eight elevator shafts stood. Six of the shafts seemed to be empty, but two, to Priya's surprise, had cars in them but no doors.

The building obviously had not been completed; there was no power, no lights, so she didn't understand how an elevator could be operational, but she was led into one of the cars along with Khan and several other men, and Appleton was put in next to her.

The car began to rise. Again, there were no doors, so she could see each empty and darkened floor as they began heading up.

Khan ignored Priya but spoke to Appleton. "These are called JumpLifts. Elevator systems for high-rise construction. The motor is on the bottom, nothing is pulling it from the top, so you can use them while the building is going up. There are construction hoists on the outside of the building, but we don't want to be out there now with this wind."

Appleton did not respond, likely, Priya decided, because there was a piece of rope tied in his mouth.

She realized both of them had been gagged so that they couldn't reveal any of Khan's plot to the B-Company men here who, she figured, had no idea what was going on.

They rose through the construction site, the wind howling on each open floor as they ascended.

Court Gentry felt the wind catch under his raincoat, pulling it up on his shoulders. This gust must have been close to fifty miles per hour, and he held on with both hands to the metal, wet from ocean spray pelting him all the way up here from the bay behind him.

It had been much slower going than he would have liked. Each step was an ordeal, and he'd not gotten far across the long arm of the jib before realizing his mistake.

There was a narrow metal catwalk within the frame of the jib; he could move along it, one foot in front of the other while in a crouch, but if he'd taken his time in the operator's cabin, he might have found a harness and lanyard, and that would have been damn helpful right now.

A long metal cable ran the length of the jib above the catwalk; it was used for workers to hook their safety lanyard onto if they needed to climb out. With the body harness all construction workers used working on high floors, the lanyard and cable would keep them safe from falling.

But Court didn't have any of that shit. He just hung on, struggled from one step to the next, and did his best not to slip on the wet metal bars.

An even more powerful gust slammed into his back; he dropped down to his knees for perhaps the tenth time in the past five minutes, and as soon as it subsided, he pressed forward, faster now, trying to cover as much of the steel jib as possible before the next blast of wind from the ocean forced him to crouch and ride it out again. He knew he was not supposed to look down, but he did, again and again, hoping like hell to see the flashing lights of one hundred cop cars making their way through the storm.

But he saw nothing from his vantage point other than a desolate construction site, a long way down from where he held on precariously.

He had ten yards or so to go before reaching the end of the jib, the tip of which was moving just ten feet or so above the roof of the building.

The jib swiveled in the wind, back and forth, and he knew this meant that, when he finally *did* make it to the end, it would be over the roof of the unfinished building for only part of the time. He'd have to jump for the roof, timing it to where the jib hadn't turned too far to the north or south to where he'd simply fall to his death.

He saw the trolley ahead, the big metal case on rollers that held the hook-and-pulley assembly and moved it backwards and forward along the bottom of the jib. It was five yards from the end of the crane itself, and he stuck his head out and looked down, again in vain, for anyone coming to his aid.

Then, as he brought his head back in to walk the last few yards, he saw them. A pair of men in black raincoats, standing there at the edge of the roof of the building.

They, like Court, were fighting the wind, adopting wide uncomfortable stances, watching him with mouths agape.

He knew in a heartbeat they were Pakistani henchmen of Murad Khan, and they'd likely been warned about the radio silence from the Indian pulling security in the tower crane, so they'd been sent to the roof to try to get eyes on the man in the distance.

And instead they found a crazy American in the foreground, three hundred fifty feet above the ground.

The men had not lifted their weapons, but Court saw squat subguns on their chests. Instead they simply stood there, trying to keep from falling over, waiting for their target to come closer and jump down.

The men didn't know Court was unarmed, but they did know he wasn't going to pull a gun and start shooting from that position. If he let go to do so, he would certainly fly off the jib and down to his death.

A new powerful gust caused Court to crouch, and as he did so, he saw both men hold their hands up to protect their faces from the sea spray.

He realized he had a few seconds to work with, though movement in the middle of a gust this powerful would have its drawbacks, as well.

He was at the trolley now, and he realized he might be able to make his way down to the hook itself and use the few feet of cable there to hang from, to swing back and forth until he could throw himself into the floor below.

Quickly, Court climbed out of the structure of the jib onto the edge, then climbed down the trolley to the hook block. The wind began to slow a little, so he dropped his head below the block, saw where the hook hung just four feet away, and then held on to the trolley with one hand while kicking his legs to swing him under the apparatus.

The men didn't have a shot at him now; he was below them, ten feet from the edge of the building itself.

Three hundred fifty-four feet above the ground, he let go of the trolley and sailed a couple feet through the air, and as he dropped, he slammed both hands onto the hook itself, catching on the wet metal with his wet fingertips.

The hook swung wildly; he was now blowing left and right with the swaying jib, and back and forth under the cable holding the hook because of the momentum of his jump. Looking up at the roof one story above him, he saw the men moving to their left to get a shot at him.

The jib he swung under came back around to the left just as he shifted away from the building, and now he saw two other men running his way on the darkened thirty-third floor, just below the roof.

One fired a round just as Court swung forward with all the power he could muster, then let go of the hook as it reached the point closest to the building.

He sailed through the air again; a fifty-five-mile-per-hour gust helped push him forward as he dropped, and he landed on the floor one story below the gunmen on thirty-three.

He collapsed his body to the unyielding concrete as he performed a shoulder roll to remove energy from his nearly fifteen-foot fall, and then he made it up to his knees.

He was exhausted, his collision with the ground had not been one of his more successful moves, and his right hip and both knees hurt.

But he forced himself to his feet, pulled his phone and his earpiece out of his raincoat, then flung the soaked garment to the ground, and this seemed to take a tiny fraction of the pressure of the wind off his back.

He then went running in search of a way upstairs.

He was unarmed, the enemy knew he was here, and two of them were just a single floor above him, surely coming his way.

SIXTY-THREE

TWELVE YEARS AGO

Omar Mufti set down his hulking Chinook helicopter in a field of saffron ten minutes north of Ismail Zai. The side door was opened by one of the two armed men in the back, and then Murad Khan and Nassir Rasool leapt out into the purple blooms.

Mufti took to the air again seconds later, then banked to the west-southwest and pushed his cyclic forward to tip his nose down.

The two KRF fighters, each armed with a powerful PKM light machine gun, remained on board, strapped into benches next to the side doors, ready to open fire to suppress any resistance when they reached their target, Forward Operating Base Salerno, in Khost, Afghanistan. They'd been told the helicopter would fly to a very specific portion of the base before it detonated, and it would be their job to hold back any attack against them if the ruse failed at the last moment.

Mufti climbed a little as he flew, but he kept his aircraft below thirty meters in altitude, because he knew Pakistani air defense radar could pick up a signal if he ventured much higher.

He would enter the Spin Ghar mountains soon, so he would be climbing then, but there he would be hidden from radar by flying through mountain passes.

He'd be above the clouds by then, and he'd have the benefit of the moon and stars to guide him, but for now he wore his night vision equipment and did his best to fly fast, to stay low, and to prepare himself mentally for his own martyrdom.

Murad Khan and Nassir Rasool had mobile phones on them, but even though it was approaching four in the morning and they were far away from anyone who would be inclined to help them, they didn't use the devices. Instead they walked through the darkness towards a single light on a lamppost in front of a farmhouse, perhaps three kilometers distant.

Rasool warned Khan that their phones might be a compromise, *everything* might be a compromise at this critical time in the mission, so they threw them into a swiftly moving stream on their way to the farmhouse, told themselves they would ask the farmer to take them in and drive them to Peshawar or some other developed area, and there the men could get new phones and a secure place to stay, along with some semblance of safety.

It was a pity about Omar Mufti, Khan thought as he trudged through the pungent-smelling saffron. It had not been the plan for the trusted former army major to die tonight. But by delivering a very powerful munition right on top of the American Special Forces base that had sent the men who attacked Ismail Zai, Omar would deal an excruciating blow to those who had disrupted the KRF's plans.

And it was also a pity about the Camp Bostick flight. The American base over the border to the north would be spared because the helicopter he'd tasked to go there had crashed right after takeoff. But, Khan told himself with his customary self-assuredness, Bagram, Jalalabad, and, to a lesser extent, Salerno would be forever changed by his actions tonight, America itself would be forever changed, and for that he had every right to be proud.

He put his hand on young Nassir's shoulder while they walked. With a tired sigh, he said, "You know, brother, I always thought this day would be the end. Now that I'm here, I wonder if it is just the beginning."

"What do you mean?"

"Twenty-five of our brothers saw you and I climb aboard that doomed helicopter. Surely they won't *all* be killed tonight. Some will be taken prisoner, and through torture by the Americans, they will never say anything other than the truth, that we were on board a helicopter that flew away before crashing in a fireball."

Nassir understood. "So . . . we are . . . dead."

Khan smiled, still weary, still stunned by the evening's events. "And we should take advantage of this, don't you think? Hide away, bide our time for our next masterpiece, use our cloaks of invisibility to our advantage."

Nassir nodded. "Where you go, sir, I will follow."

"Then," Khan said, "someday . . . you will follow me to India. And what we do there to the Hindus will surpass what we do tonight to the Americans."

The two men walked on through the night, towards a light in the distance, and towards their future.

After ten minutes of flying, the Huey piloted by Court Gentry was close enough to the first of two helicopters headed towards Afghanistan to where he strained to find it out his windscreen. Even with the night vision gear, however, there was so much terrain below them and clouds above them that he could not yet identify a massive Chinook.

He chanced a glance down to the radar again. "We're coming up on it. Should be at our one o'clock, a couple miles."

Court was flying at fifty meters above the ground, low to be going this fast, especially with his lack of skill, but it occurred to him that the helicopter they were chasing might be even lower.

"Look down on your side," he told Zack.

Zack himself peered through the windscreen and his side window. "Got it. Fucker's nap-of-the-earthing it. Starboard side, one mile. Can this thing go any faster?"

"Negative. We're closing on it, though. Get the boys ready."

Zack spoke into his radio now. "Starboard side, Two and Four. Time on target is about one mike."

Pace and Lennox were on the starboard side of the cabin, so as soon as they made it within range of the helicopter, two guns from Golf Sierra would have line of sight on it.

Court was as high as he could fly while remaining below the thick sheet of clouds, but every few seconds he ran into even lower wisps that obscured his vision.

Finally, after coming out of a gray cloud bank at twenty-five meters, he could see the BV-107 in his NODs, less than half a mile away now.

Lennox spoke over the intercom. "That first helo that went down didn't have its bomb prepped yet. The dudes in this helo have had fifteen minutes to get it ready, so it's anybody's guess if we're gonna catch the full monty if we blow it out of the sky."

Hightower opened the window in the hatch next to him; cold wet clouds blew in at 165 knots as he pushed the suppressor and barrel of his rifle outside. He clicked the transmit button for his mic. "No factor. We take down that helo by any means necessary."

Court knew they were almost within range; his heading would keep them there, and his speed would eventually move them past the first air-craft, so he concentrated almost solely on his terrain radar now. They were still a few miles from where the fun would really begin, at the beginning of the mountain range, but he could see on the avionics that the ground below him was rising and falling more sharply every minute.

The pilot of the enemy transport ship ahead and on his right was, it was patently obvious, far superior at controlling his aircraft than was Court. He flew ten meters over the ground, rose and fell smoothly with the terrain below him, and did everything right.

Court, on the other hand, was giving the five other men of Golf Sierra the bounciest, jerkiest helicopter flight of their lives. It would be hard for them to aim accurately, but Court knew better than to fly much closer to the enemy helicopter, lest he crash into it or into the ground in the process.

He'd try to carefully creep over to within 150 yards, and trust the aim of the men jolting around like rag dolls in back to shoot accurately.

Zack broadcast into his radio now. "Shooters, go for the cockpit and the engines. If we can take down the aircraft without the bomb detonating, then we might live to get a shot at the other one."

Less than a minute later, just after Court banked closer to the BV-107, putting his aircraft about 175 yards off the enemy's port side, Zack gave the order to open fire. Lennox and Pace pressed their triggers on the starboard side of the Huey, making educated guesses about how far to lead their aim so that their rounds would hit their target.

They each fired a magazine to no effect; it appeared like the other helicopter did not even realize it was under attack. The two men reloaded quickly. Redus and Morgan, strapped facing the other direction, turned their bodies around to try to get their own weapons on target, but it was impossible to do so without the potential of hitting the men on the starboard side.

Court wasn't watching any of this; he was flying so low and so fast he didn't take his eyes off his windscreen for a second.

Until Zack yelled, "Break left!"

Court jacked the cyclic left. He had no idea why, but almost instantly he figured it out.

Tracer rounds from a pair of light machine guns lit up the sky in front of his windscreen.

The enemy helo was firing back, and they had better weapons for this battle.

And a better pilot, Court reminded himself.

All the men in the back of the Huey sloshed around with Court's intense and inexpert aerobatics; his helicopter flew only ten meters above the ground before he leveled the rotors, and quickly the two men on the starboard side began firing frantically again, desperate to take out the machine guns on the helo, if not knock the entire aircraft out of the sky.

The enemy guns kept their fire up. Court climbed and banked and dove to try to make himself a hard target, but this had the effect of making accurate fire from his own aircraft virtually impossible.

Lennox and Pace each dumped another magazine at the enemy; the pilot of the BV-107 climbed a little over hilly treetops, and more machine gun tracer fire swept close to Court's aircraft, forcing him to bank away again.

Lennox yelled from the back, "Keep it steady, Six!"

Court's eyes danced quickly from his view out the windscreen, his altimeter, and the terrain radar, and he saw that the land rose sharply dead ahead of him, but the enemy helicopter was flying over a creek that would allow him to remain at a lower altitude.

Court transmitted for the entire team now. "Port side, get ready, you're up!"

He was telling Redus, Morgan, and Hightower that they would be engaging the helicopter, which made no sense to any of them since they were on the opposite side of the fight. But before they had a chance to ask for a clarification, Court pulled the cyclic hard to the right, raised the collective for altitude, and began banking closer and closer to the enemy helo.

Lennox and Pace emptied mags as they neared the enemy, but the flight was so erratic they were doing little more than waving their barrels in the general direction of the helicopter and pressing the trigger, hoping for dumb luck to end the threat.

Court increased his bank to the north, and soon he'd shot behind the enemy helo, chased all the way by machine gun fire. He was above it now, maybe thirty meters higher, breaking in and out of the low clouds, and he continued banking until he found himself aft of the twin-rotored helo and on its starboard side. He dove back for the deck, above the northern edge of the winding creek bed, and the dive increased his speed. Soon Redus and Morgan entered the fight with their rifles just behind Hightower in the left seat, and Zack himself began firing a moment later.

Court flew with his rotor just meters away from a hillside on his right, but he remained over the creek bed, less than forty yards distant from the enemy at some points.

The other helicopter's machine guns were quiet through this. Court didn't know if they were both reloading or if they were, instead, just repositioning inside the cabin to fire out the starboard side. But no matter the reason, he decided he needed to take advantage of this. He banked slightly to port, closed even more on the big helicopter, and the three Golf Sierra shooters fired furiously.

Kendrick Lennox, out of the fight now because he was on the starboard side, unhooked his retention strap and crawled across the belly of the cabin. He jabbed his gun between Morgan and Redus and opened fire just as they began reloading mags.

Hightower saw what Lennox was doing. "Kendrick! You're gonna get tossed out!"

Jim Pace reached back with a gloved hand and grabbed Lennox's pant leg, giving him a modicum of protection if Court had to put the helo into another crazy banking maneuver.

Court listened to the incredible amount of gunfire from the four operators, and he knew they were expending ammunition at a staggering rate. He was just about to tell them to try to conserve until he got even closer to the enemy when machine gun fire again began pouring out of the cabin of the BV-107.

Court reflexively banked away to the right, then realized what he was doing and stopped his turn, just as his rotor clipped a cluster of bushes on the hillside. He righted the craft, knew he couldn't bank right again or he would hit the hillside, and if he banked left he would only close the distance between his ship and the enemy's guns.

So he did the only thing he could do: he yanked back hard on the cyclic, jolting his aircraft slower and allowing the enemy to get in front of them.

This took him out of the line of fire of the machine guns, but it also threw the four men in back hard against the rear bulkhead.

His aircraft was fifty feet above the creek now, and directly behind the BV-107, but he'd have to build up speed again to go after it. He'd just pushed the cyclic forward, however, when an intense light in his windscreen bled out his night vision equipment.

He hurriedly pushed the PVS-24s high on his head and then looked at the spectacle in front of him.

The enemy helicopter burned as it rolled across the rocky creek three hundred yards off his nose. The sound of the explosion came just after.

Court immediately began to climb, lest he fly through the fire and falling debris.

"What the hell just happened?" Zack asked, stunned.

Redus answered. "I was aiming for the cockpit. Might have gotten lucky."

Next to him, Morgan said, "Bullshit. I hit the rotor and he augered in."

Court was already picking up speed, banking away from the helicopter crash and looking for the other enemy helo on his radar. He found it, some five miles ahead, and he brought his heading to an impact course.

Hightower said, "Didn't look like an ANFO explosion." He turned to Court. "Can you catch another one?"

"Yeah," Court said. "Do we have the ammo for another fight like that?"

Zack shook his head. "Not like *that*. I'm down to three mags." The other men chimed in that they were all down to less than half their ammo.

Court raced to the west, heading for the helicopter still hell-bent on making it into Afghanistan.

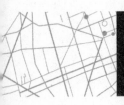

SIXTY-FOUR

PRESENT DAY

As he raced through the large, dark, empty, and open thirty-second floor of Express Tower Two, Court Gentry wanted to call Priya to get any updates about what was going on. But he didn't dare take the time, because he knew he needed one thing right now that was even more important than information.

He needed a fucking gun.

Men were coming for him, this he knew, and he also knew the only place he was going to find a gun was in the hands of one of the men who would, no doubt, try to use it on him.

He ran to the southwestern corner of the building as fast as his feet would take him, towards a stairwell there. He assumed there was one at each of the four corners of the building, as well as a bank of shafts in the center of the room, though he was reasonably sure there would be no working elevators.

Still, with four stairwells, there were four locations from which to descend, and he could only hope the men upstairs would split up before coming down to find him, not knowing where he'd go.

He arrived at the corner, running light on his feet to listen as best he could for any sounds that might tip him off to danger. As he did so, he desperately looked around for something he could use as a weapon. The whipping wind blew plastic sheeting violently, maintaining its hold on four-foot-high stacks of wallboard. Long lengths of rebar lay in rows, and construction workers' tool belts lay unattended in a pile, safe here from theft because the ground floor of this structure was held by gangsters.

Court scanned the tool belts as he ran, ready to grab something to use against an armed man, but he gave up this endeavor and flattened his back to the wall next to the exit to the stairwell when he thought he heard rushed footfalls approaching through the noise.

The tip of an Uzi Pro 9-millimeter jutted out; Court could tell the man holding the gun was moving with care but also with speed, and when Court dove onto him from the side, the impact sent the man tumbling to his right. They were a dozen feet or so from the edge of the floor and the three-hundred-fifty-foot drop, and the misty wind slammed both men's bodies as Court tackled the man onto, and then over, the four-foot-high stack of wallboard.

The Uzi remained in the man's clutches, but Court grabbed the gun hand's wrist with his own to keep the weapon out of his face.

Court had been fortunate to reach the stairs before the man came out onto the floor, giving him the drop on him, but he had not been fortunate in his choice of enemy. This Pakistani was big, taller than Court, built to quickly shake off a bone-crunching side attack. He shook Court's hold off the gun, so Court launched off his powerful legs and closed the short distance between their bodies, knocking the man onto his back as he grabbed the wrist of the gun hand again.

Still, the Pakistani held the Uzi firm.

Court's enemy had one objective in life at present: to hold on to the gun so that he could shoot the American. Court, on the other hand, had two: he had to get control of the gun as well as prepare himself to deal with the inevitable arrival of more attackers.

The two rolled around near the edge of the floor, neither able to land a strike because of Court's intense focus on the Pakistani's right hand and the Pakistani's desperate need to hang on to the weapon there.

Together they made it back up to their knees, both working their way up to their feet to employ kicks, but the wind spun the men around suddenly. Court went for a head butt and missed, and then they began to fall again, slipping on the mixture of sea spray and construction dust.

Court swiveled on the way down and slammed his right shoulder into the man on his back as he hit the concrete, and this knocked the wind out of the Pakistani.

Both men sent their free hand towards the Uzi: Court to confiscate it and the enemy to protect it.

The Pakistani fired a burst of rounds, striking the ceiling, but Court knew to keep his body and his own hands away from the end of the little barrel.

A pair of men in black raincoats appeared around the side of the stack of wallboard; they were armed with Uzis as well, and their guns were up, sweeping in Court's direction.

The American rolled his body over the top of the Pakistani on his back, threw all his weight and energy onto the right arm of the man, and guided the Uzi in the man's hand towards the new threat.

Simultaneously he let go of the man's wrist and grabbed the gun with both hands, then shoved it forward with all his might.

This caused the Pakistani's finger to catch on the trigger, and Court held the gun, adjusting aim, just as the two men attacking were about to fire on him.

Court shot them both dead with a firearm that was not entirely in his possession.

He slammed his head back into the man on the ground behind him, cracking his nose, then rolled farther, onto the Uzi totally, and then off the man, his hands wrenching the gun away from the stunned and injured Pakistani.

Court lay on his back, exhausted, as he turned the little weapon around, just as the man with the broken nose got his now-free hand on a knife on his belt.

Court shot him once in the forehead from three feet away.

Still on his back, the American swung the Uzi around in all directions he could see, unsure if there were more attackers. Seeing nothing but the whipping sea spray blowing into the open floor, hearing nothing but the whistling of the wind and the ceaseless patter of blowing plastic tarp, he pushed himself up to a seated position, then climbed to his feet.

He slung a fresh Uzi from one of the two new men's bodies around his neck, dropped the old Uzi, and grabbed the weapon from the last man, taking off the sling and jutting the barrel and little foregrip into his pants at the small of his back.

Armed with dual automatic weapons now, he started again for the stairs, but he stopped himself, turned, and looked back.

He had an idea.

Three dead bodies lay there, just ten feet from the edge of the floor. He moved to them quickly and grabbed the first one by the ankles.

Forty-five seconds later, he was back at the stairs, moving up, his weapon at eye level, scanning for a target. And as he did this, he tried to call Priya.

She did not answer, and Court took this as *very* bad news.

Priyanka Bandari, Ted Appleton, and eight Pakistanis stepped out of the elevator shaft on the thirty-third floor, into the high and howling winds whipping through the concrete structure.

A single man stood there in a raincoat, an Uzi waving around in front of him and a radio held to his mouth. He looked concerned, and without so much as an explanation, this caused all of the six new security men to lift their guns to their shoulders and fan out.

Priya and Appleton were pushed by Rasool over to a large orange freight container, its roof just a couple feet short of the twelve-foot ceilings on this floor. He pulled a knife and cut the gag off Appleton, then told the older American to untie the veil in the Indian girl's mouth.

Rasool said, "We will need your voices to beg for your lives when we call your friend."

While this was going on, Khan conferred with the lone man remaining on this floor.

Priya understood the majority of the Urdu they spoke as he shouted to Rasool. "Three more men not reporting. They went after a guy that came

from one of the cranes, jumped, then landed on thirty-two. I heard shots."
After a beat he added, "It's got to be the American."

Priya realized Cobalt was just a floor below them now, but she didn't
know if this was good or bad. She'd assumed Khan wouldn't detonate the
bomb prior to the heavy rains coming; he only needed to affect a few dozen
city blocks and not the entirety of the city, after all. But now that his
weapon was clearly under threat by an enemy he couldn't get control of, he
was talking as if he had no qualms about killing hundreds of thousands.

She stole a glance to Appleton, who looked back to her, then towards
the orange container just behind her.

"That's it."

"That's what?" Priya asked, but before the American answered, she understood. "Oh. *That's* it?" She regarded the simple-looking container. It
was several times larger than she'd expected the bomb to be, and it was
terrifying to stand so close to it.

Rasool spoke Urdu to the seven security men on the floor, told them
B-Company had been ordered to stay on the ground floor, so it was up to
them to kill this one lousy American operator who had designs on getting
to and disabling the device.

They each took a position behind a vertical column holding up the roof
to the building, and they peered through the dim light, trying to discern
any movement at all on this floor, which was difficult to do in the wind and
the poor light.

Khan noticed Priya staring in horror at the shipping container. He
stepped over to her. "The walls are lead-lined. The fuel rods inside won't be
exposed until just before the bomb detonates, when the walls collapse out,
exposing the radioactive material. I'd hoped to watch this happen on a
camera feed on my phone while in the back of a luxury Eurocopter on my
way to Karachi, but unfortunately your friend's actions mean we might all
be right here when I blow this city to hell."

As the security men began to fan out, Rasool answered a call on his
mobile, then turned to Khan. "It's Jai. He says he has Bari on the phone
for you."

Khan rolled his eyes, then extended a hand. "Fine, I'll talk to brother
Palak, perhaps for the last time." He then shouted to his security officers as

they moved from column to column, waving their submachine guns in the process. "Find that American!"

Murad Khan took Rasool's phone, put the call on speaker, then spoke in Hindi to Palak Bari, the Indian-born Muslim and the head of B-Company.

Bari said, "Jai says you are at the device now, and the storm is blowing hard."

"Yes. The enemy is approaching."

"*What* enemy? The old CIA man you told me about? I hear the authorities don't know a thing."

"I have the CIA man, I have the girl working with him. I *don't* have their asset, the one they call Cobalt. He's in the building, he's killed three of my men one floor below us, and he is coming this way."

Bari paused a moment. "What are you saying?"

"I am saying we might need to activate the device early."

"In high winds? With no rain? Are you mad? You'll kill fifty thousand Muslims."

Khan's own estimate put the number much, *much* higher, but he didn't say this.

"What else can I do? If we don't eliminate this American before it's too late, all our years of work will have been for nothing."

"I'll send all my men up there to find him."

"No!" Khan countered. "I don't want to see any B-Company on the floor. They'll only interfere. The decision is made, Palak. My hand has been forced. I must detonate the device if the American gets any closer."

Bari said, "Don't do it!"

But Murad Khan ended the call, handing the phone back to Rasool.

SIXTY-FIVE

TWELVE YEARS AGO

For the first time in almost twenty minutes of flying, Court could see the moon and the stars. He'd come out above the clouds, not because he was so high above the ground but rather because he was in the mountains now, and even though he was only flying 150 feet above the earth, he was over ten thousand feet above sea level. They were just ten minutes away from the Afghanistan border, closing fast on the BV-107 that was carefully picking its way through the mountain passes, obviously to hide its radar signature.

Court looked down at his onboard radar to try to judge his distance, but he immediately noticed a new signature moving to the southwest of him. After watching the blip a few seconds, he began to wonder if it was the same helicopter that had flown north out of Ismail Zai as if it were going to Peshawar. That would have put it behind Court, but if it had changed directions, he thought its speed might have put it about where he saw it on the radar, just entering the mountains, heading to Afghanistan.

He actuated his interteam radio. "One, we've got a new problem."

Zack turned to him. "Tell me."

Court pointed a gloved finger to the radar. "The guy who went north out of the base . . . it looks like he's turned and is heading towards the border now, south of us."

"Shit," Zack said, looking at the blip on the screen. "He's heading to Khost."

"Yeah. It's either Chapman or Salerno."

Hightower spoke confidently. "They'll go after Salerno. Much bigger target, more personnel, more to damage."

Court thought this was probably correct, so he pushed any worry about Julie from his mind and asked, "Which one are we going after?"

"How long till we get eyes on the helo we're tracking now?"

"A minute and a half. Maybe two."

"If we take it down fast, can we head south and cut off the last helo before he gets to Khost?"

"We're northwest of him. We could set an intercept course to try to meet up with it at the top of the mountain range. It will be close, and the air will be thin." Court showed his indecision on his face. "I . . . I don't know if we have the power to fly that high."

Zack said, "Stay on current heading. We'll get the one we know we can reach, worry about after . . . after."

"Roger that."

Court knew Zack was making the smart decision, but if Court had been in charge, he would have broken off his chase of the helo ahead of him and instead raced down to get the one that was heading in the general direction of Julie.

Still, he did as ordered and began looking through his windscreen to try to find the second helo.

They had it in less than two minutes. Through his NODs, Court looked ahead into a misty valley below him and caught the sparking of static electricity popping off the twin rotors of a helicopter. The pilot was clearly using skill instead of speed, doing his best to stay as low as possible, trying to hide in the mist.

The valley rose quickly ahead of him, and Court knew he'd be forced to climb through a series of snow-packed peaks before clearing Spin Ghar on his way to his target.

His current heading would take him away from Jalalabad and towards Bagram, so Court determined this guy was on his way to deliver a dirty bomb over the largest U.S. military base in Afghanistan.

Court had his Huey much higher, over a ledge that looked down into the valley, and he realized he would catch up with the enemy craft as it climbed up to his position to pick through the mountains.

Court transmitted on the interteam radio. "Port side, you're up. Less than a minute."

Redus said, "Keep it smooth this time, Six."

"Tell you what," Court snapped back. "I can fly it smoothly into a mountainside, or I can go where the terrain takes me. Your call."

Zack said, "Can it. Both of you."

The engagement with the second BV-107 started very differently than the first. As Court came up aft of the now-climbing aircraft, he was surprised to see streams of tracers racing at impossible speed out of the lowered rear hatch, two fingertips of light trying to reach out and touch the Huey racing up from behind.

Court jolted the helo to the left and to the right, finding himself on the defensive from the beginning of the fight.

He managed to fly to the north of a rocky outcropping that took him out of the enemy's line of fire for a moment, and he was thankful for this, because he saw the sparks and flashes as enemy machine gun rounds struck the top of the peak, tearing into the stone and sending it flying.

Court went lower and came out around the other side of the rock, so close his single-blade rotor blew feet of loose snow from it, and when he swung back around, immediately Redus and Morgan began firing at the enemy, just fifty meters ahead on the left, flying at the same elevation.

Court strained to go faster, diving down until he was just a few feet over the snow and rock, trying to position his ship to the starboard side of his enemy so that the guns jutting from the rear of the enemy helo couldn't come to bear.

When the Americans' rifles ran empty, Lennox and Pace traded them, handing their loaded weapons across the floor of the cabin to their team-mates and taking the others to reload.

Court's maneuvering silenced the enemy machine guns, for a moment anyway, so he tipped his rotor towards the Chinook and closed even more.

Redus and Morgan emptied their teammates' guns, exchanged them again across the cabin floor, and dumped another magazine at the fleeing aircraft.

Court chanced a look out his side window and saw impacts up and down the fuselage of the enemy, and flames erupted from the rear near the rotor there.

As Court feared, the enemy guns began again, and instantly he felt the shudder in his aircraft as it was raked with machine gun fire.

He heard a grunt in his headset; he didn't know who made the sound, and he began to slow the 412 to get some distance from the enemy, but quickly the machine guns stopped.

He watched as the helicopter twisted to the south and began plummet-ing away, followed by a streak of fire that flared out his night vision equipment.

He flipped up his NODs as he banked in the opposite direction, nar-rowly missing a rocky peak, struggling to get as far away from the enemy as possible.

Compared with the two other helicopters Court had seen crash this morning, the explosion of the Chinook on his left was, unquestionably, five times the size. A massive fireball erupted, followed by a shock wave that slammed into everyone in the Bell 412.

The dirty bomb had detonated here in the rugged mountains.

Zack didn't even comment on the incredible sight in front of them, he just said, "Who's hurt?"

"It's me," Lennox said. "Just a little shrapnel in my leg. I'm good."

Jim Pace came over the radio now. "He's got an eight-inch piece of decking sticking through the side of his thigh. I'm leaving it in, I'll tourni-quet the leg till we can get him to a medic."

Zack didn't hesitate. To Court he said, "Head south. We're going for the last bird."

Court banked hard and came around to a heading of 180 degrees. As he did this he had to maneuver to avoid a sheer cliff face, and then bank back to the right to follow a rising valley.

Zack asked, "Are we high enough to broadcast on the UHF back to Chapman?"

Court shook his head. "You can try, but we're still a thousand feet below the peak of the range between us and Chapman."

Zack got on the UHF, transmitted on various frequencies, but gave up after less than a minute.

He reached over into Court's body armor and took the three rifle magazines remaining there; he put one in his own chest rack and handed the other two to the men in the back. After doing this, he said, "You think we'll reach the last one?"

Court responded, "We can try to intercept it right at the top of the mountain range. It's our only play."

"The tone of your voice indicates there is a 'but' coming."

"But," Court said, "it's nearly fourteen thousand feet in altitude up there. I don't know if we can go that high." Court turned to Zack now. "And you guys are down to your last few magazines."

"No, we're down to *your* last few mags. Like you said, kid, this is our only play."

"Flying time from Spin Ghar to FOB Salerno is just a few minutes. It's even less to Chapman."

Zack said, "You're gonna have to be a better pilot, and *we're* gonna have to be better shots."

Court flew in silence a moment, racing for the last helo. Then he said, "The guy who trained me, his name was Maurice. Anyway, he had this mantra, said it over and over."

"What's that?"

"Proximity negates skill."

"What the hell does that mean in this situation?"

"If we can't hit him with the rounds we have on board, I'm gonna fly us right up his ass."

"I don't think I like Maurice very much," Zack said, and Court flashed a rare but brief smile.

The men flew on, Court's sweating hands controlling the aircraft along with his feet, his eyes still darting from instrument to instrument, then back up again to what lay before him. Craggy snow-capped mountain peaks loomed high, and somewhere out there off his nose was one more helicopter with one more bomb.

The Huey containing the six men of Golf Sierra lost more and more power the higher it flew, and the men on board could feel the effects of the high altitude. It was hard to catch a breath, and they all became light-headed, but they pushed on, Court watching the mountains ahead of him as well as his radar.

The last KRF helicopter was moving much faster than Court's helo, but Court had the angle on him, flying south on an intercept course. He figured he'd only be able to make one pass at the Chinook, because if they didn't shoot it down in those few seconds when their paths intersected, then the enemy helo would negotiate the last high peaks much faster than Court's little Huey could turn and catch up with him.

Court said, "We'll be on him in two minutes. Wait till we are close, then dump everything you can into that cockpit. I *will* fly straight and level to give you a chance, no matter what they throw back our way."

Everyone rogered up to the plan, and then Court glanced at Zack.

"One shot, boss."

"Starboard or port side?"

"Plan for both. He'll come from port, I'll go over him heading south, then he'll show up on your side. Everybody have ammo?"

Zack said, "One full mag each, more or less."

Court's rifle remained by his side, but Zack had stripped it of its magazine and had even taken the round out of the chamber to load into one of the mags.

"Hey, boss," Pace called from the back.

"Yeah?"

"Kendrick is unconscious. He's out of this fight."

"He strapped in?"

"Affirm. He's prone in the cabin."

"Just you and me on the starboard side, then. Sling his rifle to your body."

"Way ahead of you."

Court said, "He should be on our ten o'clock a mile out, moving through the mountains. Try and spot him."

"Got him," Morgan said. "He's lower, easy to see because of the snow."

"Tally!" shouted Redus.

Court didn't even look, so concentrated was he on the mountains around him. He just flew as fast as he could and waited for all hell to break loose.

And when it did, it came from his helicopter, not the enemy's. Morgan and Redus fired burst after burst from their weapons; the enemy helicopter raced closer and closer below them. When their rifles were empty, they dropped them in unison and pulled Glock pistols from their hips, firing as fast as they could as the helo disappeared under their feet.

An instant later, Hightower and Pace opened fire. Court had overflown the enemy, so he began a slow and careful bank to the west to pick up the pursuit and to help keep his team's guns steady.

When Zack's rifle emptied, he, too, drew his pistol and fired out the open hatch window one-handed. Pace had Lennox's gun up and into the fight now, but he quickly ran dry.

Court had seen sparks on the enemy helo's fuselage, but it flew on, faster than Court's helicopter. He put himself on a pursuit heading but quickly realized he wasn't catching up to his enemy.

Zack spoke with a tone of frustration. "We're Winchester on rifle ammo. About half our pistol ammo is gone."

Court's own frustration threatened to get the best of him. He shouted, "I can't get any closer. Their helo can fly higher and faster than mine."

Zack said, "That doesn't make sense. He's loaded down with a big-ass bomb and a couple of dickheads with machine guns!"

Court said, "He's got two engines, more power, and a higher operating ceiling. Plus I'm loaded down with a bunch of dickheads of my own."

Zack said nothing for a second. Then, "What if you weren't?"

"Meaning?"

"Meaning, what if we flew over a nice patch of snow, and I made the guys in back bail out. The four of them with all their gear, that's a half a ton. They've got beacon transmitters. Rangers would pick them up in an hour or two. That would give us some more speed, right?"

Court shook his head. "Zack, we aren't shooting that aircraft down with your handgun."

Zack acknowledged the validity of Court's statement with a frustrated groan.

Then Court had an idea. "But there is a way."

"Tell me."

"All five of you bail at the next ridge, I go on, try to catch up to him."

"And then?"

Court shrugged. "I use this aircraft to take him down."

Zack said nothing at first, then, "Kamikaze? You serious?"

"Yeah."

"You willing?"

"Yeah."

Zack said, "Okay. The guys will jump, but I'm staying with you."

"Bullshit. I don't need you."

"I can dump some pistol mags into that fucker before you hit him. Maybe we get lucky."

"No," Court said. "No sense wasting two lives when we only need to use one."

Zack made a long, slow sigh. Then he said, "You don't strike me as the kind of dude that gives a shit, but you'll get a star on the wall at Langley."

Court focused on looking for a snowy mountain peak ahead, but he said, "I don't give a shit."

Zack communicated the plan to the men in the rear of the helo; Pace assured him he had the decking out of Lennox's leg and his bleeding under control and would help him once they were on the ground, and then Court gave the men a one-minute warning.

The enemy helicopter remained in sight, climbing over one of the highest and one of the last crests of the mountains before it would dive back down into the flatlands of Afghanistan on the far side.

One after another, the two closest men behind Court reached up and slapped him on the back. He was concentrating too hard to acknowledge them, but at that brief moment, for the first time, he felt like he was part of a team.

Zack's pilot-side door was cracked open; he was ready to leap out on Court's command.

Just ahead, Court saw a snow-covered rise that his skids would clear by no more than ten feet. Looking it over as carefully as possible in his NODs, he couldn't make out any rocky mountainside jutting through the accumulation.

"Ten seconds," he said into the radio.

Everyone unstrapped themselves and waited to jump into the unknown.

"Now!" Court shouted, and Zack leapt out the pilot's door; the other men leapt from their places on the deck of the cabin, with Jim Pace pulling Kendrick Lennox off the deck as he went, cradling the man's head and neck as they fell.

Suddenly Court was all alone, one half mile behind the last enemy helicopter, which itself was barely two or three minutes from passing into Afghanistan.

SIXTY-SIX

PRESENT DAY

Court squatted in the southwestern corner stairwell of Mumbai's Express Tower Two, his submachine gun at the ready. He wiped sea spray, blood, and grit from his right eye, then carefully peered around the corner.

A quick glance was all he needed, and then he brought his head back around, out of the line of sight of anyone out there.

The floor was bare concrete, from one open side of the building to the other, with vertical support beams interspaced evenly throughout.

Exactly like the floor below.

And in the center of the room, he saw the walls of a bank of elevator shafts, six in all. They were empty and dark, and, Court assumed, they were waiting for the stage of building construction when electricity and cars and machinery would be added to make them operational.

He took a second, equally brief look around the corner, and then he brought his head back again and leaned against the wall, sighing in frustration.

He'd seen several people on the floor. He saw Khan; he was standing by an orange forty-foot shipping container, closer to the eastern side of the unfinished space, maybe twenty-five feet from the edge of the floor, which itself was thirty-three stories aboveground.

The big shipping container would be the bomb, of this Court had no doubt. It was an efficient way to move it, and plenty large enough to line it with lead to keep the radiation inside. He imagined there would also be a computer terminal inside the forty-footer, so the weapon could be controlled from within.

In his second look, Court had also seen Priyanka and Appleton and at least four or five security men fanned out, maybe more.

There were building materials here on this floor as well, and Court realized the stacks of boards and piles of rebar, along with the support beams every fifty feet or so, could provide him with some cover if he were to advance.

And he would *have* to advance, since he was forty yards away from where he needed to be on this floor.

But first, his earpiece buzzed in his ear. He was getting a call from Priya's phone.

It rang several times; he got lower to the floor and looked around the corner again.

He couldn't hear much outside of his earpiece because of the plastic tarps tied down to building materials slapping in the wind just outside his stairwell, but he didn't see any of the security men coming his way at the moment. He knew that could change at any time, so his plan was to give up the call and attack the attackers if they came close enough, and then advance through the floor towards the dirty bomb and the men protecting it.

Finally, he answered the phone.

"Who is this?"

It was quiet for a moment, and then the voice of the man who Court had spent the last dozen years assuming was dead answered his question.

"You are the one they call Cobalt."

"And you're the one they call Pasha the Kashmiri."

There was a chuckle. "I haven't heard that name in a long time. So . . . you and I. We share some history, do we?"

"Yes" was all Court could say to that. "I thought you were dead. I had no idea you would come back to life twelve years later as an even bigger asshole than before."

"Well," Khan replied, "let us both hope that our interaction in the present goes well. I have Priyanka in my custody. I will release her unharmed if you come up to thirty-three and give yourself over to my men without a fight." He added, "I will grant you the opportunity to save her a second time."

Court said, "Once was enough. She's on her own now. I'm getting the hell out of here."

Now Khan laughed again. "Why is it I don't believe you?"

"We'll add 'lack of trust' to your long list of shortcomings."

"Yes. Lack of trust. I've told my people they have ten minutes to find you or I will detonate the device."

"If you do that, it will be really hard to come back twelve years later."

"But I will have achieved my mission, and I will journey to paradise."

"How about you tell your boys to hurry up and come find me so you can delay your trip?"

"Who are you? CIA? Or are you, like Theodore, ex-CIA?"

"Doesn't matter who I am. All you need to know is that when people like you go down the wrong path, I'm the guy who comes in to bring them to the end of the road. It's as simple as that."

"I can kill Priyanka right now. Would your anger force you to reveal your location?"

Court saw two men approaching, twenty yards away. One covered for his partner from behind a column while the other moved forward, and then he covered for the other man's movement. They bounded like this proficiently, and Court knew his phone call was coming to an end.

"How about this?" Court said. "*Don't* kill Priya, and I'll reveal my location right now. Deal?"

"Very well. It's a deal," Khan said.

"Cool. Gonna hold you to it." Court leaned out around the corner, shot the bounding security man through the face with his Uzi, then sprayed a short burst at the man behind the column, hitting him in the elbow and spinning him to the floor, writhing in pain. Court fired another controlled burst into the man's back, ending him.

Into the phone he said, "I'm over here."

Suddenly he heard racing footsteps, but they didn't come from the thirty-third floor. Instead the sound was coming from the stairwell below him. Men were ascending quickly, heading to the sound of the gunfire. Court launched himself out onto the floor, crawled behind a large stack of rebar, and went flat, for both cover and concealment.

The footsteps entered the floor, walked a few feet, and then stopped.

Then he heard a voice shouting something in Hindi.

Sneaking a glance over the top of the rebar, he saw a big middle-aged Indian man along with three younger men; they were just twenty feet away, they were all armed with pistols, and they regarded the two dead Pakistanis with confusion.

Now the older man shouted, "Khan?"

A conversation started across the room. Court thought these men looked like B-Company, and he realized at any moment these gangsters could look around the other side of the rebar stack and find him, but after thirty seconds of talking that Court could not translate, the four men holstered their weapons and began walking forward with their hands up.

Court didn't know what the hell was going on, but he decided he'd use this distraction to get closer to the action.

SIXTY-SEVEN

TWELVE YEARS AGO

Omar Mufti looked down at the gloved hand he'd just pulled away from his stomach. Even with the night vision goggles he wore, he could see the blood as it dripped from his fingertips.

He'd been shot in the gut. Looking over to his copilot, he saw the man's head hanging forward, and blood splatters covered the broken windscreen in front of him. The young man had been shredded across the chest and neck, and if he wasn't dead yet, he would be in seconds.

Mufti looked back over his shoulder and saw one of his two fighters lying there, just in front of the massive bomb constructed of artillery shells that was lashed to the deck. The fighter was strapped in, so his body hadn't fallen out of the helicopter's open side door next to him, but he was clearly dead, missing most of his right arm.

He couldn't see the other fighter, didn't even know the man's name, and as he flew, he wondered how the hell he was supposed to detonate the device over Salerno if he didn't have the detonator in his hand.

This conventional ANFO bomb, just like the RDDs in the other helos, would only go off if a handheld plunger wired to the device was pushed. The plunger was still in the back with the fighters there, and Mufti realized he'd have to land the helicopter to go back there and find it if he was the last man alive on the aircraft.

He thought about what had just transpired. He had recognized the Pakistan Army Aviation Corps Bell 412 as it strafed his helicopter, obviously, as it was the same aircraft he himself had flown in to Ismail Zai over an hour earlier. It had, no doubt, been hijacked by American troops on the ground back at the base and had flown here to intercept him.

Flown poorly, this he'd noticed, but flown nonetheless.

Mufti knew nothing about the other two aircraft that had made it away from Ismail Zai. He'd given the pilots a strict order of radio silence, and he'd heard no transmissions at all, so he could only hope they had avoided the 412 and were now flying over the flatlands of Afghanistan towards their targets.

He couldn't see the Bell helicopter behind him, but he wasn't overly worried about it. His aircraft could easily make it over the 4,500-meter peak of the mountain range just ahead, and while the Huey variant might eventually be able to muster the power to do the same, weighted down with men with guns, it would be much slower than the BV-107.

The Huey had its one chance to defeat Mufti and his mission, and though the enemy had done a lot of damage to him and the others with him, he could still pilot the helo to the target.

He just needed to ignore the pain in his stomach, to keep his wits about him, and to fly another ten minutes or so to reach Salerno.

But first, he had to find a place to land to retrieve the detonator.

There, up ahead, was a flat spur in the saddle between a pair of high mountaintops. It was large enough to land on, and though he didn't know how stable the snow would be under it, he saw brown rock and earth poking through the accumulation, so it looked to him like it could be terra firma.

This was a risky move; only a pilot with the experience of Mufti would dare try it, and even then, only as an act of desperation.

He began to slow as he neared his landing zone.

Court Gentry could feel his helicopter failing him. He checked the gauges, saw that the oil pressure was good, as was the engine output, but the thin air up here at such a high altitude robbed the aircraft of lift and forward motion.

But still he climbed. It was either climb and stay in pursuit, turn around and go back to Pakistan, or crash, so he didn't feel he had much choice in the matter.

His indicated airspeed was barely 30 knots, down from the 165 he'd been getting at low, straight, and level flight, but he pushed on, kept his eyes on the outcroppings all around him, as well as the radar, which intermittently flashed the last helicopter's position ahead whenever there wasn't a mountain peak obstructing the radar return.

The Bell 412 shuddered; he looked and saw he was running low on fuel, but it was the lack of oxygen that kept him from gaining on his target.

Except that he *was* gaining on his target. To his surprise the radar signature showed on his screen again, and it appeared as if his enemy had drastically slowed down. They were at the very top of the Spin Ghar mountains now. Court didn't have a clue why the hell the man would take this moment to reduce his speed, and he wondered if his team had, in fact, crippled the helicopter as it had passed beneath them moments earlier.

Court pressed on, watched his airspeed, struggled with the controls, and prayed for one brief moment of luck where he could slam his aircraft into his enemy's and end the threat, once and for all.

Omar Mufti brought his big helicopter to a hover, then lowered the collective slowly, testing the landing area by touching his tires gently to the snow, then waiting to feel if anything gave way.

As gradually as he possibly could, he descended the last several centimeters, and he put the aircraft down, his hands on his controls and ready to yank his ship back into the air at the first sign of instability below him.

But the Chinook came to a solid rest on the saddle between the twin peaks.

Hurriedly, Omar Mufti unfastened his three-point harness, winced with fresh pain as he climbed out of the copilot's seat, then turned back around to look for the detonator.

There, just behind his seat, the other fighter sat, his back to the wall of the fuselage. He'd been shot in the left collarbone and he was wounded badly, but he still held his PKM machine gun in his right hand. It rested across his lap, and in his blood-covered left hand was the detonator. Mufti grabbed it, checked the cable, and saw that it was still attached to the massive bomb, farther back in the cabin.

"I can fight," the man said weakly.

Mufti nodded to him, shouting back over the roar of the rotors above. "You might have to. Watch for that helicopter."

The man's eyes were unfixed, but he nodded, and Mufti left him there by the open hatch and slumped back down in his seat.

He wanted to check his own wound again, but he didn't take the time. Instead he put his hands on the controls, wrestled the helicopter back into the thin air, and pushed the controls forward for momentum.

He'd gone no more than fifty meters; he could see the last ridgeline of the mountain range dead ahead, and he smiled, knowing he could dive down on the far side of it, all the way to the farmland and scrubland of Afghanistan, and travel ten meters above the ground all the way to his target. He was almost home free now, had just increased the throttle a little for his last climb of his life, when suddenly the belly of a small helicopter shot over the top of him, its skids missing his front rotor by no more than a few meters.

Mufti couldn't believe it. The American pilot must not have known the Bell 412 had no business at this altitude, or else he just didn't care.

Right before his eyes, the Huey began to slow and to turn in a tight bank; it lost altitude in the process, and to Mufti it appeared the pilot was not very skilled, otherwise he would have known to make the turn less steep, but he came back around, face-to-face with Mufti's aircraft, and then he began lumbering slowly forward.

It took seconds for Mufti to realize the man intended to crash into him.

"Brother! Brother! I need you!" Omar Mufti shouted to the wounded gunman in the back, and then he took evasive action, turning to the north, diving lower, even though he'd soon have to climb out of the dive if he wanted to avoid slamming into the last ridgeline.

The green Pakistan Army 412 whizzed by on his left, one meter away from rotor-to-rotor contact. Mufti pulled full power and started his climb to the west, and just then, the fighter behind him lay down on his PKM machine gun.

Court had been surprised to come upon the BV-107 as it came out of a hover, and he'd dived for it from above, barely overshooting. Then he'd turned around to try again to ram his helo into the enemy craft, but the other pilot had managed to avoid him.

And now, as Court banked around as tightly as he could without crashing, turning to pursue the enemy for another try at a kamikaze maneuver, tracer rounds lit up the sky, like a glowing bullwhip, desperate to strike Court between the eyes.

Court dove; he was mere feet over the snow, but the Chinook climbed, and Court's heart sank when he heard the crunching sound of bullets ripping through his aircraft from above.

Suddenly the rotor noise changed, the controls shook in his hands, and he fought to keep the aircraft steady.

The BV-107 was higher, one hundred yards ahead now, and the gunfire had ceased, but Court realized he was losing control, facing a mountainside dead ahead, and though his enemy seemed certain to just clear the top of the ridge, Court's helicopter didn't have a chance in hell of making it over.

He fought and fought his cyclic, pushed pedals to try to keep the nose pointing in the right direction, but soon he realized he was going to crash.

He caught a glimpse of the big helicopter, seconds from disappearing over the other side of the mountain. Court pulled back on his collective as hard as he could, then popped his harness off with his left hand.

He threw open his door and, traveling at thirty knots just twenty feet above a steeply angled snow-covered mountainside, he leapt from the helicopter. He plummeted through the black air, slammed into steeply angled and soft-packed snow, and began tumbling down the slope.

He heard his helicopter impact higher and slightly to the north of his position, but he was fully involved with trying to stop sliding and rolling any farther down the mountainside and didn't even look at the crash.

After thirty or forty yards, he skidded gently into a rocky outcropping, then rolled to his knees, fighting his way back to his feet. Looking up, he saw the twisted wreckage of his helicopter on a ledge; the lack of fuel and the lack of oxygen kept it from even burning, and he saw the ridgeline, some hundred yards higher, just as the Chinook disappeared over the top of it.

He began climbing through the snow because he had one last play in him. If he could get to the summit, he might have line of sight that would allow him to get picked up on his UHF radio by Chapman or Salerno. The enemy helicopter would be over Khost in just minutes, but if Court could alert the bases before the Chinook got there, they could identify it as hostile and shoot it down.

He used his legs, his arms, even his belly to climb, struggling for every footfall. The snow, even after the brief avalanche, was deep and mostly soft.

He would have been exhausted undergoing this even if not for the high altitude. But he was at 13,500 feet, the air was impossibly thin, and every breath was a deep and audible effort.

He climbed as fast as he could, aware he'd freeze to death up here within a couple of hours, but all that mattered to him now was reaching the top of this mountain and getting a message out.

SIXTY-EIGHT

Julie Marquez saw the images on her screen, and she knew it was her job to make sense of them before anyone else could. The satellite feed had just been restored; one of the Reapers was back over the target now, but there was still no radio contact with any of the ground forces, still no contact with the Blackhawks that approached from the south, just minutes away from Ismail Zai.

She saw the fires; some had burned out since the last time she'd laid eyes on the base forty minutes earlier, but there were new blazes, evident on thermal cameras even through the cover of cloud and smoke. She focused on the largest, zoomed and focused again, and tried to figure out what she was looking at.

Hanley and Vance were darting from workstation to workstation, mostly concerned with getting communications reestablished with the ground commanders, but that wasn't Julie's job, so she blocked out the chaos around her, looked at her monitor, and tried to evaluate the massive burning item just in front of the location of the hardened bunker.

It was the size of a vehicle, and she thought it must have been a large tanker truck that had caught fire, but she couldn't be certain, and its crumpled shape confused her for a moment.

Then she put it together. Though she was just looking at a fuzzy heat signature of hot metal some sixty feet in length, she finally discerned that this was no truck.

No, from the twisted mess of the still-intact piece of machinery, she could ascertain that it had fallen from the sky.

Softly, almost to herself, she said, "Helicopter."

No one heard her—they all had their own jobs, after all—but then she said it louder. "Helicopter!"

Hanley was shooting by in front of her workstation; he turned to her without breaking stride. "EH-60s are inbound. ETA is ten mikes."

Julie shook her head. "No. There is a crashed helicopter at Ismail Zai. A large one. Looks like a CH-47. It's still burning."

Hanley stopped now, rushed around to her side of the monitor to see what she was looking at. "That flare? You are saying that looks like a Chinook?"

"Yes, sir, and it impacted with the tarmac and burst into flames. Not from a great height."

There were other heat signatures visible that appeared to be humanoid. Some lying still, some moving around. Various small fires glowed through the cloud cover. But the burning helicopter was the only thing that mattered right now.

"Why is there a helicopter there? It's not ours?"

Julie looked up at Hanley, started to answer his question, but then he answered it himself. "Delivery vehicle."

Julie nodded. "And they had the capacity to build three or four bombs."

"Where are the other delivery vehicles?" Hanley asked.

To this, Julie said, "They are either in that bunker, or else they got away."

Hanley spun away from Marquez, grabbed Vance by the arm, and shouted loud enough for most everyone in the TOC to hear. "Inbound enemy helicopters. Alert Salerno, J-Bad, Bagram, Bostick. They might look like CH-47s. Anything that isn't supposed to be on radar is a fucking hostile!"

Vance ran to a workstation and got communications officers working, though he didn't even understand what the hell was going on. There was a moment of shouting, men and women trying to get clarification, trying to understand the intelligence, but then a young radio operator stood from his desk and shouted above all the other voices.

"Sir! I think I'm hearing from Golf Sierra!"

Hanley spun to the man. "Patch him on the overhead."

The room fell silent, and then there was a scratchy connection sound on the overhead speakers.

Hanley pressed the transmitter on the communications officer's table. "Sierra One? This is Rooster. How copy?"

But the man on the other end of the radio call couldn't hear him.

Court was exhausted, starved of oxygen, and slowly freezing to death. He was on his knee pads in the snow, his shaking fingers trying to manipulate the UHF radio frequency selector on his chest while looking out over the lowlands of Afghanistan, all the way to the faint glow of Khost under the clouds, dead ahead.

He'd transmitted on multiple frequencies, but now he switched to yet another freak, and he repeated his message.

"Golf Sierra Six, broadcasting in the blind! Say again, Sierra Six is broadcasting in the blind. Be advised, hostile aircraft inbound, time now. ETA, imminent. Helicopter bearing Chesapeake colors and logo is hostile. Say again, hostile. The target is Khost."

Court couldn't see the helicopter; his night vision equipment had been ripped off his helmet during the fall, and the BV-107 had been traveling without exterior lights. Still, he looked across the clouds, saw pockets where he could make out farmland below, and he widened his eyes to pull in as much light as he could.

The first glows of dawn would begin at any time, but they weren't here yet, and he cursed the darkness.

He was about to change freaks and try again when a faint voice came through his headset.

"Golf Sierra Six. This is Salerno. Your message was garbled. Say again?"

The men and women in the TOC at Camp Chapman hadn't made out much of Sierra Six's message, but Julie Marquez understood. He was talking about hostile aircraft inbound.

Hanley got it, too; he looked to Julie, then said, "They're using Chesa-peake transport helos to disguise the bombs. Alert Bagram, J-Bad—"

Julie shouted across the room at her boss. "Khost. He said the target is Khost!"

Hanley spoke back into his microphone. "Sierra Six, did you say Khost?"

There was a quick pause. Through the scratchy radio speaker, he heard, "Affirmative, Rooster. Impact imminent!"

"Salerno or Chapman, over?"

Now everyone in the TOC realized there was a chance a radioactive dispersal device might be coming their way. The room again fell into utter silence.

"I lost him in the mountains, but he's heading—"

The transmission faltered; the words came through as squelch.

"Shit!" Hanley said.

Julie stood from her workstation, took off her headset, and headed for the exit of the tactical operations center. She walked through the door, but once she was outside, she broke into a run.

Thirty seconds later she was standing in Court's unlocked cage in the Golf Sierra pit, and she grabbed one of his left-behind weapons. It was an HK rifle; she slammed a magazine into it, grabbed two more off a particle-board table, and ran back out the door.

She heard the sound of a helicopter as soon as she came back out of the pit. While helo traffic was ubiquitous here at Khost, even in the middle of the night, she oriented herself to its origin and began running for the fence line where she and Court had exchanged their first kiss the afternoon before.

She didn't make it to the fence; she stopped in the middle of an open area some two hundred yards away, and she tossed her spare magazines into the dirt and sand next to her as she scanned the sky.

She didn't see the helicopter; it was flying black, it was flying low, and this told her all she needed to know to satisfy her that it was hostile. She raised the rifle, scanning the low darkness back in the direction of the mountains to the east, and the helicopter noise grew louder.

Two CIA security officers, both armed with M4 carbines, ran up behind her. A man with a southern drawl said, "Miss? Put the weapon down! The hell you doin'? Only Ground Branch and security are allowed to carry arms."

She ignored the man for an instant, still trying to make out the helicopter in the dark. No, she wasn't a Ground Branch paramilitary operations officer like Court, but she had been an army sergeant, and she sure as hell could shoot something the size of a helicopter with a rifle.

She saw movement ahead in the black, beyond the fence.

"There!" she shouted. "It's hostile! It's hostile!"

The men, both unsure, raised their weapons towards where she indicated. The younger of the two, this guy sounded like he was from Boston, said, "Negative, that's a Chesapeake! Lower your weapon, miss!"

And then the base klaxon erupted, a wail that could be heard for miles around, telling everyone there that an attack was imminent.

Julie Marquez opened fire on the helicopter; it was two hundred yards away and just passing over the wire into the base.

The men with her hesitated, but the young woman was so self-assured that they themselves soon began shooting.

Omar Mufti had wanted to hit Salerno; it was the bigger target, and he knew exactly where the command center of the base was, near the barracks where hundreds of American Special Forces would be sleeping.

But less than a minute earlier he came to the realization that he wouldn't make it that far. His lifeblood running down into his boots and his brain growing foggier by the second told him he would pass out in moments. Chapman was three kilometers closer than Salerno, just a turn to the south and he'd be on top of it, so he decided to fly to the geographical center of the base before detonating the dozen artillery shells he had wired together behind him.

Now he crossed over the outer fence on the northeastern side of the CIA camp, and incoming fire raked the belly of his craft. He heard more rounds impact with the rotor above him, and even *more* fire streaked by on his left and right, visible through his night vision.

He kept flying, juking a little to the left and then back, and then another burst of fire hit his cockpit. He felt an indescribable pain in his right shin, knew he'd been shot again, and immediately he recognized he could no longer apply the right rudder.

More rounds pocked the already damaged windscreen, spiderwebbing it in front of his face, and Mufti began banking hard to port.

He reached down for the detonator in his lap, fumbled with it a moment, then lifted it up.

Court Gentry's voice had gone hoarse in the high altitude. His nose bled, his eyes burned in the cold, but still he peered down the mountain, through broken clouds, his eyes on Khost.

His message had only partially gotten through, that much he understood from Hanley's repeated questions. He switched frequencies, again and again, trying to find someone closer who could pick him up.

Utterly exhausted, operating on adrenaline alone, he tried one more time.

"Sierra Six! Any station this net, please reply. Say again, please—"

Before him a white light flashed over Khost, silhouetting low clouds for miles around, like a lightning strike from below, not from above.

But it wasn't over FOB Salerno. It was to the south.

It was over Camp Chapman.

Court Gentry dropped facedown into the snow. He felt tears of exhaustion and frustration and pain and terror freeze on his face as soon as they left his body.

He passed out as the first hues of the morning sun began to glow faintly in the east, a beautiful background that went wholly unnoticed by anyone who happened to be on this mountainside due to the bright fireball glowing in the foreground.

SIXTY-NINE

PRESENT DAY

Priyanka Bandari watched while B-Company men appeared on the thirty-third floor, all walking towards her position with their guns holstered. Still, the Indians came from all four stairwells; they were armed, and it appeared to Priya as if they outnumbered the Pakistanis, two to one.

She and Appleton were no longer gagged, but she kept quiet as the men neared. There was nothing preventing Khan from putting a bullet into her at any time.

As Jai appeared in front of her, he motioned for the rest of his men to stay back, away from the container and the people standing near it, and then he walked up to Khan.

The Pakistani shouted in Hindi to Jai. "I told you to keep your people away from—"

But Jai interrupted. "And Bari just told me otherwise. We took the construction hoists on the outside up to thirty, climbed the stairs for the rest of the way."

"We have everything under control here!" Khan insisted.

"Do you? Is that why three of your bullet-riddled men just dropped thirty stories and crashed down in the dirt next to the covered drive at the front entrance?"

Khan said, "It's still just one man. We'll get him."

Priya took the opportunity to speak. She motioned at the container and to Jai she said, "This is a dirty bomb. He's going to detonate it over Mumbai in eighty-kilometer winds blowing over the city."

It was obvious to Priya that Jai *knew* it was a dirty bomb, but he clearly did not want it to go off right now. "I am taking control of the device."

The Pakistani guards who'd been out hunting for Cobalt reconverged on the scene; they waved their guns crazily at the fifteen or more Indians, at the same time shifting their eyes towards the dark corners of the floor, worrying all along that Cobalt could still be lurking close by.

Jai said, "We will wait until the rain comes, or we will not detonate the device at all."

Khan said, "Then send your men out there after Cobalt. If we kill him, then we're back on schedule."

This seemed reasonable to Jai. "Fine. Your men working with mine. We check every part of this building until we find him."

"Thank you," Khan said.

Jai held out a hand. "In the meantime, give me your phone. Bari says that is your detonator. I will hold it for safekeeping."

Khan held a phone in his hand, and he passed it over to Jai. "Hurry! Find him and kill him."

Jai and his men turned away from Khan, Rasool, Priya, and Ted Appleton, and they fanned out in teams of two, augmenting the surviving Pakistani security men, who themselves again began hunting for the American assassin.

Khan spoke to Rasool in Urdu now, but Priya understood. "Of course, what Jai doesn't realize is that we have no way of knowing if Cobalt has contacted anyone else. We can't wait for them to search a skyscraper for one man if the police are on the way."

Appleton whispered to Priya, interrupting her from listening in on the conversation. "The phone he gave to Jai. Was that yours?"

She realized Khan had been holding *her* phone, talking to Cobalt before the Indians arrived. She started to turn to yell to Jai, but before she could, she saw Khan produce a silver phone from the pocket of his raincoat.

This, she knew instantly, was the detonator.

Priya was only five meters away, and Khan was another five meters to the edge of the floor that looked out over the city of Mumbai. As soon as he began tapping on his phone with his finger, she ran towards him, catching Nassir Rasool by surprise.

Khan looked up just as Priya reached him; he started to pull his phone closer to his body, but she reached forward and slapped the device, knocking it out of the Pakistani's hand. It bounced on the concrete and slid all the way to, and then over, the ledge.

Nassir Rasool lifted his pistol, aimed at Priya's back, but just as he was about to fire, Appleton slammed a shoulder into him, disrupting his aim.

Priya caught the round high in her right shoulder, and she tumbled facedown, landing less than a meter from the precipice.

Rasool spun and fired at Appleton from contact distance. He hit the retired CIA station chief in the stomach, and the man doubled over, then fell to his knees at the edge of the shipping container.

Court had run down the stairs to thirty-two, then crossed the entire open floor at a dead sprint, fighting the wind as he did so, until he came to the stairs on the opposite side. He was now in the northeast corner, closer to where the bomb was upstairs, and he took the stairs quickly but quietly.

He heard a couple of gunshots above him, and this masked his approach, as did the whistling gale-force winds, but these things also masked the footsteps of anyone coming his way.

He turned on the landing in the stairwell and found himself face-to-face with a pair of B-Company men.

Their pistols were up and they were switched on, but Court slammed his body hard against the wall as he fired a full-auto burst at the men just feet away.

Their shots missed his torso by inches, while three of his rounds struck the lead man in the upper chest, and a fourth hit the second man in the left cheek. Both shooters fell past Court, with the rear man dropping dead on the landing and the lead point man, clearly also dead, sliding all the way down the stairs to the lower floor.

The American continued ascending, knowing he'd just revealed his position.

He came to the top of the stairs and started to peek around the corner in the direction of the shipping container, but before he could do so, gunfire from the western side of the dark floor began pocking the concrete doorway around him.

He saw where the fire was coming from, and he also saw if he went low, they'd lose their angle on him because a large forklift was parked between his position and theirs.

Court dropped to his knees and crawled across the floor with the Uzi swinging in front of him, until he found a place to hide behind a four-foot-high stack of wallboard sheets positioned just five feet or so from the western edge of the floor.

He knew his enemy would still think he was in the stairwell, so he'd bought himself some time.

He pulled the second Uzi Pro out of his waistband, took the mostly spent magazine out of the first weapon, and jammed it into a back pocket. Then he crawled around to the end of the wallboard, thinking he might have a view from here of the area around the shipping container.

Nassir Rasool knew what to do without being told. With both of his prisoners dead or wounded, he headed to the back of the orange shipping container, opened the door, and stepped inside.

While he did this, Khan stood over Priyanka Bandari. She held her bloody shoulder and looked up at him helplessly. He said, "You think you've accomplished something important, but you have merely inconvenienced me. With a little time, I can program a detonation on the device itself. I don't need my phone."

He left the young woman there on the ground, bleeding on the concrete, and stormed over towards the container. Just then, gunfire in the northeast stairwell caused him to duck for cover, and he pulled his own pistol, began looking for a target there.

He saw nothing himself, but others, either his men or the Indians running around on this floor, did, because gunfire from multiple locations shot up the doorway and stairs.

Assuming he had a brief respite from any attack from that direction, Murad Khan stood up and ran into the back of the shipping container.

Court poked his head around the stack of wallboard as more gunfire struck the stairway some twenty feet behind him and on his right. He squinted into the high winds, looked across twenty-five yards of floor, and saw the container. The rear door was open, but he couldn't see inside. He did see Ted Appleton, however, pushing himself up off the ground, slowly and weakly. Closer to the edge of the floor, on the same western side where Court was positioned, Priya Bandari rolled onto her side, even more slowly than Appleton had moved.

He saw blood staining her right shoulder area. Her eyes were open, and in seconds they locked on Court's. To his surprise, she shouted at him. "Call my phone! Tell Jai that Khan is detonating the bomb right now!"

Court snatched his phone out of his pocket, hit the one-digit code to call Priya's phone, then poked his head above the wallboard.

A man stood fifty feet away, waving an Uzi towards the stairwell. Court shot the man before the Pakistani ever realized he was in danger.

Court heard the call answered, but no one spoke, so Court shouted. "Jai! Khan is detonating the device now! If you and your men help me stop him, I won't fire on you!"

There was a brief pause. Then the man answered in English, "What do you want us to do?"

"The Pakistanis are your targets now. You deal with them, and I'll go for Khan."

When Jai didn't say anything, Court shouted, "Listen, asshole. I called the police twenty minutes ago. You have to stop this bomb from going off and then you have to get the hell out of here. Nothing else should matter to you right now!"

He heard the man shout in Hindi, and then Jai said, "You stop Khan! We'll do the rest."

Court had no idea if Jai would be true to his word, but when he heard fresh gunfire rocking in different parts of the floor, he got the idea that the two other forces present were now at war with each other. He hoped like hell that would buy him the cover he needed for a twenty-five-yard sprint across open ground.

He stood and began running, holding his Uzi Pro with his right hand, sweeping it back and forth for any target that happened to be shooting at him, because he had no other way to discern friend from foe at the moment.

He closed on the open rear door of the container, saw Priya looking at him from her position on the ground near the ledge, saw Appleton struggle to stand, and realized the old man had been shot in the stomach.

But Court put Appleton out of his mind, Priya out of his mind, because the bomb was priority number one right now.

He made it to within ten feet of the open rear door, then slid down on the wet concrete on his butt. He heard gunfire close, but he wasn't sure if he was the target or not, so he just kept sliding until he popped back up to his feet and dove headfirst through the open door.

He found himself face-to-face with Nassir Rasool, who had his gun up and pointed at the opening, but Court's momentum and his low angle of attack caused the Pakistani to fire high over the diving man. Court slammed into Rasool, knocked the man's weapon onto the ground outside the container, then rolled with him on the metal flooring.

Court finally got his Uzi into position, and he fired a burst into the man on the floor with him just as he began to shout something.

A string of 9-millimeter rounds to his chest killed him instantly.

Rasool did not have the strength or skills to match Court, but the man had cost Court time that he desperately needed.

Court looked up just as Murad Khan spun away from the computer monitor in front of the device, bringing his own pistol to bear on the American.

Both weapons, Gentry's and Khan's, were held at full extension, pointed at each other's face. Court was on the floor; Khan stood a few yards away from him, next to the computer monitor.

It was a standoff. Each man was certain to kill the other if either fired.

Khan forced a thin smile. "You're too late."

Court moved up to a sitting position, his weapon locked at the end of his arm. "We're still here, aren't we?"

Khan sniffed out a laugh. "I could have detonated it instantly with my phone, but your little friend Priyanka threw it off the building."

"That why you shot her?"

Khan did not respond to this. Instead he said, "I was able to initiate the countdown here, but you didn't leave me time to remove the countdown clock that I'd already programmed into the brain." The Pakistani shrugged. "It doesn't matter. Only a few people in the world would be able to stop the detonation of this device, and none of them are in south Mumbai during a monsoon." He laughed a little. "I will die, but I will die knowing that I have achieved paradise."

Court swallowed hard. "How long?"

"Till detonation? It's assured. You can't stop it. Does it even matter how long?"

"From where I sit, yeah."

Khan shrugged, as if it made no difference. "One hour. In just one hour the entire landscape of—"

Court interrupted. "Good enough." And then, "Ted?"

Murad Khan held his gun on Court, but he looked up to see Ted Appleton standing in the entrance to the container. The former CIA man had Nassir Rasool's pistol in two bloody hands, it was pointed at Khan, and he said, "For Aimal."

Murad Khan started to shift the aim of his weapon up to Appleton, but before he could, Ted squeezed the trigger, a shot rang out, and Khan fell back against the little terminal.

Court shot Khan a second time, tagging him in the forehead and sending him face-first down to the floor of the shipping container.

As Court pulled himself up to his feet, Appleton collapsed just outside the entrance to the container.

SEVENTY

TWELVE YEARS AGO

U.S. Air Force pararescue men in a UH-60 helicopter picked up Zack Hightower and four other members of CIA Ground Branch cell Golf Sierra from a snowy mountain ledge on the Pakistani side of the border just after sunup. One of the paramilitary operations officers had an ugly wound to his leg, but he wore a tourniquet and a pressure dressing and was deemed stable by the Air Force men. Another operator, Keith Morgan, had broken his ankle on impact after jumping from the Bell 412 and was bitching about it enough for the medics on board to realize he'd be fine, as well.

All the men suffered raging headaches from altitude sickness.

These five men had activated their beacons, but the last member of Golf Sierra had not. Zack Hightower had demanded the pararescue flight search the area to the west, and though the pilots thought this would be a low-probability endeavor, the wreckage of a Huey was soon spotted, and then the figure of a man facedown in the snow on top of the last ridge of the range before Afghanistan was seen by a set of keen eyes on the UH-60.

Two pararescue men roped down and brought the unconscious operator up in a gurney pulled by a winch.

Zack and his team finally landed at Chapman at six thirty a.m. The fires had been put out but there was damage and devastation all around the northeastern portion of the camp. Fortunately, as far as Zack was concerned, the pit, Lima Foxtrot's building, and the intel building and the TOC all appeared to be unscathed.

Kendrick Lennox, Keith Morgan, and Court Gentry were all placed on litters and put in a truck like they were produce for the drive to the base hospital.

Zack Hightower, Jim Pace, and Dino Redus walked off the flight line under their own power, feeling strange doing so, because they had so little gear still with them. They'd lost their rifles, their ammo, their backpacks; they were just three beat-up guys with raging headaches walking alone through a chaotic base that had just suffered an attack.

Nobody paid any notice to the men at all.

Both Pace and Redus stepped into the Golf Sierra pit, but Hightower saw a lone man standing by the Lima Foxtrot building next door. It was Walt Jenner, Foxtrot Six, standing outside his hooch and smoking a cigar with a shaking hand. Jenner was thirty-five, ex–Delta Force, and one of the toughest of the young guys in Ground Branch.

Zack limped over to him. "Hey, Walt? You okay?"

Jenner just looked back at him with distant eyes. After a moment, he said, "Anderson bought it."

Zack Hightower had known Duane Anderson, Foxtrot One, for well over a decade. He sighed and closed his eyes, almost too tired to mourn. "What happened?"

"Command building was wired. We blew a door and found a group of Chinese nationals, they were jamming the satellite or something. We started rounding them up and one hit a det switch. Hays and Ng are wounded. Ng will be okay, eventually. Took another half hour to bring the sat back online." Jenner took a drag on the cigar and said, "It was fucked up." He shrugged. "Not as fucked up as things back here, though."

The younger man tossed his butt on the ground, turned, and went back into the Lima Foxtrot pit without saying another word.

Court Gentry woke up in a hospital ward with eight beds, all of them occupied. He saw Morgan rolling by on a gurney, but the rest of the wounded he saw were not paramilitaries; they were security officers, base logistics, foreign-contracted food service. There were shrapnel injuries and burns, and Court had a sinking feeling he'd been triaged in a room with the less severely wounded, and it made him wonder who was in the room where the gravest injuries were.

He looked down at his arm, pulled out the IV that had been jabbed into it, and climbed off the gurney. His body and head ached, his face felt like he'd been badly sunburned, but though his shirt had been cut off him, he was still wearing his soaking-wet pants, so he left the room and began walking down the hall of the infirmary.

A nurse stepped up to him and put his hand on Gentry's chest. "Hold on there. You haven't been released."

Court could see outside the front door of the infirmary. With a confused tone he said, "Where are we?"

"Chapman. Where'd you think?"

"But . . . radiation?"

The nurse shook his head. "None of the sensors tripped. We got hit, but it was with conventional explosives. Now . . . let's get you back on the gurney and—"

Court pushed by the man, walked for the door.

"Hey! Hey!" the nurse called from behind, but Court wasn't listening.

He was thinking about Julie. He hadn't seen any other wounded that he recognized from the TOC, nor any CIA analysts at all, for that matter, and even when he looked in on other rooms housing wounded personnel, he saw no one who looked familiar apart from Ng, a guy on Lima Foxtrot he barely knew.

Stepping outside, still bare-chested, he turned to head towards his portion of the base. He could hear the fire engine sirens and the heavy machinery behind him, far from this location, and he felt great relief that, even though the bomb had obviously injured and probably killed personnel here, the detonation was hundreds of yards away from the people he knew and worked with.

He bypassed the Golf Sierra pit, the Lima Foxtrot pit, and stepped into the darkened intelligence building.

It was full of people; it looked the same as usual, but Court looked at Julie's workstation and found it empty.

He turned around at the door, deciding to head to the DFAC to see if she was there eating breakfast.

Matt Hanley exited the intel building, just behind him. "Six?"

Court turned around.

Hanley gave off a look of shock. "Jesus, Six. You okay? They told me you'd had some exposure and they'd given you something for pain. You look like you've been set on fire."

"I'm okay." It made sense to Court now, he was on some sort of drug that was making everything feel foggy. "What happened here?"

"We caught a conventional blast. No fallout to worry about, but that VBIED was a big sucker."

"Who did we lose?"

Hanley said, "Six fucking Rangers. *Six*. Another thirteen wounded. Two Team Ten guys didn't make it, two more are injured. Lima Foxtrot One is dead, too, and pretty much that whole team got beat to shit."

"Damn," Court said, and he started to ask about Julie, but Hanley continued.

"On your team, Morgan will be fine. Broken ankle. Lennox has a lot of rehab to look forward to, but he'll keep his leg." Hanley shrugged. "Good news is, the rest of you guys are all heading home, too."

"Why?"

"*Why?* Didn't you hear? You got your man."

Court cocked his head. "The SEALs ID'd Khan's body?"

"Negative," Hanley said. "Khan was in the last helo that made it out of there."

"How do you know?"

"SEALs and Rangers rolled up multiple KRF shitheads at the scene. Prelim interrogations have four different captives saying they saw Khan, and some unknown personality named Rasool, run up the rear hatch of the last helicopter pre-takeoff." Hanley shrugged. "From what Zack said, there's no way to know the order you boys shot down those two Chinooks. We'll do DNA testing on any scrap of ground beef we find at the scene here, I'm sure, but there's a sixty-six percent chance he died on the Pakistani side of the border, so we might end up having to take their word for it."

"How many did we lose here at Chapman?"

Hanley sighed. "Eight dead. Thirty-some-odd injured."

Fuck. "Who died?"

Hanley sighed again. "Ed Phillips and Mike McKenzie from Logistics; Heinraker and Petrie from Security; Marquez from Analysis; Singh, Richards, and Novack from Operations."

Court hadn't heard clearly, but his body trembled. "Marquez? Julie . . . Julie Marquez?"

Hanley cocked his head, surprised. "The analyst? You knew her?"

"Knew?" He suddenly felt sick, weak-kneed.

Hanley put a hand on Court's shoulder. "She didn't make it. I'm sorry. Damn, kid, I didn't know you guys were friends, or I sure as shit would have led with that."

This didn't make any sense to Court at all. *He* had been the one to go outside the wire. She was an analyst. Here. Safe.

He croaked out a single word. *"What?"*

"Hell of a thing. We're counting ourselves lucky that it wasn't ten times that number of casualties. Marquez put together what was going on before the rest of us, even before you radioed, and then she grabbed a weapon from your cage and linked up with two Agency security officers. They ran towards the perimeter, and they were the first to engage the inbound hostile."

Court fought the urge to vomit.

"We assume that's why the helo detonated at the northeastern edge of the camp, and not right in the fucking middle."

Hanley added, "Marquez saved my life, and the lives of pretty much all the other people still with a pulse you run into around here." He looked at Court. With a little shrug he said, "Not that I think she'd give a shit, but she'll get a star at Langley."

In a hoarse whisper, Court croaked, "She wouldn't give a shit."

He turned away from Hanley, began walking back to the pit. Hanley called after him, but when Court didn't respond, the group chief let him go.

But Court didn't go in the building; instead he continued walking, all the way across the base to the area where the helicopter detonated.

It took him a couple of minutes to arrive, and once there he saw the fence line, looked for the place where he and Julie had kissed early the evening before, and he found it burned and charred, along with the ground around it.

Court dropped to his knees, stared at the mountains, stared at the sky, and he had no idea how he was going to survive this fresh, indescribable pain he now felt raging in his heart.

SEVENTY-ONE

PRESENT DAY

Court stepped out of the shipping container, leaving the eight-ton dirty bomb behind, and he moved to a wounded Ted Appleton, who had dropped the pistol and now lay on his back on the ground outside the rear of the container.

Court knelt down to put pressure on the man's wound. "Nice work for a station chief. I saw you in the monitor's reflection. He was too fixated on me to notice you."

The older man ignored all this. Instead he said, "Radiation. Shut the damn door."

"Why? The bomb is going to go off anyway."

"You can stop it."

Court stood and shut the lead-lined door, and as he did this, he asked, "How?"

"You were Agency. Agency has plans on that computer in there. They know how to stop the countdown timer. I was involved with nuclear pro-liferation plans in India, remember?" He coughed, and blood expressed out, down his chin. "The highest-ranking person you know at CIA. Get them on the phone, send them pictures of the equipment, they'll have a plan to shut it down. Either remotely, or they will talk someone through it here."

Court said, "The highest-ranking person I know at CIA . . . she wants me dead."

"Well," Appleton replied with a weak laugh. His voice grew weaker with each word, but he managed to say, "Maybe she wants to save half a million people even more."

Court knew not to bet on it, but he also knew this was his only option. "Got it."

Appleton let out a long gasp, and then the older man's eyes rolled back into his head. Court knew death when he saw it.

He'd seen it far too many times before.

He ran over to check on Priya, still lying near the edge of the building, and as he did this, he noticed that the gunfire around the floor had stopped. He looked over towards the stairwell and saw Jai being held at gunpoint by Mumbai police tactical officers. Dozens more black-clad cops filed into the space, pushing B-Company men to the ground. Court dropped his weapon and kicked it away before he was noticed, and then he knelt down next to his technical specialist for this mission.

"Hey, partner. Let me take a look."

Priya winced with pain as he probed her wound. "In and out. The cops will dress it. Stop the bleeding. You'll be fine."

"The bomb?" she asked weakly.

"Still a problem," Court confessed, then said, "but I'm working on it."

"How . . . how are you working on it?"

"You have to trust me. Tell the police that the phone they get off Jai is going to ring in a few minutes, and on the other end of the line is going to be someone who can help them dismantle that bomb before it detonates."

"Where are you going to be?"

The Indian tactical squads were converging quickly; he could hear authoritative voices and pounding footsteps approaching.

"I've got to get out of here if I'm going to make this work."

Priya didn't understand, but she nodded. Court smiled at her, held her hand a moment.

Then he stood up.

"Stop!" a man shouted, but Court raised his empty hands, stepped to the edge of the building, then spun around, facing the cops. As they converged, their weapons pointed at him, he rose to the balls of his feet, then stepped back off the side.

His hands caught the lip of the floor, and he swung his feet in, then dropped the eight feet or so on the next level. It was an awkward landing; he twisted his knee in the process, so he limped off, as fast as he could, for the stairwell.

Five minutes later Court was on the twenty-eighth floor. He found what was clearly going to serve as a bathroom, but now it was just a concrete box with plumbing connections and holes in the walls where doors would soon be, provided the building was still standing in an hour's time.

He sat on the floor, his phone in his hand, and his earpiece in place.

The phone rang, then was snatched up on the other end.

"Brewer."

Court closed his eyes. All he could do was try.

Brewer's voice was annoyed now. "Suzanne Brewer. Who's calling?"

Court took a slow breath. Just as the woman began to speak again, he said, "It's Violator."

Brewer was taken aback, that was clear from her voice. "*Violator?* You know we are hunting you. Why the *hell* are you calling me?"

"You want me, right?"

"It's not me. I'd rather you crawled off into a ditch and died quietly. But the policy here is that you are a target."

"Good. That's what I want right now."

"What game are you playing?"

"I didn't call you on an encrypted app. Get your people tracing my line."

He assumed she was already in the process of doing this, because she just repeated herself. "What game are you playing, Violator?"

"I'll save you some trouble. I'm in Mumbai."

She sniffed. "Sure you are."

"Your techs will confirm that soon enough, but you don't have much time."

"What does that mean?"

"I'm going to sit tight for a few minutes, see how fast you can cobble together an Agency hit on my location. I am in Nariman Point, southern tip of the peninsula."

"Why are you telling me?"

"Because if you don't help now, there isn't going to be anything left of this city."

To this, Brewer said, "What did you do?"

"You wouldn't believe me if I told you. There's a dirty bomb, and it's going to detonate in about fifty-two minutes."

Brewer didn't know what to make of this, obviously, but it was also obvious to Court that she was focusing on the wrong detail at the moment when she asked, "And where are *you*?"

"I'm sitting on the floor right below the fucking bomb, Suzanne. Listen, I know you will send shooters, that's what you do, but if you want to be a hero, then you will get NSA to call a number I will give you, and they can tell the Mumbai SWAT guy who answers how to turn off the detonation countdown."

"How do you know we can—"

Court interrupted. "You are going to be a very busy girl over the next hour, but if you do everything right, then you'll be the biggest rock star on the seventh floor."

"I'll be the biggest rock star on the seventh floor if I put a bullet into your brain."

Court laughed. "Not if everybody who made it happen and twenty percent of a city of twelve million people died in the process. You'll never get your credit." Court couldn't believe the hoops he was having to jump through right now to get Brewer to do something for the good of humanity. "Two birds with one stone. Save a couple million lives and get a chance at bagging me."

"How do I know you won't leave as soon as this conversation ends?"

"You don't know that, but I *do* know you are wasting very precious time, so I'm going to give you that number now, 'kay?"

He gave Brewer the number to Priya's phone, which by now should have been in the hands of the team leader of the Indian tactical unit. She read it back to him.

"That's it. Chop-chop, fifty minutes and counting." He added, "Good-bye, Suzanne."

"But—"

"Stop this detonation. Do the right thing for once." He added, "You might be surprised how good it feels."

Court hung up. This was all he could do. He put the phone down on the floor, then stood up and began hobbling off towards the stairs.

EPILOGUE

TWELVE YEARS AGO

Court sat in the rear of the C-17 Globemaster, looked out a portal at the snow-capped mountains of Afghanistan below him, and told himself he sure as hell wasn't going to miss this place.

He gazed slowly around the massive cabin of the aircraft. There were nine flag-draped caskets on the floor. Two more had died from their injuries since Hanley gave him the number of KIA, but one of the dead was a Chilean contractor and therefore not on this flight.

One of the caskets in one of the rows contained the body of Julie Marquez, but Court hadn't gone to look for it. He couldn't bear it. Instead he just sat there, let his walls thicken and his heart chill, and he told himself this shit was just part of the job.

Redus and Morgan sat together a few seats down; Morgan wore a cast on his elevated right leg, and Redus spit dip into a can as the two men talked quietly. Beyond them, Kendrick Lennox was on a stretcher at the moment, but Court had seen him hobbling around some on crutches before takeoff, so obviously the operator was going to be fine.

Jim Pace and Zack Hightower stood over with what was left of the Lima Foxtrot team, sitting on a row of benches on the opposite wall of the cabin. There were three men ambulatory, two men on stretchers, and, Court knew, one of the caskets on this flight belonged to Duane Anderson, the men's team leader.

The Lucky Fuckers, the analysts had called them.

No, Court decided, that name *wasn't* going to stick. He wondered if Goon Squad would, but this quickly left his thoughts.

Hightower looked Court's way, then turned and crossed the cabin, came and sat down.

Zack said, "You still look a little freezer-burned on your face."

"It's fine." Court wasn't in the mood to talk.

"Good. If I didn't say it before, I should have. Sorry about Marquez. That chica was a fuckin' hero."

"Yeah." Court looked out the portal, the brilliant sun forcing him to squint. He held his face there a long moment, but when it became evident Zack wasn't leaving, Court turned back to him. "What?"

Zack ran a hand through his short dirty-blond hair. "Look. A person you cared about died. I get it. It's tough. Believe me, *I* know. I've been dealing with that shit on an industrial scale for the past decade, kid."

Court sat up straighter now, gave his team leader a hard look. "You and Hanley were planning on giving me the axe when this was all over for shooting Redus."

Zack said nothing.

"But I want to stay your Six, Zack. I've shown you I have what it takes, despite my fuckup in Lahore."

Hightower gave no hint what he was thinking. He just said, "I don't need an operator on my team who's carrying around a death wish."

Court shook his head. "I don't have a death wish. I have a *kill* wish. Put me in front. I need to be first man through the door. Through *every* door."

Zack looked back to the other men on his team. He took a long time to speak, but when he did, he said, "Gentry. I decided days ago. You aren't going anywhere. You're my Six."

Court nodded.

Hightower stood. "Get some sleep." And then he walked off, past the caskets, heading towards the front of the plane.

Court closed his eyes, thought of Julie, and then closed them tighter, as if he could somehow squeeze away reality.

PRESENT DAY

Priyanka Bandari had been living quietly in the weeks since the insanity with Murad Khan, other than tending to her wound and meeting with government officials, who grilled her over and over about everything that had happened.

They also asked about her uncle, and to this she played as dumb as possible. Her tactic seemed to work, because Arjun had left her everything in his will, and no one was holding that up.

She'd moved into a small but elegant apartment in Worli; it was safe and secure, though she'd already broken into the building's CCTV system, both out of habit as well as out of a newfound paranoia.

She met friends for dinner from time to time, she cared for a neighborhood alley cat that she was considering making her own, and she read books about computers, planning on starting coursework at the university to obtain a more advanced degree in information technology.

She was poring through one of these tomes in her bed just after eleven p.m. one Wednesday night when her phone rang on the table next to her. Assuming it to be a girlfriend, she picked it up without looking.

"Yes?"

"Let me take a guess. Hurts like hell to point at the sky."

She recognized the voice instantly, and she smiled. It was Cobalt. She said, "I haven't had a need to. But, yeah, I imagine that would hurt." She added, "It's getting much better, though."

"Good."

"Are you still in India?"

"Long gone."

"I guess you won't miss it."

The American laughed. "I wasn't bored." He added, "Where I am now . . . I checked the newspapers. Apparently Mumbai still exists."

"Thanks, in large part, to you," she replied.

"*And*, in large part, to you. Do you know how much time was left on the countdown clock?"

"I was told it got down to two minutes and four seconds."

"Shit," Cobalt said. "That must have been stressful."

"Not for me. I passed out. Woke up in the hospital." When the American did not speak, she said, "The American government came to my room. To talk about you."

"I figured as much."

"They were *not* friendly."

"I figured as much," he repeated, then added, "Listen. Seriously, whatever you told them . . . it's fine."

"I told them the truth. That you were a selfless hero."

Another little laugh carried over the phone line. "Good. Maybe I'll get a plaque out of this."

She laughed at this. "Sorry, but they hate you for some reason. I'll have to make you that plaque myself." Finally, she said, "Is this just a social call?"

"I wanted to check in on you. And I wanted to tell you that your uncle would be very proud."

She felt tears welling up in her eyes. "That is nice of you to say."

"It's true."

She wiped the tears away, then said, "Wherever you are, I really hope you aren't in any more danger."

"None at all. I'm on vacation." When she didn't reply, he said, "I promise."

"You've earned it."

"How about you?" he asked.

"I'm unemployed, so . . . every day is a vacation right now."

"Well, you are a bright woman. You can do anything you want."

"I'm thinking about going back to school. The real world kind of sucks."

"Tell me about it," Cobalt said. "I wish you all the best."

Priya sniffed back another tear. "We made a good team, didn't we?"

"Absolutely we did."

She hesitated, then said, "Julie. The girl who you told me about. The one Khan killed twelve years ago. Do you think this will take some of the pain away?"

She heard a long sigh from the man on the other end of the line. Then he said, "I don't know. Julie's death is what got me into that mission in Algiers, and that's what led me to Khan in Mumbai. So I guess her death, in a funny way, ended up helping to save a lot more people a dozen years later."

Priya said, "My uncle used to say, 'When one door closes, another door opens.'"

The American replied, "Honestly, I've only seen that happen in prison."

"You've been to prison?"

With mirth in his voice, Cobalt said, "Look at the time. I won't keep you. Take care of yourself, Priya."

"Take care of *yourself*," she said, then added, "Courtland."

The Americans had told her his name. She hesitated using it, but wanted to see his reaction.

He said, "People who want me dead call me Courtland. Among other things. You can call me Court."

He then said, "Good night, Priya."

"Good night, Court," she said, and then she disconnected the call, put the phone down on her bed, and smiled.

ACKNOWLEDGMENTS

I would like to thank Trey and Kristin Greaney, Allison Greaney, Joshua Hood (JoshuaHoodBooks.com), Brad Taylor (BradTaylorBooks.com), Rip Rawlings (RipRawlings.com), James Yeager and Tactical Response, Jack Stewart (JackStewartBooks.com), JT Patten (JTPattenbooks.com), and Joe and Anthony Russo.

I'd also like to thank, as always, my agents Scott Miller at Trident Media and Jon Cassir at CAA, along with my editor, Tom Colgan, and the other remarkable people at Penguin Random House: Sareer Khader, Jin Yu, Loren Jaggers, Bridget O'Toole, Jeanne-Marie Hudson, Christine Ball, Craig Burke, and Ivan Held.

And a very special thanks to Ridhi Shandilya in Mumbai for helping with vital location research and information about India.